H.A.L.O. UNDONE

A BROKEN H.A.L.O. NOVEL

JILLIAN NEAL

Written by Jillian Neal

Published by Realm Press

ISBN: 978-1-940174-45-7

Library of Congress Control Number: 2018944902

First Edition

First Printing – May 2018

Many thanks to Ann and Ann – for your friendship and your help, two things I needed more than you will ever know.

CONTENTS

1

GRIFF

"I should've shot you the first time I met you." I stared down T-Byrd, one of the idiots who was supposed to be my brother in arms, and all that other shit they shovel into your skull in Basic. I willed him to be some kind of mirage or one of those visions you get when you're high on pain killers or something. Normally, I loved the guy like he *was* my brother. Today, not so much. "I'm gonna give you a chance to repeat what you just said to me. But think on it before you do because if you seriously think I'm going to do what you just said I was gonna do, you've lost your damned mind."

In true T-Byrd format, he was laughing- hysterically, I might add. "Dude, you should see your face right now."

If you served in Special Forces long enough, you figured out a few things. The ability to do a thirty-mile run with an eighty pound ruck is handy when, say, you're fleeing insurgents on foot. Endurance is a thing just like keeping your mouth shut and not bitching about living in hundred-degree weather with hundred-percent humidity while you're stuffed in a ghillie suit like a sardine in a deep fryer. But the two skills that will save your ass day in and day out are the ability to tell when someone's lying and being able to effectively tell a lie without getting caught.

I ran my hand through my hair and then gripped the thick oak desk I'd had delivered to my corner office four years ago. How the hell I'd come to have a job that required a desk I still hadn't figured out.

Here's the thing though: T wasn't lying. You don't work with a guy for seven long-ass years and not know their tells, Beret or not. He'd actually gone and done this and now I was going to have to smash his face into the pavement, which was a far more appealing prospect than actually doing the thing he'd just informed me I was going to do. "I'm not fucking around, T. If you're shitting me, say it because I'm about to shove your head through that concrete wall and hang a frame around it. I don't give a damn what all we've been through together."

This only elicited more laughter. His guffaws echoed against my skull. I ground my teeth until my molars protested.

He quieted down and gave me his signature eye roll. "Come on, Griff, you haven't had a vacation since we started this security firm. You work every weekend. You work every holiday. It's fucked up. I'm sending you to Vegas not Valdivia."

I shuddered at the mention of the Chilean city where we'd spent far too much time doing far too many things I didn't care to remember.

"What's he bitching about now?" Smith Hagen, the guy who was going to be demoted from being my best friend if he knew anything about this, strolled by my office and leaned in. His hulking frame took up the majority of my doorway.

"I'm not bitching about anything," I ground out. "Tell him he's a moron." I shoved my finger in the general vicinity of T-Byrd.

"Hey, T, Griff says to tell you you're a moron." Smith smirked. *Asshole.* "Oh, is this about the Vegas thing?" His smirk turned into an all-out freaking grin. He actually chuckled. I made plans to have both of my best friends' faces permanently mounted onto my office walls. They'd fit nicely right between my Distinguished Service Cross and my Medal of Honor.

"You knew about this and decided to keep your mouth shut? What the fuck is wrong with you?"

"Honestly, bro, I wanted to see the look on your face when he told you. He was supposed to wait 'til I got here just so I could enjoy this moment. Based on that fact, I agree with the moron status."

"Hey," T huffed. "He was about to take on yet another client. I had to get to him before he signed the contract."

"I guess I'll allow that." Another chuckle erupted from Smith. Here's the thing about my best friend - if NASA, the army, and some badass tattoo artist hijacked Professor X's lab to create the ultimate soldier, they would've created Smith Hagen. He's not someone you want to piss off but typically he's pretty chill, the very reason we're friends. Well, that and the fact that we'd marched straight through hell on numerous occasions and always had each other's back.

Instead of him coming through for me this time though, he slipped into negotiations. He cleared his throat. Never a good sign. Smith was about to tell me something he knew I didn't want to hear. "He's right, you know. We all got out of Walter Reed, got our discharge papers and a slew of medals, and you started working. You never so much as took a day to piss around. It's a week in Vegas. Drink too much. Sleep too much. Blow some money. Hell, get yourself blown. You're literally getting paid to get laid."

"Precisely what I was trying to tell you," T vowed. "But you know I'm just a moron. I'm worried about you. You've upgraded your normally hot-headed status to full-on asshole lately. You need to get the hell out of Lincoln. That's for damn sure."

"Get out of my office." It was the only phrase I could come up with. Clearly, I needed to up my repertoire of threats. I'd been out of the army too long, getting soft. I was no longer accustomed to having to threaten people a dozen times before my second cup of coffee. That was it. My synapses were under-caffeinated. Damn them.

"No," T huffed. "It's for charity, man. It won't kill you."

"No, but what doesn't kill me might make me kill you." Oh, that was a good one. Need to remember that. "Seriously, a bachelor auction. Are you high? That doesn't even sound legal. I don't know what you're smoking but the street value has to be insane."

I got another eye roll from T. "Legal? You're worried it's not legal. Who the hell are you?"

"It's sketchy as fuck," I snapped. "Some chick is supposed to bid on me? Who even came up with this?"

Smith laughed. "We were Berets, the kings of black ops. The shit we did. The shit we still occasionally do under the guise of an everyday government security firm. Come on, sketchy as fuck could be our team motto."

"Does the Department of Defense know about this?" I demanded.

Another round of hearty laughter filled my office from my former friends as they helped themselves to the chairs in front of my desk.

"It's a charity bachelor auction, Griff. Organizations do them all the time. The DOD doesn't give a shit about it. Plus, it's for Homefront Heroes. They actually get money to vets that need it, unlike most of the charities that say they help and don't. They helped Maddie pay for what we couldn't cover of little Olivia's eye surgeries last year. Do it for Chris." Smith still choked over his name. It had been four and a half years and we still couldn't say their names.

The calendar on my desk distracted me from the gut-punch of pain. I amended my original thought. It had been *almost* four years. *Almost.*

"Do not..." I shook my head. That was low. "Don't you fucking go there. That's a bunch of bullshit right there. Don't you go pulling him into this shitfuckery you've decided to sign me on for."

"How about you don't make me pull rank on you." T levied another blow.

"In case you haven't noticed, I haven't had a uniform on in years so you can take your rank and shove it up your ass so far you choke on it. You may have gotten to order me around back in the day but you do not actually outrank me," I reminded him.

"Oh, that reminds me, you need to be in your blues for the ceremony thing at the end when they give the money to Homefront

Heroes. Don't forget to pack them." He acted like the only part of my diatribe he'd heard were the words *uniform* and *years*.

"T, man, I need you to get your head out of your ass so you can hear me. I am not going to Vegas to be purchased for charity. If this whole deal was the other way around, and the women were the ones being bought, you and I and the entire Department of Defense would be ripping people's heads off and busting balls with no mercy. Rightfully so. I'll write Homefront Heroes a check myself, right now. But this," I lifted the brochure he'd placed on my desk, "this isn't happening."

"You're not being purchased," T came right back. "You're agreeing to take some woman out to a few formal dinners, to a brunch, and to attend a ball. That's it."

"Sounds an awful lot to me like my cock is going on an auction block."

"Better than being cock blocked though, right?" Smith laughed.

"So, help me, man. I have three pistols in arm's reach that you can't see. Don't tempt me."

This time I earned the coveted double eye roll from my team members. "Yeah, you two keep rolling your eyes. Maybe you'll locate your brains back there." My own brain started creating new and more colorful curse words for this shitastrophy. Oh, that was another good one.

"Once a weapons sergeant, always a weapons sergeant." Smith shook his head.

"It'll be good for your people skills," T tried.

"I don't need to improve my people skills. I'm good with people."

"You are good at *killing* people but not necessarily talking to them," T reminded me.

Smith smirked and switched back into negotiation tactics. He was going to pay for this. "So, you're saying if some smart, sweet, gorgeous woman wants to spend a little time with you and your cock, you're not interested?"

A Beret is really only as good as his ability to adapt, so I switched tactics. Ordering myself to leash my rage, I attempted to get him on my side. I filled my chest with air instead of fury. "That is not what I'm saying. I have long been a fan of women of every variety. They're all fucking amazing and have, on numerous occasions, made me certain there is a God. They make the whole damn world spin. My cock is practically the freaking fan club president, but we" —I gestured to myself and then to my crotch— "prefer it if we have some say in who we're spending time with." I sank down in my chair and reminded myself that I was a grown-ass man who didn't have to do anything at all. I no longer took orders from the army.

My ability to effectively tell a lie had just come through for me again. There was *one* woman. One who'd ever convinced me this world wasn't a fucked up cesspool of hate. One who'd made me believe heaven was actually wherever she existed. One who'd been... everything. And there would only ever be one. Because as it turns out this world *is* completely fucked up. And because life loves to twist a knife already buried to its hilt, Smith was just one of the reasons I could never have her again. But the idiots sitting in my office bought my bullshit about being a fan of all women and that's all that mattered.

"Hey, Smith, man, let me talk to him for a second." T's request came off as an order. I hadn't heard that tone in quite some time. What the hell was going on? Maybe he hadn't quite bought my lie. *Shit.*

Before Smith could follow T's order, Rylee, our own personal ball-buster poked her head in. "Smith, Mrs. Kendrick is here."

Smith sighed. "Doubt she'll be Mrs. Kendrick much longer. Not after I show her the pics I got of her husband and not one but two of his mistresses last night. Griff, man, take him up on his offer. This job occasionally sucks. Have a gin and tonic or four and blow through a few Benjamins for me while you're there." He closed the door on his way out.

He was right. This job did occasionally suck. What job didn't? But catching the cheaters was a very small part of our security gig. We also helped find missing and runaway kids. We help find criminals the cops couldn't get their hands on. Hell, last year we helped a half-dozen men and women who'd been adopted as babies hunt down their birth parents so they could help with medical issues. We did all of those things to keep from ending up with the same reputation of a few of the government security firms out there. The ones people vaguely knew about because they all had a sketch factor higher than the Empire State Building. We took on the small, pro bono cases to cement ourselves in humanity, to remember why we'd ever signed on to be Tier One assets of the United States Depart of Defense. Eighty-percent of our cases came with classified dossiers that included words like weapons trades, foreign cybersecurity hacks, and terrorist shields. The other twenty kept us sane.

As much as it sucked to have to watch it through a camera lens and show it to whoever hired us, knowledge was power, right? Besides, they weren't all cheaters. Once, I caught a guy taking dance lessons behind his wife's back so he could take her dancing for her birthday. Nothing wrong with that.

Keeping the people who hadn't yet realized what a shithole this world is from figuring it out seemed like a noble effort. It was the same reason I'd joined Special Ops. I do the things no one wants to do, or even know exist, so everyone back home never has to think about them. No one has to be afraid of the inevitable wolf at the door. Believe me, there is always one there and there always will be. Keeping people safely inside whatever version of reality made them smile made my own personal hell a little easier to swallow. At least I slept on occasion now. That was something.

"How long have you known me?" T's question jerked me back from my own inner monologue.

"Right now I'm thinking too damned long."

"I'm serious, Griff." And he was. Damn this reading people thing I'd been trained to do.

"Long enough to expect you not to pull shit like this." I wasn't letting it go.

"Fair enough, but if you'd get over yourself for the better part of a minute maybe you'd figure out that you *need* to do this."

The way he'd emphasized need was weird. What the hell was he up to?

I rubbed my temples attempting to rid myself of the constant tension that resided there. "Look, we can sit here all damn day playing who's better at lying and who's better at telling when someone's lying. By the way, both of those would be me. But why don't you just tell me why you did this?"

He shook his head. His amused expression only served to make me determined to add some kind of antler hat to his stupid head when I framed his face in my wall. "I can't do that so how about you trust me when I say, there's more to this than you know and I *need* you to go to Vegas and just be. Take a week. Be...happy. Hell, maybe take a whole lifetime to do it but I'm not letting you out of this. You deserve to go. Get packed."

We went through the Q course and jump school together. Hell, we'd shared barracks and patches of sand all over the Middle East. I'd know Master Sergeant Thomas Byrd almost a decade. He was the guy always cracking a joke no matter what we had to do. I had never, in all of that time, in all of our training, on the most grueling days when I wanted to quit, every single day in that hospital while I had my leg reconstructed out of rods and pins and it hurt so fucking bad I asked him to just shoot me and put me out of my misery, ever heard him speak so earnestly about anything. Never. "Is this for a case? Is someone in trouble? Just...what does 'I need to go' even mean?"

"Yeah, man, someone's in trouble. You. We thought about having an intervention but we couldn't decide between beer or tequila shots for a damned-and-determined-to-be-miserable party. It's high time somebody stepped in to give you the one thing you've always needed but never really been able to have." Half joke. Half honesty. I didn't know what to do with this version of T. The one thing I'd always needed but couldn't have is the one thing I'd kept from him, from the entire team. It was the one part of myself I refused to give up for the good of the brotherhood.

My traitorous gaze shifted to the combat vest folded under my helmet on one of my bookshelves. When had my own eyes stopped taking orders from my brain? Damned good way to get yourself blown to hell in the field. Oh yeah, I almost forgot. My entire body took to doing whatever it wanted whenever I thought about her. The all too familiar ache slammed through me again, like a bullet but worse because there was no suture or any amount of painkiller that would mend the wound.

Unable to believe what I was about to agree to, I let my eyes close for an extended blink and there she was. Like someone had maliciously tattooed her gorgeous form and that smile that I knew sprung open the gates of heaven on my eyelids.

The way she used to whisper my name echoed against the recesses of my skull. The way my touch could always make her tremble burned in my fingertips. Her hungry moans ricocheted through my mind. The way she laughed when I cracked a lame joke took station in my ears. The way she spread her legs for me. The slight shadow at the apex of her thighs she revealed at my instruction. The marks of my teeth I'd leave there. The spice of her creamy musk danced on my tongue. The tight, hot, silky channel where she took me in and made me certain she'd been formed just for me. The only place I ever belonged.

The way she sank her teeth into her bottom lip when I got her close. The way she came for me, screaming my name, calling me a god, and begging for more. It was always right there. Right between my shoulder blades. Directly under my skin. On the highest cloud when my boots were soldered to the ground. Always just out of reach.

2

HANNAH

"Hey, Rach," I called from my office again. By the time I got on the plane the next day she was probably going to have fired me from being her friend and her employer. Assuming you could actually fire your employer, which I was not sure you could. The point is she was going to hate me.

Rachel's fiery red curls bounced as she whisked into my office. She adjusted her glasses and then shook her head at me, forcing her to have to make a secondary correction of them as they slipped down her freckled nose. "You are not a horrible person. This is absolutely what you must do. It's so freaking romantic I'm devastated I didn't come up with it myself. Soulmates. Uh..." she checked a notepad she was carrying. "What he said to you in the hospital. The way you make each other feel. The fact that neither of you have gotten over the other and...oh, let's check the combat vest picture T sent again."

"You made notes on how to make me stop freaking out?" That was actually supremely logical.

"Hannah, this is the fourth time I've been in here and it's barely ten o'clock. It was more efficient to make notes. Plus, I'll be able to type them up and send them to you tomorrow when you text me another dozen times before you get on the plane. Now that I think of it, I should've booked you an earlier flight. We're ripping off the bandage remember?"

"What if he hates me for doing this to him? I'm basically forcing him to spend a week with me." All of that was true and yet Rachel's list was incomplete. There were so many memories, instances when he'd let his guard down in the last few years, that I would never share with anyone, not even the girl who helped me keep Palindrome Design running. I was never quite sure what to do with girlfriends anyway. When you move around every year and a half your entire childhood, friends are variable. Griff and I were not.

Rachel pursed her lips. If you've never been on the receiving end of a glare by a redhead, you don't know the power of those green eyes that are obviously telling you you're being ridiculous. I sank my teeth into my tongue to keep from saying more.

She jerked my cell phone off the massive desk I'd had Liam, my carpenter, construct from an old barn door we'd rescued for a job out in Boulder but hadn't ended up using. She entered in my passcode, touched my texts app, scrolled for a second, and thrust the image of Griff's old combat vest, the one I couldn't stand to see due to the rips and the frays from bullets that thankfully hadn't penetrated, toward my face. And there it was. A ragged photograph of me he'd methodically covered in clear packing tape to keep it from getting ruined no matter what he had to do, that he'd kept in a concealed pocket.

The picture was pressed to his heart by a body armor plate, the very thing that had kept him alive. It was hidden from sight until T had revealed it on the med evac helicopter that had taken Griff to the hospital in Germany. The profound meaning of its location wasn't lost on me. I pushed the phone back toward Rachel. "I can't look at that anymore. It's narcissistic to look at a picture of myself so often."

That wasn't really it. Every single time I allowed myself to open my text messages and search for that image, my ribcage tore itself apart, my heart escaped and took up residence in my throat and compressed all of the air from my lungs. Much the same breathless reaction I had whenever I actually got to see Griff, only more painful. What if he hadn't come home? Over half of their team hadn't. I'd allowed my family to hurt him, to ultimately tear us apart. I was going to fix this. I owed it to him, to me, and to us.

When I'd finally broken down and called T-Byrd a few months ago to ask if maybe he'd help me talk with Griff about everything that had happened, he'd told me about the photograph. It was the one thing that had kept me going in all of this planning for the auction.

Rachel cleared her throat. "If he can't have you, he'd rather go on and die. He doesn't want to do life without you anymore. He can't. Those were his words, Hannah. All his, while lying on a hospital bed. There is nothing more honest and raw than a man hovering between life and death saying things like that to you. He's just being stubborn. Sometimes a woman has to get a guy to snap out of it. That is your Vegas mission, my friend. Go forth and conquer the Beret," she commanded.

Rachel's words sent another wave of determination through me. I was going to do this. My stubborn Green Beret was going down. In fact, he was going down in every possible way I could possibly mean that. I tried to hide my smirk over the deliciously naughty thought.

Suddenly, the phone in her hand was ringing. Rachel's eyes rounded and panic sparked in their pine green depths like a warning flare in a forest. "It's Smith!"

"Under the pillow! Put it under the pillow!" I pointed to the settee near my office door. Ever reliable, she stuck it under one of my grain sack pillows and stacked two more on top of it. We stared at the ringing heap like we'd somehow pulled the pin out of a grenade and the pillows would protect us from the detonation. When the incessant ringing finally stopped we both slumped in relief.

"Wait?" Rachel's hands landed on her hips. "Why are we hiding from your brother's phone calls? It's not like he could have overheard what we were talking. He's not that good."

"Says the girl who did not grow up with a brother who's a Green Beret and a father who's a general. It's like being raised by the entire CIA, NSA, and FBI all at the same time."

The phone blared again from its cushioned bunker.

"He's going to keep calling and eventually he's going to call me to find out where you are," Rachel reminded me.

But it wasn't the number of times Smith called that had me concerned at that moment. Flinging pillows off of the phone, I stupidly prayed I would see Griff's name instead of my brother's. He used to call me every few weeks, usually in the dead of night, and force small talk for a few minutes. Eventually he'd confess in a haggard choke that I swore ripped my heart into a thousand delicate strands only he could weave back together, that he just needed to hear my voice and know that I was okay. He hadn't called in two months. I was not okay and we were not doing this anymore. My father and my brother could just get over it.

But Smith's name, not Griff's, glowed infuriatingly on my screen. Another round of guilt tugged on those fragile glass strings comprising my heart. Smith was more than my big brother. He was my best friend. I had no right to keep avoiding him.

No one else knew what it was like to grow up as army brats, the son and daughter of the General of the entire Fourth Infantry Division. Our father was a force. He was a theater commander during one of the two Iraqi wars. For the other one he was the commander of a brigade combat team. He was also a two-time commander of joint task forces in Kosovo and Korea, and an advising chairman to the Joint Chiefs of Staff. Oh, he was also a distinguished graduate of Army War College. Yes, that's a thing. He had a dozen other impressive titles bestowed on him including the coveted Cadet Bridge Commander right out of West Point. In army lingo, all of that basically means no one, and I mean no one, defies my father, Four Star General Gerald T. Hagen. Until now.

I rescued Smith just before he had to listen to my voice mail message again. "Hey, bro." I cringed and tried to regulate my breathing. He'd been trained to pick up on the slightest note of hesitation in your tone, to study how easily you drew breath, to know precisely when someone was lying. They all had.

"What the hell is Mom doing?" he growled in my ear.

Mom. Of course. All of the air pent up in my lungs came out in a relieved hiss. I prayed he was distracted at that moment. I could definitely discuss our mother. Just so long as he didn't want to know too much about my upcoming plans, I'd talk to him about Mom all freaking morning.

I giggled. "Do you mean specifically at this moment or in a more general sense?"

"Hannah-B," he warned. I rolled my eyes at the shortened version of my childhood nickname. "I mean specifically right now why the hell does she keep calling me about hiking?"

I bit my lips together trying to imagine the look on his face when I explain our mother's latest endeavor. In that instant, I missed my big brother like crazy. "Well..." another giggle erupted, "...she read this book about the woman who apparently decided it would be a good idea to spend three months hiking some trail to find herself. So, now, Mom's decided she's going to hike some trail that leads to some kind of hot spring thing."

"Dear God."

"Yeah. According to her, skinny dipping in the hot spring is necessary for the self-discovery."

My brother sputtered profanity and what was probably coffee. I doubled over laughing. "Jesus, Hannah, I did not need to know that."

"Oh, yes. Yes, you did because I will not be the only person on this planet that has to bear that knowledge. Also, you're welcome."

"You are such a brat."

"But you love me."

"Only occasionally," he goaded. "She asked me how long it took us to hike a mile when I was doing Pathfinder training."

"And you said?"

"Not long."

My grin was now a permanent fixture on my face. I half-wished I'd been on the line to hear their conversation. "And she told her recent time and you said what?" I'd already had a similar discussion with our mother.

"That if it took her an hour to go a mile and a half she needed to get it in gear. Then she asked how she could improve her time. I told her I often found that I really picked it up and put it down when I was being shot at." Army life. You can either laugh or cry at the realism. I chose to laugh. I almost always did.

"Wait 'til she sends you a picture of her pack."

"This isn't funny. She's gonna get out on some trail, remember that she really doesn't enjoy sweating, figure out that no one on some hippie-loving, skinny-dipping hot spring trail gives a damn about who her husband is, get herself lost, and then I'm gonna have to come find her."

"She's not completely helpless, bro. She's quite good at most everything. But there is always the possibility she might not like hiking and might require your assistance in getting back. So, you know, have fun with that."

"Holy fuck, she just texted me to ask about the thread count of the sheets we used when we were in Chile. Sheets, Han. Sheets. Oh, and now she wants to know if a higher thread count will make her pack heavier."

I'd made the mistake of sucking down some water before he'd said that. I choked and half managed to swallow before another round of laughter burst from my lungs. "Mom never quite got how awful your living conditions were when you were serving."

"Clearly."

"She didn't like to think about it. Neither did I for that matter."

And just like always my big brother sighed and his voice snagged on all of the memories he'd never share. "I'm home now. Hell, I even own more than one set of sheets."

"Yeah, I know, different sheets for different women who make their way to your bedroom."

His refusal to comment spoke volumes. To Smith, I would always be his baby sister, much too young to discuss things like sex, or love, or lust, or anything else he deemed inappropriate for my young ears. You'd think I was still twelve.

"Why the hell does Mom need to find herself? I thought that's what Dad took her to Paris to do last year."

"Yeah, well, I guess she wasn't *in* Paris." I kept up our banter. It was our thing.

"I'm not sure she's *in* her right mind."

And here was where we were going to argue and then agree to disagree. "Come on, Mom was the quintessential general's wife. She gave up forty years of her life to follow Dad's career and to raise us almost completely on her own, since he was always off fighting somewhere. She's just feeling a little out of sorts. She's not in charge of blood drives, or recommended reading lists, or post school supply drives, or support groups for service members' families anymore since Dad retired. Give her some time to figure out life after the army. Besides, Dad's home all the time now. I think he's getting on her nerves."

"Dad didn't want to be away as much as he was. No one ever said serving was easy," he countered.

"Cut her some slack. She sacrificed everything for us," I demanded.

"Then you do the same for Dad."

"Fine." Slack was not exactly what my reunion with Griff would elicit but Dad was tough. He'd survive. "I mean, if Mom wants to go get naked in some hot spring, we should support her."

"I will pay you money never to use the word naked when you're referring to the woman who gave us birth ever again. Seriously, name your price."

I glanced out my corner office windows to the Japanese lilacs set against the lush green grass of the Front Range. I'd worked hard to be right where I was. "Last time I checked, big brother, I made more money than you," I teased.

"Yeah, so I heard. I have your *Country Living* interview framed in my office right beside your *Colorado Home* feature, by the way. I'm really proud of you Hannah Banana."

Another round of emotion clogged my throat. "Thank you. You didn't have to frame them. You could have just stuck them on a bulletin board or something." Having my big brother's approval and pride meant the whole world to me. The fact that I was about to disappoint him and piss him off made it even harder to swallow.

"Says the girl who managed to keep us supplied in dip and Snickerdoodles even when we were imbedded in the field."

"I do make a kickass Snickerdoodle and still don't tell Mom about the dip."

Smith chuckled. "My lips are sealed. Hey, I checked out that article on the suites you redid at The Obelisk Hotel. Impressive as hell, sis. Breaking into the industrial market."

"Thanks." My heart triple timed its normal rate. Discussing Vegas with Smith was not a good idea. I had to orchestrate my plans perfectly. If T had followed orders, and I'd never known a Green Beret that didn't follow them to the letter, Griff had already been informed that he was going to spend a week in Vegas. I couldn't afford for my nosy big brother to suspect anything. No associations. No lilt in my voice. Nothing. Smith remained quiet. He was waiting on me to fill in more detail. Ugh.

"I actually didn't really like the commercial aspects. I prefer making people's homes a place they want to be, somewhere the world doesn't have to exist for a little while. But that project was good for business." I refused to refer to the name of the hotel or the city. It would henceforth be referred to as *that project*. That project I did in the past. Not the one I just finished two weeks ago. Not the one that landed me squarely in the sights of an Interior Design Firm of the year award. Not the one that would be the pinnacle of the career I'd thrown everything into. Not the final piece of the puzzle that had just scored me chatter amongst the Forbes Thirty Under Thirty crowd. Nope. Because none of those things mattered anymore.

How incredibly stupid did Griff and I have to be to believe, even for one more moment, that something so incredibly magical, so right, was just a spectacularly orchestrated coincidence that meant nothing at all? That it was just all an illusion, a gut-wrenching trick of the universe. I was tired of being stupid. I'd fought hard to become one of the top designers in the Midwest. But that fight was nothing compared to the one I was willing to put forth to prove to Griff that all of the reasons we shouldn't be together were nothing more than dust on something beautiful. They could be wiped away. We could reveal what needed to happen. We could wash away all we'd been through. He could stop pretending he doesn't have a limp and scars both visible and invisible. I could stop pretending my heart had ever been whole without him. It was either going to be forever, somehow, or I was going down in flames. There would be no white flag this time. I refused to retreat. I refused to back down no matter what he said. I'm a four-star general's daughter for crying out loud.

"I'll bet." My brother's voice jerked me out of my own personal keynote address at the conference of How Hannah Hagen Can Unfuck Her Own Life that had been going on in my mind for the last two weeks. I heard a few more mouse clicks and wondered what he was up to. "Ah geez. Cosmo. Really? Palindrome Design's own Hannah Hagen designs sexiest suites in Sin City. Has Dad seen this?" Disgust flooded his tone.

"I have no idea but I doubt Dad reads Cosmo too often." I needed to get him off the phone. "I have a silk supplier in Vietnam. She owns an organization that supports educating women about their reproductive rights so I worked out a deal where we used silk from there for the blind folds and tie-ups in the rooms. I was able to make a huge contribution to the organization and it will be ongoing since those will need to be refreshed every time a new guest stays in the suites." Take that, bro. Smith didn't even try to disguise his gagging noise. Checkmate. "How the fuck do you know about tie-ups and blindfolds? No wait. Don't answer that. I don't have time to kill anyone today. I'll pencil it in for this weekend. I'll need a name and address by then."

I rolled my eyes. "Very funny." I didn't actually have any experience with being tied up or blindfolded but maybe that was all about to change. It was probably a good thing Griff was just as well-trained as my big brother. There was a decent chance he'd need those hand-to-hand combat skills when I announced to my family that they could all go suck a lemon because I would be busy sucking Griff.

Smith had taken it on himself to protect me for my entire life.

Dad wasn't around so he stepped in. That all had to change. I did not need to be protected forever.

"Wait a second, Mom just sent me another picture." I heard Smith's mouse click and I drew a measured breath. "Holy fuck, have you seen this pack?"

Thank you, Mom. I would listen to her tell me all about the hot springs or whatever else she wanted just for the gift she'd given me by providing a distraction. "I told you," I supplied.

"Does Dad know she has his Leatherman duct taped to one of my old rucksacks?"

My mouth dropped open. Our father's Leatherman tool was his prized possession. Mom had given it to him when he'd made Colonel. His name was engraved on it. Dammit, I needed Dad to be in a good mood. "Are you serious? I didn't notice that. I only saw the rolls of toilet paper she taped to the pack. Don't tell Dad."

"He's going to shit an entire latrine."

"That's putting it mildly."

"I gotta go, Hannah. I'll take one for the team and call her. I'll try to talk her out of this insanity."

"Thank you."

When he ended the call, I sank down on the settee letting the relief soak through me. Now, if only I could keep him from calling and interrupting me next week while I was in Vegas all would be well. The key was going to be to remind Griff that we were made for one another while getting him to temporarily forget whose little sister and whose daughter I was. I was under no delusion this was going to be easy.

3

GRIFF

I slung my tactical duffle on my bed still furious but still going. I couldn't even figure out my own insanity at this point. Despite my best interrogation techniques, T had given up nothing more than the insistence that I *needed* to go.

"Bro, you're seriously going to pack for a week in Vegas in your army duffle?" Voodoo, yet another army brother, asked like that was the dumbest decision in the world. He was lounged on my bed throwing my popcorn in his mouth while he and Smith watched the showdown at Wrigley where my Cubbies were going to mop up the field with the Sox.

"You know we have a big screen in the living room. Why are you two parked in here?" I grumbled.

Smith, who also happened to be my roommate and therefore did have more right to my room than Voodoo, was pacing. The Sox had loaded the bases at the top of the eighth but Rogers was up. "Would you stop wearing out my carpeting? His shoulder's still jacked. He can't hit. My boy Johnny isn't gonna let me down now."

"Yeah, well, he let them load 'em up. And we're in here because T said to make sure you actually packed. Also, it's my house. I can pace wherever the hell I want," Smith reminded me. He'd been making comments like that more and more. In his defense, it was true. He'd bought the house. He'd put down roots or whatever the hell people like him did. He asked me to move in because at the time I could hardly walk and he couldn't lift his arms over his own head. We'd figured if we bunked up we could help each other out and put more money into the security firm.

I hadn't really intended to stay this long. The idea of getting my own place had its appeal. For one, I wouldn't have them crawling up my ass about this trip I was being forced to go on. For another, our own personal vagrant, Vince "Voodoo" Grimaldi, wouldn't be over here eating my groceries all the damn time. I just hadn't pulled the trigger. Something about a permanent address irked me. I hated the finality of it. I'd been a motherfucking Green Beret for the best years of my life. I was never in the same place more than few months. Go in. Get the job done. Get out. Stability just wasn't something I required.

"Strike three!" The much welcomed guttural cry sounded from the speakers beside my television.

"See." I pointed to the Sox players pouting on their way back to their dugout. "Johnny likes to fuck with 'em. Let them think they've got a chance in hell and then snuff it out."

Smith grunted what was likely a half-agreement and settled back on my bed. As a commercial for jock itch cream came on, we all cringed.

"Hey, that reminds me I got you something for your trip." Voodoo stood, stretched out his bum knee, and then headed for the door.

"Jock itch cream reminded you of something you got for me? I think it's gonna require crayons for me to explain how seriously fucked up that is."

Voodoo rolled his eyes. "Jesus, I hope you use every damned one of the things I got you because you are seriously in a mood lately. Should'a got you some Midol, asswipe." He made a quick trip to the living room and hurled a massive box of condoms at me when he returned. I caught it with one hand and narrowed my eyes. "I got you the industrial sized box at Costco. As your former medic, I figured it's my job to keep your package crab free."

Smith smirked. "When the hell did you start shopping at Costco? You get married and have five kids in the last two weeks or something?"

"Nah, remember a few months ago when they hired us to come in and figure out which of their employees was taking shit out of the stockroom? They offered me a membership when I caught the girls doing it. And, dude, have you seen how cheap the liquor is there? Now, I helped our boy Griff get his grumpy-ass rocks off. Win. Win."

Smith laughed outright. "Have you even tried out your new equipment since you got it?" he asked me.

The new equipment he was referring to would be the rod that was fused to what was left of my femur along with the metal hip joint the good army docs had installed. There was also the matter of the reconstruction that had to be done on my cock. That was just as awful as it sounds like it would be.

"I'm not saying I hate both of you but I'd definitely unplug your life support to recharge my phone before my battery was even really gone." I shoved the condoms in my bag along with a wad of Ranger rolled T-shirts. Being an ass was a preferable option to answering his question. I'd made sure my new equipment worked just fine on his little sister, more than a few times in the last few years. "I'm not getting laid. I'm getting *purchased* because when Sergeant What's-His-Name yanked me outta line and said, 'Haywood, we think you're the man for the Q,' instead of saying, get ready, get set, go fuck yourself, I said 'sure, why the hell not. I'm just as much a macho masochist as the rest of you losers.'"

Both of my friends shook their heads.

Voodoo tried again to soften the blow. "Man, come on, some beautiful woman is going to *pay* for the opportunity to spend the week with you. In Vegas. Probably be kinky, too. 'Cause you know what happens in Vegas and all that shit. Wish T'd signed me up."

"You want to go instead. Be my guest," I offered. The words kinky and beautiful rushed another image of Hannah to the forefront of my dumbass brain. Her brother was less than five feet away from me. My next tat should just be the word douchebag on my own forehead.

"Can't. Heading to Austin this weekend. The Grimaldi reunion is at Mom and Dad's this year. I told you this. I even invited you."

"You tell me a lot of stuff, Voodoo. Doesn't mean I listen." I shoved three pairs of dress pants in the bag, grimaced, and took them back out. Damned army training. I smoothed them and located my uniform hanging bag. My blues were concealed inside. I swallowed the bile that rocketed to my throat. The last time I'd worn them, hell the last time I'd looked at them, had been to attend funeral after funeral after funeral. Seven in all. And I'd had to go in my damned wheelchair. If I never had to wear them again, it would be too soon. Oh wait, apparently I was wearing them for some fucked up ceremony where my pride was being auctioned off to the highest bidder. I could meet women on my own thank you very much. Just because I hadn't didn't mean I couldn't. I'd had the best. No one else would ever even come close.

"Hey, Griff, maybe you oughta use some of those rubbers to fuck yourself...sideways," Voodoo snarled.

"You are pretty much being an awful human being right now," Smith confirmed. Okay, that last remark was clearly over the line.

"Sorry. I have the very same feeling I always had just before we stumbled into a shit pile about this whole thing, just so you know. V, sincerely, I'm sorry. Give the family all my love." Family wasn't something I necessarily got but the Grimaldis had always welcomed all of us into theirs anytime any of us wanted to make the trip. V's mama had birthed nine children of her own and lived in her kitchen. I'd even fled to their expansive home in Austin when I'd pushed too hard too fast and had to have yet another surgery six months after the first three. Mama G had taken me in, fed me pasta and sauce until my eyeballs were floating in garlic-infused olive oil from their motherland, and she'd put me to bed where I'd stayed for days.

"I will but I'm not bringing you any of Nana's cannoli."

Smith smirked. "That's rough, V. But not unwarranted." He morphed his smirk into a scolding glance and shot it directly at me.

If Voodoo was holding out on his Nana's cannoli maybe I did need a vacation. I started to offer up another apology but he waved me off. "Just fix whatever the hell has your panties in a wad."

"Yeah. I'll work on it." How fucked up was it that the only thought I had at that moment was that the light pink G-string I'd stripped of Hannah four years ago, the night I'd lost my fucking mind and had driven to Denver, was still hidden in my bedside table drawer.

If T-Byrd had ordered me to spend a week in Vegas drinking, gambling, and sleeping I wouldn't have minded as much. It was the whole ridiculous bachelor auction that galled me. Being forced to spend an entire week with some woman who'd want, at the very least, some decent soldier to entertain her wasn't going to work. I wasn't decent. I was damaged. And there wasn't a single person who could do a damned thing about it. I had nothing to offer anyone at all.

I had to get out of that room. The men who'd stood by me through it all didn't deserve my shit. "I'm gonna get in a run," I informed them.

Rushing into the exercise and weight room Smith and I had set up, I switched on the treadmill and ordered myself to stop being a prick.

Pain speared from my hip all the way down to my left knee as the treadmill whirred to life. It always did. It always would. Clenching my jaw, I took the first step. Walk before climb. Climb before run. My physical therapist's instructions pounded in my head to the tune of my Nikes on the belt.

Rhythmic beeps from the treadmill, as I increased the speed, assaulted the background noise of the game in the other room. The searing pain intensified as I forced my legs to move faster. Hannah's bright blue eyes and the most perfect smile on this planet or any other formed in my head. The vision of her arching into me in the back of my Jeep had kept me fighting for years.

I had to walk so when I stole chances to see her I'd be able to lift her up into my arms. I had to be able to rotate my hips just the way she preferred when I had her under me. And most importantly, I had to be able to protect her, even if she'd never really be mine. My goals would never change.

4

HANNAH

Slinging both of my large, pink-striped bags from Victoria's Secret into the empty chair on the opposite side of the table, I grinned at the nuthatches as they dive bombed a spilled cone of butter pecan ice cream. The universe was clearly on my side that afternoon. Not only had Victoria and whatever her secret might be had the lace camis I'd been lusting after, they also had the most perfect see-thru babydoll nightie in purple and in my size. On top of that, I'd also just snagged a coveted outdoor seat at my favorite downtown ice creamery. When a girl voluntarily has the hairs ripped out of her va-jay-jay, she totally deserves strawberries and cream in a purple cone for supper. I don't care what anyone else says.

Besides, I'd taken the whole afternoon off to do just this: prepare. It was the first afternoon I'd taken off since the last time Griff had shown up at my apartment. I'd lied through my teeth to my entire staff about why I couldn't come in that Monday morning and what to do with all of my appointments and phone calls. Hell, I would've diagnosed myself with the plague if it meant having him at my place longer.

"Had a feeling I'd find my little girl here."

I gasped and manage to dip my head into my scoop shoving it up my nostrils as my father helped himself to the seat previously occupied with more satin and lace than I'd be able to get through in the next week, even if Griff and I never left my suite. A few dribbles of ice cream splattered on my favorite jeans.

"Daddy!" I coughed out. Running the back of my hand over my face, I searched for napkins I'd clearly forgotten to pick up again. Dammit. "What are you doing here?"

My father glared at the bags he'd set on the ground. I watched him mentally count backward from ten. I knew that look. I'd been on the receiving end of it since I was six.

"Had a doctor's appointment up here. I went by your office afterwards. Your secretary said you were out running errands."

"She's not my secretary, Dad. She's my assistant."

As usual, he ignored my edit. "I put two and two together and assumed I could probably locate you at one of your usual haunts. If you don't want to be found, Hannah, change your patterns. That's basic cordon and search training."

I bit into the side of my mouth to keep from rolling my eyes but my jaw unhinged anyway. "Except that I'm not an insurgent and my usual haunts don't need to be cordoned nor do I have anything worthy of searching. This is Denver. It's a beautiful evening. I'm having ice cream. You should get some. It's amazing."

"Yes. Your mother dragged me out here for something called a pear wine something or another. I still don't understand the purpose of an ice cream shop speakeasy. Seems ridiculous. United States government outlawed them. That should've been that."

"It's not a real speakeasy, Dad. It's just for fun." I shook my head. "Never mind." Fun was not necessarily something my father understood.

"Please tell me that isn't your dinner." He gestured to my cone which I was squeezing slightly harder than was really advisable.

"I...uh..." Okay, telling my father what I'd done to earn an ice cream dinner was not happening. Besides, no amount of torture would warrant dessert before veggies for General Hagen. "It's just a snack. You've been walking all over the city. What did you need?"

"I hiked less than two miles according to my Fitbit. Would've been handy to have had this in the desert. Your brother's suggestion that I get one was spot on." Of course it was. Everything Smith did was *spot on*. "But I did have a question. What is this nonsense your mother is carrying on about? Some kind of trail hike?"

"It's not nonsense to her. She wants to go hiking. What's wrong with that?"

"She never liked to hike when I was in the army."

"Well, people do occasionally acquire new hobbies."

"When your brother was in Cub Scouts and you were a baby, I took the family to some waterfall near that post we were stationed at in Georgia. You slipped on a rock and got your sandals wet. Your mother got mad at me. I assumed she didn't care for hiking."

I glanced skyward, squinting into the setting sun. *Universe, come on, you were doing so good there for a minute.* The cool metal grate of my chair was suddenly irritating my ass. Centering my gaze back on my father, I prayed patience would travel in on the deep breath I took. "Dad, she got mad at you because my panties were soaked and they were rubbing me raw and I loved those sandals. You didn't understand why I was crying. You also didn't want to turn around and go back. It had nothing to do with Mom and hiking." I honestly didn't remember the incident but I'd heard the story numerous times from my mother.

"Never surrender. You know that."

"Yes, but I was four and miserable so surrendering might've been the way to go in that scenario."

"I don't understand you when you say things like that, Hannah."

The ending of that sentence was unnecessary. He didn't understand me. Hard stop. I attempted yogic breathing I'd learned in the one class Rachel had managed to drag me to. It proved unsuccessful. Clearly the instructor was no match for the general.

"Does she want me to go with her?" He glanced at a nearby table that a couple had just abandoned. Grabbing a clean napkin they'd left behind, he handed it to me. "You still have ice cream on your nose, little one."

Grinding my teeth, I scrubbed my face. *Little one. Ugh.* My accomplishments never seemed to matter. To my father, I would always be a clumsy little girl with wet shorts, squishy sandals, and ice cream on my face. I had to concede that some things would never change. "I get the feeling Mom wants to do this on her own."

"Understood. And you'll be on leave for R and R next week?"

I considered his question. If I went through the mental gymnastics of trying to explain that civilians called it a vacation, I would only have to be there longer and I had a pedi appointment in a half hour. "Yes." There. One syllable. Precious little to fuss over.

"And you think traveling unaccompanied is a good idea?"

Translation: traveling unaccompanied was *not* a good idea and insisting that it was would only be further proof that I didn't make good decisions. "I'll be fine, Daddy." Hopefully, I wouldn't be unaccompanied for long. In just over twenty-four hours' time, I'd have placed my bid on the man I intended to spend the rest of my life with no matter what my father had to say about it. However, I suspected telling my father I'd be with a well-trained, highly-skilled weapons sergeant from the Green Berets would be ranked several steps worse than traveling alone.

"I worry about my girl." And just like that I melted.

"There's no need for you to worry. I promise. I've been out there a bunch for work lately. Remember?"

"Yes, but I felt better knowing people there were expecting you. You never really explained what happened with you and First Lieutenant Simpson. Perhaps he could escort you. He seemed ready to settle down. He's an officer with a promising career ahead of him. For several weeks, you two seemed quite happy together."

I shuddered at the mere mention of the last asshole my father had set me up with. The truth was, I'd endured a half-hour of our date before I got Rachel to send me the standard fake emergency text so I could leave.

I'd told my father I liked him, however. Proof lying will almost always blow up in your face. I'd endured my lie for a few weeks and it had ended up hurting Griff. Definitely not worth it. He'd stopped calling right about the time my father had informed my brother that I was getting serious with Marc. It didn't take a genius to figure out that Smith must've mentioned something about it to Griff. "Yes, well, I got tired of not being allowed to order my own food and of him referring to himself in the third person. 'First Lieutenant Marc Simpson class of 2015 would like to order a filet medium rare and my date will have a salad.' I'm begging you, Dad, stop trying to fix me up."

Concern deepened the light wrinkles on my father's face. "Did you want the salad?"

"No. He never asked me what I wanted."

That earned a noncommittal grunt. Standard army-speak for there must be another side to this story. There wasn't but that didn't matter. "Getting through West Point is quite an accomplishment. He should be proud of his work. But if you don't care for a Point grad, another friend of mine from the air force is stationed over at Nellis. Maybe I'll just let him know you'll be in town. Perhaps you could have dinner with him and his wife. His son just came out of the Air Force Academy. He's back home on leave as well."

"No!" The awkward glances from people walking down the street let me know I'd been a touch too adamant. The very last thing I needed was one of my father's old buddies to keep tabs on me and to try to fix me up with his bratty air force officer son, while I was on a mission all my own. I cleared my throat and attempted to summon patience. "No, Daddy. I really do not need the entire air force tailing me on vacation. I'll be fine. I swear."

My father eyed me curiously. *Shit.* Suspicion furrowed his thick brows, more gray than black now. "You'll be aware of your surroundings at all times?" His questions were always ninety-five percent commands.

"Yes, sir." I knew how to play the game.

"Are you meeting a man I don't know out there, Hannah?"

"No, sir." Since Griff had no idea I would be there, we weren't technically meeting and Daddy definitely knew him. He just also hated him. Still, it wasn't a complete lie. Unfortunately, my conscience layered a dose of guilt on top of the ice cream I'd consumed thicker than the chocolate syrup I'd forgone.

"And you will not let anyone order a drink on your behalf or provide you one you did not watch the bartenders prepare?"

"Yes, sir."

"Is all of that going with you on your leave?" He gestured to the lingerie bags at his feet.

"You don't really want me to answer that do you?" I broke form.

"You will return to your room alone each night of your R and R?"

"Daddy."

"I had to try." He stood and planted a kiss on top of my head. "Be careful and maybe call your old man next week and let me know you're okay. Both of my girls are deploying. I don't much care for it."

I offered him a grin. Maybe I was too hard on him. "Now you know how Mom and I felt every time you and Smith left."

"Believe it or not, I felt the very same way every time your brother went out as well, little one. Have a nice leave." He waved as he walked away.

5

HANNAH

The next morning, filtered light from the expansive windows I paid a fortune to call my own taunted my eyelids. Whimpering, I rubbed my eyes. I should've smelled coffee. I'd methodically set that stupid coffee maker to start at five. Of course, I'd never actually gotten that timer thing to work right. Realization took a split second but then panic shot me up out of the bed.

"No, no, no! There cannot be light. Light is bad." I jerked my phone off of the bedside table yanking the charging cord from the stupid little box that connected it to the plug. "Fuck!" The battery was dead. No battery no alarm. The familiar hum of the fridge and my bathroom fan were missing.

"Oh no!" Bolting toward the bedroom door, my freshly manicured toes collided with the footboard. "Ouch! Dammit!" Pain seared from my feet all the way up to my eyeballs. Gripping my foot, I hopped on the non-injured one and made it to the door. Flinging it open, I hobbled to the kitchen. "Ouch, ouch, ouch, ugh, ouch." I flipped on light switches as I went. Nothing.

I spent one split second cursing Denver Energy, my apartment complex, my throbbing toe, and the lack of coffee in the darkened maker. I grabbed the battery powered clock Daddy gave me last year for Christmas from my junk drawer. Seven thirty. "No!"

I headed to my front door still clad in my favorite torn pajama pants and the Maroon 5 tank top I'd owned since long before Adam Levine had moves like Jagger.

My neighbor, Mrs. Lipscomb, was in the hallway staring up at the sun blazing through the atrium windows in the entrance. "We pay a small fortune every single month to live here. Why is the power out again?" I screeched.

She offered me a sympathetic smile. "Looks like they still haven't worked out that issue with the substation. I have a percolator. I can make some coffee once I light the stove." Without my glasses on or my contacts in, her face was a little fuzzy.

Remembering that my sweet neighbor had nothing to do with our constant power issues, I shook my head. "I have to be at the airport in an hour. I have to be in Vegas this afternoon."

"I saw that article about the hotel you redid out there. So sexy. I told George we really ought to book ourselves a weekend trip."

Every single one of my meticulously made plans was going to evaporate into thin air if I missed my flight. I forced what had to be a pained smile. "You and George should definitely go. I'm so sorry, Mrs. Lipscomb, but I've got to get out of here. Griff's waiting on me in Vegas only he doesn't know that yet."

"Is Griff that handsome young man who used to be in the army whom occasionally visits you and stays for breakfast?" She edged close enough for me to see the mischievous grin painted on her features and the shimmer of the sunlight in her eyes.

"Yes. That's him."

"Well, honey, you better go. I know true love when I see it. I used to send my George a letter every single day sealed with a kiss when he was over in Vietnam. My best friend, Margie and I had a plan for the day he finally came home. As soon as they lined up to get off the boat, she started shouting at the MPs holding the barriers that protesters were breaking into cars. They took off to stop the non-existent break-ins and I took off toward George. Met him on the gang plank. He swept me up in his arms and kissed the heck out of me. When he finally set me back on my feet he asked me how I'd managed to get up there. I'll tell you this, it was my scheming that impressed him enough to propose that very night."

A genuine grin replaced my forced one as she stared just past my head as if that precious moment in her past was painted on my apartment door. "Breaking through the barriers is precisely my plan."

"Well, if you need someone to distract the MPs, so to speak, I'm your woman."

"You have no idea how badly I might need something just like that. Thank you for the offer." Racing back into my apartment, I flung off my pajamas and simultaneously yanked on the jeans I'd thrown on my floor the night before all while wiggling out of my tank top. My hair got hung in the balance. I fell forward onto my bed and had to slow down to untangle myself.

"I'll have a few hours before the dinner auction after I get there. I can shower and get ready then." Having no time to contemplate my own sanity since I was in fact talking to myself, I crammed my makeup bag into the toiletry bag I'd packed the night before and shoved my glasses on my face. Grabbing my contact case, I stowed it in my purse, threw on my favorite old bra, a pink long-sleeved T-shirt, and gathered my luggage and my courage. I sprinted out the door. As long as there was no traffic on Peña, I might just pull this off.

When I stumbled under the weight of my luggage as I made it back into the hallway, Ms. Lipscomb grabbed two of my bags and headed down the stairs towards my truck. "You go get your man, honey. We'll be here cheering you on."

"Thank you." I threw my arms around her just before I threw myself in the driver's seat. It was almost eight in the morning and who the heck was I kidding thinking there might not be traffic on Peña Boulevard? Flooring my jet black GMC Canyon pickup, that was my prized possession, I whipped around a Cadillac whose driver clearly didn't have places he needed to be.

I also pled with the universe. "Please, please let me get on that plane. I swear I'll volunteer more at the food bank, and I'll do that

Siblings of Soldiers thing Mom wants me to do, and I'll donate all of those clothes I know perfectly well I'm never going to be able to fit back into to the church." I made good time until I hit the onramp construction at Tower. Tapping my left foot and my hands on the steering wheel, I willed the Buick in front of me to move it.

Twenty minutes 'til takeoff. My empty stomach seized. My heart beat out a frantic S.O.S. And my stupid brain finally rushed the one detail I'd been refusing to confront to center stage. If I wasn't there to bid on Griff that night at the auction, someone else surely would. He was kind, and gorgeous, and funny, and brilliant. But in terms of a bachelor auction, it was that faded scar just above his gorgeous hazel eyes, the way he looked like he'd been carved out of solid steel and chiseled with a blade, and that half-smirk he frequently sported that said he was thinking something dirty and would likely say it if given the opportunity, that had me worried. I wanted to cover the man in ice cream with chocolate sauce and lick it off of every square inch of him slowly and thoroughly and any other woman would want to as well.

He'd be required to spend a week in the company of some other woman and it would all be my fault. Frustration and devastation went to war in my empty stomach. Bile shot to my throat burning a path through my chest. It was laced with my own stupidity. The power in my building went out at least once a month. I should have made a contingency plan. This was why my brother was the Beret and not me.

Never surrender, Hannah. There is always a way. This time, my father's voice bolstered me instead of irritating me. There had to be a way.

I drove up over the curb and sped through the grass to pass a Budget bus carrying passengers from the rental car lots to the airport and flew toward the east terminal.

Not caring in the least how much I'd end up paying for taking up a space in the closest lot for an entire week, I threw my truck into park, hoisted my bags out of the back, and sprinted to the ticketing counter.

Thrusting my phone into the dude-at-the counter's face, I gasped for breath. He looked like a twelve-year-old. Maybe he was some kind of Doogie Howser of the airlines. There was a stitch in my side from my sprint but I'd have to get over it. "I have to get on this flight. Now," I demanded of the man-child running the ticketing counter. "I'm TSA pre-checked."

Counter dude, complete with a man-bun, spent thirty precious seconds taking another sip of his coffee then licking his lips. He took another ten to give me an incredulous glare. Bastard. With the speed of dial-up internet, he took my phone and held it under the ticket scanner. "It leaves in ten minutes."

"I'm aware of that. But I *have* to be on this flight."

He shook his head. "There's no way you'll make it through security that fast. Seems you're another example of why blonde jokes are always right." Another sip of coffee was taken. I resisted the urge to throw it in his face.

"I don't have to go through security. As I just mentioned I'm pre-checked. You have no idea the kind of planning this required. Have you ever tried to get a Green Beret to do something without them knowing it? Have you ever tried to convince someone that even if your family would be impossible from now until forever that doesn't mean you can't be together? No, you haven't, because if you had, you'd let me go so I can get on that plane."

That was when my morning went from shitty to all out fucked up. Still stuck in his molasses routine, it took him entirely too long to lift the phone on his station to his ear. He dialed three numbers. "Security, we have a potential threat at ticketing."

6

GRIFF

"S'pose I should be thankful for small favors," I muttered to myself as I shoved my laptop bag in the compartment over my seat. T had sprung for first class. Rescuing the Sports Illustrated and Major League Magazine from the bag before settling into my seat, I surveyed the plane.

Besides space to extend my leg, the reason T had probably gone for this seat, first class afforded me the opportunity to keep an eye on the boarding passengers. A couple with twin toddlers attempted to manage the kids and their bags in the barely existent aisle. One of the kids was already wailing. The guy offered me an apologetic glance as he passed my seat.

"Hey, if people can't handle a screaming kid on a plane, they need to man the fuck up," I offered. It was possible the conditions I'd lived in had slightly altered my version of discomfort but I was trying to be a better human.

"Thanks," the guy nodded. "If all else fails, we have cookies for them."

"Solid plan."

No amount of me trying not to be an ass made the whole thing more palatable, however. On top of everything else, I wasn't a fan of commercial flying. I'd jumped out of more planes than I could count. Frankly, I'd much prefer to have been given an oxygen mask and chute when I'd boarded. Nothing like the feeling you're being dropped into the unknown without a pack or pull cord.

Every time I sat on a plane as it ascended to the skies, the ghosts of my past stormed through my head. The rolling lift. That momentary lurch. The manufactured quiet. Military aircraft never gave a fuck about your comfort. They were loud enough to drown out thoughts of where you were headed and what might greet you when you arrived.

Every time I flew now, breathy memories shoved their way into my lungs when the fuel-laced air was forced in through the exhaust system right as the wheels were tucked into the plane. I couldn't stop them. I wasn't entirely sure I wanted to.

A backpack almost collided with my face. "Watch it," I snarled to the idiot-owner of said pack. He stopped with his pack in my face, blocking the way for everyone trying to board behind him. For some bizarre reason, he was talking into a hand-held camera.

"No worries. I have arrived on my flight and Vegas is anxiously awaiting my arrival. I know you're all asking yourselves why your man, Gig-splainer is doing a video on Saturday but just let me tell you. It's because I'm going to Vegas, bitches! Click the subscribe button so you can keep up with my trip and if you haven't purchased my autobio, what are you even doing with your life? Get your copy of *Gig-splainer Does Life All the Way to Paradise*. Catch you later, my gigs! Don't forget to subscribe. Click that button. Buy my book. Merch link is in the description. Subscribe!"

He panned the camera, much to the irritation of the forty people behind him all waiting to get to their seats, and then settled in the seat beside me. Great.

The way I saw it I had two options. I worked for a top-level government security firm. I could not be on camera so I could block my own face from the lens or I could rip the damned thing from his hands and stomp it into the floor of the plane. I went with an altered version of my second choice, only removing the camera from his grip but not crushing it under my boots...yet.

"Oh, are you a fan?" He offered me his hand.

"A fan of what?" I snapped the lens cover on the device, turned it off, and shoved it in the side pocket of my own seat. He would not be taking it out again on this flight.

"Of me, obviously." He stared at me like I didn't have enough sense to get in out of the rain.

"I'm going to go with no, I'm not a fan. I also can't be on camera, so keep that shit out of my face."

"Wait, you seriously don't know who I am?" Utter shock formed on his features.

"Don't know. Don't care. Whichever you need to tell yourself works for me."

"Dude, I am *the* Gig-splainer, famous YouTuber, my autobio just hit the NYT, I have like a quadrillion follows on Insta and Snap. I have the blue checkmark on my Twitter. I even have my own merch line. This nail polish," he pointed to his obnoxiously blue fingernails, "totally mine."

Okay, maybe I'd somehow missed takeoff. We'd clearly crashed on the runway and now I was officially in hell. "Look at that," I sniped. "I was so busy sitting on this plane I must've missed the boat to Give-a-fuck-istan." At least Satan had left me with my sarcasm when I arrived.

"Wait. You're going where? Did you say something about a cruise?"

"Oh, my dear God." It was always a bad sign when my brain began reminding me of all the ways I know how to kill a man without the use of a gun. In this situation, I wasn't necessarily above the idea.

"Last year, me and one-hundred lucky subscribers went on the YouTuber cruise. It. Was. Epic. Woot! Woot! Like it was just good, man, you know? Just good. Like we were there and they were there. And everyone was just...there. You know?" Clearly, this idiot was high. There was no other logical explanation.

"Did you just woot on a plane?"

"It's my thing. Woot! Woot! Gig-splainer here to explain yo' life." He proceeded to perform a dog bark while he cranked his hand above his head. What in the actual fuck?

"I could literally not care less about what your thing is, Jizz Stain, do not do that in my presence again. Ever." Life needed to start using some lube if it was going to continue to fuck me over like this.

The plane lurched forward and taxied down the runway. Damn. Now I was stuck in a seat with the very reason this country has to put instructions on shampoo.

"So, what're you doing in Veeeeggggaaaasssss?" He drawled the city's name out into more syllables than could possibly have been in his I.Q. I'd happily take the two screaming twins over Jizz Stain and his Twitter followers.

"We don't have to chat. It's a complete misconception that just because I have to endure your presence in my life for the next three hours, we have to communicate," I pointed out.

"My friends-with-bennies, Wiggleswarm, she's a YouTuber too but she doesn't have as many subs as me, went on the pill so we don't have to worry about miss conceptions. Get it?" He elbowed me. Never a wise move. Then he proceeded to howl with laughter.

I ran my fingers through my hair mostly to make certain my brain wasn't bleeding from the current torture I was enduring. The DOD needed to get on this. Put Jizz on his cruise ship with our captures. They'd break in under twenty-four hours guaranteed. "I am rapidly running out of reasons not to stab you."

"I seriously cannot believe you don't know who I am. But, dude, your arm. I think I like injured my elbow. You are ripped."

"And yet you just keep talking."

"You run some kind of fitness channel on the Tube or something? That pay well? Been thinking about adding another channel."

I said nothing. There was no safe way out. Any answer I provided would only force me to endure more of his incessant narcissistic drivel. At that very moment, the plane lifted off of the ground. I was trapped and alone. No amount of army training or Beret PACE methodology was going to help. I'd been spotted so evade and escape techniques were out. He was going to keep talking and I was going to end up having to store him in an overhead compartment. It was inevitable.

"Where are you staying on your vacay?" he chirped.

Assuming he'd decided I was going to Vegas for a vacation, I drew in a deep breath of recycled air. "Wherever you're not."

"I'm doing a show at The Obelisk. Pretty sweet if I do say so myself."

Fuck me.

He continued, because of course he did. "After my show, I'm gonna do this live thing where I go out on The Strip and take comments on my latest 'Splainer vid series - 'Chicks and Their Monthlies.' After that, Wigs and me are going to Denver for a mountain trick shoot that should bring killer views."

I clenched my jaw but clearly the trauma to my brain was extensive and the words spewed forth despite my efforts to dam them back. "Their monthlies?"

"Yeah, I'm not afraid to get into real life, you know? Like that's what my channel is all about. Real life. I did a series where I explain to girls about their bleed weeks. Got a ton of views."

"And your plan is to go out and ask women about their menstrual cycles while you're in Vegas?"

"Yeah. Like in-depth, too. I want to hear from my people. Answer their questions. It's basically my job to explain it. It's like my gift to the women of the world. You get it?"

"No. But what I'm most baffled by is your insane belief that women need you to explain their bodies to them."

"See, you don't get my purpose, man. If I don't explain it, who will? It's my brand."

"The women of the world really should not have to put up with the sheer amount of shit free-flowing out of your face right now. They've been through enough. We've worn them out collectively with all of our utter bullshit. Leave them the hell alone." I felt genuinely sorry for every single person lacking a Y chromosome that was in the state of Nevada at that moment.

However, on a personal level, occasionally the universe gives you the thing you need most. I wasn't going to have to kill the extra paddle on the douche canoe. Some fantastic woman with god-awful cramps and a real perspective on life was going to do it for me and I would gladly tell any judge willing to listen that he had it coming. Hell, skip the judge. I'll help her hide the body.

"Hey, I bet you totally do know me. You've read my autobio, *Gig-splainer Does Life All the Way to Paradise*? You read it and didn't know it was mine because it totally doesn't say 'by Gig-splainer.' It says by Nelson Q. Linn because that's like my real name but not the name I go by which is obs Gig-splainer. All of my followers are my gigs and giggettes. That's what I call them. The 'all the way to paradise' part had to be a smaller font because it wouldn't all fit on the cover with my name. Basically, I'm a national hero. I totally made my publisher put a close-up shot of my face on the back cover. You know, so if any of my followers have worries or nerves about kissing, they can just practice on my face. I'm there for my people, bro."

Never before had I ever wanted to punch myself in the face. I ground my teeth instead and shifted in my seat. The dull throb I was more than accustomed to began in my hip. It didn't hurt nearly as bad as my head but, hey, he was the national hero, right? "How old are you?" I demanded.

"Nineteen."

"How the fuck does a nineteen-year-old even have an autobiography? You have no life experience."

"Uh, duh, I keep telling you I know stuff and I explain it to people."

At that moment, God himself must've decided I'd suffered enough because the flight attendant stopped by with the liquor cart. "Can I get you anything, sir?"

"No, but you can do something for me. I am too old, too tired, and entirely too sober for this." I framed Jizz Stain's face with my hands. "Either find me another seat or leave the cart here."

Three hours later, I stifled the guttural groan that threatened to tear from my lungs as I forced my body into a standing position to disembark the plane. My ass ached from the seat in coach and my leg felt like someone had set it on fire. Still, it was better than what I would've had to endure next to Captain Braincells in first class.

I could walk it out once I was off of this godforsaken jet. Besides, the flight had given me ample opportunity to come up with a plan. Going to this ridiculous bachelor auction was not happening. I'm not some kind of desperate loser. I may not have many fucks left to give about this life but when I do give a fuck it's a good one. I've been known to blow Hannah's mind more than once. Hell, with her, I could do it more than once an hour. The surgeons had done right by my junk. It had gotten my baby off repeatedly every time I'd snuck down to Denver.

Hannah's form swayed through my mind again. Shaking my head, I tried with everything I was to force the memories away, something I was going to have to learn to do a better job of. She'd moved on. She needed to. God, I wanted that for her. I wanted her to have the kind of life she deserved. Killer career, a million reasons to smile every damned day, kids. All of the things she'd always wanted. The things I just wasn't certain I could give her.

She was with someone now. Someone whole. Someone who wasn't me. My mission was to figure out how to be okay with that. There was no reason I couldn't blow off a little steam this week. Maybe it would even help but I wasn't going to be forced into it.

I had my checkbook with me. I'd write a hefty check to Home-front Heroes, surely more than I'd ever garner at some auction. If my team wanted me to vacation, it was going to be on my terms. End of story.

With every step I progressed down the jetway, my leg loosened up. I was almost to a normal gait when I entered McCarran International. Thank God. Like a dumbass, I'd packed in my duffle so when I picked up my luggage it would be apparent that at some point I'd been in the military. Nothing drew attention more than an injured serviceman. I didn't need people's thanks or their awkward pity. I just couldn't do it today. It had been my job. I tried to do it to the best of my ability but I'd failed my team. My failures had nothing to do with the American people. They'd deserved better.

A repetitive clanging sound and obnoxious neon lights assaulted the air. Pressure built in my skull. Rolling my eyes at the slot machines in the freaking airport, I headed to baggage claim. The casino at the hotel would be every bit as deafening and twice as annoying.

"Great locale for a vacation, T," I grumbled to myself.

I fell in with the throngs of people heading toward the turnstiles. Stale rubber, cheap liquor, and sweat. The scents of Vegas. It was going to be a long-ass week.

Jerking an army green duffle bag off of the rolling belt, I grimaced and started to set it back down. It wasn't mine.

"Oh, that's probably mine," a guy called from a few feet away. Definitely not regular army but also not Special Forces. He had the look but not the scars. Lean muscle. Slightly overgrown haircut, not the standard high and tight. Clean shaven. He'd seen some stuff but he'd never even dreamed the kind of shit we'd done in his worst nightmares. I tossed the pack his way. "Thanks," he offered.

I gave him the standard nod.

"Hey, are you here for the bachelor auction tonight?" he sidled closer.

And here's where S.F. training came in handy. If I took too long to answer, it might be somewhat apparent, if he had any training at all, that I was lying. However, since I was not going to that auction the extended pause I offered gave credence to my lie. My brow furrowed. "What?" If I weren't there for the auction, I wouldn't know it existed.

"Sorry. I thought you might be. Homefront Heroes is having this bachelor auction thing. I got roped into participating. Figured if you were looking for a duffle, you might be here for it, too." He offered his hand. "Staff Sergeant Ryder Mathis, 101st."

As fucked up as it was this was one of the weirdest parts about retirement. I could tell people what I did, where I had been stationed, who I was. I wasn't sure I'd ever get used to it. "Sergeant First Class

Griff Haywood. Seventh Special Forces Group. Have a good friend who's also a Screaming Eagle from the 101st."

Ryder looked appropriately impressed. "Oh yeah? Who's that?"

"You know Maddox Holder?"

"Mad-dog, hell yeah. Dude's crazy."

"Hence the nickname." I offered the kid a half-grin.

"Wait did you say Special Forces Team Seven?"

"That's what it used to say on my tags."

"Bet you have some stories."

I chuckled. Yeah, that was the one thing we all had. Most of them we didn't want.

"Bet you won't tell them either." He offered me a genuine grin.

"That'd be a safe bet."

When his brow furrowed and realization lit in his eyes, I regretted not lying about my former position. "Holy shit. Team Seven. Man, are you serious? You're one of the guys who runs Tier Seven Security. You all took Northeastern Iraq on your own, before our boots even hit the ground. You dismantled that chemical weapons facility. You're in all the Tactics and Techniques textbooks now. You all got Medals of Honor."

The air in my lungs compressed. I couldn't bring more in or release the valve. I couldn't breathe at all. I should've kept my mouth shut. "Might'a done something like that," I forced out in an odd choke. Ryder must've crawled so far up his instructor's ass he'd memorized the whole freaking Tac and Tech manual.

"Fuck, man, you lost half your team. I almost forgot that. I'm really sorry."

He almost forgot the one thing I never would. I refused another response.

Offering me that pity I loathed, he carried on just like a good little soldier. "How long are you in Vegas? I'm supposed to wine and dine some chick for the week but you gotta let me buy you a beer. We owe you a helluva lot more than that so let me step up. I'm at The Obelisk. Where are you staying?"

"I'm sure I'll see you around."

"Yeah, give me your phone. I'll put my number in."

"No." I shook my head. At that moment, Ryder was entirely too...much.

He laughed. "Right. Special Forces. Here's my card. If you hit a bar later, text me." He handed over a standard army business card. I shoved it in my pocket and vowed to lose it as soon as possible.

By the time I turned back to the luggage turnstile, my bag was the only one making the loop. Throwing it over my shoulder, I forced my boots to the shuttle that would take me to my rental car. T better have gotten me something worth driving.

The Vegas sun was out in full force. It glowed almost as brightly as The Strip. I settled my Oakleys on the bridge of my nose thankful for the cover. Sweat dewed on my neck while I waited on the shuttle. I'd been living in Lincoln too damn long. I clearly wasn't accustomed to the heat. Someone caught my eye through the windows of the airport. A cheerleader blonde ponytail whipped out behind a shadowed form. She was coming off of a flight that had just arrived. But she moved away from the window too quickly for me to make out much else. Something about the curvature of her spine and length of her legs was familiar.

I shook my head. Great, now I had a bum leg, half a dick, and I was losing my mind.

Twenty minutes later, I was handed the keys to a four-door navy blue Jeep Wrangler. It was a decade newer than the one I'd bought with my first combat paycheck. I threw my bag in the back, just like I used to do every single day. My ass sank into the seat just like it always had. Instinctively, I slid the key in the ignition and let my right hand fall to the gear shift.

My mind scrambled. The years in between were too variable for me to discern the past from my present. I turned to stare at the passenger seat half expecting her to climb in beside me, to grin up at me, to tell me to get her away from every expectation the general heaped on her. I'd always been her escape and all in the world I wanted when I gripped that all too familiar steering wheel was to run away with her again. Fuck. Me. Now.

7

GRIFF

I dropped a decent tip in The Obelisk's valet's hand mostly because I couldn't stand to drive the damned thing anymore. Bracing for the onslaught, I made my way into what was admittedly one of the nicest hotels in Vegas. I'd come out here with my first platoon for one of our military balls long before I was selected for Q training. The thing you had to admire about The Obelisk was their sheer dedication to their own theme. You damn near needed a machete to get through the fabricated rainforest and a massive waterfall sat front and center out the entry doors.

Lining up behind what had to be a few other victims of the bachelor auction, I pretended to be interested in the massive aquarium behind the front-desk employees all efficiently checking people in. I couldn't stomach another round of former-soldier reunion chatter so I eavesdropped on a customer frantically discussing something with another attendant. "My purse has been on me all day. Now, my husband's medicine is gone. Someone must've taken it while we were in the casino."

"Mine too," another woman fussed. She glanced around nervously and leaned closer. "The medicine we use so he can...you know."

I grimaced. Poor guy.

"I am very sorry. We do keep security very tight but I will let them know and we'll keep an eye out for the missing medications. Be sure to check your room just in case it's there," the attendant instructed.

"He might've left it in the bathroom, I suppose," one of the women considered. "We were out late last night." The other nodded her agreement.

I moved on from that conversation. A sign advertising the bar at the Bare Pool Lounge caught my eye. Tits weren't something I ever minded getting an eyeful of. Maybe this wouldn't be all bad.

I lingered behind the guys all discussing the auction as they headed toward their rooms. Letting them clear out, I stepped up to the counter and handed over the hotel paperwork T had provided. "Griffin Haywood. I'm supposed to have a suite."

"Yes, sir. Welcome to The Obelisk." The woman smiled as her fingers flew over her keyboard. "You're in one of our Villa suites. They were just completely redesigned. You'll love it." She handed me a brochure, two key cards, and then a legit set of metal keys. What the hell? "That's for your private backyard pool." She pointed to one. "And this is so you can access the secluded wing where your suite is located."

"I have a private pool?" Clearly, the remaining members of Team Seven really thought I needed to get laid.

"Yes, sir. You also have access to a twenty-four-hour chef and your own personal concierge. If there's anything you need, don't hesitate to ask."

"Yeah. Thanks."

"Here's some information on the bachelor auction tonight and the shows going on at the hotel during your stay." She thrust another stack of brochures into my hands. "You can leave your bags here. I'll have someone bring them to you."

"Nah. I got it." People waiting on me generally set me on edge. It certainly wasn't something I was accustomed to, and I'd spent the last few years nurturing the chip on my shoulder. I wouldn't even let the nurses push my chair in rehab.

Heading toward whatever these Villa Suites were, still avoiding onlookers, I flipped through the first brochure hoping to find a map. When Jizz Stain's face greeted me on the show brochures, I dropped all of the information on entertainment into the nearest trash can cleverly disguised as a boulder.

There was no mistaking the distinctive ringing of slot machines and collective rise in volume as I neared the hotel casino. Around another few turns, I passed fancy-ass murals and sconces down another hallway and was almost to the door that would lead me to whatever exclusive room I'd been assigned when all noise was vacuumed from the very earth itself.

My mouth was suddenly drier than the desert I was standing in. "Holy fuck." My own gasp seemed to sucker punch the rest of the air out of my chest. I stared at the back page of the brochure that contained a short paragraph about the designer who'd redone the Villa Suites. And there she was. Her headshot stared up at me.

Owner and Lead Designer, Hannah Hagen, of Palindrome Design out of Denver brings her own brand of sensual class and refinement to The Obelisk Villa Suites. There was even a quote: *'I wanted to create a retreat within the hotel itself. I kept the themes of understated elegance, indulgence, and forbidden romance in every hand-picked detail. I want couples from every stage of life to rediscover what made them fall in love. It's the kind of place I'd love to spend a week with someone I love.'*

This time the blare of alarm bells wasn't coming from the slots. They were lodged in my skull. There was no fucking way. I never told anyone about her. No one. Her father was the only one who knew about us and he'd made it abundantly clear that I was never to tell anyone else. How the hell had T...? No. It was all some kind of sick coincidence. It had to be. *'If you'd get over yourself for the better part of a minute, maybe you'd figure out that you need to do this.'* T's insistence slammed through me again along with the fact that he'd rented me a fucking Jeep to drive around this week. My bag tumbled down my arm and fell to the floor. The hotel surrounding me swam in my vision. The words forbidden romance and her wishing she could spend a week here with someone she loved backstroked through the bile in my gut.

Holy shit. If T knew...who else had figured us out? There was no fucking way Smith knew about this. Not with all that shit he was shoveling about my new equipment. Not with the way he'd been damn near giddy about me coming here.

My hands shook as I fished my phone out of my pocket. How could T have done this? How could he have traded one brother for another? That's not how we worked. That was fucked up beyond all recognition. The damned phone slipped from my sweaty grip and landed on my bag. *Get your shit together, Haywood.*

Finally managing to call T, I paced in the corridor. If the next words out of his mouth weren't "What the hell are you talking about Hannah for," I was going to fly home and murder him. Four rings and then voicemail. Fucker. It took several deep breaths for me resist the urge to hurl my phone against the nearest indoor tree.

"Sir, if you have a key to the Villas, I'd be more than happy to escort you to your room." One of those twenty-four hour concierges offered me a concerned smile. His deep British accent and thinning black hair made me wonder momentarily if I was about to be whisked away to a few London rooftops via an umbrella and a song. I was fairly certain I'd already lost my mind so I probably looked like an escaped psych ward patient out for an afternoon stroll. I had to know if she was here before I went about accusing the men who had never let me down.

Slowly, an idea formed in my mind. "Yeah. I have the key." I held up the set I'd been given.

"Right this way, sir."

As I followed the dude in a three-piece complete with white gloves down the corridor, the only available option I had locked into place.

"My house isn't this big," tumbled from my mouth when he opened the French doors to the suite. That got me a polite chuckle. Another thought dogged my already addled mind. "Does everyone involved in this auction have a suite like this?"

"I'm not at liberty to say, sir. Can I get you anything? Draw you a bath? Perhaps give you the tour of your suite? Fix you a drink? You must be tired after your flight."

"I'm fine and also capable of bathing all on my own. Who's paying for my suite in particular? Thomas Byrd? Does that sound familiar?" Hannah had more talent in her tiniest toes, the ones I most loved to suck, than I'd ever hoped to have in my lifetime. But she better not have spent her hard earned money on this for me. Shaking my head, I tried to forcibly remove the idea that she was even there. That was insane.

The ponytailed woman who was racing through the airport sprinted through my mind again. There was no fucking way.

The concierge drew a measured breath. "I wouldn't know, sir. That kind of thing is handled with the front desk staff."

"Right. One more question, is anyone else assigned to this suite with me?" The army did it regularly. Maybe Homefront Heroes figured we could all bunk up. That would explain all of the space.

"This is your suite alone, sir. No one else will be here unless you should invite them to stay."

There went that idea. Excitement and panic took sides and duked it out in my gut. I dug in my pocket and slammed the tip into his gloved hand. "Can you just...go?"

"Certainly, sir. If I can be of any assistance, don't hesitate." He pointed to a phone on the table near the massive seating area. "If you'd like to turn on the pool heater, just flip the switch by the back door."

I spared the suite a quick glance. I could see a massive bed in the bedroom off of the seating area. The room looked to be half the length of the entire suite. If I didn't know every intimate detail of my Hannah, I would never have recognized her in that suite. But every single thing my mind registered reminded me of my baby.

A small table by the door for setting down your keys. She made everyone in her presence welcome no matter where she was. Her softness was there in the flannel blanket on the sofa. The covering on the bed complete with a folded blanket at the end. Pink peonies in an antique vase were situated on the eating table. They were her favorite. The bed was full of thick white throw pillows, the kind I usually teased her about owning too many of. The motion in the scrolled iron of the deck chairs reminded me of the sway of her hips. The turquoise water in the pool beyond was the precise shade of her eyes. If she wasn't there now, it was obvious she had been.

Shaking my head, I waited on the concierge to leave me to lose the rest of my mind. As soon as the doors closed, my plan took shape in my mind. If she was there, she'd have a room. There were at least a dozen ways to get a room number out of a hotel attendant without making them suspicious. None of them were legal but that would never matter. I just needed to figure some reason to get an attendant to call her room. If someone made a call to a room from inside the hotel, they never used a standard ten-digit number. When they called, the last three or four numbers would almost always be the number of the room they were dialing. The best way to get information out of people is to make them believe you already know more than they do. If I could convince someone she was already in the hotel and that I expected to meet her, there was a good chance they'd be forthcoming with info. I just needed a believable backstory.

8

HANNAH

"I'm sorry but can you drive any faster?" I begged the Uber driver currently taking me to the hotel. I could've pedaled a bike faster.

"Traffic's bad. We only get paid if we're moving. I'm getting you there as fast as I can." The guy made precious little effort to pacify me.

"Sorry." I hoped I'd get more flies with honey. "I just need to already be at The Obelisk. They had to gate check my luggage and apparently that means you get your luggage very last." *And then you took fifteen minutes to show up at the airport even though the app thingy said you were two minutes away*. I ground my teeth.

"Yeah, I get it. You're in a hurry." He made sure I saw his eye roll in the rearview.

Shoving my hand into my massive handbag, I reveled in the smooth cardboard binding on my sketch pad. Digging deeper, I landed on my favorite worn Brazilian leather case Smith had sent me when I'd graduated from art school. I kept my beloved set of Blackwing pencils in there. I rubbed my thumb back and forth over the stitching. My typical soothing technique wasn't quite cutting it that day. Not to mention the fact that I was going to have calluses on my thumb.

Cocktails were being served at five and the silent auction dinner was at seven. Winners were announced at nine.

Relinquishing the pencil case, I grabbed my cell phone and touched T's name on my favorites list.

"He's called me three times. He knows something's up," was T's greeting.

My heart sank through my stomach and landed somewhere near the paint-splattered kicks I was wearing. "What did you say to him?"

"I haven't answered. I don't know what he knows. I guess if something went wrong with the hotel, he might try to call me. Maybe it doesn't have anything to do with you." Regret ate at T-Byrd's words.

I hated for him to blame himself for anything. He'd helped me so much. "We're the only people who know I'm on my way there."

"Yeah, so maybe he's calling about something else." T didn't sound like he believed that any more than I did. Somehow, he'd figured something out. He was a Green Beret and as their slogan says, they are second to none. Something must've tipped him off. "You know, he could be trying to back out of the auction tonight. I could see his wheels turning this morning when I dropped him off at the airport."

"You think that's it?" Hope reared once again in my chest. Maybe he hadn't figured me out.

"Could be. He'd probably try to get me to agree to forget about it in light of him making a donation to Homefront Heroes. If I agreed, it would alleviate his guilt."

"I'm almost to the hotel. I'm going to pray you're right. If he calls you again, answer and tell him he has to be there tonight."

"You got it, sweetheart. Just promise me you'll find some way to make this work so that Smith doesn't end up hating all of us. Remember we're family, okay? And we're the only family Griff has."

"Believe me, I would never do anything to break up The Sevens. I have no intention of playing Yoko in this situation."

T's chuckle eased a little of my nerves. "Good. Because that did not end well for John."

"Let me get through to Griff. Then I'll work on my brother."

"Then go make it happen, Hannah Banana." he teased.

"I'll get you for that later. We're pulling up to the hotel."

"Good luck."

"I'll get out here," I opened the door before Uber-guy had fully stopped. "Thanks!" Slinging my handbag over my shoulder, I grabbed my suitcases and raced through the side entrance doors. My computer case bounced against my knee. Grimacing, I rearranged the bags quickly, and continued my sprint.

Thankfully, people who saw me coming got out of my way. I gave my typical grin to the bronze mermaid statues near the atrium. I loved the motion in the sculptures. Their desired liberty evident in the arch of their spines with their breasts exposed and their hair thrown back. It was both invigorating and depressing. Freedom allowed only if it was captured in hardened, immovable bronze. I understood them.

Counting the seconds until I could escape to my suite to wash my hands and put in my contacts, I shoved my glasses back up my nose and rushed toward the front desk. I'd been here so many times it was second nature now.

Batting a leaf from the indoor rainforest out of my way, I whipped around some old lady demanding a photograph with two overly-muscled men in Hawaiian shirts. They seemed to be debating giving in to her request. She took it upon herself to pinch their asses. Only in Vegas. I rolled my eyes.

"Man, listen, I don't know what to tell you. The delivery is outside the kitchen doors. Your manager has tried calling her cell a dozen times. Hell, I've been calling her all morning. I don't know where she is but we've got to find her before you start checking people into rooms that don't have whatever the hell is in those boxes."

My feet froze just prior to my heart stalling. Air trapped itself in my lungs and refused to vacate. His voice. My God I would know that voice anywhere, a raspy rumble with a liquid chaser of pure sin. I peeked out around the clump of palm trees and there he was. My previously stalled heart flew. My head spun. Even thirty feet away, I could make out the harsh angle of his jaw and the expanse of muscle threatening the cotton trying desperately to keep him contained.

"I thought Ms. Hagen's work for the hotel was already completed." The attendant looked utterly confused. Poor guy. He had no idea who he was up against. Every plan I'd so carefully orchestrated shattered like glass in my hands. It wasn't until that moment that I realized I didn't have a Plan B. I hadn't arranged for any contingencies. He was supposed to see me at the banquet tonight. I was going to bid on him and spend the next week in bed with him. We'd fuck, and talk, and make love, and fuck some more, because there was a difference and we both knew it, until I convinced him that there wasn't anyone else I would ever want.

"If her work was done, would I be standing here?" Griff gestured to a mostly empty tool belt slung around his waist. Where the hell had that come from? It didn't matter. Him in a tool belt would fuel my fantasies for the rest of my life.

It took entirely too long for the panic to make its way into my stubborn brain. What was I going to do now?

"I don't think she's checked in yet. Let me try the suite she usually stays in," the attendant lifted the phone receiver and Griff leaned in.

My traitorous feet eased two steps closer to him. I didn't have my suite yet or anywhere to hide. I could make an escape to one of the bars or the casino but I was carrying all of my luggage and all of the pretenses and the lies I'd told myself about this week suddenly weighed even more than all of my bags.

Griff popped the knuckles on his right hand while he intently watched the man dial the phone. It was his tell. He did it when he was about to do something that made him nervous. What had I done?

The man brought the receiver to his ear but obviously no one was in my room to answer. A moment later he hung up. "I'm sorry, sir. She's not in her suite either."

"It's fine." Griff stepped back. "I'll find her. Thanks for your help."

"I'm sorry I couldn't help more."

"You gave me everything I needed to know." Griff stated cryptically. He'd just gotten my room number. The attendant may not have known that but he probably hadn't grown up with a pack of Green Berets.

Ice cream splattered jeans, a worn out shirt, paint-covered tennis shoes, and my glasses was not exactly what I wanted to be wearing the first time he saw me but it was going to be now or he would set up camp outside my suite. It was who he was.

"Griff." I stepped out of my makeshift hideaway as he passed by. "I'm right here."

9

GRIFF

"Hannah?" I choked. She had to be some kind of mirage. "What are you...? How are you...?" Fuck it. I didn't even know what I wanted to ask her first. All I seemed capable of doing was staring at her.

Her long blonde hair was indeed pulled back in a ponytail. The synapses in my brain seemed to all fire at once. Part of me had to know how this all had come to pass. Other parts, larger parts, wanted to drag her into my arms and refuse to ever let her go again. Wait. Where was the fucker she was supposedly so happy with now?

"You know, it's probably not great for business for my clients to think I'm not where I'm supposed to be." She gestured back to the man I'd just effectively conned her room number out of. That little mischievous grin that always turned me inside out was planted on the most beautiful set of lips in this galaxy.

"Guess I should've thought of that." Those six words were entirely too difficult to push from my mind to my mouth. What the hell was wrong with me? "Boyfriend?" Great, now I'd resorted to caveman vernacular. At least the word I'd managed had two syllables. That was something.

"There was never a boyfriend, Griff. I lied to my father and told him I was getting serious with some prick First Lieutenant he set me up with. It was all a lie. I wanted him off of my back. I'm so sorry I hurt you. I tried to call and explain. I'll only ever want..." She halted abruptly.

"What?" She'd only ever want *what*? Surely not me. That...just couldn't be. We could never be a thing. Life didn't like me that much.

She shook her head. "Are you angry with me?" Devastation cast those pale blue eyes of hers, the ones I swear I wanted to drown in, the very ones framed by her adorable tortoiseshell glasses that I rarely got to see her in. Angry? How the hell could I ever be angry with her? She was my own personal conquering angel sent from heaven to pull me up out of the seventh ring of hell.

"No. Why would...?" Back to single syllables. Shit. "Never." That was marginally better.

"You weren't supposed to see me until tonight. I wanted to at least be wearing clean clothes." She pulled that bag of hers that was big enough to pitch for cover, if things in this rainforest got rough, over a light pink splatter on her right thigh. My face did something I wasn't quite expecting. It smiled. God, she always made me smile.

"Ice cream?" I asked unnecessarily. I knew my girl better than I knew anything else in this whole fucked-up world.

She gave me a sheepish nod. Heat bloomed across her features, the precise shade of the shirt she was wearing. She looked like a tall glass of pink lemonade and I was the loser in the desert who'd somehow managed to forget his canteen for his two-hundred-mile hike. I was done for. Stick a fork in me. I was going down and I knew it. "Wait. What's tonight?" Her words slowly filtered through what portions of my brain that were still functional.

"The auction." Now even she looked at me like I was losing it.

"Right. That. Wait, did T make you come here?" Her eyes closed and her teeth sank into her bottom lip. I lost all ability to breathe. My cock, however, was suddenly alive and well. He damn near saluted her through my jeans. "Hannah?" I needed some answers. I'd do anything in the world for her but I needed my orders. I'd been an army grunt most of my life. Life worked when I followed the plan.

"T didn't make me come. I got T to make *you* come. This was all my idea. I'm sorry. I shouldn't have..."

"Hey. Stop." I took one step closer. Then another. And one more. She was temptation incarnate. I'd had her in my bed two weeks after I'd first set eyes on her. I was a rat bastard for that and when it came to her I was also a weak-ass motherfucker. The vulnerable skin of her long feminine neck contracted as she swallowed harshly. That was it. Somebody find me a fucking white flag. I eased the bag off of her shoulders, set it on her suitcase, and pulled her into my arms.

"No apologies." My eyes closed of their own accord. I inhaled her sweet, vanilla cream scent. Her slender form fit against me like two pieces of a puzzle finally locked into place, just like it always had. "So... I was supposed to show up at the auction thing tonight and you were going to bid on me?" I still wasn't sure I had this straight. The intoxication of holding her in my arms only furthered my own confusion.

She nodded against me and strengthened her hold around me. I swayed her back and forth in the middle of a rainforest, in the middle of a hotel, in the middle of Sin City. Yeah, my life made absolutely no fucking sense at all.

An ache centered in my rib cage when she lifted her head to stare me down. My chest protested the absence of her heat. "Didn't really occur to me until I saw you Beret-ing that attendant that I should never have tricked you into coming here. I can't believe you're not mad. I just didn't know what to do. I kept calling you and..."

"I didn't answer," I supplied for her. "I was trying to give you and your new guy a chance. Smith told me your dad said you were happy. I have a damned calendar where I x-ed off the days I made it without driving to Denver and taking back what's mine. It killed me every time I let it go to voicemail. You should be mad at me about that." Hey, look at that. An actual sentence or two.

"I was the one who told the lie. If I'm going to be mad at anyone, I should be mad at myself."

"I'm not mad about the auction. I'm actually...relieved." And I was. Kind of. I still had no idea how she saw this whole thing working. "Wait. How does T-Byrd know about us? Did you tell him? I never..." I couldn't verbalize the single truth about all of the lies I'd told. The secret I'd kept from my brothers. The chink in the armor. The weakest link. Our ultimate downfall.

"I didn't tell him..." The rest of a confession hung on her tongue. Didn't have to have any kind of training to see that.

"Ms. Hagen." A middle-aged woman rushed up to Hannah. I ground my teeth and reminded myself that other people were allowed to talk to her. It was just that I hadn't gotten to in what felt like years.

"Oh, Ms. Mallory, uh, this is First Sgt. Griff Haywood. He's an old acquaintance of mine. He served with my brother. He's in the auction tonight. Griff, this is Megan Mallory. She's a representative for Homefront Heroes."

What the actual fuck? Old *acquaintance*? Served with her brother? Maybe that damned plane had crashed and after my initial greeting by Jizz Stain the YouTuber, and I'd gotten my one-way ticket to some kind of Amazon rainforest in hell. That was the only thing that made any sense at all.

Only, Hannah would never be in hell. Angels don't get sent there.

"Lovely to meet you. Thank you for your service." Ms. Mallory's smile reminded me of a drill sergeant I'd had in Basic. He'd always smile just before he'd order you to sweep all of the sun off the sidewalks or fill sandbags with a spoon. I managed a nod. For some bizarre reason, she looked far too pleased with my appearance. "Hannah, the gift bags I need you to stuff are in the ballroom. Can you meet me down there to start setting up?"

"Uh..." Hannah's eyes closed for an extended blink. "Maybe. I just need to get checked in and shower. I'll be down there as soon I can."

"Sergeant Haywood, I can't wait to hear more about your service this evening. Hannah, do remember no one is supposed to be fraternizing with the volunteers until the auction." With a quick nod, she went on her merry way.

Fraternizing with the volunteers?

Hannah glanced around the crowded entrance. The check-in

lines were now almost ten people deep. "I'm so sorry about...everything. I promise I'll tell you every single thing I did to arrange all of this and how T-Byrd knew." She pulled her phone from her pocket. "I missed my original flight. I really need a shower and apparently I have to be down at the ballroom to help set up. Palindrome Design in one of the sponsors. If you're not furious with me, I was hoping to get to spend every moment of the next week with you."

"What the fuck was all of that about me being an acquaintance of yours and fraternizing?" Okay, maybe I was a little pissed. Not at her. Never at her. But at something I couldn't quite put my finger on yet.

Hannah's teeth sank into her bottom lip and my cock immediately came up with all kinds of other things, better things, she could do with her lips. I decided I wasn't angry just maybe mildly irritated, mostly because I still had no fucking clue how I'd gotten to this rainforest purgatory. Because it couldn't possibly be hell if she was here and yet if she was trying to get away, this definitely wasn't heaven.

For one thing, that Ms. Mallory chick was here and then there were the real reasons we could never be together—her father and her brother, also known as my best friend. If I somehow really did get to spend a week with my baby tucked up in that made-for-fucking suite, without Smith finding out, then we'd talk about heaven. Of course, if she was just here and I couldn't really have her, hell itself couldn't be worse than that.

She gestured her head slightly to the left. I watched Megan Mallory disappear into a crowd that had spilled out of the casino. Once she was out of sight, Hannah slumped. "Me arranging for you to be here just so I can bid on you goes against the ridiculous policy she set for the auction. She just kept on and on with rules for this. It was weird. It's the first Homefront fundraiser she's done and she's adamant that it go off without a hitch, I guess. It also goes against the contract I signed as a sponsor. We give a lot of money to Homefront Heroes because I believe in the work they do. I don't want to mess up the relationship. Guess I'm still not so good at following rules when it comes to you." Heat climbed seductively out of the V-neck of her shirt. It swirled up her neck and settled high in her cheeks. Definitely not hell.

"Neither of us were ever real good with rules."

She wasn't shouldering the blame for me.

A glimmer of light shone in her eyes. A sizzle of heat shot down my spine and, once again, my cock reminded me that he didn't give a rat's ass about Smith, the general, rules, morals, doing right by anyone, or anything else. He just wanted to be buried deep inside her. Never ever take advice from your cock. He's basically an idiot. I knew that but damn, that guy was insistent.

"Just let me go wash the ice cream off my crotch and get those stupid gift bags stuffed." She sighed.

An involuntary groan vibrated up from my gut. Visions of my tongue lapping ice cream off of her crotch, as she'd so eloquently put it, danced in my brain. My cock seemed to believe this was a forgone conclusion. He wanted me to volunteer to be her own personal shower. God knows I can get my baby girl sloppy wet. So fucking weak for her.

Shaking off thoughts of me lathering her up just prior to me drilling into her up against a shower wall, I managed a nod. "Need to return the tool belt anyway." I gestured to my waist.

"Where did you get that?" Her grin still held a mixture of shame and that adoration she always had when she looked up at me. Adoration I would surely never deserve.

"Did a little Googling. Figured out there was construction on the fifth floor. Dropped by there. Gave some guy a twenty to let me use it for an hour. Had to look like I work for you to get them to call you. Never go into a battle without your uniform and all that shit."

"Guess you can't take the Beret out of the man, huh?"

"I've tried but it doesn't seem to work. They soldered it into my brain."

"How'd you figure out I was here?" She still wouldn't meet my eyes. Instinctively, I brushed her delicate chin with my callused fingertips and lifted her face. A slight shiver worked through her. My touch still made her do that. All of the years and all of the fucked-up things I'd done hadn't tamed our fire at all. The one thing I would always crave was the one thing I couldn't ever really have. This universe was severely fucked-up.

"The way T kept saying I *needed* to come and do this. He was so serious about it and he's never serious. Then they gave me a flyer about..."

Realization rounded those sorrowful eyes that were wreaking havoc with the torn fragments of my soul. "Me redoing the Villa suites. Dammit. How could I have forgotten they were giving everyone those now? I put it in our freaking contract. I also never thought anyone would actually read the flyers."

I laughed. Jesus, first I smiled then I laughed. Two things I hadn't done much of since Smith had mentioned that Hannah was getting serious with some shit-scraper. I still had no fucking clue how I was supposed to make this work. Who knew what? What was safe to say? What did she want to happen this week? Despite all of that I was laughing like a fool. Probably, because that's what I'd always been for her.

"Thanks for not being mad at me." She stood on her tiptoes and brushed a kiss on my stubbled jawline. I grunted out my approval. "I'll meet you in the ballroom at five."

"Five." I watched her be waved through the check-in line. Guess doing work for the hotel paid in more ways than one. And then, I watched her disappear down the corridor because that was the way our relationship worked. One of us always had to disappear and I needed to remember that.

10

HANNAH

As long as I lived, I would never forget the parade of emotions I'd just witnessed marching through Griff's eyes. It still made no sense to me how he'd ever been embedded deep in enemy territory and had managed to fool people into believing he was whatever persona he'd been forced to put on like a mask. His eyes always gave him away. I could read him like a book. Maybe it was only me that could read him with ease but after what I'd just done to him, I didn't deserve that honor.

Sealing myself inside my suite, I slumped back and allowed the cool metal door to ease the fiery shame burning through me. My bags and the few remaining fragments of my dignity fell to the Ateliers Pinton rug I'd picked for the suites because the detailed motion in the designs was erotic if you knew what you were looking for.

Joining my bags, I slid down the door until I was seated on the ridiculously expensive rug.

He'd said he wasn't angry because he refused to allow himself to be angry at me. He'd lied to me and to himself. How had it never occurred to me that maybe he didn't want to be forced to spend a week with me? Maybe he would've liked to have had some say in it. I'd driven up to Lincoln three times in the middle of the night in the last two months but it wasn't like I could pound on my brother's front door and demand to see Griff or show up at Tier Seven for a chat. I'd been blinded by my own determination to get my man and not break up The Sevens.

When it all boiled down, love or not, I was using him. I wanted to have all of the things I wanted and I didn't want to deal with the consequences, whether real or perceived. I know something happened the night my father caught us all those years ago. Griff couldn't keep things from me no matter how good he was at lying. I may not know the specifics but I know something happened, something that kept him from telling me goodbye.

I'd been determined to get it out of him so I could deal with it. My plans had spilled into my fantasies as well. Once we'd dealt with my family, he could play the hero in all of my dirtiest dreams. Lately, they'd come by the dozens, always starring him. Just like he'd taught me all about vanilla sex when I was nineteen, he could teach me all about dirty sex now. I never wanted to experience any of my fantasies with anyone but him. Instead of explaining that to him, I'd just arranged to have him at my disposal.

I owed him better than this. Ms. Mallory was just going to have to find someone else to stuff her bags. I had to talk to Griff.

I hung my head in a silent prayer that I'd be able to make this up to him and my eyes locked on the ice cream stain on my jeans. "Dammit, Hannah, why do you have to screw everything up?"

Climbing up off of the floor, I marched to the shower, turned it on, flung off my clothes and allowed myself exactly six minutes to shower and re-dress. Then I was going to start at the very top and make all of my confessions to the man I loved.

The steam from the shower fogged my glasses. Okay, six and half minutes. Shower, redress, contacts, then Griff.

11

GRIFF

"Much obliged, man." I shook Joe's hand as soon as he restored the borrowed tool belt to his own waist.

"You want to do my work for me, I'll let you do that, too," he teased.

"I've done a little construction in my time. Trust me, you don't want me touching that wall." I was always better at destruction than restoration, came with my weapons sergeant title. You want the bridge to go up in flames at the touch of a button? I'm your man.

"Hey, you want to see a picture of my little girl? She's so cute. She's with her mama right now but I get to see her next weekend." Joe retrieved an old cell phone from his back pocket. Clearly my heart still had something left to give after seeing Hannah walk away again because it ached for this hardworking guy who was hanging sheetrock for his little girl. He thrust a picture of a toddler, with her short brown hair pulled up in a bow, in front of my face. She had her father's deep olive coloring and his grin.

"She looks like you." I offered Joe a smile, not that it would do anything to solve the fact that he'd made a baby with a woman he couldn't live with for whatever reason.

"You think?"

"Hell yeah. Got your smile. See." I pointed to her grin.

"Yeah. She kinda does, doesn't she? I need to plan something fun to do with her. I want her to like staying with me, too," Joe explained. "Her stepdad makes lots of money." He shrugged. The rest of the story was unnecessary.

A confessional was housed somewhere deep in the soul of every man picked for Q training and every man who ultimately completed Robin Sage, the final step to becoming a Green Beret. We sure as hell would never qualify for a cleric's collar. The beret would have to do. I'd seen it a hundred times with every single one of my brothers. People tell us things. No rhyme or reason. When we're around, they talk. Maybe they sense that we can keep our mouths shut when we need to or that because we'd seen the very worst of humanity, we could offer them something to make things better. Perhaps it was because we carried the weight of the world on our shoulders already, so what's a few more stories if it helped lighten their own loads.

"Take her to get ice cream with every topping she can think of," I instructed.

He studied me. "I can do that but it won't be as good as Disneyland."

"You never know. It might be better but you have to remember the most important part." I buried the memories of how I'd acquired this knowledge. Joe didn't need to bear the burden of my demons. They were mine to fight. Ultimately, they would be mine to slay.

"What's that? The toppings?"

"No. Just listen to her the whole time she's with you. No matter what she wants to talk about, listen to her. And thanks for the belt." I slapped him on the back and headed to the elevator. My own little ice cream loving girl and I needed to talk but not before I ripped T-Byrd several new shitholes.

To keep from obliterating him on the elevator, I dug deep and forced myself to recall just how I'd met Hannah. Smith's daddy was all too thrilled to host the newly minted Team Seven to dinner after we were assigned to Fort Carson where he was the head bastard in charge. Didn't particularly matter than Special Ops didn't fall under

Two Star General Gerald T. Hagen's command. He ran the fucking Fourth Infantry. Everyone on that base slopped up his shit.

Smith had let everyone know when his father had earned his third and fourth stars just before he retired but I refused to give the fucker an inch, not after he'd done what he done to his own kid. My own father might hold the record for being the biggest shithole in Idaho but General Hagen, he had to be a world fucking champ. Who signs their own kid up to get killed just because they're pissed?

When the commander of the Fourth Infantry tells you come to dinner at his house on the golf course, you fucking show up. I should've stayed at my apartment. I should've defied orders. Instead, I'd stepped into the bastard's home, locked eyes with his daughter, the most amazing woman on this planet, and had fallen head over boots. She was only nineteen. Nineteen years old. The worst part was I didn't care. I was that much of an asshole. I popped her cherry two weeks later. On the douche scale, I'd tipped the canoe somewhere out in the middle of the Pacific without a paddle.

The thing was the first time I set eyes on her I knew she was different. I didn't think about her age because I was in awe of her. That part hadn't changed.

All of the reasons I couldn't have her hadn't changed either.

Mercifully, the elevator doors parted on the first floor and I hotfooted it to my suite despite the throbbing in my hip. White-glove dude smiled. "Can I get anything for you, Mr. Haywood?"

"Mr. Haywood is my old man. It's Sergeant Haywood and I'm good. Thanks." Perfectly capable of opening my own damn door, I stepped inside without any assistance and had my phone to my ear a half-second later. This time the traitor actually answered. "You better fucking start talking and if the words Smith knows about me and Hannah and he's fucking fine with it aren't located somewhere in your explanation then you can just take my name off of your precious security firm. Team before individual. You betrayed him. You betrayed me. What the hell is wrong with you?"

"You done?"

"Talk. Now."

"She is worth every bit of chaos she's gonna bring to our table and you know it. There. I talked."

"And who the hell are you to decide that on my behalf, T? Who died and made you the head universe shitter?"

"Off the top of my head, Chris did."

I'd been throat punched twice in my life. A few fuckwits in Saudi got to me before I finished them. Those punches hadn't tangled my vocal cords the way the words T had just stated did. I swallowed down raw rage. It burned hotter than the fireball whiskey the boys in my old neighborhood used to cook up. "So, what? Chris isn't here anymore so now you're in charge of fixing all of us?"

He had the audacity to huff. "You never thought you'd get hurt did you? It never even entered your mind that somebody would have to check the SAPI pouches on your vest. When the medic told me to pull your plates, I prayed there'd be something in there. I knew you didn't have any family and I was covered in your blood. I knew you needed something to live for or you weren't going to make it. And I reached in there and pulled her picture out. Not only her picture but her *taped* picture. We only tape up the ones we're terrified to lose. You know that and I sure as hell do.

"So, you go on and hate me, and quit your job, and do all of the shit you just threatened to do, but no one told me you were in love with her. Seems to me one of your favorite phrases, when we were under fire used to be– 'bullets will always talk and they'll always get the point across.' Fitting because they told your story. If you'd never been shot, I wouldn't know. But I do know and I also know you've been nursing a broken heart over her for years. How many assholes get lucky enough to have the woman they want also be the one that wants them? Jesus. If you'd pull your head out of your ass long enough, I bet the two of you could come up with some way to get Smith to see that you're better together than apart. He loves her. Hell, he loves you. He may not ever want to think about what the two of you do in bed but I know he wants her to have everything in the world she wants. And man, she wants you."

My entire being seized. My heart refused another beat. The blood that had previously been pulsing in my head sank slowly downward washing me of a little of my righteous indignation. A dozen questions I wanted to ask staged a revolt on my tongue. I needed to know if he understood that my recklessness and complete disregard for the power her father wielded was why Chris wasn't at home with his little girl and his wife. I wanted to ask him if he hated me for not telling him. Had he figured out that what happened to us was all my fault? I wanted to know if he really meant that about Smith wanting Hannah to have everything, even if everything included me. I wanted to tell him what the general had done when he'd caught me with her. I wanted him to know why I couldn't do this to her or to Smith. I dammed back every question and every comment behind my teeth save one. "Why didn't you just tell me she's why you signed me up for this?"

"Because she wanted that moment, man. She's had it all planned out for weeks. She told me you'd been down to see her a few times. I already knew. Whenever you came into work looking like hell but smiling like you'd just won the damned lottery, I knew it was because of her. She wanted to walk into wherever this thing is being held and be all dressed up for you. You know how chicks are about shit like that. She was so excited. I couldn't mess that up for her. I figured you'd catch her before she got her moment though. Once a Beret and all that."

My pulse timed the silence. I had no response. I'd robbed her of her moment and that wouldn't even make the top ten list of shitty things I'd done to her.

T cleared his throat. "Why don't you just give her what she wants? Would spending a week in Vegas with the love of your life really be so bad? At the end of the week, I'll talk to Smith with you. I'll tell him how I found out and that I know once he gets over his rage he'll see how good the two of you are for each other. If he starts swinging his fists, I'll even take a pot shot or two for you. I would never betray either of you. I did what I thought was right and I stand by my decision."

"I don't think this is going to be as easy as you seem to think it is,"

I choked over the broken shard from the full confession I could never make.

"And I don't think this is going to be as hard as you seem to think it is." Of course he didn't. He didn't know the story. "Try on my way of thinking for a little while. Make the jump. Let's see where we land." Yeah, *let's see where we land*. The gamble every HALO jumper takes every single time he leaps out into thin air with faith in a mask and a sheet of nylon.

Half the time you landed in the zone you were supposed to be in and all was as good as it could be. The other half you landed in enemy territory or in your own territory but the rest of the good ole US of A's military started shooting at you because they didn't know you were going to be there. Worst case, you landed alone and had no fucking clue where you were, where the rest of your team was, or how to find your way out. Any way you went down, you were fucked until you figured out what you were doing.

Before I could point that out to T, a soft knock sounded on my door. "Sorry I said all of that shit," I ground out.

And T laughed because that's what he did. I'd proudly served with the guy for years and the truth of it was, sometimes his laughter was the best bandage you could ever ask for. "For what it's worth," he added, "I should've told you."

"I think she's at my suite door."

"Then let her in, man. All the way in."

"Yeah. God knows I owe her that much."

"Yeah, He does know that."

I made my way to the door and uttered the two words I should've said a long, long time ago. "Thanks, T." Call Ended flashed on my screen as I swung open the door.

And there she was. Glasses gone, face scrubbed clean, damp hair cascading over her shoulders in loose waves, and no longer wearing ice cream stained, ripped jeans. Now, my girl sported a white off-the-shoulder little cotton dress that showed off her ripe, dewy breasts in stunning perfection. My sweet baby was so provocatively innocent my mouth flooded with saliva and my cock took up T's banner. *Just give her what she wants.* It worked out to his advantage that what she wanted was precisely the thing he wanted to give her.

She extended her hands which currently contained one of my old Cubs caps. The last time I'd escaped to her apartment in Denver, she'd threaded her ponytail through the back, ordered me to her truck, and had driven until I wasn't even sure we were in Colorado anymore and I didn't care. We'd gotten busy in the bed of that truck three times and that was all that had mattered.

"Peace offering," she whispered.

What in God's name did she mean by that? She didn't need to offer me anything at all. I sure as hell didn't deserve it.

It took me a split second to realize that white-glove dude was still ogling her devastatingly spankable ass. An infuriated growl kicked up from low in my gut. Fucker needed to tread very, very lightly or the last thing he'd see coming would be my fist. I narrowed my eyes and slammed the door in his face.

Her brow furrowed. My blood ran hot and thick with possession. She'd wanted a moment. As she stared up at me with those sky-blue eyes colored with confusion and pain, I knew what my mission would be. I'd give her every possible kind of moment I could think of for the next week. By the end, I'd figure out some way to convince her that I wasn't worth giving up her family and that's what it would require. I couldn't tell her what her father had done. She loved the shit-stain. I wouldn't rob her of that as well. I'd taken enough from her.

Slipping the hat from her fingers, I tossed it on the couch and then backed her up to the wall. I pinned my hands on either side of her shoulders, caging her all for myself. I was a bastard. Couldn't change that fact any more than I could change my former army MOS.

Her chest rose and fell in rapid pants, presenting her gorgeous tits as an offering all for me. Her mouth parted and I swore the zipper on my jeans was going to leave a scar on my cock from its teeth. Poor guy had enough scars from being rebuilt, so I decided to give him a little something.

"Griff?" she breathed my name like a sinner's prayer because that's what I turned her into. And just like always, I was determined to do it again. "Don't you want to talk?"

"Right after I do this." I leaned in, pausing millimeters from her face, close enough that every breath was shared between us.

"After you do what?"

"What I should've done when you stepped out in front of me in the lobby."

12

HANNAH

It was wholly unfair that my entire body always reacted to his touch like it was the connection point when you hot-wired a car. A jolt of electricity shot down my spine. I arched into him. This time his growl wasn't a warning of incoming danger, like he'd given his attendant, who'd apparently spent a little too long staring at me. No, this one was a warning of incoming force.

I licked my lips expectantly. His hungry gaze locked onto my mouth.

Until he'd gotten out of the hospital, there had been years between our stolen kisses. I knew the bitter taste of his absence and I wanted nothing to do with that anymore. In the relatively short life of my design career, I'd accepted awards and hefty paychecks for my work. I'd been recognized by other artists. It was all great. I loved what I did. I loved turning over the keys after I turned a house into someone's home but none of that ever made me feel alive the way he did.

The air stalled in my lungs so it was convenient that I could steal a little of his in the breath he trapped between us. My eyes fell to half-mast. I always closed them when he kissed me so I could memorize the flavors of his lips, the motion of his tongue, and the grip of his massive hands when he took possession of me. Those memories kept me going when he was away.

Like any good soldier, he stormed me. His lips swept in with unrelenting devastation. Heat he'd detonated rippled outward from my core. I was a goner. There wasn't even time for an S.O.S. I had no desire to be saved anyway.

His tongue dove past my lips and his left thigh split my legs, forcing the loose skirt portion of my sundress upward.

An embarrassingly loud groan vaulted from my throat. He feasted on it like it was the very thing that would sustain him. I couldn't seem to make my brain understand that this time it didn't have to end. I wasn't taking no for an answer anymore. Every synapse I possessed was currently occupied with what I needed to feel, not what I needed to say.

Desperation urged me onward. "Touch me," I begged as he allowed me breath and trailed kisses down my neck. He readjusted his good leg to give himself more stability as his hands abandoned the wall and wrapped around my waist. "Yes," I whimpered. My body began to rock back and forth against his injured thigh.

The sensations he wrought with his lips were too powerful to be contained or immobilized. Raw masculinity rolled off of him in potent waves. The light minty scent of his soap and musk of his cologne teased at my nostrils. I gulped in a deeper breath and there it was. That scent of gun powder that clung to him always. Like a lit firecracker on the Fourth of July just moments before it shattered and spilled its light out in the night sky. Danger and explosive passion were fused in his skin and comprised the sheen of sweat on his brow.

His hands, callused from years of shooting without gloves, slid to my thighs. He pushed until he revealed the white lace panties I'd worn for him. The thundered groan he offered up was worth a hundred times whatever I'd paid for them. If we kept this up they were going to be ruined.

There was no room for either shame or decorum between us. That wasn't us anyway. I rocked harder against all of that muscle and sinew constrained by worn denim. His entire body was a sight to behold. All of the scars he'd been forced to wear only enhanced the dangerous beauty of him. It wasn't fair he had to cover up the might of his thighs or the definition of his chest and abs and yet I was selfish enough not to want anyone else admiring what was mine.

His left hand latched onto my ass. He pulled me higher, sliding me further up his thigh, closer to his cock. High enough that I was no longer on my feet. I'd been in his room less than three minutes and I was already flying. Yeah, my brother and my father could take a long walk off a short pier.

Using the wall for leverage, I ground against him now. My nipples strained against the satin of my bra. He brushed his thumb along the lace between my legs, teasing me, coaxing me. I burned for him, a willing sacrifice heaving myself on the pyre.

After another long exploratory session conducted by his greedy tongue into the heat of my mouth, I wrapped my left hand around the back of his neck and my right hand found purchase against his erection, so hot and heavy I knew I wasn't the only one burning. A low groan tore from his lungs as he lifted his head and stared me down. I continued to stroke until his eyes closed to preserve the ecstasy between us.

When they opened once more, he'd lost the gentlemanliness beaten into him by the army. Need burned in his eyes. "Feel how wet you are for me, baby. So needy for me aren't you? Tell me." His demand was a scarred rumble that rippled over my heated flesh.

"Yes," I choked. "You make me so wet." My entire body throbbed. Yes, this was what I needed, wanted, refused to live without anymore. A knot of pure desire pulsed behind my mound to the frantic rhythm of my heart. My blood raced through my veins.

I had no use for his polite army breeding. That wasn't my Griff. That was what he'd been ordered to be. I wanted who he was.

His stubble chafed my chin. The friction was intoxicating. I lost myself in the rough caress. The tension locked in his muscles as he kept me bracketed on his thigh came from the precious little restraint he clung to. And this was precisely why I had to make my full confession to him before we continued. I wanted no restraint from him. I needed him to understand that.

But my body still wasn't up for talking. Another arch of my spine rolled my clit against the wet lace and ropes of muscle between my legs. I choked back a plea for more. It felt so good. It would be greedy to beg. I wasn't certain I could even contain more.

And yet, I would always want more of him. There would never be enough time, enough kisses, enough conversations, enough meals together, enough orgasms to ever satisfy me.

"Come on, Hannah, baby." My name sent one last shockwave through my skin. "Let me have it. Come on my leg. Fucking soak me down with your juices. Let me clean you up with my tongue."

The rough scrape of his words sent a convulsive shiver throughout my body. My lungs forgot how to take in air. My mind centered on him, flat-lining any other information that was absolutely unnecessary. My entire being tensed in preparation. Pleasing him was always the crowning moment of my own satisfaction.

"That's it. Just let it come for me," he soothed.

Awash in a sea of his voice and his pure male scent, I threw myself forward, and clung to the only anchor I would ever need.

The quick raps on the door ripped the orgasm from my fingertips. "Sergeant Haywood, I have some paperwork you'll need for the auction tonight." The demanding click of Ms. Mallory's voice rushed the lust from me and replaced it with panic. Another knock, this one faster and more irritated. How many times had she already knocked? Had she heard me moaning or him demanding for me to come?

"Please let me in," she pressed insistently.

I wiggled until Griff set me on my feet. A tremble I couldn't halt marked what had been stolen from us. Every curse word I'd ever heard and a few he made up on the fly seared out of his mouth. If someone had actually set him on fire, I don't think he could possibly have looked any angrier.

"She can't know I'm in here," I mouthed silently.

"Too fucking familiar," he ground out, scooped me up into his arms, and stalked to the bedroom. I was perfectly capable of walking and hiding but I also wasn't complaining. My man was nothing if not a rescuer, a savior, and a provider. Three of the items on the lengthy list of things I adored about him. He stalked into the massive en suite bathroom. "Why isn't there a shower curtain?" His hot breath made me dislike Ms. Mallory even more.

"It's a steam shower. The entire suite is supposed to be about losing your inhibitions. A shower curtain goes against the whole idea. I'll get in the closet."

"That's the first place she'll look."

"Not if you don't let her in," I pointed out.

"Fine but stay quiet because when I get rid of her we're getting you right back where you were."

"What are you going to say to her?" My pulse sent constant reminders that this could be a PR nightmare. He stared at me like I must've forgotten all of his training. "Right. You got it. Sorry."

I received only a frustrated grunt as he sealed me inside the closet and then inside the bedroom.

13

GRIFF

She'd been a half-second away from coming on my fucking thigh. Any dude with a sac knew how fucking hot that was. Hell, eunuchs knew how insanely hot that was. For me, an idiot with a bum leg because my thigh had been obliterated, her sweet juices dripping out of that innocent lace onto my jeans would've brought about healing no army doctor could ever provide. My preferences when it came to her marched in by the dirty dozen. I never would've washed them, would've loved brushing my hand over her sweet cream on my jeans and remembering how I'd gotten it there.

I pulled off my T-shirt and flung it on the couch as I sped toward the door.

Fury ricocheted through my veins. It sizzled from the tip of my scalp down to my boots. I scrubbed my hands through my hair and adjusted Griff Jr. who was pissed the fuck off on Hannah's behalf. Pressing my palms to my eyes hard, I blinked away the pops of white light and hoped it would be enough to confuse my opponents. I flung open the door.

"Sergeant Haywood, sir." White-glove dude's eyes rounded as he took in my biceps and my six-pack. Back in the day, Smith and I would occasionally walk around Fort Carson with "shock" painted on his chest and "awe" painted on mine. Damn, I needed to stop thinking about Smith while Hannah was in my closet. Besides, I wasn't just showing off. I had a plan and being shirtless was part of that plan. "I did try to tell her that you had company. She's..." he paused, "rather insistent."

"Thanks. And tell me your name. I need to stop calling you white-glove dude up in my head." I tapped my forehead.

Confusion intensified the wrinkles around his eyes making him appear ten years older. "My name is Fred Jones, sir." Every single Special Forces operative loves when the universe provides us material. I'd just been given gold.

I narrowed my eyes. "Are you serious with that shit? That is legitimately the worst fake name I've ever heard and I've made up some doozies in my time. I told the head of a foreign liaison office in the Sudan that my name was Tian Tee. Get it? Okay, yeah, you don't get it. For real though, what's your actual name?"

He looked mildly frightened, which is precisely the way I preferred for him to look. If he thought I was going to forget the fact that he up and thought he could stare at my baby's sweet little ass, he was mistaken. "I assure you, sir, that is my name. Perhaps I could phone my mother if that's required." Ah, so Jones had something to prove. I could use that.

"If your mother actually named you Fred when your last name is Jones, two of the most common names ever, you should hash that shit out with a shrink. Seriously, I'll pay for the first session. That's messed up." I turned to Ms. Mallory enjoying her bewildered expression almost as much as Fred's. I needed them off balance and I needed her to forget that, according to Fred, I had company in my suite. "Did you need something?"

Her mouth hung open stupidly.

"For the love of God, tell me you needed something. Do you have any idea how long it's been since I got to take a nap?" I added a yawn and popped a nonexistent crick out of my neck for effect. Shock people with your entry and then make them feel they did something to offend you, like waking you up, and they'd become putty in your hands.

"U-uh..." she stuttered.

"Have anything to do with those?" I pointed to a stack of stapled packets clutched in her hands.

"Oh...." She stared down at the papers.

"We playing twenty-questions? Come on now. Sounds like?"

"Sorry," she cringed. "Yes, uh, here's your badge for the auction and your number. You'll uh..." her eyes landed on my chest once again. I might've flexed a little. "Um..." She actually cleared her throat. I couldn't wait to tell Hannah this story. I couldn't wait to make her laugh. And that was when I realized how absolutely fucked I was. One week would never be enough. I'd just be feeding the addiction and worsening the withdrawal when it was all over.

I refocused when Ms. Mallory remembered what she'd come to tell me. "You'll need to mingle with all of the guests throughout the cocktail hour. There will be dancing and then we'll announce the winners after dinner."

"Cocktails, dancing, dinner, winner, got it." I took the badge and gave a quick scan to the packet of information that turned out to be a list of acceptable places to be seen with the woman who wins me. I flipped the page to reveal a lengthy list of rules for the auction and how a gentleman should behave. Ten fucking pages worth of rules.

She really was worried this was all going to blow up in her face. Probably should've thought of that before she decided auctioning people off was a good way to make money. "I'll see you tonight." I closed the door before any questions about me having a guest could be asked or even remembered.

I glared at the door. If you can hear a knock through it, it's not soundproof.

The plush rug under my boots would mute my footfalls but I needed to hear what was going on outside my door. Hannah stepped out of the bedroom. I shook my head at her and touched my finger to my own lips. My baby had lived the military life her *entire* life so she knew what was up. Silently, she took a seat on a chair out of sight from the front door.

There was a peephole. That shit was getting covered up as soon as I'd dealt with this latest situation. Theoretically, hotels all used quality fisheye lens in their peepholes so only the people in the room can see out and not the other way around, but the quality of the lens was key. Cheap lens and people outside the door could catch an eyeful of whatever was going on inside the room. Should've remembered that before I had Hannah grinding on my thigh.

I stepped to the side and pressed my ear to the door. I heard nothing.

We weren't in the clear yet. There was a decent chance Ms. Mallory would remember Fred's reasoning as to why she should've left me alone and knock again.

Left to their own accord, the average human with a relatively short attention span would debate something in their own minds for less than twenty seconds. I needed Fred to keep his mouth shut about me having a guest.

On her own, Ms. Mallory would decide she'd misheard Fred as she'd seen no evidence of anyone else in my suite, and I'd given her a plausible explanation as to why it took me so long to answer. In just a few seconds, she'd go annoy the piss out of some other guy. It's always easier to trick someone than it was to convince them they'd been tricked. We humans don't care for the idea that we're so very, very fallible. She'd much prefer to believe she knew what other humans were doing at all times. That sense of control was her drug. We all had one. No one without some deep need to maintain authority came up with a ten page list of rules for an event.

"Did you say he had a guest in his suite?" Ms. Mallory's question was audible. "I was certain she'd be in there."

"I must've been mistaken. Perhaps it was one of the other rooms I'm attending," Fred supplied. So the guy wasn't all bad. Maybe I'd cut him a little slack.

"Maybe," Ms. Mallory's tone maintained her doubt. "It doesn't really matter anyway, right? He's just a volunteer. This whole thing will be great for Homefront Heroes. That's all that really matters." Yep, it was brewing right there just under the surface.

Fred, theoretically, had nothing to do with the auction and yet she needed his assurances. Knowing what someone wanted more than anything else always gave you the upper hand.

14

HANNAH

"Is she gone?" I mouthed. My heart continued to hammer home how stupid I'd been to have arranged all of this. Why did there always have to be so much at stake when I was with him? Why couldn't the universe just cut us a freaking break? I could already see the clickbait blog titles now: Design sponsor of bachelor auction for charity gets caught.

Griff nodded and joined me on the couch. "Come here to me," he ordered. I grinned at his determination to follow through on our previous mission but I wasn't going to be distracted again.

Reaching, I scooped up his baseball cap and rubbed my thumb along the worn rim. "I need to talk to you first." When I refocused on him, it finally slapped me across the face that he was shirtless. "Did you seriously take your shirt off to distract her?"

And there was my cocky smirk. My God, I loved this man. He waggled his eyebrows. "Shock and awe, baby doll." He pointed to each of his pecs in turn.

It took a rather extreme amount of effort for me to trap my giggle behind my lips. My cheeks reddened from the task. I shook my head at him. "I like to think of both shock and awe as belonging to me, Sergeant."

He scooted closer. His right hand rubbed my knee and his fingertips disappeared under the skirt potion of my dress. It took even more effort than it had taken me not to laugh to deny his questing hand. Our magnetism wasn't going to be denied and the delight in his eyes had returned. I hadn't seen it in so long. Every time he'd come to Denver there'd been insistency, and desperation, and love there, but never delight. "You're not jealous are you?" He weighed his words, part kidding, part worried he'd actually upset me.

My eye roll was involuntary. "You do have a very high opinion of yourself."

His chuckle was half-haunted. It pricked at my heart. "I definitely don't."

Leaning closer, catching that underlying scent that made me lose my mind and my inhibitions, I brushed a kiss on his cheek. "I am not jealous but I am taking this opportunity to say that for the next ten disagreements we have I reserve the right to flash my tits at you and therefore win."

This time his chuckle was genuine. He narrowed his eyes. "Do I get to touch them or do I just get flashed but can't touch? Torture is against the law. The DOD said so."

The giggle I'd been keeping at bay sprang free. I batted his right hand from my leg and he latched it onto my rib cage instead. When he wiggled his fingers, I jerked away. "Do not tickle me!"

"Why? It's fun."

"Griffin Duke Haywood."

"Damn, full name. You trying to scare me, Hannah B? Now, tell me, do I get to touch or not?"

My lips pursed and I kept my arms pinned to my sides in an effort to keep his fingers away. "Fine you can touch as long as I win the argument."

"Half the time, I also get to use my mouth," he continued his negotiations. His earlier thrill was still alight in those hazel eyes. The sun from the patio doors highlighted the faded scar above his right eyebrow. Yep. I was done for. "Fine but I get to choose the times you get to do that."

He took one moment to consider. "I agree to this arrangement." He offered me his hand. I knew what was coming. When I shook on our deal, he took hold of my hand and yanked me into his lap. Gravity and Griff, the two fundamental forces of nature I could never fight and would never want to.

"We have to talk. I need to apologize," I insisted.

"What in God's name do you have to apologize for?" He cradled me against him. Warm muscle enveloped me completely. The satin covered steel of his skin pressed against mine and made me long to strip bare so there was no longer anything between us.

Weak against his strength and my own complete lack of resolve, I nuzzled my head on his substantial shoulder. I went as far as to brush my lips on his neck. The touchpoint sent another round of sparks directly to my pussy. But I would not be weak this time. I had to apologize. Only, my hands had gone rogue and were clearly no longer taking orders from my brain. I ran my palms over the firm planes of both shock and awe.

"Mmm, honey, you keep doing that and the Department of Defense can come try to drag me away because I'll be torturing you in every delectable way I can think of."

"I'm sorry I tricked you into coming here." I lifted my head to stare him down.

"What?" That was the second time that day he'd looked utterly confused. Another round of guilt walloped through my stomach.

"I shouldn't have gotten T to help me do this to you. I should've come up with some other way to see you. You should've had the option to not have to be auctioned off. I mean..." I climbed out of his lap and began to pace. "I'm pretty sure after that kiss and all of the other"—I gestured to the approximate location on the wall where he'd had me on the knife's edge of a climax I would never forget —"that you do still have feelings for me but I shouldn't have just assumed that." I shrugged and increased my pace in the tiny vestibule where I'd had large antique dressers installed that served as storage space. "I got T into this. It wasn't fair to either of you. I jeopardized one of the most important relationships in your life. I'll apologize to him, too."

In one adept move, he stepped in front of me halting my progress. "Look at me." Anger riffed in his tone. I lifted my eyes from his chest to his face. The intention in his gaze kept my feet locked to the cool tile flooring. "The sixteenth of March. You were standing behind your mom in the entryway of the biggest house on post. It had that dark Parquet flooring that popped when you walked on it. You had on this..." he gestured to his own shoulders, "...white tank top thing that had the word love spelled out in flowers. And a pair of cutoffs that were so short I almost came in my uniform as soon as I laid eyes on you. You looked so annoyed your brother's whole stupid team had been invited to dinner and you had to be there.

"I have no fucking clue what else went on that night. I kept trying not to stare at you but, my God, it was like telling me not to breathe. Not ten seconds before we all got there we'd been harassing Chris about Maddie. I'd sworn I was never going to fall in love and then you looked up at me, and smiled, and blew all of that straight to hell." He grinned and tucked a strand of my hair behind my ear. Every vocal cord in my body strangled on the memories. He recalled every detail. "You were drinking something from Starbucks."

"A mocha coconut frappucino. They'd finally put a Starbucks near the PX. I was so excited," I filled in a few details of my own.

His half grin spread liquid warmth through me. Every moment of that night was etched in my memory as well, along with every moment I'd been in his presence in the last seven years. They sat on my chest like a lead weight.

"Yeah, I know. I used to have you one waiting for you in my Jeep, when you snuck out of the general's house, but that night all I wanted was to taste it off of your lips."

I grinned up at him. "As soon as I saw you, I wasn't annoyed that I'd had to stay to meet the team anymore. I was trying so hard to be cool. I tripped when you offered me your hand and I spilled my coffee all over that shirt."

He grinned. "You've never been too good at getting all of your food to your mouth, baby doll. Then you cursed, and your daddy almost birthed live cats over your language, and I fell hopelessly in love with you. And absolutely nothing about that has changed."

"Daddy has never understood my affinity for pretty things and the word fuck. But you looked miserable down in the lobby." I would never be able to wash away that remembrance no matter how many good ones he replaced it with. I'd hurt him deeply.

He quirked a pained half-grin I couldn't decipher. Even his eyes didn't give away what he was thinking this time. "When I was in the field..." grumbled from him. The sound reminded me of the noise the tanks at Fort Carson made they smashed their way over the gravel out by the airfield. "The things you didn't know could be what got one of your team members killed. I knew something was coming. Made me a little nervous that I didn't know what it was. If I'd had any clue that you were the beautiful incoming bombshell, I wouldn't have looked miserable. I would've been so fucking thrilled to see you I would've been able to give you your moment." Regret ate at the last word as it slipped out of his mouth.

"My moment?" I didn't understand.

Before he explained, I was lifted back up into his arms. He settled us on the couch and tucked me against him once again. "Can't stand that you thought even for a second that I wasn't still in love with you. I'm going to hold you until I know you've gotten over your epic bout of insanity."

"It must not have been too bad of a bout. I wasn't going to just let you walk away. I did get you out here." I was still a little proud of myself for that.

"You did do that and now you're apologizing for it. Still don't know what that's all about."

"It's not just tricking you into coming here. I had a whole agenda of things I wanted to do with you while we're here. My head ran away with my heart again and all of that."

"You are aware that one of the things I love about you is that you never take no for an answer. Your stubbornness and wild schemes turn me on."

Bliss popped and fizzed under my skin. My grin spread the width of my face. "That works really well for me."

"I'm glad but let's hear about this agenda of yours. You make me a list of everything you want us to do this week and I'll make every last thing on it happen."

Of course he would. He was Griff and if I asked him to bring me home an entire constellation of stars he'd fly up there, leap out into space, and capture every single one for me. "I know you would." Guilt clawed away that bliss that had existed in my chest a moment before. "But I have no right to use you that way. I never even asked if you wanted to come here. I took total advantage of your love and willingness to spoil me rotten."

"Maybe so, but we're still nowhere near even."

"What?" Even? What the hell did that mean?

"You remember that night about three months after I got sprung from Walter Reed when I showed up at your apartment the first time after I'd moved in with...into the house?"

His omission of my brother's name spoke volumes. He was still determined to keep us in separate worlds. That would never work. "I remember." His eyes closed sealing off my cipher to him. "Griff, what's wrong?"

A harsh breath escaped his lungs. "I was losing my fucking mind that night. Couldn't think about anything but you. Fuck. I needed you so bad my entire body burned like I'd been doused in lighter fluid and your brother had struck a match. I was..." His jaw clenched.

"Scared," I supplied readily though that didn't quite cover it. When he'd beaten on my door at two o'clock that morning, he'd been terrified.

He nodded. "Yeah. 'Cause I wasn't sure...everything was going to work the way they kept saying it would. I couldn't imagine what kind of a life I would even have if I couldn't feel the way it feels deep inside of you. I'd lose my mind if I couldn't see the look on your face when we're together, hear the sounds you make for me, feel the way you love me. I'd buried seven of my brothers and still couldn't breathe. It was like I'd run out of emotion before I was even close to running out of pain. I couldn't even see until you let me in your apartment. Then I just..."

"Stop." I wrapped my arms around his chest. "You didn't do anything wrong. What we did that night...it was exactly what I wanted you to do."

"I used you," scraped from the depths of his throat where his admission must've been mired in shame. How had we never talked about that night? "I'm sorry, Hannah."

"Stop it. Right now. This has to stop. Don't you see what we keep doing? We keep swallowing these lies because we're so hungry for each other."

"Smith." The single word escaped his tongue. He stared me down. Weary caution darkened the golden flecks in his eyes until they almost disappeared.

I knew this particular mountain in our relationship would take an endless amount of time for us to traverse. I was fine with that. Patience was something I'd acquired in the last several years. "Yeah, we need to talk about him and a lot of other things. We're not going to keep ly..."

"Do you really think...?" he cut me off. I sealed my lips shut already knowing what he was likely to ask. "You really think this will work?"

"By *this* do you mean do I think we can spend a week here without Smith finding out?" He was so not getting where I was going. *Men.*

"Yeah. That."

"I don't care if he finds out anymore as long as you're okay with that but I will never come between The Sevens. I think we could stay down here for a long time and he'd never know, though. He's aware you're supposed to be on vacation for a week."

"I'm an asshole for doing this to him."

"No, you're not. You're an amazing friend to him for not wanting to hurt him. I know he's just as much your brother as he is mine. Maybe even more so but this is sounding kind of incestuous so you get where I'm going. I don't want to hurt him either but I'm getting tired of hurting us, too."

His arms circled around me tighter, crushing me to his chest. "I can never hurt you."

I dammed back the fact that every single time he insisted we couldn't be together it hurt me. Now, wasn't the time. I had to walk this mine field with extreme care. I was the general's daughter and the Green Beret's baby sister. I knew how to follow a plan even if I did occasionally get ahead of myself. "You never told me what moment you were talking about."

He tucked my head under his chin. "T said you wanted to surprise me in the ballroom tonight, all dressed up for me or whatever. I'm sorry I ruined that."

Another flash of heat bloomed across my cheeks. "I did want that but this was way better."

"I wasn't going to come in there tonight," he confessed.

My mouth dropped open as I lifted my head. "You were going to ditch me?"

"I didn't know I was ditching *you*. Every freaking time I thought about spending a week with some woman who wasn't you it made me sick," he confessed earnestly.

It was by nature of their positions and their careers that Berets often heard confessions. Smith had explained this late one night when I sat in the hospital room with him after one of his surgeries. Watching men die often elicited a seemingly insignificant story they wanted to share one last time. Being a savior brought on the same effect. People tell them things because they seem like gods in armor, unstoppable, unbreakable, and without remorse. But they weren't gods and their armor could be lifted from their bodies. They were mere men and those men needed someone to shoulder every single one of the confessions thrust upon them often at their weakest moments. T had readily agreed when I asked him if he was sure I was the person meant to help Griff carry the lockbox of confessions he housed in his soul. I was thankful he'd shared that one.

"I love you," I whispered.

"I love you, too, so fucking much."

"Then let me go get ready for my big moment. I get to spend the week with a man I love so much it hurts."

He stared at me as I cemented the truth between us. It hurt every time we chose to inflict the pain on ourselves instead of bringing the scars out into the light and allowing them to heal. Somehow, I would convince him of that.

"You never told me about your agenda."

"I'll tell you tonight after the auction when I get to order you around." I joked and laughed instead of cried. It was often the role of the army wife. I'd learned from the best.

"I do not mind being ordered around by you at all but I meant to ask if you need some cash, baby. I don't want you spending your money on me."

I gave him another one of my signature eye rolls. "It's for charity and I have plenty to give. Besides, I have to do this on my own." I traced my short fingernails along his collarbone loving the way his body shuddered at my touch. "If I don't, then I can't make you do my bidding for a whole entire week."

His left eyebrow raised and I earned myself another one of those cocky grins. "I take it I'm not going to be doing your laundry or cleaning out your suitcases for you."

"Definitely not. I'm hoping we get extremely dirty this week. Cleaning is off the table altogether."

"Oh honey, believe me, if you need someone to get you dirty, I'm reporting for duty."

"I was hoping you'd say that but I really am sorry if any of this put you in a bad place or if I caused you to be mad at T."

"I'm not mad at T or at my girl. I'm...fucking thrilled, honestly."

"Me, too."

15

GRIFF

One of the last conversations I'd ever had with Chris replayed in my head as I helped Hannah escape my suite without Ms. Mallory, high queen of the bachelor auction, discovering her. We'd been in Iraq for eight months and every day I lost a tiny fragment of my own sanity. Chris called me out, told me to take a walk with him. He knew I was coming apart at the seams.

Nothing made sense anymore. I'd gotten an email from Hannah from the hidden address she'd set up so her brother would never know who they were coming from. She'd poured out her heart to a screen and I had no way to answer her, to reassure her, to promise her I'd figure out some way to hold her in my arms again.

The demon who'd taken up residence in the chip on my shoulder kept tempting me to tell Smith and then to inform him that as soon as we got home I was marrying her and the general could just deal. I couldn't remember why I'd ever wanted to join the army, or to be a Beret. I couldn't remember enough of the things I'd needed to run from to figure out who I was running to. I couldn't remember why we kept fighting a snake with more heads than we could ever sever from the body.

If I closed my eyes, I swear I could still hear the muted puff of our footfalls in that godforsaken dust that would cake inside our boots and clog every damned weapon I was in charge of. There were days when the dust storms would blot out the sun. You couldn't tell which way was up. Like drowning in air and shooting into a cloud that occasionally shot back. If I concentrated, I could still feel the permanent grit in the air that whipped your skin with every lash of the wind.

Chris had asked who I was missing so badly. I'd told him no one. He called me a flat out liar and for once I didn't argue.

"You've been missing someone since the first mission we went on. Since you've never said a word about her, I took that to mean I shouldn't ask. She pretty?" His smile said he was willing to let me spill everything gnawing me in two from the inside out and that he'd keep his mouth shut.

"Fucking gorgeous." I couldn't do it anymore and Chris would never have asked for her name.

"When's the last time you heard from her?"

I shook my head. He'd understood. Sometimes hearing from them made it better, made it bearable. Sometimes it made it so much worse it was like inhaling fire. The thing was you never knew if it would help or if it would hurt until the phone call was over.

"Might could get you a sat. phone. You could try to call her," he'd offered. We hadn't seen a satellite phone in ten weeks and even if he could've located one it was him that needed to call home. He had a six-week-old baby he'd only been able to see in a few grainy pictures Smith had managed to get downloaded with his old Toughbook, a classified internet network, several unclassified servers, and most likely two cans and a string. Besides, my calls always had to be made far away from my brothers.

"Fuck off, man," I'd supplied which was Special Ops speak for thanks for trying.

He'd chuckled. "S'posed to be another sand storm today according to the illustrious army theater weather predictors."

"Guess I'll clean out the guns again tonight. Can't fucking wait." I could still hear the disdain in my own voice.

"Day in the life..." he'd supplied expectantly. I was supposed to fill the wind drenched silence.

"You ever get so sick of looking at all of us you want to quit?" I'd finally asked.

"Every damned day of my life. And if T doesn't quit snoring I'm gonna shoot him," he'd joked.

"Like I said, I'll have you a clean gun tonight."

His laughter was whipped away in the incessant breeze. "I just try to make the weeks at home heaven so I can endure hell with you losers. For what it's worth, I wouldn't want to walk through it with anyone else. You all know that, right?"

"Yeah, we know."

"I figure the days at home in bed with Maddie where I bring her coffee and she orders pizza that we eat on for days so neither of us has to get up are so good I can't complain about the fucking moon sand in my sleeping bag." He kicked the fine dust with the toe of his boot. The ensuing cloud choked out what was left of my patience. "You can't know heaven until you've seen hell kind of thing," he'd concluded just before we were greeted with mortar fire in the distance.

Shaking off the memories, I knew he was right. If I could have this one week of heaven with Hannah, I could go back to living in hell, which was pretty much anywhere she wasn't. I wasn't an idiot. I knew she wanted me to agree to tell Smith about us. If she went as far as to lie to her father about a made-up boyfriend, then he was still a fixture in her life she kept dusted. She had no idea what a confession would detonate, the people we would hurt, the people we would infuriate. I would never allow her to be caught in the crossfire and I could never look either of them in the eye and tell them what the general had done to keep me away from her.

Digging deep in my seabag, I located the survival kit I still carried with me everywhere. Fetching a roll of electrical tape, I placed two pieces over the peep hole and then viewed my suite in a whole new light. Everywhere my vision landed, it conjured up images of Hannah splayed out all for my taking. The warm pink flesh she kept hidden from everyone but me, soaked and ruined at the force of my hands and my cock.

Every horizontal and a few vertical locations in the suite beckoned. Places where I could turn her into a limp pile of pure satisfaction over and over again.

Tossing my bags in the bedroom, I flipped on the shower. She wanted a moment. She wanted to make me drool, to make me ache with need, to make me fucking burn with it. And I was going to give her every single thing she wanted that week if it was the last thing I ever did.

16

GRIFF

"Damn." I halted my progress half way to the ballroom. I'd forgotten that badge thing I was supposed to wear. Reminding myself of the prize that came at the end of this ridiculous auction, I turned back to rescue the badge. I was so fucking anxious to see her I'd left a half hour before cocktails were set to be served. Couldn't give her the moment she was after if I wasn't there when she arrived though, right?

I'd seen movies. I knew what I was supposed to do. She walks in. I struggle to breathe much less speak. None of that would have to be forced. That was my reaction most every time I saw her. I march in, tell her how beautiful she is, sweep her off her feet, cue the montage where I either let her run to me and I lift her up in the air or I hold onto her hands and spin her around in Central Park while the seasons change in the course of one song, and then whisk her off to my room.

"Back so soon, Sergeant?" Fred smiled.

"Forgot that badge thing with my number on it." I allowed him to open the suite door for me this time.

"Then how would Ms. Hagen know whom to bid on?" Mischief glimmered in his eyes and I narrowed mine.

"Who?" I never missed a beat.

Fred chuckled. "She's a doll. I learned her name while she was here with her design team but didn't get to speak with her. Beautiful girl and quite the talent. Since she did march into your suite, sir, I have to assume you two know each other well. I have no idea how she arranged all of this but that woman with all of the rules seemed rather insistent that she find Ms. Hagen. I didn't care for her urgency. Tread carefully and remember, I'm happy to help if I can."

Okay, so he had me but that didn't mean I had to give anything else away. "Just bear in mind that she's mine and I'd kill for her. Wouldn't even tax me honestly."

"American soldiers." He allowed his deep British accent to free flow now. "I assure you I will keep that in mind. Perhaps while you're here you could lay down your arms so to speak. Indulge in her. Might make her happy."

"I'll keep her happy, Fred. But thanks for the advice." Stalking back into the room, I located the paperwork for me to be freaking sold and headed back to the ballroom.

It was still twenty minutes before the event was set to start when I arrived. The band was tuning their instruments. The metallic peal of an electric guitar split through the thick expectation that hung in the air. There were a few other victims standing around with bewildered expressions they were trying to conceal with bravado and might. It was the way of the military from the Marine Corps Devil Dogs all the way up to the Special Forces Snake Eaters. None of us were sure what was going to happen and that was never a comfortable feeling.

"Hey, I thought you weren't in on this?"

It took me a minute to remember his face and then another to recall his name. Ryder Mathis from the airport made his way over.

"Never said that," I reminded him.

Genuine humor played in his features. "You are awfully unapproachable."

"And yet here you are." I grinned at him. Now I was making small talk with relative strangers. Hannah made me a better person. There was no denying that. "I'm just giving you a hard time, man. You know anything about how this all works?" I gestured to a long row of tables with black cloths draped over them. There were twenty cardboard boxes wrapped with white butcher paper lined up along the table. Odd decor for a military event. The boxes reminded me of those Valentine holders the teachers used to want us to make back in grade school.

The lights weren't low enough for the candles scattered around the room to give the desired romantic glow I assumed they were going for. Vintage recruitment posters from all of the branches blended into the bland walls. One thing was certain, my baby hadn't been in charge of decor. The room held none of her class and none of the polish she put on every project she worked on. There were gift bags stacked on one of the back tables. Clearly, someone had stuffed them while she was in my suite.

"Yeah, so apparently, we all have a box. Our pictures are on them." He pointed across the room. Narrowing my eyes, I couldn't quite make out which box had my picture from across the long ballroom. If T had been in charge of supplying a pic, it was likely one of me looking like a dumbass passed out with an oxygen mask strapped to my face or one of me burrowed down in mud like a pig with a rifle and a helmet. I started to pray that it wasn't my bootcamp picture but then remembered it didn't matter. Hannah had seen all of the pictures of me like that. She knew a few of the things I'd accomplished and what I'd had to do to get the job done. She loved me anyway. T was right. I was one lucky motherfucker just to have that. I didn't deserve to have her for my whole life anyway. The thing was, she deserved a whole life.

Mathis marched on jerking my attention back to the table. "The chicks will fill out their bids and drop them in the cut-out slot. Ms. Mallory announces the highest bidders at the end of the night." He shrugged. "Should be fun, right?"

Oh, I would be having fun in a few hours when this thing was over and I whisked my baby back to that suite and kept her there for a week. As for him, I couldn't answer that. "Guess that depends on the bidders doesn't it?"

"Yeah. Guess so."

Three other men all in suits approached. We participated in the ridiculous male practice of sizing each other up. Ridiculous only because I could take them all on with one fist. They seemed to come to the same conclusion.

Mathis offered them nods. "This is Seth Seeger, Mike Watson, and Drew Morris. We met at the pool a little while ago. Guys, this is Griff Haywood. SF Team Seven." He added a great deal of weight to the words *team* and *seven*.

"Do you think they at least got women our age?" the Watson guy asked.

"No idea." For Watson's sake, I hoped he got someone he could have fun with.

"They had to make a donation to even get to bid so that's something I guess," he continued to rattle off information.

"What the hell does that have to do with anything?" If his point was that at least the women making bids had money, so that somehow made them better, they were all about to find me extremely unapproachable. So unapproachable that I knocked his ass through the back wall to get him away from me. I crossed my arms over my chest to keep from strangling him just yet.

His eyes made it to the approximate size of a half-dollar. "Nothing really. Just that at least they're familiar with the organization. I'm doing this for a buddy of mine. Homefront Heroes is helping him pay his chemo bills."

Okay, so Watson was one of the many, many people on the planet who didn't think before he spoke. That didn't make him a bad guy just an idiot. "Give your friend my best."

He nodded and then lifted a glass of wine off of a tray as it was shoved under his nose.

"That'll be seventeen-fifty," the tray-wielder informed him.

Watson spit back the sip he'd taken. "For one glass? I thought drinks were compliments of Homefront Heroes."

"Some drinks are but not this wine." He gestured to the credit card reader on his hip and held out his hand. "This is a new plum wine out of California. It's rather expensive." The waiter waved his fingers back and forth like Watson was just going to hand over a credit card due to his summoning. "The terroir is evident in the taste."

"It's kinda...weird." Watson scowled at his glass. "I don't want to pay for it."

"You're probably just getting the flavor of dog." I rolled my eyes.

Wine guy scowled. "For your information terroir is the environment in which the fruit is grown not something a consumer of hops would ever understand I suppose. And it's terroir not terrier."

"To-may-to, to-mah-to. All I'm hearing is dog," I countered.

At that moment another dude in a tux exited the kitchen area with a tray of what appeared to be glasses of Jack. My own personal hero. I waved him over. The waiters shared a quick glare. I lifted a glass of whiskey from the tray. Every male nearby followed suit. "I told you they weren't gonna drink that much less pay for it," whiskey guy reminded wine guy. Oddly, he had no credit card reader on his apron. The all too familiar tightening in my gut and twinge in my bad hip said something wasn't right. Dammit. What was this wine idiot up to and why did I always have to notice everything?

"A refined pallet is something that has to be cultured, not that members of the armed services would understand that." The wine guy puffed up like he'd invented the yo' mama jokes and someone had given him the Nobel Prize of comebacks.

"Oh, dude, leave the sarcasm to the professionals. You're gonna choke on the shit and hurt yourself," I ordered.

Ryder's cohorts all chuckled as wine guy slunk to another group of soldiers.

Suddenly, Ms. Mallory was upon us. "Sergeant Haywood." She gave me a quick nod. "Lovely to see you this evening. I am sorry I woke you earlier."

"No problem." I downed a sip of Jack and reveled in the burn as it centered in my chest.

Another woman who appeared old enough to have seen the turn of two centuries butted her way into our group.

"Oh, Ms. Rutherford, welcome." Ms. Mallory straightened like someone had shoved a yard stick up her ass to perform a tonsillectomy. "Gentlemen, this is Victoria Rutherford. This is her first Homefront event but I know she's going to be... generous this evening."

"Boys," Ms. Rutherford traced her index finger down Watson's arm. The clogged scrape of her voice sounded like she'd either been smoking ten packs a day for the last seven decades or she'd swallowed the motor off of a lawn mower.

Watson cringed and managed to step back discreetly.

Two other women of equal age flanked Ms. Rutherford. They were all dressed in red, white, and blue sequined gowns. "These are my gals, Gladys and Edith," she whirred. We all smiled at the original Golden Girls in our midst. And no one was shocked when Ms. Rutherford whipped out a pack of Pall Mall's and lit one up.

Still unable to remove that yard stick, Ms. Mallory gripped Ms. Rutherford's wrist. "You can't smoke in the hotel, ma'am. You'll have to go outside."

Ms. Rutherford rolled her eyes and took a long drag. "Honey, if I'd lived my whole life fussing over rules I never would've spent the last fifty years being happily married to seven of my husbands. The eighth was a center ring shitshow." She paused to drown her lungs in another round of nicotine and bury the rest of us in a smokestack. "I married him for kicks but that wearing a red clown nose and cape to bed got old faster than I'd planned. With him we were able to use the same cake we'd had at the wedding for his funeral." She laughed at her own joke. "Normally, I let them hang around longer than that."

I chugged the rest of my Jack. Ms. Mallory's eyes goggled. "She wasn't married to all eight of them at once. They, uh...all passed...in their own time...I mean."

One of the women, rasped her index finger along my jawline. My stubble caught in the knit gloves she was sporting.

When she coughed and then batted away the smoky haze, I used the slight veil of emphysema to escape. Mathis had the same idea and followed me out.

Turning back toward the door, my mouth dropped open of its

own accord. Holy mother of God she was stunning. At some point in my life I'd clearly done something right because damn... just damn.

The skin tight dress in black and white should've been illegal. The sky high heels she was wearing framed her ass in an offering I intended to own. Her tits spilled over the low neckline. She'd pulled her hair up in one of those loose twist things, showing off her delicate neckline. Those legs went on for several miles. Savage possession twisted hard in my gut. *Mine* was the only word my mind was capable of understanding. All fucking mine. All for me.

"Holy fuck, look at her," Mathis all but purred.

Utter hatred took up residence in the marrow of my bones.

Hannah's eyes met mine. I was fairly certain music swelled from somewhere. Surely that shit wasn't all in my head. Her sweet grin melted a little of the hatred I'd acquired recently. She headed my way.

"Damn, why do they always go for Special Forces?" he whined.

"It's the scars, man. You gotta have the scars."

17

HANNAH

M*ine.* I didn't have to hear him say the word to see the warning flare in his eyes as he stared me down. I wanted nothing more than to sink into the possessiveness armored in his battle-ready stance. As soon as I laid eyes on him, my body required that I be near him at all times. I shouldn't have been so obvious. I should have mingled with all of the men up for auction but when it came to him all bets were off. Rules were made to be shattered into a thousand unrecognizable pieces. If Ms. Mallory figured out that I'd arranged for him to be here, so be it. I'd deal with the fallout later.

He handed his glass to a guy standing beside him. His laser-sight radar locked onto me and he edged two other men out of his way to get to me in the fewest number of steps. "My God, sweetheart, heaven couldn't possibly be more beautiful than you are." Okay, so he was making my moment every possible clichéd thing I could ever have dreamed it would be. What can I say? When I pick out the guy I want to spend the rest of my life with, no matter what it might cost me, I do it right. "Isn't there someone I can fucking pay so I can get you out of here now?"

"I don't think that's how this works," I reminded him.

"Then we need to fix it because I'm gonna need a metal fucking baseball bat to beat back the assholes staring at my baby."

"There are lots of women here. Besides, I only want you. No one else could ever keep me satisfied." I prayed he'd take that in the dirtiest possible way. The craving grunt my flirtation elicited said he'd gotten the message loud and clear.

"You keep tempting me like that I'll throw you over my shoulder, fly you back to my suite, tear that dress off of you, and take you so hard you feel it for the next week and that'll just be the appetizer."

Another two quick steps and I was fully in his space, close enough to catch his scent and to be enveloped in his heat. Sergeant Griff Haywood in a charcoal gray suit, ladies and gentlemen, it was a sight to behold. "That's definitely on the agenda."

A tray of wine glasses slammed into my arm. "Ouch!" I winced and instinctively gripped my bicep trying to rub away the ache. The glasses rocked back and forth ominously and the carrier of said glasses looked embarrassed but managed to stabilize the tray enough to keep them from toppling.

"I'm sorry, ma'am. I didn't see you there."

"How the hell did you miss her standing here?" Griff shot angrily. Here was the thing about soldiers—they were bred to protect the people they loved at all cost. Occasionally, that meant they overreacted ever so slightly. "She's the fucking sun, asswipe. You can't miss her. The whole universe should revolve around her."

My heart turned to the consistency of a warm puddle. "Griff, I'm fine." I let my eyes plead on my behalf because he wasn't listening. Instead of noting my insistent gaze, his eyes zeroed in on the red mark on my arm. Then, in an epic bout of stupidity, the wine guy shoved his tray under my nose. "Wine, ma'am?"

"I don't care for wine, thank you." I never liked the taste. I'd do champagne on occasion but I was perfectly happy with a good beer, a Cubs game, and my man.

"Are you certain, Miss? This is plum wine from California. Quite delicious for the refined palate."

Griff's eyes narrowed. "When she said, 'I wouldn't care for any,' what exactly did you hear her say, fucker? Was that too many words for you?"

"That she was almost as uncouth as you clearly are," wine guy retorted.

My mouth hung open. He clearly had no idea whom he'd just pissed off. This wasn't going to end well for him. If Griff had his druthers, the guy was likely to be chewing both the wine and the glasses that contained it.

Apparently, his brain cells were involved in some kind of argument rendering him completely insane because wine guy pushed the tray into me again. I stumbled forward this time. Griff steadied me. Rage was locked in his features. That suit couldn't quite conceal the flex of his biceps. "If I were you, fuckstick, I'd take a very long walk the opposite direction," Griff snarled.

"I promise. I'm fine." I leapt in. "Let's go...speak to Ms. Mallory."

"No witty comeback for that, soldier?" the waiter spat. Oh, this was bad. Very, very, very bad.

"You got something you want to take up with me, you take it up with me. You leave her the hell out of it."

"It's only seventeen-fifty a glass." He explained to me like Griff hadn't said a word and gestured to a credit card reader on his hip.

"I do not like wine," I emphasized every syllable. "And drinks are supposed to be provided by Homefront."

"Then I suppose you two deserve each other," the waiter spat. "No class at all between the two of you."

"Oh, let me see if I can get a slow clap going for another one of your brilliant comebacks. Seriously, go back to your village. I'm sure they're missing their idiot. What is your deal anyway?" Griff demanded.

"What is my deal?" the waiter turned on Griff and actually shook a finger in his face.

"Dear God," I whispered, "please do not make me have to call my brother to help hide this guy's body."

"My deal is that I'm here delivering wine to unappreciative servicemen when my father should have chosen me as the sommelier at the winery instead of my ridiculous brother. Oh, he went off and joined the National Guard," the waiter shrieked. "Well, what about all of the years I spent tending the plums? Tell me that. What was all of that for? Oh, *he* went off to Iraq and is a hero."

Griff's lips folded under his teeth to keep from laughing. The wine nutjob would live to see another day. Several curious onlookers moved closer.

"That's rough, man." Griff nodded. "Really. That's just shitty. I'm sorry for your self-indulgent insanity. Narcissism is a real bitch."

"Is there a problem here?" An older man with an Obelisk Hotel name tag on his suit approached. His gaze moved from me, to Griff, to wine guy. "I'm sorry. Who exactly are you?" he relieved wine guy of his tray. "Why aren't you wearing a uniform?"

"Plum wine is the way of the future," the idiot seethed.

"Let's go." The man escorted wine guy out.

As soon as he was out of the ballroom, Griff and I both started laughing. Our laughter together was one of my favorite sounds. The others included the guttural groan he gave when he came deep inside me and the sleepy way he said my name first thing in the morning.

"I'm losing my edge." Griff sighed. "I kinda feel for the guy."

"You're not losing your edge. He is clearly losing his mind in plum wine."

"Rough way to go down, that's for damn sure." He winked at me and I fought not to propel myself into his arms. This stupid auction needed to hurry up and be over with but the events of the evening were ripe with opportunity so I took them up on their offer.

"Guess we can both empathize with a dad who does something crappy to his kids."

I watched Griff's brow furrow as he grabbed two bottles of craft beer as they went by on another tray. The tops were already popped. He handed me one. "What did the general do, sweetheart?" Molten fury popped and oozed behind the practiced calm he tried to portray.

"I was hoping you'd tell me," I came right back determined to figure this out one way or another. Whatever my father had said to him before he'd deployed that first time with Team Seven held the key to why Griff was so determined to keep us a secret.

"You want to dance?" he gestured to a few other couples who were getting to know each other on the dance floor as the lights lowered. So that's how we were going to play this. Disappointment crashed through me but I was nothing if not stubborn.

"I think I'll go place my bid first." I let him off the hook for the moment.

He smirked and my heart fluttered. That smirk would always be my undoing. He knew it and was using it against me. I'd get him for that later.

"Bidding on anyone special?" He shook his head at me.

"Very special."

18

GRIFF

So, Hannah had figured out that her father played a huge part in the reason we couldn't really be together for any length of time. My girl was cut from the same cloth as her brother. Steady determination, dogged stubbornness when they wanted something done, and a head full of smarts. She knew perfectly well that one of us would have to give something away to get the other to make a confession. Dammit. I didn't want to keep shit from her but her father's actions would infuriate her and then devastate her. I refused to play a part in that.

"Hi, I'm Savannah," a brunette stepped in front of me and presented her hand, presumably for me to shake.

"Nice to meet you," I supplied out of forced habit. I'd momentarily forgotten that I was one of the pieces of meat up on the hook for this event.

"What happened to your eye? It's weird looking." She pointed to the jagged white brand from shrapnel that had flown between my goggles and helmet one night in Djibouti. I didn't tell people that actually cared about me how I'd earned all of my many scars much less some chick trying to decide if I was worthy of bidding on based on the markings I'd collected.

"What happened to your manners?"

"I was just curious," she smarted.

"Me, too."

She spun on her heels and found some other victim. Two other ladies about my age made their approach. If this was how most women felt when they went in bars, I needed to apologize to all women everywhere on behalf of my kind.

"Hi, I'm Trina and this is my sister Becca. Our big brother's a marine. He's in Kuwait."

Unable to keep my eyes off of Hannah's delectable little ass as she bent to slip a piece of paper in the box with my picture, name, and rank, I managed a nod. "Name's Griff Haywood. Give your brother my best and send him some baby wipes, some eye drops, and some Copenhagen. He'll appreciate it." I stepped around the ladies and headed toward Hannah. I ran into another red, white, and blue sequined roadblock in the form of one of the Golden Girls I'd met earlier.

"You are a piece of Grade A prime rib, honey, and I am up for a meal," she drawled. "Most gals my age are looking for someone with a pension and an unsigned power of attorney to play doctor with, but not me. I want a hunk of man who'll make me look like I've been run over by a mayonnaise truck when he's finished with me. I got money when my first two husbands kicked the can. Now, I need a stud."

Making a return trip back to me, Hannah was close enough to hear her proclamation. Her right hand flew over her open mouth as she stopped in her tracks. Meanwhile, I tried to remember how to make my own lower jaw join with its top half and how to keep the beer I was drinking from making a rapid return.

"I'm one hell of a knitter, too. When your hotdog gun gets cold after I've left, I could knit it a sock to remember me by. I made a few for some of Gladys's boyfriends. Just keep that in mind." The woman winked at me and then went on her way before I recalled how to blink.

"Hotdog gun?" Hannah gasped as she swept in protecting me from other bidders. "Is that to go with the mayonnaise?"

I shuddered. “Never say that again. Never. Just...never. Also, you know those roast beef clubs you make me when I come to Denver? I need you to never put mayo on those again. I can basically never have mayonnaise in any capacity for the rest of my life.”

“You got it.” She bit her lips together but couldn’t quite contain her giggle.

“You know how I said I wasn’t mad about this whole auction thing?” I finally spluttered.

“Yeah, I feel the need to apologize again. Also, I promise to make it up to you and I promise no one will outbid me.”

“I’m holding you to both of those promises,” I assured her.

Despite her laughter, those cool blue eyes of hers carried a storm of shock and sorrow. She still felt bad about the auction. “And here I was hoping you’d hold me up against a few walls, the side of your personal pool, the custom tile I designed for the showers, and to the bed,” she teased.

I cocked my left eyebrow in intrigue. I’d hold her up against most any flat surface I could find. She needed to remember that it was me who’d stopped taking her phone calls. I was just as much to blame for this shitshow as she was. Our world just didn’t work when we weren’t talking. “It’s a good thing I love you.” I wrapped my arm around her.

She brushed a sweet kiss on my cheek. “I’ve always thought so.”

“Come dance with me,” I demanded. “I need something that will make me stop thinking about what my dick would look like in a knitted sock.”

Hannah dissolved in another round of giggles. “I had no idea it would be like this. Where on earth did some of these people even come from? That girl over there just told me I should’ve bought this dress in a bigger size.” She pointed out the woman who’d asked about my scar.

“And you didn’t bitch slap the shit out of her? I’m shocked,” I teased her.

“I thought about it but I love this dress and she looks like a hair-puller. What I want to know is who are all of these people? Where did Ms. Mallory find them? I know all of the board members for Homefront Heroes and none of them are here."

"No idea, sweetheart. All I know is you look so fucking gorgeous in that dress I honestly can't wait to get you out of it."

"Thanks." She gave me a bashful grin that had my cock taking up far more real estate in my pants than it had been a few moments before. "Hey, you know, if you really want a cock sock I'll knit you one. Nana taught me how a few years ago when I was home one summer and missing you."

I'd met her grandmother once and couldn't quite picture the sweet lady who'd fussed over the entire team like we were her own flesh and blood crafting thermal penal outerwear.

"To make cock socks?"

"No." She continued to giggle. "But I could improvise."

"Dance. Now."

"Yes, sir," she breathed across my ear.

I grunted my approval, set our beers on a nearby table, and dragged her into my arms on the dance floor. She melted into me and any sign of irritation from being hit on by Betsy Ross's slightly younger and far more perverted sister evaporated into thin air.

She laid her head on my shoulder and buried her face against my neck. Yeah, I was all good. If she'd forget to ask me again about her father, I would've been damn near perfect. "Hey." My whisper lifted a few stray strands of her air. I inhaled the perfume of her that wafted to my nostrils. "You know I would never have agreed to spending a week anywhere with you if you hadn't arranged this. So, thank you for always knowing what I need better than I do. I promise I'll make this everything you want it to be. Okay?" Her guilt was unnecessary. I wanted her to leave it behind and focus only on the two of us and the things we could do here for the next seven days.

Her head lifted and my shoulder instantly felt abandoned. "Thanks for saying that. I needed to hear it." Her eyes made a cursory glance around us. The music and low lighting in the ballroom provided a slight smoke screen, a concealment from the insanity surrounding us. Or maybe it was the actual smoke filtering from the Golden Girl's cigarettes. I couldn't be sure.

"Can I tell you something?" she whispered.

"Anything in the world, baby. You know that."

She gave a slight nod. "You know that night that you apologized for earlier? The first time you came to my apartment in Denver?"

"Yeah." I had no idea where she was going with this but if she was talking I was absorbing every word.

"I've been trying to practice how to tell you this. You're going to think I'm lying to you," she hemmed.

"Hey, come on, it's me. Just say it. Whatever it is."

"I hated how freaked out you were. When you're hurting, it hurts me, too. Please know that."

The flare of my nostrils from the harrowing memories brought more of her vanilla cream scent to my lungs, calming the storm in my gut. "Keep going," I urged. There had to be more.

"It killed me that you were scared but that night was...amazing." Her eyes closed as if she couldn't be in the presence of whatever was coming next. "It was amazing because you didn't hold back with me. You were...unrestrained. You let me have all of you. I want more of that. I want *all* of that."

Shame. She'd closed her eyes out of shame. "Look at me," I demanded. When her eyes flickered open, they were pools of confusion and pure, unadulterated need. "Mean what you say, baby. It takes everything in me to hold back with you. Are you saying you don't want that? Are you telling me..."

"I'm telling you I want you in every possible way I can have you but mostly I want..."

"What, Hannah? Tell me." Urgency swamped my veins. I could barely breathe. I was choking on what she wouldn't say.

"I want it hard, rough, hungry. All the things we always are for each other but without you thinking you have to be gentle with me. Tie me up, hold me down, all of the dirty things you could ever dream up right down to the most depraved and filthy fantasies I know you have about us. I want to do them. I want you to leave marks on my ass. I want to feel so empty when I'm without you all I can think about is being full of you again. I want to ache with it. I want to see the evidence of your possession on my skin. I want to be used by you. I've always wanted that and…I was…"

"Scared to ask or ashamed to admit that?" My cock burned in my trousers. I looked down to make certain they weren't actually on fire.

She swayed slightly to the music. Heat from the cradle of her thighs further amped the fever in my groin. If she'd reached her hand down my pants and had wrapped her fingertips around me to tug, I swear I couldn't have been hungrier for her. Dammit. I still couldn't be sure I hadn't died on that plane. If she was real and really saying all of this to me, this had to be heaven, but men like me, we don't get to go to heaven. If for no other reason than the fact that I wanted to protect her above all others, but the craving to corrupt her ran a close second. I'd burn in hell for the things I'd already taught her.

"Both." A tremor that probably registered on the Richter scale worked through her body. My sweet, sweet baby. Her eyes were seeking some kind of beacon, something to guide her right into my arms and into my bed. If she needed a guiding force, I would always be that for her. "Those are the things that were on that agenda I had for this week. Right at the very top of the list is to do every single filthy thing you can come up with for us to do. I want that. I need that," she all but begged.

With that declaration, the depraved side of my soul won the ongoing battle between good and so very, very bad. Jerking her closer to let her feel exactly what her admissions were doing to me, I buried my face in her hair right beside her ear. "I have one question, sweetheart." My tone carried more than a single note of warning. It was a whole fucking sonata full of it. "How wet are you right now? How wet did it make you to finally tell me what you need from me?"

She whispered two words that cemented the plans surfing on the blood surging to my cock. "I'm soaked."

"Good because from the time I get you inside my suite you'll have less than one full minute before my cock is buried deep inside of you. No foreplay. Just me taking what I want. You want me unrestrained, honey, I'll show you just how ruthless I can be."

"Please," she whimpered.

"Now."

19

HANNAH

I'd just propelled myself headfirst into the eye of the hurricane and there was nowhere else I wanted to be. It brewed right there under the invisible armor Griff kept wrapped around his skin. I'd held his darkest desires in my hands only once, the night he'd finally broken down his own walls and had come to me. I needed to hold them again so together we could heal his self-inflicted wounds.

There was something malignant wrapped up in his mind. I had to rid him of it. The only suture for the survivor's guilt he'd lived with for so long he could no longer see through it was complete acceptance. Whatever he blamed himself for, whatever it was that he had wrapped up in a box with our relationship, I deserved to know it, to hear it, to wipe it from existence.

The way he dragged me out of the ballroom said I'd gotten through at least the first layer of Kevlar. The plates underneath would be another war all unto themselves.

I should've felt guilty for leaving before dinner had even been served but this was far more important. Not to mention the ache between my legs was unbearable. The quick motion of my steps wasn't quite enough friction to bring any relief. I needed him just as much as I needed to make certain he knew whatever demons he was trying to slay on his own, I was right there to fight beside him. The check I would write at the end of the night was why we were even attending this bizarre soiree anyway. Our presence was not required.

The corridors were choked with people out for a taste of Vegas nightlife. People oohed and ahhed over the rainforest motif as the lights from The Strip filtered through the doors.

Griff made quick work of slicing through the crowds. He unlocked the entrance to the villa suites and fished his wallet out of his back pocket. Before I could ask what he was doing, he'd pulled two twenties out and restored the wallet all with one hand. The other was still being used to keep me right beside him. It was woefully unnecessary but I wasn't complaining.

Halting beside the doors to his suite, he slapped the bills into the attendant's hand. "Do me a favor and take the night off, Fred. I'll take care of anything we might need." His tone held every weight of an order from the weapons sergeant of Special Forces Team Seven.

The attendant grinned. "I understand, sir. I'll give you a little time. If you should need anything, I'll be around...just not too close."

Griff dismissed him with a nod. Another wave of heat washed through me and then centered between my legs. If I'd bothered to wear panties, they would've been soaked. The dress was too tight. There would've been a panty line. Besides, I wanted as few obstacles between us as I could get away with. He wanted to take me without foreplay. I was more than ready. The important part would come after. When I assured him that his desires were also mine, that he could lose himself in me and feel no shame, that we could find healing together.

The lock on the door turned with an audible click as he closed it behind us. The dark fire in his eyes burned away most of his practiced restraint. He shed his suit jacket and tossed it on a nearby chair. I prayed he'd toss away any inhibitions he held as well.

"Tell me," I urged again. "Tell me exactly what you want to do to me. Don't think, Griff. Just feel."

"Oh, I'm gonna feel, baby. Feel how tight you are when I haven't warmed you up. Feel how sweet you squeeze around me when I pound into you. Feel how slick and wet I make you. I'm going to feel myself fucking you raw. Just need to make sure your mouth isn't writing checks your sweet little pussy lips can't cash." The deep timbre of his voice shot jolts of need through the cream coating my lower lips.

"Why don't you come see for yourself?"

"I intend to. What's under that dress, honey?"

"Nothing."

A low thundered groan accompanied the harsh male shudder that signaled another slip of his control. My breaths were much too quick. I squeezed my thighs together desperate for relief from the achy heat gathered there.

"Say it one more time, honey. Tell me you're sure you want me to lose control with you."

"I want you to lose everything with me. I'm not a china doll, Griff. You can't break me. I want all of you, even the parts you're afraid to show me. I've always wanted those."

He popped the knuckles on his right hand. I fought not to throw myself at him, to do whatever it took to convince him he didn't have to be nervous with me. He was still worried he'd do something I wouldn't like or that if he showed me the demons he tried so hard to keep caged I might run away. I wasn't going anywhere. Not this time. "I don't need you to be a soldier for me, Griff. I want the warrior that existed deep inside of you long before you signed on the dotted line with the United States Army. Show me what you think about when I can't be with you."

That did it.

With savage possession armored in his drive, his long legs ate up the distance between us in two determined steps. "You want to hear my depraved thoughts when I'm not with you, honey. Fine. Hike the skirt of that dress up. Then bend over that couch and show me what belongs to me. Right fucking now."

His eyes followed the sway of my hips, right and then left, as I shifted to scoot the skirt up. My ass jiggled as I worked the cotton lining to my waist. An untamed growl hummed from the base of his throat.

I managed a breath that came in harsh gasps as I turned to face the rolled arm of the Chesterfield sofa. I'd picked this piece specifically for this purpose. Soft, cushioned material to provide a canvas for brutal passion. Every nerve ending in my body quivered. A hint of fear skimmed the periphery of my awareness. But my own personal halo was far too neat and shiny. It needed to be shattered and my own personal HALO jumper was the man for the job.

"Show me," he ordered. I could almost hear the chains he'd bound the warrior in scraping along the cage walls as he yanked against his own restraints.

Spreading my stance, I balanced on my high heels, and did as I was told, folding myself forward over the arm and bracing my elbows on the cushion below. I turned to stare him down. Reverence and greed went to war in his eyes. "Take me." I fed the wolf I knew he needed to free.

20

GRIFF

If there was such a thing as the sweetest sin, it was my baby offering herself up on the arm of a couch and begging for the beast I did my damnedest to keep caged. And he'd been deprived of her for so fucking long I had no hope of denying myself or her.

Laying the condom from my wallet on the couch, I'd freed my cock from my trousers in two quick moves of my right hand. I jerked my boxer-briefs down low enough to get the job done. She wanted to know the things I'd ultimately burn for, the things I wanted from her but would never take without her prompting. Fine. I'd hate myself later. Right now her bare pussy was swollen and creamy, ripe to be ravaged. I'd never be strong enough to walk away from the only piece of heaven I'd ever hold in my hands.

The spice of her arousal filled my lungs as I stepped behind her. I gripped the globes of her ass too far gone for any kind of tender touch. I kneaded her pliant feminine flesh. She wanted marks. I'd make certain she could see where my hands had lain.

A quick gasp sprang free from her. My cock lengthened and throbbed, such a weak motherfucker for my baby. Weight of restraint racked in my balls, more than I could bear.

She wanted me to lose control, wanted me to take exactly what I wanted. Done.

Gripping my cock, I traced my head up and down her slit once, twice, slicking my tip with her honey. I was a fucking inferno for her and the only relief was so deep inside her neither of us could tell where I stopped and she began. "So wet. Does thinking about me fucking you so hard you forget your own name make you drip for me?"

"Yes," she panted. "Please, Griff."

Her hips rocked upward. The sound of my name snapped the chains I roped myself in when I was with her. The bare lips of her pussy were swollen and pink as they brushed by my cock and tempted my sac. Bare all for me. She'd wanted this all along. Fuck, she'd planned this. And the thing that I couldn't rectify was that she'd planned this all for me.

She spread her stance farther, incinerating any hope I'd ever had of keeping my dirtiest demons at bay.

"Take it, baby. Take it all," I demanded as I speared through her in one dedicated thrust. Because that is what I needed more than I needed the next beat of that half-shattered organ in my chest. Desperation filtered through my veins. The blood required to pump through my body demanded that she allow me to own hers.

Unable to help myself, I withdrew a few inches and then slammed into her again with brutal force. I didn't want to see the scars from the skin grafts and reconstruction on the left side of my cock. Only she could make me whole. I sank deeper with each pass, seeking the holy water that would wash me clean.

"God, yes!" she screamed. Oh fuck, it was on. She arched her spine and I gripped her hair the way she'd gripped my heart, forcefully and with no reprieve. I rode her hard and still needed more.

Untangling my hand from her hair, I gripped the top of that dress that drove me to the brink of insanity, jerked the bodice down, and let the weight of her gorgeous tits spill through my fingers. Her nipples pressed insistently against my palms. With every thrust of my hips, she soothed the constant ache that resided there. With every slight withdrawal, she somehow tightened as I barreled back inside.

There was no room within her for me to be anything other than the man I'd been put here to be, a fierce protector and ultimately a dirty corrupter of her.

My hands scraped to her hips. My thumbs dug into the flesh of her ass once more. I worked her open until I could see her sweet little puckered rosebud seeking with every thrust of my hips. She'd asked me to show her what I wanted. I wanted her to come with my thumb teasing her ass.

I stroked her opening. She shook and gasped out my name.

"That's it, baby. You said you wanted filthy. This is only the beginning. Scream my name for me so I know how good it feels."

"Yes," whimpered from her.

I snapped my hips against her thighs hard and fast, even deeper this time. My redemption was there in the depths of her. "My name. That's all I want to hear from you."

"Griff," groaned from her as I pressed deeper between her cheeks with my thumb. Her body seized, cinching tight against my hand and my cock.

The grip of her pussy tore a deep guttural growl from my lungs. Another ragged shiver worked through her. Fuck it, I couldn't fight it anymore. Every blood cell in my body surged toward my cock with a boatload of cum. Metallic silver glimmered in my peripheral vision as I stared down at her. The unopened condom wrapper that had fallen off the back of the couch and landed on the cushion she was currently gripping with everything she was glared back at me.

Dammit. Thing probably wasn't even necessary but I didn't get to decide that for her. Letting her feel the calluses on my hands, I shoved the skirt portion of her dress further up her back as she screamed out my name. Her channel cinched around me constantly, tight pulses that threatened to decimate me. She milked away my every weakness. The vice grip of her pussy choked out my every failure, silencing the howl of my demons. Her heat consumed me.

She squeezed her thighs together and dug her nails into the

couch. That's how my baby always came, hard, fast, and with an intensity that made me weak. Then she'd curl up in my arms, sweet little sex kitten, and let me soothe away all I'd done.

I made one more pounding thrust, reveling in the perfection of her, before I pulled away and unloaded all over her ass. Spurts of my cum dripped over her gorgeous curves. It had been so damned long and the erotic sight fed the darkest fragments of my soul. I just kept coming.

Shutting my eyes made no difference. All I could see was the fantasy I'd just lived out until white pops of light shattered across my lack of vision. I gripped the sofa until I could bear weight on my hip without wavering. "Stay just like that one more minute, sweetheart," I whispered. Locating a towel from the wet bar, I wiped her clean of my seed.

When she finally stood, shame gut-punched me. She stumbled forward. Her body was still flushed from her climax. I caught her and held her against me. The former twist she'd put in her hair was undone. It hung in tangled hanks over her shoulders. The clip caught in a few stray strands. The dress, God, I couldn't stand that I'd been rough enough to have contributed to the disheveled garment oddly shoved under her breasts and over her ass. Keeping her tucked close to my chest, I managed to unzip the damn thing. I watched it slink over her slight curves until it gathered in a puddle of satin at her feet. "Baby, I didn't mean..."

"Stop." She lifted her head and placed a finger over my lips. "You were perfect."

I brushed a kiss on her fingertip and stepped back, quickly working through the buttons on my shirt. Shrugging out of it, I eased it over her shoulders as she slipped her arms through. I lifted her up into my arms and set to make up for taking her like a cheap one-night stand. Settling on the couch, I eased her adorable feet out of the strappy heels I'd left her in for the purposes of fucking her blind.

Her lips were swollen even though I hadn't gotten to kiss them yet. Next time, I promised myself, I'd take my time with her. There'd been no room for words or promises or anything else just then. Confusion fed the shame swirling low in my gut.

Guilt mortared itself inside my brain as soon as enough blood flow reversed course from the head below my belt to the one on my shoulders.

"Griff, I'm serious. That was amazing." Her voice was rough, almost anxious.

"You deserve better than that and you know it." Disgust perforated my tone. She was everything and I'd treated her like nothing.

"I deserve better than the very thing I'd been fantasizing about since that first time you visited me in Denver?"

"You fantasized about me slamming you up against the side of a sofa and coming all over your ass?" I was incredulous and had no plans to hide that from her.

"My fantasies about you occasionally get way dirtier than that," she admitted. "Despite what you, and my brother, and my father think about me, I'm not a little girl. I'm a full grown woman and I refused to be ashamed about the things I want or the man I want them from."

Her bringing up Smith and the general right after we had sex was not a good sign. In fact, I couldn't recall a single time she'd ever done that in the years that this non-relationship had been going on. Quite honestly, I'd take Smith to the mat over who loved her more. I didn't even know love was an actual thing until I met her.

As for her father, no man who'd done what he did to his son could possibly love his daughter at all. She adored her big brother and he'd all but signed his death sentence. General Hagen wanted to control her not to love her.

"I never want you to be ashamed for anything, sweetness. If you want to...push the boundaries of what we've done in the past, I'm all in, but you have to understand that me loving you more than life itself means I want to protect you from everything that might hurt you. That includes me." There. She wanted feelings, she got them.

"I do not need to be protected from you. I wish you would let yourself have something you want without convincing yourself you didn't deserve it."

My brain still hadn't fully engaged so I participated in the male tendency to grunt instead of speaking. Only thing I knew for certain, I'd never deserve her.

She lifted her head off my shoulder and brushed a kiss on my cheek. "I was unaware that one of the inhibitions you wanted to lose was the cock sock." She traced her fingernail along the V-neck of my undershirt and gave me a mischievous smirk.

"You're going to call Trojans that from now on aren't you?" I forced a mirthless chuckle.

"Definitely." Her giggle erased a little of my own confusion. If she wanted to turn up the heat, I'd set the whole fucking world on fire for her. I just had to get my head on straight.

"I didn't quite mean to lose that one. You had me so fucking turned on I'm tempted to say I forgot the damned thing. Full admission though, I love the way you feel with nothing between us. Like my own personal piece of heaven. I swear it feels like a fucking drug when I'm inside you. You're the only thing that..." I couldn't lay that on her. What the hell was wrong with me?

"I'm the only thing that what?" Fervency darkened her sky-blue eyes like night had vanquished the day. The truth shimmered there in her starlit gaze. I'd always thought of her as my own personal sun but this was different. People believed light revealed the truth. Soldiers knew the truth came to life in the flickers of fire watch. Night held secrets the daylight would never see because it couldn't contain the weight of the pain. I refused to deny her the authenticity she deserved.

"That makes me feel like I never got hurt, like I'm...a whole person."

Her eyes closed and I loathed the words I'd spoken aloud. She always disintegrated my barriers like they'd been constructed of nothing more than residue and gunpowder. "I love you," she whispered.

"I love you, too, baby, but we both know that isn't enough. Don't worry about the condom. You know you're the only person I've been with in years. Probably not even necessary."

"We do *not* both think it isn't enough and you don't know about condoms being necessary either. None of what you just said is true. It's just what you've chosen to believe. The doctors said it might be more difficult for you to make babies not that it was impossible and I don't care. I want you. If babies come out of that, great. If they don't, that's fine, too. I love being your own personal heaven. Of all the things I am or ever will be, including a mother, that's the most important to me."

Damn, she was setting me straight that night or at least she was trying. And fuck me if it wasn't somehow working. I reminded myself that she'd said it didn't matter several times but we both knew deep down she wanted kids.

There was slight damage to my vas deferens from the bullet that had shattered near my groin. I'd stopped going in for the tests after the first one showed a significantly lower than average sperm count and motility. Yet another reason, after this week, I had to figure out how to make her understand that she'd ultimately be happier with someone else.

21

HANNAH

A few weeks after Griff and I had started dating secretly, I'd talked Smith into taking me to hang out over at Chris and Maddie's house with the rest of Team Seven. Griff had done a decent job of acting like he was amused I was there, just Smith's baby sister, along with my brother and T-Byrd who were really the only members who would say much around me.

I was an outsider, a slight weakness to their tight cohesion. There was a reason Special Forces never hangs out with the regulars, as they refer to other soldiers. The secrets between them were an iron bond that both kept them alive and forever afraid to break the chain.

When Smith wasn't paying attention to us and everyone else was distracted, Griff would whisper the evening's itinerary near enough for me to hear. "Chris'll throw everyone out in an hour, sweetness. Meet me outside the Enlisted Club. I'll take you anywhere you want to go."

The E Club was always our place. My father only ever went to the Officers' Club, of course, and Special Forces would never show at the E. He'd park his Jeep in the back near the dumpsters. I could run there from my house so my father never missed my car. Griff always took me where I needed to go, straight into his arms. Biding my time without a great deal of patience that evening, I'd managed to give nothing away. His countdown was constant fuel to the fires he kept burning low in my belly. My control slipped with every warning.

Desperate to be near him, I'd wiggled my way into a circle of conversation between my brother, Griff, and Chris. Laying my head against my brother's shoulder, he'd wrapped his arm around me protectively like any good big brother would. The conversation had continued on despite my presence.

They'd been discussing something they'd done in training that day. With his greedy gaze occasionally locking between my thighs when the slight breeze ruffled the hem of my skirt, Griff had managed to focus enough to answer Chris's question. "*Yeah, but we don't have to dismantle things the way they're put together.*" He taken a long, satisfied pull on his beer. I'd caught a glimpse of his tongue and had shivered against my brother. He'd offered me his jacket. "*You don't have to take it apart piece by piece. We can blow the damned thing to hell or we can tear it apart in chunks. Your choice,*" Griff had concluded.

You don't grow up the way I did without learning a thing or two. I planned to blow Griff's insistence that Smith and my father never know about us straight to hell and if that didn't work, I'd tear it apart, chunk by stubborn chunk.

"Where'd you go, baby?" The husky rumble of Griff's tone in present-day jerked me back from my reverie.

I grinned. "I was thinking about that night I made Smith bring me over to the bonfire at Chris's just so I could see you before we snuck out. Do you remember that?"

"I remember every single moment I have ever gotten to spend with you. You hopped out of Smith's truck in a freaking mini-skirt right as Chris lit the fire pit. For a second, I thought the damned thing had sparked without a match because you looked so damn hot. It took everything in me not to march over, pin you up against that truck, and kiss the hell out of you." He paused as if the memories needed a moment to breathe. "I remember what else we did that night, too, after I got you back to my apartment."

My heartbeat quickened. I swore I could feel my own pulse

between my legs. I remembered as well. Suddenly, Griff was no longer beside me on the couch. He was on his knees before me, positioning himself between my legs.

"I'm about to ask you a question and I want the truth," he demanded as his hands skated up and down my thighs. I spread them automatically. His scent surrounded me in his shirt as the fabric spread and fluttered against my skin. His hot breath whispered over my bare pussy.

"Always." The word hitched a ride on my breathless pant.

"Did I hurt you, baby? Are you tender from what we just did?" Hot-leaded intention was locked and loaded in his darkened gaze.

There was no right answer, dammit, and he knew it. His thumbs circled higher. He licked his lips. My legs spread farther. My clit went to war with my brain. I didn't want him to think he'd hurt me. He'd never forgive himself but his implied offer to make everything feel better was a temptation I had no hope of denying. "Just a little tender," I confessed in a haggard choke. That was true. The only pain I had resided in the absence of him. A quick moan escaped when his roughened fingertips brushed the thin skin at the apex of my thighs.

"I bet I can make it feel better, baby."

The involuntary arch of my spine scooted me closer to the edge of the sofa. The rolled hem taunted the back of my thighs. "Yes."

"I can make it better just like I did that night."

"God yes." I shuddered against his tender touch and the seductive memories. I wanted to steep myself in both.

His fingertips teased at my pussy and my entire body was on high alert. I was still swollen from his earlier force. The nerve endings were raw with need.

"I remember every single thing about you that night. So fucking beautiful. The way you tasted. I wanted to drown myself in your sweet heat, baby. The way you spread your legs for me. How wet I got you on my tongue. You love when I fuck you with my fingers but you crave my mouth, don't you?"

"Oh God, yes," I choked on the admission.

"And you know I love you bare and creamy for me, don't you, baby?"

My teeth sank into my lower lip as I managed a nod.

"And you did this for me, didn't you?"

Words became a foreign concept when he delicately circled his thumb at the apex of my slit, preparing me. My eyes fluttered closed. I wanted only to feel.

"Answer me," his demand was laced with greed. I knew it wouldn't take much to shatter all of the rules and obligations he'd heaped onto his own shoulders. I just needed to locate the words.

His fingertips continued to feather over the lips of my pussy. Just enough teasing friction and pressure to make me weak. *Speak Hannah.* I whimpered instead. That smirk of his formed readily on his features. Damn him.

Summoning my own inner determination, I channeled my best sex goddess tone. "I don't think you have any idea how much pleasing you turns me on."

A flash fire of undiluted sin lit in his eyes. "Your very existence pleases me, Hannah. My God, how could I ever ask for more than that?" His tone was a wounded warning, refusing the very things I desperately desired and what he was ashamed to give.

"I know you want more than that." There. Not the most eloquent statement but his fingers were still tracing over my pussy and it was the best I could do under the intoxication of his touch. An involuntarily shiver quaked through me. A low hum of approval rumbled from low in his gut.

"Tell me, Griff," I begged, pushing him constantly closer to the cliff of pure arousal. A real relationship and an unending well of my love for him was at the bottom. I just needed him to trust me, take the leap, and free fall one more time. I'd be the thing that took his breath away but I'd also restore it.

Coasting my own hand down my torso, I captured his and pressed his fingers between my lips, right where I needed them to be.

His nostrils flared and the dark fire in his eyes intensified. His jaw worked visibly damming back the things he needed to say with the might of his molars. Using my middle and ring fingers I gathered my own dew and lifted them to his lips.

"Tell me," I whispered as he abandoned my pussy and wrapped my hand in the strength of his own. His tongue guided my fingers into the heat of his mouth. I groaned from the sensation as he began to suck. My legs opened farther in a desperate invitation, needy for his ministrations somewhere other than my hand.

"You want to hear all of the filthy depraved thoughts I carry around with me? That's what you're telling me?"

"Repeatedly," I urged.

"I'd turn your gorgeous ass over my knee. You want marks, baby, I'd leave you with marks for the months I've spent thinking you were with another man. Then I'd put you on your knees, feed you my cock, make you suck away the fucking agony I've been through thinking you weren't mine anymore. Nothing I've tried works. Nothing satisfies me even for one damned minute. Nothing but your lips wrapped around me while I come down your throat."

"Oh my God." I chased the air my lungs begged for and wet heat coated my lower lips. Yes. This. This was precisely what I wanted.

"Oh, I'm not done, honey. Not by a long shot. How fucking long has it been since I've buried my face between these fuck-me thighs? Too damned long I know that. I'd spend hours here, honey. Hours. Make you raw from coming on nothing but my tongue so many times, you begged me to fill you full of my cock just for relief."

"Yes." If he wanted me to beg, I was more than happy to oblige. My body rolled and writhed against the cushions. Victory fed the need surging through my veins.

"I'd take you to bed, baby. Take you to my bed and sate my cock on your tight, wet pussy until I ruined you. But that's only half of the things I want." He leaned in. His tongue swirled around my clit as he coaxed my lips apart.

An anguished sound of my own pure need purred from my mouth. One single brain cell kept up the fight. "I want to know the rest," was half-lost in my own eager moan. Despite my declaration, I laced my fingers through his thick brown hair and pressed his face between my legs.

Another swirl of his tongue preceded him coaxing my clit into his mouth to suckle. My body went boneless with satisfaction. My hips undulated to the rhythm of his licks. He lifted his face much to my dismay. His smirk couldn't quite disguise the raw hunger in his eyes. "I don't think that's what you really want right now, sweetness. Look how wet you are for my mouth. My baby's so needy for my tongue she can't even stay still for me. Let me make it feel better." Before I could agree, he went back to work.

His teeth scraped gently down my folds. I was soaked. The friction set me on fire. That lone brain cell who'd tried to hold out waved a white flag. I gave in to the persuasion of his mouth. As weak and wet as he made me, when he drew my clit back into his mouth and sucked in earnest all of the fragmented pieces of my world aligned and then shattered into tiny, unrecognizable pieces as I groaned out his name.

I shook. My vision clouded with my own ecstasy. My thighs clamped tight against his stubbled jaw but he wouldn't allow me to close him out. My legs were going to be chaffed. Somehow that only turned me on more.

He knew me. Knew the rhythm and friction I needed. Knew exactly how to make me come. I tensed so hard my muscles protested as the rapid spasms began. The sweetest agony. He lifted his head only when he'd wrung me dry. My own cream glistened on his lips. He licked them like a prisoner devouring the final vestiges of his last meal.

"The other things I want are only slightly more honorable than the ones I already told you. I want to put my body between you and anything on this entire damned planet that might ever hurt you. I want to be able to give you every single thing you want, every single moment of every single day. I want to fix it so that I'm the only man who ever gets to taste you like that. I want to know I'm the only man who's ever moved inside of you. The only man who makes you moan that way and knows how you tighten up with every thrust. I want to put you in my bed and piss a fucking circle around you so there is no question who you belong to. There. That's what I want."

Wow. The sheer amount of honesty he'd just laid at my feet had to have cost him most everything. "Will you look at me, please?" I spoke as soon as the orgasm released me from its clutches. His eyes lifted to mine. "I need you to understand that I want both sides of you. I want most everything you just said you needed." Maybe not the literally marking his territory confession but I got it none the less. "You are capable of giving me every single thing I will ever want or need because you unto yourself are both of those things."

He managed a haggard nod but I hadn't convinced him, not yet. "Guess we should get back to the Mad Hatter's Bachelor Auction, huh?" He'd come up with a reason for us to leave much too quickly but I knew I'd dismantled a little of his armor. I had a week to rescue him from the parts that still had him ensnared.

I wrinkled my nose. "Want to get the chef to bring us some wings here first? They're almost as good as yours."

"Bullshit. Nobody's wings are as good as mine. You take that back," he ordered as he rose to his feet, towering over me, and then let me cuddle into him when he settled on the couch.

"I said almost." With my own teasing grin planted firmly on my face, I reached to the phone on the table behind the sofa and dialed the chef assigned to the suites.

22

GRIFF

An admittedly decent platter of wings and shame swirled in my gut when I guided Hannah back into the peckers-on-parade ballroom. The band had moved on from top twenty current hits to playing *It's Raining Men* because of course. I still couldn't believe even half of what I'd admitted to her. Not that I could've stopped myself. With her, I disintegrated into nothing more than guilt and dedication.

I'd zipped my baby back up into that dress that was hot enough to fry my few remaining brain-cells. She'd removed the wayward clip from her hair and let her long blonde waves fall all over her shoulders. I'd just fucked both of us into oblivion and I was already harder than the barrel on a sniper's long-gun.

Watson circled nearby before he spotted us by the door. Narrowing his eyes and shaking his head, he made his approach. I knew what was coming and braced for impact.

Hannah narrowed those killer baby blue eyes. She'd clearly seen his knowing smirk as well. Great.

"Did you go somewhere?" Mike huffed. "I didn't see you at the dinner."

"Army not teach you to feed yourself or something, Watson?" I countered.

"How did you got a woman like her to go back to your suite ten minutes after you met her?" He spoke through his clenched teeth.

"You know what really is funny?" Hannah snapped. I couldn't help but grin. "The fact that you somehow think speaking through your teeth is going to render me deaf."

The guy needed to see about having a speed bump installed between his brain and his mouth. "Sorry," he offered. "Not like you didn't disappear though."

"Yeah, well we were enjoying a few minutes of not being here," I huffed.

"You're lucky. This whole thing is strange and I'm an intelligence analyst so I would know."

"Intelligence, huh? That explains so much." I rolled my eyes. He hadn't noticed that his fly was open so he lived on as the clear example of every joke ever made about military intelligence. "Strange how exactly?" This whole thing was more than a little shady but I was curious what Watson had picked up on.

"That chick..." he gestured to the woman who'd asked about my scar, "...had never heard of Homefront Heroes. Apparently, Ms. Mallory invited her to attend this afternoon. Her grandfather is some Vegas hotelier or something."

"So, she's like Paris Hilton?" Hannah's head cocked to the side and she screwed her mouth up into her thoughtful pose. My gaze zeroed in on her lips with scope-honed precision. She did the sexy mouth thing when she sketched as well, only she had more peace about her when she was designing.

"I guess." Watson shrugged.

"It is weird that none of the other board members are here. I've done tons of charity events for Homefront and the board always attends," Hannah continued.

I logged all of the information being thrown my way.

Before I could take a stab at what was actually going on, Betsy Ross was swaying before me and shaking what appeared to be a pom-pom made of knitting yarn. The next time the band declared that it was raining men she beat out the hallelujah back and forth with what had to have been her replacement hips. Not that I was one to judge since I was sporting a replacement as well.

"Hope you two are up for gettin' down and dirty." She pointed to me and Watson in turn. "Vicky gave me one of her spare pills for now and one for later. I'm ready to be bent over the barrel so I can salute all fifty states." She punctuated the last three words with more alarming hip gyrations. "God. Bless. America!" This time she slapped her own ass with each word.

Hannah's eyes were the size of hand grenades as she stared up at me in horror. "Wow," she mouthed.

"Yeah, I'm going to have to bleach my own retinas," I concluded. But the constant twitch of the woman's eyes was actually more concerning than what we'd just witnessed.

"Da'fuck?" Watson gasped.

"See, swearing helps. Keeps you limber so you can duck the bull-shit raining from the ceiling right this moment."

Watson actually stared up at the ceiling so we still had some work to do but then he summed, "Those women are nuts."

"Certifiable with an entire finished basement and three-car garage of what-the-fuck-is-actually-happening."

A slight pop and muffled scratch of a microphone drew everyone's attention to the dance floor.

Megan Mallory cleared her throat twice. "All right, ladies, it's time to get your final bids in. Gentlemen, why don't you line up here on the dance floor for a final viewing."

"Final viewing," I spat. "I'm either at a wake or this is the part of some kind of ritual sacrifice just before they start stringing people up on spits."

"At least it's almost over," Hannah pointed out hopefully. "I promise I will make all of this up to you."

"You naked all week. That's the only thing that could possibly make this better."

The slight dimple in her right cheek made an appearance as she gave me a sexy grin. "But I brought so much lingerie."

I considered for a moment. "Fine. But those are your only two options. Naked or lace. Or maybe my Cubs jersey."

She fucking saluted me with a husky, "Yes, sir." My cock saluted her right back. Weak bastard that he was. Damned woman would always be able to get away with murder with me and she knew it. "I love you, Griff."

"I love you too, baby." I winked at her. "I'm more amused than angry. I swear."

"I know."

I brushed a kiss on her cheek and begrudgingly followed Watson to the parade of the ritual sacrifice.

"Okay, so you two have to already know each other, right? I mean you just said you love her," he leapt as soon as he decided Hannah was out of earshot. "And I'm pretty sure her hair was up when she got here. It's not now."

"Nah, I profess my love to any random blonde with legs like that. Don't you?"

"You're hilarious."

"Agreed. Also check your fly."

He quickly fixed his zipper situation. "Seriously, if you're together why are you in a bachelor auction?"

It was always cute when regulars tried to interrogate Special Forces. "Here's the thing. We're actually here on a mission with Pentagon Intelligence. Betsy Ross's sister over there." I pointed to one of the sparkler sisters. "She's a foreign national and we suspect she's smuggling sensitive CIA information she found on an encrypted copy of Zelda from an old Nintendo that was labeled: CIA Black Operations—Do not steal."

"Wow! Are you serious? You're CIA?"

"No, dumbass. Shut up and strut." I shoved him forward as the guy ahead of us fell into line on the stage. If there was one thing all members of the military could do, it was march in a straight line.

I'd survived the Trek, as we lovingly refer to it. Three days alone in the Uwharrie National Forest hiking miles from point to point with only a map, a compass, and an eighty-pound rucksack. There was no talking, no one but point sitters that spoke only your next coordinates to you, and sure as hell no Hannah waiting on me at the end. I could walk around a fucking dance floor for two minutes even if I was currently being cat-called by the original backup singers for Tony Bennet. I needed to get the fuck over myself.

Spying a cute brunette who'd come to stand near Hannah and who was grinning at Watson, I nudged him. "Looks like somebody's interested."

"She's cute right? We danced a few times. Name's Bethany. She's an anesthesiologist. Says she wants to get wild this week in Vegas."

Apparently Vegas just loosened everyone's inhibitions including my own. "I gather you're the soldier to help her do just that."

He chuckled. "I will definitely be feeling no pain."

"Look at that, my boy. Now that was a decent joke. I knew you had it in you."

A half hour later, Ms. Mallory was finally reading the winners' names.

Slowly but surely, cautious men were paired up with eager women and began discussing hanging out for a week in Vegas. Mathis and a couple of the guys he'd introduced when I'd arrived were displaying every sign of nerves. "Be cool, man. It's just a thing," I offered them a phrase The Sevens frequently told each other.

"Says the guy who already knows who he's spending the week with. Those crazy old women are still here," Mathis spoke under his breath.

"There are still lots of guys here too," I pointed out.

Ms. Mallory continued working through the stack of winning bids. Bethany, Watson's hopeful anesthesiologist, edged toward him. His grin expanded and I genuinely hoped they had a great week. Tired of all of the pretenses, however, I had my arm wrapped around Hannah. I was entirely out of fucks to give about someone knowing she'd arranged for me to be here. I figured five minutes for Ms. Mallory to get the rest of the winners read. Another two for Hannah to write a check and then I could escort her back to my suite and make up for taking her like I'd been deployed for all of my adult life and had finally gotten leave.

Ms. Mallory continued to flip through bids. Bidding on humans would never be okay in my book. I'd seen too much, rescued too many, and hadn't been able to rescue enough. Still, I kept my mouth shut.

The winning bidder for Sergeant Ryder Mathis is...Ms. Victoria Rutherford."

The elderly woman strutted up to the stage waving a stack of hundred-dollar bills. I cringed. Poor guy was going to have his hands full. Ms. Mallory continued before I could offer him some helpful info.

"The winning bidder for Lieutenant Mike Watson is...also Victoria Rutherford."

"What the fuck?" leapt out of my mouth.

"Wait. There can't be two guys for one girl," Hannah protested. "This isn't some kind of reverse Beach Boy's song. If she's the highest bidder for both of them then one of them has to go to the second highest." God, I loved that woman. On top of just being the world's most perfect human specimen her media sarc was always on point.

Ms. Mallory went on despite our protests. "The winning bidder for Captain Seth Seeger is also Victoria Rutherford."

The men standing around me with mouths hanging open all shot me pleading looks as Victoria and her two sequin-drowned friends went about pinching them on the ass.

"Okay, back the fuck up," I demanded. "How are you allowing this? They didn't know they were signing up for an orgy at the nursing home."

"Sergeant Haywood, you're Ms. Rutherford's final win."

"What?" Hannah shrieked. "I bid ten thousand dollars on him!"

Now I was not only dumbfounded by the fact that this scam of a fundraiser was allowing one winner for multiple men but what the actual hell was she thinking? "Babe. My God. Are you serious with that number right now? She actually bid more than that?" I gestured to Betsy Ross's wealthy dick-dealer.

"She has eight dead husbands, honey." The woman who'd offered me a knitted dick scarf, fanned cash in Hannah's face and I fought not to vomit. "Now get out of my way. My friends and I have a big night planned."

Victoria Rutherford, however, appeared to be seething. What the actual hell was going on? Suspicion I had no choice but to acknowledge slithered over my skin when I noted wine-guy waiting in the wings of the ballroom for someone.

Stunned to the point of numbness, I huffed. "You wrote out ten fucking pages of rules for this bogus fundraiser yet you didn't come up with one that would prevent some kind of sick geriatric sword dueling contest?" I demanded of Megan Mallory. She ignored me. Never a good idea. "You better come up with an answer and you better do it now."

Panic broadcast from her features. Oh, yeah, there was something extremely fucky about this whole thing and I was going to prove it. "Nothing about this fundraiser is bogus. Nothing. Do you hear me? All checks are to be made out to Homefront Heroes. I'll see you all here for the dinner tomorrow. Please enjoy your stay in Vegas." With that, she grabbed several stacks of papers, her briefcase, and a few file folders. Then she stormed out of the ballroom.

Watson was busy begging his anesthesiologist to still spend the week with him despite every disturbing thing that had just happened.

I was a fucking weapons sergeant. They told me where to shoot and I blew whatever it was straight to hell. Thinking quick on his feet and getting us out of bad situations was Chris and T-Byrd's job. When the perverted knitter grabbed a handful of my ass and twisted, however, I decided I better come up with a plan.

When she went back for a second grab, realization slammed through me. Her fingers palmed my wallet, that time, not my ass. Wine guy's credit card reader centered in my mind. He didn't have a uniform or a nametag because he didn't actually work for The

Obelisk. I would've bet the insane amount of money Hannah had bid on me that his credit card reader also had a skimmer attachment. So, that's what this was about.

Never slap a woman. Never slap a woman. Never slap a woman. Besides she'd probably like it. I repeated the mantra in my head. "Never pinch me again. Ever," I growled.

There was something rotten in the Happy Days retirement village. I had to figure out exactly what they were up to, how they were doing this, and what parts wine-guy and Megan Mallory played in it all. I had one week to reveal their underbellies.

"I cannot believe this," Hannah fumed. "How...just how?"

"Listen to me, this week, you and me, we're still doing all the things you wanted to do. You got that. Nothing has changed. Not a single damned thing. But I need you to keep MacBeth's sequined-witches distracted for a minute."

"Okay," she readily agreed.

"Watson," I bellowed. "Get your ass over here."

He seemed to have placated Bethany so he joined our ranks. Our winning bidders looked none too pleased when we huddled up. "Seegar, you're a Captain? That's what she said right? And you, Mathis, didn't you tell me this afternoon you're a Staff Sergeant?"

"Yeah, I'm a Staff Sergeant."

"Did you tell them you're Airborne?"

"Yeah. They asked what I did in the military." Concern plagued his eyes.

"Figured that as well."

"What does that have to do with anything? Why do they care what we do in the army?" Watson huffed. God bless him and his dumbass life.

"Never mind." I managed a quick eye roll. "I'm not entirely sure what's going on yet but do me a favor and do not sign anything at all in their presence. Especially not a credit card slip. You got me? Not even a note to your mama where they could find it. Nothing. And for the love of American cheeseburgers in the desert do not give them any personal information at all. Make up a new hometown, school, hell, if you're Catholic, plan a belated bar mitzvah because you just became Jewish. They chose four of us so we're in this together. Leave no man behind. You got that."

I received two exuberant army yes sirs and one guttural hoo-ah so I was making my point.

"Wait, so I'm supposed to say I'm Jewish even though I'm Episcopalian?" Watson asked.

"Dude, what the hell do you know?" Seeger demanded of me.

"He's Special Forces, man, listen to him," Ryder urged.

"Tomorrow night at dinner," I continued with my orders despite Watson's utter confusion about life in general, "I'm going to be late. I need the three of you to keep them entertained."

"But how do you know you're going to be late?" Watson demanded.

I stared him down. "Tell me something. When you came in here did you notice a big-ass rainforest in the lobby?"

"Yeah. Duh."

My eyes were going to lodge themselves in my fucking skull dealing with this guy. "K, I'm gonna need you to go stand in it, real near a few of the trees, because we need to get some oxygen to your brain."

"You want me to do that now or tomorrow night during dinner?"

"Holy Mother of God. No! Just...forget the trees. Here's what I want. You somehow survived Basic so this shouldn't be new to you. When I say something, you do what I said. No questions. So, tomorrow night I'm going to be late to dinner and you're going to be early and keep our wicked step-grandmothers from noticing that I'm late. You got that?"

"I guess. Well...but what did the rainforest have to do...?"

"Nope. Nada. If you have more questions, you write them down and give the paper to Mathis here. If he thinks it's not a stupid-assed question, then you can come ask me."

23

HANNAH

I couldn't believe this actually happened. Who were these women? "So, eight husbands, huh? Most of us can't even find one," I mumbled, still trying to keep them from overhearing the orders Griff was giving. It probably wasn't really necessary. They were all tipsy and excited with the spoils of the auction.

"Oh, honey, you have to know where to look." Ms. Rutherford took another long drag on her cigarette. I tried not to breathe. "Money helps. Men like a woman who can fend for herself and someone with a backbone. You must be a Pisces. Too sweet for your own good."

"Actually, I'm a..."

"That's the truth from the horse's mouth right there," one of the other woman interrupted and tapped her ashes in the champagne flute I'd grabbed off of the table when I realized that Griff was going to be forced to entertain these women and it was all my fault. Even Ms. Rutherford looked disgusted.

"Guess I'm not drinking that," I ground out.

"Adds to the flavor, honey."

Bile singed up my esophagus and ignited my tongue. "No, it doesn't. Not to mention the fact that it's incredibly rude."

"You get, what, eighty, ninety trips around the sun, girly." Ms. Rutherford shrugged. "If I'd worried about being rude, I'da been miserable for most of my eighty-three trips. My fourth husband, Robert, always said take what you want. Nobody's going to give it to you."

"What do you do for a living, dear?" The other woman, the one who hadn't yet done anything truly reprehensible, asked. Her tone, however, reminded me of cough syrup. Sweetened-coated bitterness that still tasted like shit.

"I'm an interior designer."

"Is that a lucrative career?"

"Guess that depends if you're any good or not."

"And are you any good?" Ms. Rutherford picked up the conversation.

"Do you like the suites you're staying in?" I countered.

"They're all right. Touch overdone if you ask me."

"Then I guess I'm just all right." Whatever Griff was doing, I needed him to hurry before I tied the tails of their sequined gowns together and pulled a fire alarm.

Ms. Mallory rushed back into the ballroom. "Ms. Rutherford, ma'am, you signed the wrong last name on your check." She thrust the offending paper in Victoria's face.

"Did I? And this is the check you're worried about? If I were you, I'd have my mind on another mistake," she huffed.

What did that mean? I scooted closer.

She shook her head and seemed to slip back into character. "Well, you know I've been married so many times I forget my own name from time to time." She accepted the pen and check. Easing to the side, I managed to spy the amount. It was made out to Megan Mallory for sixteen-thousand dollars. That made absolutely no sense. Even if she'd only bid one dollar more than I had on Griff that only left two thousand for each of the other men. That was impossible. That doctor I'd met earlier, while the guys were parading around the dance floor, said she'd bid a whole paycheck on that Watson guy.

"How much did you bid on Griff?" I demanded.

"A lady never reveals her secrets, Ms. Hagen," Victoria scolded as she re-signed and then initialed the check.

At that very millisecond, I arrived at the end of my rope. The bitch was going down. There was a man standing in the room who I was desperately in love with and he was desperately in love with me. How many people even get that? Not many.

He needed to be rescued from his own self-appointed sentence to hell and I was the only one who'd ever been able to get through to him. Rescuing a victim is difficult. Rescuing a hero is damned near impossible and I did not need this horrid woman fucking up my plans. "Oh, I don't think so, *honey*. Why didn't Ms. Donahue and Mr. Goodwin attend this event, Ms. Mallory? Why wasn't the board here? And how the hell did you allow one woman to win four men? And why is that check made out to you and not Homefront? Perhaps I should phone Mr. Goodwin because I will not have Palindrome Designs associated with a charity that's not completely on the up and up."

"I did nothing wrong, Ms. Hagen. You're welcome to call Sandra if you'd like. But do be sure to mention to her that the owner of Palindrome Design clearly had someone come to the auction she intended to bid on despite that being explicitly prohibited in the contract *she* signed."

I ground my teeth but decided to take a cue card from all of the Berets in my life. Never give away all you know. Despite her returned threat, I hadn't asked about calling Sandra Donahue. I'd threatened to call Mr. Goodwin. Was she aware of what she'd just said or was that a slip? Would she prefer I call the head of the board or was she of the opinion that telling me to do something was the quickest way to get me to balk? Perhaps Ms. Donahue would be angrier about all of my arrangements with Griff and she wanted me to get cut from the list of distinguished donors to Homefront Heroes. "Is that a threat, Ms. Mallory?" was all I could come up with.

"I could ask you the same question, Ms. Hagen."

Only problem with my plan was that I didn't have all of the extensive training Berets receive. My job did not require that I threaten people too often. On occasion a subcontractor would screw something up and I'd have to let them know it needed to be fixed but I was in the market of making people happy. I liked it that way.

I wasn't sure how to read Ms. Mallory and my favorite Beret was still giving orders to a group of men all staring up at him like he was their only hope of getting out of this alive. You could take the armor off of the hero but you could never take the hero out of the man.

Suddenly, he was standing beside me. I was aware of his presence before I lifted my eyes to his. It was stupid and I should've been focused on everything wrong with this auction but just then what I really wanted was that rush I always got when he folded me into his arms like I was the only thing in the entire world that would ever matter.

"What the fuck's going on here?" he demanded in that low guttural growl that shot a spike of awareness through my nerve endings.

"Seems Ms. Rutherford signed the wrong last name on her check." Okay, so I sounded a little like I was tattling but I was tired and this was seriously fucked up. "Her sixteen-thousand dollar check."

"Interesting," was his only comment. He was so much better at this whole thing than I was. He obviously knew something was up but gave nothing away.

Just then one of Victoria Rutherford's cohorts started fanning herself. "All of this excitement has given me heart palpitations...or maybe it's just you." She waggled her eyebrows at Griff.

"I doubt that's it," Griff countered knowingly.

"Shock and awe sometimes give me palpitations," I teased under my breath while everyone else was distracted with a woman in a red, white, and blue sequined gown snatching an unused napkin folded like a fan to mop her brow and then her bosom.

With my favorite half-smirk planted on his features, he shook his head at me and chuckled. Being able to laugh in a bad situation was Survival 101, something else I'd learned from my mom.

"Well, Sergeant Haywood, I do hope you and Ms. Hagen have an enjoyable week despite the fact that it's been more than obvious you both knowingly broke several rules in regards to the auction. Do remind Ms. Hagen of that from time to time." With that, all sense of humor that I'd conjured a moment before was scoured from the air around us.

Griff's eyes narrowed a half-notch. His jaw cocked to the side as he stared Megan Mallory down. Almost instinctively, she stepped back. Smart woman. My lips folded under the weight of my teeth when his suit coat bulged from the force of his biceps flexing. Team Seven used to have several mottos. Their favorite was, "burn the house, torch the skyline, and fuck the world." That was precisely what was about to happen.

"I need you to get something straight, Ms. Mallory, so listen up. I am not Sergeant Haywood. I am Sergeant First Class Griffin Haywood weapons expert from Operational Detachment Alpha 1167. Heavily trained and medal-bearing in foreign internal defense, black ops, hand-to-hand combat, special reconnaissance, and unconventional warfare. Ms. Hagen runs an extremely successful design firm not to mention all of her charity work. I doubt she needs me to remind her of anything. But you might want to remind yourself, from time to time, that Berets only find themselves in a fair fight when they haven't planned their mission well. And I *always* have a plan."

Ms. Mallory's harsh swallow revealed her nerves. "I'll see everyone at dinner tomorrow evening. Enjoy your stay, Sergeant Haywood." Ms. Mallory stormed toward the door once more.

"I intend to." Griff lined up and took a final shot. Based on the frantic look in Ms. Mallory's eyes, he'd hit the bullseye.

"Well, Haywood is going to be just a little late for dinner tomorrow," that Watson guy announced rather loudly.

Griff turned to stare him down. Apparently that was the wrong thing to say. "Dude, are both of your brain cells arguing currently or something? Keep your mouth shut," he rasped quietly.

"She's hosting the dinner. I thought she might want to know you're going to be late. It's polite."

"Were your parents cousins?"

I choked back laughter but Griff swiveled his head and shut his mouth when he noticed Ms. Rutherford and her friends staring at him.

"You ready, baby?" He grabbed my hand.

"Sure." The heat of every gaze in the room scalded my cheeks.

"Where do you think you're going? I paid good money for a week with the four of you. She can go. You're coming to the bar with us," the woman who'd wanted to know if my career was lucrative informed him.

"No, ma'am, you didn't. *She* paid to have a few dinners and a brunch with us. Nothing more." Griff pointed to Ms. Rutherford.

I watched every minute movement of the exchange. "You know, honey," she sauntered closer, "you can learn a lot from a more experienced woman." With her gloved hand, she traced down the buttons of his shirt. I wanted to vomit, preferably on her. "We could have a good time. She's nothing. She's barely even legal. But after a week with me you'd have so many tricks of the trade you could have any woman you want."

Since my age was still something Griff felt guilty about, I leapt. "Excuse me, I am far more than legal!" I fumed but Griff shook his head. "I'm..." His arm whipped around me with lightning speed and his hand wrapped gently over my mouth.

"Do not say another word," he commanded. Too shocked to have spoken anyway, I managed a nod. What the actual fuck was going on? "Few things, I do not need the education you're offering up. Trust me. And she is everything. Every single thing. In fact, she's not just everything she is the only thing. You got that?" With that, he lowered his hand from my mouth and draped it over my shoulder. Then he half-dragged me out of the ballroom.

"Mm, mm, mmm, I would not mind being manhandled by that one," Ms. Rutherford drawled as we made our escape.

I turned back just long enough to see that wine waiter approaching Ms. Rutherford and her friends. He no longer had his tray.

"What are we going to do now?" he whined to Victoria. "You promised me a check."

24

GRIFF

"What is going on? Why did you cover my mouth?" Hannah huffed as soon as we were out of the ballroom.

"We're going by your room to get your stuff," I informed her as we escaped toward the Villa Suite corridor. "We'll talk when we get to my room." Her legs may have gone on for miles but she was struggling to keep up with me in those heels. I forced myself to slow down. She clearly hadn't given them enough information if they were still trying to goad her birthday out of her. She was safe. I repeated that phrase in my head for the rest of our march to her suite. It stood to reason that if they were that interested in a few lowly soldiers' credit cards, Hannah's would've delighted them.

"It's never a good sign when you start giving me orders. Talk now." She slipped her key card in the door and stared up at me. Her eyes were pools of confusion, exhaustion, and irritation.

"Thought that's what you were wanting from me?" Hey, I could dodge like a pro. Not a problem.

And I earned myself her I-am-officially-pissed expression. "Pretty sure you knew I meant in bed."

"Might've picked up on that." I sealed the door shut behind me.

"I'm not sorry I covered your mouth. It was necessary. I am sorry if I freaked you out though."

"I didn't so much mind. I just want to know why it was necessary?"

Dammit, I still didn't have this all figured out and I sure as hell didn't want to scare her. She wanted a week for just us and, my God, I needed that more than anything in the whole entire fucked-up world.

Grabbing a sturdy looking side chair from nearby, I wedged it under the door handle. Hannah's eyes rounded with dread. "Griff, what is going on?"

"Come here to me." I took a seat on the sofa in her suite. It was in the same location as the one in mine but the decor in her room was different. No hard edges. Big, fluffy cushions and pastel colors. The entire place felt warm, just like my own personal sunshine. Like she'd designed the suite for herself. "Baby, do you want us to stay in here instead of in my suite?" Truthfully, I hoped she'd want to stay in mine. I'd already worked out attack and counter attack points for my space but I wanted to give her the week she wanted just as soon as I figured out exactly how devious The Little Shop of Horrors backup singers really were.

"No." Hannah eased beside me on the sofa. She threw frantic glances back to the door a few times before staring up at me. "I want you to tell me what you figured out and I want to know how that awful woman bought all of you for so little money. I mean, compared to my bid. I also want to know why there's a three-thousand dollar Henredon arm chair in front of my door."

"I haven't quite figured everything out yet." The words tasted like battery acid on my tongue. I had to get some answers. In any other scenario, I'd call Smith and talk it out. That certainly wasn't an option this time. "The chair is just a precaution. I will keep you safe, baby. You know that."

Contemplation weighted her gaze. "I do know that. I never feel safer than I do when I'm with you. But why do you need to keep me safe from the *Charlie's Angels*' outcasts?"

"Hey, that was a good one." I was genuinely impressed. Neither of us were old enough to watch that show.

"Talk, Griff," she ordered. "You're the one Victoria Rutherford bid on. There's something weird about this auction and the amount of money and all of that. But none of that explains why you think I'm in danger."

I momentarily debated sticking to army protocol in case of capture—name, rank, number, and nothing else. She had me bolted to the fucking sofa with those eyes. I certainly couldn't escape. And here's the thing, I didn't want to. Buying myself one moment more I inhaled one long heavenly inhale of her scent. Sweet vanilla cream filled my lungs and bile swirled in my gut. If anyone tried to hurt her, I'd kill them. No questions asked. "When I first saw Victoria, I suspected she was a black widow."

She stared at me like I'd grown another head out of my ass or something. "You thought she was a spider?"

"It's a term used for women that kill their husbands off for insurance money."

Both her eyes and her mouth opened wider. "Oh my gosh. I thought stuff like that only happened in movies."

"I have little to no proof and now I'm not so sure that's it. Did you notice how one of her friend's eyes kept twitching?"

"Yeah. I think her name is Edith. I thought she was just drunk."

"She was tipsy but not drunk enough to have done that to her eyes. Edith said something about Vicky giving her two pills. Made me curious how often they share pills. Like I said, I have precious little proof of anything. Then, it hit me."

"What hit you?" she scooted closer.

"I love you my little impatient princess," I teased her.

"Would you just tell me what hit you before I do?"

"You're adorable when you threaten me," I continued to buy myself more time.

"Griff!"

"Fine. When Edith was pinching all of our asses, she wasn't just indulging in sexual harassment."

"What was she doing then?"

"She was making grabs at our wallets."

"Are you sure?" she gasped. "We were all standing there. If she'd stolen one of your wallets, everyone would have seen her."

"Hence the pills. Whatever meds Victoria is handing out, Edith took too much. As fucking nuts as they all are I'm betting she doesn't go around acting quite that insane on a regular basis."

"Oh my...fuck." She slumped back against the sofa. Defeat seemed to settle on her cruelly and I couldn't stand it.

"I don't want you to blame yourself for any of this," I gestured back toward the three-ring circus in that ballroom. "And I know you're going to."

"Griff, someone tried to steal your wallet and someone else is killing off her husbands. This is a major clusterfuck and it is my fault we're involved in it."

"Stop it," I summoned my best soothing tone and guided her into my arms. "None of this is your fault. If I can catch these broads, doing whatever it is they're doing, they'll be exchanging their sequins for orange jumpsuits. I think that plum wine guy is in on it."

"Did you hear what he said when we were leaving? He said they owed him a check."

"I know. I'm just not sure if they owe him a check for pedaling wine at this thing or if they offered to split the money from the credit cards I'm betting he skimmed tonight."

"Why would they have hired someone to serve wine at an event hosted by another organization? Obviously, he knew he was skimming credit card numbers."

"Agreed but never get set on one outcome or one bad guy. Every possibility must remain in our sites if we're going to figure all of this out. I don't like to state things with any certainty until I know for sure."

25

HANNAH

Of course that's what he would say. He knew what he was doing. Bracing my elbows on my knees, I let my head fall into my hands to keep from looking at him. All of my stupid scheming trying to give us a real chance and a vacation and he was going to spend it catching criminals.

Why couldn't one of my stupid plans ever work out? The realization of everything he'd explained sank through me like I'd submerged myself in icy water. Chill bumps charged down my bare arms. "If that awful woman kills men, what about you? What if she tries to...hurt you?" I had no idea why he was so worried about me. She didn't kill women. "And what about those other guys?"

"I'm not sure that's what she does. And we'll all be fine, sweetheart. She would only want to kill any of us if she stood to profit from it. I haven't signed over any life insurance policies lately. She chose most of us because we were among the highest ranking soldiers at the auction. Theoretically, we have the most money. Higher credit card limits. Shit like that. Not sure why they chose Watson. He's only a lieutenant. He can't be making that much."

"Except that his family is *the* Watson family of Wally Watson Chicken Company. They're in all of the grocery stores. They have those commercials with the people dressed up as a mother chicken, and a dad chicken, and then chickadees, only the chickadees are actually taller than the mom and dad. They sing and cluck around about how chickens from the Watsons are the tastiest. I bet they make tons of money." I recounted what the anesthesiologist had told me about Mike while we chatted.

"You are fucking brilliant." Griff grinned.

"That girl that thinks he's cute told me that. I didn't come up with it on my own or anything. The commercial is cringe-y but clearly someone in that family has enough sense to run a national chicken supply company."

"Doesn't matter who told you. At least it makes sense. Maybe brain power skips a generation in his family or something but if they make a shit ton of money in chicken why did he join up?"

"According to the Bethany, his father makes all of them serve before they can start drawing from the vast family accounts."

"We're going to do some reconnaissance tomorrow night during the dinner. I'll catch the cock sock knitter and her cohorts and we'll have our week. It's just a thing."

"Don't give me your 'it's just a thing' thing. You and Smith say that before you have to go do something ridiculously dangerous and I'm already about to throw up." Still trying to think through a haze of panic in my head I suddenly realized what he'd just said. "Wait. You said we're going to do some reconnaissance. You're actually going to let me help you do this?" This wasn't exactly how'd I wanted to spend a week in Vegas but at least we'd be together.

"Of course. I need some help. How good are you at CQB?" He laughed but he'd clearly forgotten who my father was. Maybe that was a good thing. Maybe despite every disastrous thing that had happened I was still wearing him down.

I cocked my left eyebrow. "Funny. But I'm actually quite accomplished at close quarters battles. I can clear a room like any good soldier."

"Damn, baby, you are the most perfect woman in the world."

I rolled my eyes. "So, that's why that Watson guy said you were going to be late to dinner."

"I swear that guy's got diarrhea of the mouth and constipation of the ideas. I'm gonna end up duct taping him in a closet so he can't fuck up this mission."

A mission. Yep. That's what this was going to become. Not a vacation. Not a rekindling of a lifetime love. Not a recognition that we were meant to be and that my family ultimately wanted both of us to be happy. It was just a mission. If I clenched my jaw any harder my teeth were going to disintegrate so I unhinged my mouth. "You still haven't explained the chair or why you covered my mouth."

"Right. Sorry. The chair is me being insanely overprotective of you. I covered your mouth because they're looking for personal information. If you tell them how old you are they have the year you were born at the very least. With a birthday and a credit card from you they could do some serious damage. It wouldn't take many internet searches to find out all about my baby. She's famous in case you haven't noticed."

"I am not famous." I shook my head. "I'm just a designer."

"A designer who's been in a dozen design magazines recently including Forbes. I don't even want them to know your name if we can help it."

"But..." Something about my whole exchange with the women had been weird. I knew it but until he'd said that it hadn't occurred to me. "They already knew my name. Victoria kept referring to me as Ms. Hagen but I've never met her before. I wasn't introduced at the auction."

His jaw tensed right along with my chest. But it wasn't until he popped the knuckles on his right hand that I started to panic. "I had a feeling they might know who you are. I will keep you safe I just need you to be extremely careful about what you say and who you say it to."

"I can do that." I reviewed everything I'd said to the three witches that night. "She said I must be a Pisces because I'm too sweet for my own good."

"Did you tell them your sign?" This time it wasn't the even tone of his voice or the way he bit at the side of his mouth that sucker punched me. It was the panic in his eyes.

"No. Edith interrupted me and knocked her cigarette ashes in my champagne glass. Even Victoria looked at her like she was disgusted."

Griff scowled and shook his head. "Bet she wasn't disgusted about the ashes. Bet she was furious she never got an answer out of you. A birth month and then year would've been like handing over a Platinum card but good old Edith and her pills foiled her plan."

I grinned at his expression. I could adapt and still accomplish all of my goals. I had to. "Okay, I'll play Daphne to your Fred but when we catch them I totally get to say 'You would've gotten away with it if it weren't for my big badass Beret.' Deal?"

That did it. All of his hardened edges softened with his laughter. "You got it, baby doll. Now, if you're sure you don't want to stay here instead, let's get you to my suite. I still have plans for you tonight, Daphne."

"Ooh, you could use that super manly orange ascot to tie me up." I giggled mostly for purposes of making him believe I wasn't completely freaked out.

"You are aware you're killing me, right?"

"You look perfectly healthy to me, Sergeant."

"Yeah, keep calling me that and I won't survive until morning. Now, come on. Let's get you moved into my suite."

I eased off of the couch and rededicated myself to the goals for this week. "Moving into your life was the whole reason for doing all of this, Griff. I'm sorry it went off the rails."

A quick wince tensed his face when he stood. Reaching, I centered my right hand over his hip bone and rubbed. His eyes closed and a quick, relieved sigh escaped his mouth. But he only allowed himself the care for a split second before he took my hand in his own. "Let's go."

"I could do more of that in your suite."

"I'm fine, baby. Let me take care of you."

I trapped my irritated sigh behind my lips. Chunk by chunk, I reminded myself as I marched to the bathroom and threw makeup and curling irons into my toiletry bag.

My calves felt like cinderblocks after wearing those stupid heels all night so I kicked them off and slipped my feet into the paint covered kicks I'd worn earlier. The suites were all on the same floor so we weren't going far.

Grinning at my change of footwear, Griff grabbed the heels and stowed them under his arm. He gripped the handles of all three of my suitcases and headed toward the door while I slung my handbag over my arm.

I winced when the corner of my sketchpad collided with my elbow the precise location that stupid wine guy had bumped into me. "Oh my God!" I gasped. "Wine guy!" My purse slipped off my shoulder as I dug into the pocket on the dress.

"What?" Griff had lifted the Henredon chair and was restoring it to its former location.

"He's in on whatever they're doing. They already knew my name. They must've told him to try to get me to buy a glass. When I didn't, he kept running into me. I had my license and a credit card in the pocket of my dress. I didn't want to bring a handbag. The pocket was the whole reason I bought this dress." Frantically, I dug farther into the entirely empty pocket. My heart located a new residence somewhere near my throat. Finally, I turned the tiny pocket completely inside out. Nothing. "They're not here. I have to call American Express. How do I get a new license? We have to call the police. They probably still have it on them."

"Okay, deep breaths for me. When he bumped into you, nothing fell out of your pocket. Come on. Before we call the cops, we have to check something." He flung open the door and marched out into the corridor.

26

GRIFF

There was an all too familiar tightening in my gut that served as a reminder that it had never lied to me. I knew before my boots had ever set down on the hot Vegas cement that there was going to be trouble. But I had been put on this earth to protect my baby and dammit that's exactly what I was going to do.

Fred offered us a kind grin when we reached my room on the opposite end of the corridor. "I take it you'll be moving in for the week, Ms. Hagen?"

"Uh..." Hannah had her hand stuck down her handbag. She was playing with that bag I'd managed to discreetly talk Smith into sending her from Brazil. I knew what she was doing but to the unknowing eye it probably did look a little odd. "Yes," she finally managed.

"Everything okay?" Fred asked.

"She can't find her cell phone," I explained as I eased by Fred and opened the door with my own keycard.

Whisking her inside, I dropped her suitcases in the entryway. My hip protested when I leaned forward and dug into the couch cushions.

"What are you doing?" She set the handbag down and turned on one of the lamps.

Breath rushed back into my lungs when my fingers brushed over the rounded corner of a card. I grabbed the Amex. Her license had fallen nearby. Breathing through the pain of standing, I held up the cards.

Clutching them in one hand, her other flew to her chest in relief. "I have never been so thankful for having rough sex with you and I was pretty damned thankful after it happened."

If she kept saying shit like that I was likely to bend her over the arm of the sofa again. "Glad to have been of service, baby."

"Should we lock our stuff up in the safe? If we go out, we can charge stuff to our rooms. We don't have to carry around our wallets. That's how all of the nicer hotels on The Strip work."

"That's good to know but hotel safes are the easiest to break into, sweetness. But that gives me an idea. Do you have a compact thing? Something with powder or that stuff you put on your cheeks?"

Giving me that sweet grin that managed to both set me at ease and enliven me all at the same time, she dug back in her bag and produced a powder compact. "What are you going to do?"

"Impress you, hopefully." I gave her both a cocked eyebrow and a cocky smirk.

"Well, you are extremely impressive."

"I live to serve, baby. Come with me. Let's see about our safe. Might save us time tomorrow night. If the Demons Three are stealing credit cards they have to be storing them somewhere in their suite."

She followed me into the bedroom closet. I flipped on the light and studied the safe. It was a standard Safelock with a keypad. If the average person knew how insanely easy these things were to open, they'd never leave anything worth more than dust in one. Hotel safes generally allowed the guests to set their own code. However, there was always a master code for the hotel staff that would work on all the safes in the building. Guests notoriously put stuff in the safe and then promptly forgot their own code meaning the staff had to help them get back in. And the previous codes were erased after each stay using the same master code to reset the safe.

To make sure the damn thing even worked in the first place, I set the safe with an easy one, two, three, four code. The safe opened. I slammed it shut and pressed lock.

Constantly aware of Hannah's presence, I turned back and indulged my lips in a quick kiss on the soft skin of her cheek. She grinned. "Are you stalling, Sergeant? I thought you had skills," she teased.

"Are you doubting my skills, honey? 'Cause if you are, that hurts. Not gonna lie."

That giggle of hers could bring about world peace. "Never," she assured me.

"Stand back and watch me work. Prepare to be amazed. I'll take appreciation in the form of applause, your undying affection, and blow jobs."

She waggled her eyebrows. "I can do all three."

"Good. You ready?" I flipped open the compact, held it close to the keypad, and huffed enough breath to make a slight cloud of powder. Turning my face away quickly to keep my breaths from ruining the effect, I waited on the dust to settle. "Seriously?" I shook my head. Powdered fingerprints were on the four buttons of the code I'd just set and only one other number. "Makes me cranky when they make it this damn easy."

Hannah shook her head at me. I hit the nine key four times and the fucking thing sprung open. Amateurs.

"Wow."

Well, at least my baby was impressed. That was something. "Never put your shit in a hotel safe. They're ridiculous."

"Not everyone has your lock picking and safe cracking skills though."

"Still. The safest place to keep things you don't want stolen is on your person. You just have to keep your head about you. You know how many people probably get pick-pocketed here while they're pointing up at the Eiffel Tower in awe standing on the viewing deck?"

She toed out of her sneakers and spun around. "Will you unzip me?"

"Anytime." I jerked the zipper down.

Once again it hit the floor and then she spun back to stare me down. "Holy fuck, you're beautiful." My eyes drank her in. Her long blonde hair teased at the swells of her breasts, occasionally obscuring her soft pink nipples. Frustration mounted in my chest. Reaching, I ran my fingertips in the slight shadows under the swells of her tits, loving the way she shivered at my touch.

Her eyes were somehow eager and questioning at the same time. My fingers scraped lower on a downward trek across the soft plain of her abdomen and the bare rise of her mound. "So fucking gorgeous."

When her tongue darted over her lips, my eyes locked there. She was the only drug I would ever require for survival. I ordered myself to slow it down. She wasn't a fucking conquest despite the number of times that day I'd treated her as such. Cradling her face in my hand, I let my thumb tenderly memorize the swells of her lips before I allowed my tongue a taste.

Her long eyelashes made a slow blink as she studied me. "Is it bad if I don't want to think about thieves and safes and everything else anymore?" she whispered.

"No, baby. The whole fucked up world will be out there tomorrow." She needed to forget, needed to be rescued from the insanity of our situation. Search and rescue happened to be another one of my specialties. "Tonight, it can wait outside the damned door."

That did it. She looped her arms over my shoulders as I drew her closer using the firm globes of her ass. The patience I was trying so fucking hard to possess went up in flames. I widened my stance and took her lips with a greedy claim. God, I needed this kiss to make promises I'd never be able to keep.

I coaxed her tongue into my mouth and rocked her pussy against the fierce bulge of my cock. I'd trade every possession I owned in this world to be able to swear to her that I'd figure out some way for us to be together forever. I'd heard her repeated pleas for us to come clean with her brother and her parents. I wasn't an idiot. Ignoring her requests punctured the fragments of my soul. Giving her what she needed, whatever it was, would always be what mattered to me. But what I'd have to take away to give her us, together, just wasn't worth it. I wasn't worth it.

So, instead of verbalizing promises that would ultimately be lies, I sank into the heat of her mouth and drowned myself in the flavors of my baby. I let her feel the weight of my insatiable hunger. My body vowed to protect her above all others. I cupped her bare ass in my hands. She arched as I dragged her between my legs. Desperation swamped my thoughts, drowning out the knowledge that at the end of this week in heaven I had to go back to hell and this trip to paradise would be the last I allowed myself. She deserved more than I could give.

My hip throbbed as I rocked her up and down against my trouser-trapped shaft. I didn't give a fuck about that or what would have to come when this was over. Tonight, I'd make her forget anything else in the whole fucking world even existed. Tonight, I'd give her everything I was or ever would be. I knew it wasn't enough but just then it didn't matter.

27

GRIFF

I'd actually slept all night long. That hadn't happened in so long I'd almost forgotten it was a thing other people occasionally enjoyed. I'd held on to her. She'd eased one of her legs between my thighs and had nestled her head on my chest and heaven couldn't possibly be any better than that.

One of the many, many perks that came when I snuck down to Denver to be with her was waking up beside my sweet Hannah, who was decidedly not a morning person. She'd grunt and groan when it was time to get up but trust me, you get your head down there between those thighs and her groans would turn quickly to moans of my name. Best fucking way to wake up there would ever be.

I dragged my arms out across the cool hotel room sheets, stretching out the kinks in my shoulders. But cool sheets were not what I was expecting. My eyes blinked in the sunlight's assault through the sliding glass doors. The covers on her side were thrown back and my baby wasn't there.

Still drowsy from actually sleeping, devastation stabbed through me the same way it always did when I woke up in her brother's house instead of her apartment. Sitting up, I remembered that I wasn't in either. Scrubbing my hands over my face, I yawned. I also needed to shave. "Hannah?" I sounded like a drunk frog as I located a pair of shorts.

"In here," her sweet voice beckoned. Wherever here was I wanted to go.

Standing, I clenched my jaw as I let my hip figure out that it was going to have to hold up my weight again. But this morning's aches and pains were almost nonexistent. Sex with my baby just made everything better.

Mildly impressed with how quickly I could walk, I scooted into the living room. There was my girl curled up in the corner of the sofa with her sketchpad and a pencil. Her hair was looped up in a lopsided bun by way of one of those cloth hairbands women always wore on their wrists. She was sporting a pair of panties, a tank top, her glasses, and nothing else. I'd seen her in a swanky cocktail dress, lingerie of most every flavor, and in ripped jeans with a Cubs T-shirt, a personal fave of mine, but this beat all of those by a mile.

"Morning, beautiful, you sleep well?" I rasped as I headed to the coffee maker.

"Extremely well. The mattresses I purchased for the suites are amazing aren't they?"

"Oh yeah, I'm sure it's the mattress and not the sheer number of orgasms I gave you last night." I pretended to be offended.

She glanced up from her sketch. "Those were amazing, too," she assured me with a mischievous grin. The pencil pouch she also used as a security blanket was open on the coffee table.

"Glad you think so because I thought we could go for a new personal best today." I switched on the coffee maker and joined her on the couch.

"If you try to give me any more right now, I think my vaj might stage a protest."

That was not at all what I wanted to hear. "You hurting?" Fuck, I'd been too rough. I knew it. She'd asked for it repeatedly. I should have had more willpower.

"Not at all. I was teasing." She rolled her eyes but then returned them to the pad.

Easing closer, I studied the room she was drawing. Looked to be some kind of office lined with windows all complete with window bench seats. A massive desk sat in the middle. Her drawings were always so real I felt like I could step into the rooms that only existed two dimensionally. "For a new client?"

She shook her head.

Okay then. "For an old client?"

Another head shake.

"Want me to go back to bed and leave you the hell alone?"

This time her head lifted. "No. Not at all." She sounded shocked. "I love when you sit with me while I sketch."

I could do this. *Just sit and keep your mouth shut, Haywood.* Obviously, that's what she wanted. She had the sketchpad braced on her bent knees. I took one of her feet and reclined her leg into my lap leaving her one leg to hold the pad. "Keep drawing." I began to massage the foot in my lap.

"You are the best thing ever. This is my favorite sketch pad so I never use it for clients."

I nodded, afraid to make more guesses and sound like a fool, so I rotated my thumb in the arch of her foot enjoying her sighs of contentment.

The intricate tat on my right pec was a sketch she'd done for me. Right after I'd gotten it, Smith had asked how I'd come up with the design. I'd lied through my teeth of course. The compass and sword that faded into a map tat would always be my favorite. I'd only had the artist change one thing about her design. Her initials were hidden at the top of the sword. What was supposed to be the N for north was actually an intricate, old world, double H design. If you didn't know what you were looking for, you'd never notice.

I tried to keep my mouth shut but I wanted to know about the room she was drawing. I wanted to know every single thing that fascinated her the way the design clearly did. "Are you designing a new office for you, then?"

"Kind of." She sank her teeth into her bottom lip and slowly her bespectacled eyes met mine.

"You're doing this on purpose. You're torturing me, right? You know I always want to know what you're drawing."

She laughed and then shook her head at me. "I am not trying to torture you."

"Yeah, right. Fine, I'll just go make myself a mug of coffee and will conveniently forget to pour some for you."

"That is cruel," she teased.

"Then tell me what you're drawing."

"I don't want to scare you," she hemmed.

"Baby, unless you've got bombs under that desk or IEDs in that rug or something that office is not particularly frightening." I did indeed get up to pour coffee, still impressed with the lack of stiffness this morning. "It's too nice to be scary."

She flipped the well-used sketch pad back to the first page and held it up for me to see. This drawing was of some kind of theater room. She'd colored in just enough for me to see the pallet she'd chosen for the room.

Black leather recliners sat before a projector screen. She'd added a few throws and pillows. There was a counter with what looked like an old school movie popcorn popper, because let's be real, movie popcorn is the best.

When my eyes landed on the framed Cubs Sosa jersey on the wall with signatures all over the back, I failed to stop pouring the coffee even though the mug was full. Coffee streamed over the sides and down the counter. The picture of the jersey wasn't something she'd dreamed up. It existed in real life. It hung over my bed.

"Shit." I grabbed a towel to mop up the coffee and tried to process this. She flipped to another page in the book. This one revealed a state of the art exercise room. I couldn't quite manage words.

"The office is for me but it won't exist until we buy a house," she confessed.

Abandoning the coffee, I forced myself to look at her. Hope and disappointment waged war in her eyes.

"Baby, please don't do this." I barely recognized my own voice but

I fought on. "It kills me. It fucking kills me to think that you dream up something I can't ever give you."

"Then give it to me." She never even blinked.

"You don't know how badly that would hurt you." There, that was almost a confession, almost a whole truth. Disappointing her crushed me. I swore my bones couldn't stand the weight of the agony in her eyes.

"I'm an incredibly strong person, Griff. The only thing that hurts me is you keeping something from me, especially when what you're not telling me is the thing that clearly keeps us apart."

"I know you believe that I couldn't hurt you but this...thing...it would hurt you. And that's the one thing I cannot and will not ever do. And not only that, but after it hurt you it would hurt him. The two people I care the most about in the whole fucking world. I...I just can't do that."

The muted ring of her cell phone shattered a little of the tension between us. Setting the sketchpad down, she dug in her bag and rescued my own savior. Whoever was calling her, I owed them big time.

"It's Smith." She flung the phone further down the couch and stared at it like it had talons.

Of course it was. Because that's just how my life always seemed to work out.

When she covered it with a throw pillow, I had to chuckle. "He's just going to keep calling."

"Maybe not. Maybe he'll give up. I am on vacation."

"Oh yeah, I'm sure because that's his style. He's an SF soldier, baby. He doesn't give up."

The ringing stopped but then started back before she even slumped in relief.

I stalked back to the bedroom. "Answer him." I closed the door and hated myself right along with the rest of the world.

28

HANNAH

"What do you want, Smith?" I demanded. Why did he have to call me right now? Why when I was about to have what should have been one of the most important conversations of my life?

"What the hell are you so bitchy about?" He sounded more hurt than shocked though so I tried to quell a little of my irritation.

"Nothing. I'm just...tired." So fucking tired of living this way and not being able to tell him how much Griff meant to me.

"You over at your new guy's house or something?"

"No."

"Sure."

"Why do you care where I am?"

"Because staying over with a guy is a bad idea. You should be smarter than that."

If I could have reached through my phone, I swear I would've strangled my brother. "Besides lecturing me why did you call?"

"I keep trying to explain to Mom that I cannot have social media accounts. She doesn't understand why I can't see the pictures she's apparently posting on Facebook. And, dear God, I hope they're not of that pack of hers because that's just embarrassing. I could hack in but that seems tedious."

I took two deep breaths. That didn't help. Counting backward from ten didn't either.

"Hannah? You there?" Smith demanded. Yep, I was gonna kill him. I did not have time for Mom or Facebook right now.

"I'm here. Just tell her you'd rather her text them to you." There. That was a workable solution.

"I'm not an idiot. I did try that. Apparently she posted something about me and she wants me to see how many likes it has." Secretly, I hoped it was a naked baby picture, because that would serve him right, or maybe that one of him when he was five and got his head stuck between the spindles on the staircase in our house in Germany and was bawling his eyes out. But the disdain was more than apparent in my brother's tone. It tugged at my heart. For the most part, all of The Sevens hated attention in any form. Smith was no different.

"Here, I'll check it, screen shot it, and text it over but I can't talk to you and do that at the same time."

"Hang on, that gives me an idea." I heard his keyboard clicking. "Is her account private?"

"No, because she doesn't understand that anyone can see it. I've tried to explain it but I haven't gotten far."

"Then this'll work." I heard him typing.

"What will work?" I told myself not to care just to get off the phone but I was curious.

"I have a few of my clients' social media account info since we catch a lot of cheaters via Facebook. I can just log in through their account and see whatever it is she's posted."

"Perfect. I'm going now."

My mind reviewed what had already happened that morning. Maybe I should've put the sketchbook away when I'd heard him get up. Maybe we weren't quite ready for that talk yet. Impatience would forever be my downfall. We had a week. I had to bide my time and take this slowly because men could be both stupid and stubborn.

The distinctive ring of an iPhone sounded from nearby. Frantically, I covered the speaker of my own phone and prayed Smith hadn't heard that. Griff rushed out of the bedroom and silenced the ring. Checking the caller, he headed back to his hideout.

"Was that a phone?" Smith demanded. Damn him and his perfect hearing.

"No...how could it be?" But my voice lilted.

"You're over at that new guy's house aren't you?"

For some very bizarre reason when God was making me, He'd decided I needed the big brother who was a hundred times more overprotective than any other big brother on the planet. "No one is here with me. Drop the interrogation mode."

"Fine. Wait, why does Mom sign her posts?"

"It took me six months to get her to stop signing her texts to everyone. Again with the lack of Facebook knowledge."

"Jesus, is she serious with this?" Smith spat. But his words were wounded, like someone had stabbed him in the chest. All of the air in his lungs came out in a pained hiss.

"What?" I tried to figure out how to put him on speaker so I could see whatever Mom had posted but I was fairly sure that would make him able to hear what was going on the room with even more accuracy.

"She can't fucking post shit like this," choked from him.

"Hang on." I switched from the phone call to Facebook. Her post was the first one in my feed. My big brother's boot camp picture stared back at me. I'd almost forgotten how young and innocent he looked before he'd gone from soldier to Beret. I glanced at her post. The blood racing through my veins froze. Oh my God. Oh my God. Oh...dear...God. How could I have forgotten what day it was? I read the words *Always thankful for my beautiful children but on this day especially, when half of his team lost their lives...* Quickly, I switched back to the phone. "Smith...I'm so sorry. I forgot what day it is. I didn't mean to. Are you okay? Do you...want to talk or anything?"

If I could have one wish in the world, I don't think I would use it to make Griff mine as much as I desperately wanted that. I think I would wish that the calendar year would go from July tenth to July twelfth so that my brother and Griff and all of the remaining Sevens didn't have to relive this day every single year. The day their whole world had been torn to shreds with no hope of it ever returning to the way it was supposed to be.

"I'm fine."

"You don't sound so fine," I whispered.

"Fucking wish Griff was here," he finally admitted and I knew how much that had cost him. Guilt swirled in the pit of my stomach. I was the reason Griff wasn't there to go through this day with the ones who remained.

Every single cell in my body longed to march into the bedroom and hand my phone to Griff. Why couldn't we all be in this together? Why would neither of them ever let me help? They didn't think I could handle what they'd been through. I had no idea what it was like to walk around in their boots but I wanted so badly to be able to ease their pain. "I'm so sorry."

"Nothing but a thing." And there it was again. I wondered how long that expression would suffice.

"Yeah. I know."

"Mom still can't put shit like that on Facebook."

"I'll talk to her."

"Same way you talked to her about her hike?" The forced chuckle was worse than any of the tears I'd heard my brother sob when he'd finally woken up at Walter Reed and my father had delicately explained that not all of them had made it.

"Yeah, something like that."

"Do a better job with this, please."

I'd never deny him anything. Not today of all days. "You got it."

"Whatever. Go have fun but not too much fun, okay?"

"I love you, Smith. So much."

"Same, sis. Be good." He ended the call and I flew toward the bedroom. Today was not the day for me to force my own agenda. Today, I had to be there for Griff. No matter what he wanted to do, or talk about, or forget about entirely, I was there for it.

He was behind the bathroom door with his phone to his ear.

"Did he hear the phone?" he mouthed.

I nodded and he cringed. "I know, okay. I know. But I'm kind of in this other thing too so any help you have I'll take."

It had to be T-Byrd. I wondered what they were discussing.

Griff's eyes narrowed. Traces of pure hatred quivered in their depths. "Yeah, I have a fucking calendar."

My heart sank slowly down to my stomach. It landed there in the storm of acid and regret. This was how Griff handled this day every year. No talking. No reminiscing about the good times. Certainly no discussion of the bad ones. No going to the graves. Nothing that had anything to do with what July 11 would always mean to us. Nothing but work and there was no talking him out of it. Occasionally, a new tattoo would appear somewhere on his form on this day. If that's what he needed, that's what we'd do.

"K, I'll text you what I find tonight." When his searching gaze found my eyes, he held out his free arm and I propelled myself into him. I clung to him with all of my might. If only I could squeeze him tightly enough to suture all of those scars he collected to prove his worth.

He buried his head into my hair and kept talking. "Yeah, we're gonna get out of here." Another long pause. "T, man, I know, okay? I was there."

I wondered what it was he knew.

"We'll do whatever she wants. But I can do that and catch some geriatric credit card thieves. I multitask well. I'm hanging up now." There was another quick pause. "No, you are not talking to her." I lifted my head, offered him what I was certain was a broken grin, and held out my hand for the phone.

He handed it over with a complimentary eye roll. "Hey, T, listen... I'm really sorry...." There were no words. I knew that. Words were insufficient bandages for what they'd survived but my God, I tried. "So sorry."

"Nothing but a thing, baby doll." Grinding my teeth, I was beginning to wonder why we hadn't etched that expression on the other half of their team's grave markers. "Listen though, he forgot what today is until I called. I'd say you're getting through to him so keep up the good work but maybe let him have a break today. Just let him talk if he will."

"He won't but I'll try."

T's chuckle was just as broken as Smith's had been. "You're probably right. Maybe just ease up then. He sounds like hell."

Another round of guilt backhanded me. How could I have not only forgotten the date but have also shown him that sketch book? I'd done nothing but cemented more guilt in his soul. I glanced at the toilet certain I was going to vomit. "You got it."

"Hey, if anyone can make him feel better today, it's you. Go take care of my bro."

"That is all I ever want to do."

"I know, Hannah Banana. Go do your thing."

29

GRIFF

"What did he say?" I ordered my voice to sound slightly more human to no avail.

"To take care of you." She stared up at me, through me maybe. I didn't need to be taken care of. I needed T to get his shit together and... I needed to do something that wasn't whatever we were doing in the bathroom.

"I'm fine. Nothing but a..."

"Thing. Yeah, I know. I told him you were fine." She wasn't a good liar and that one was a doozy.

"Oh yeah?"

"No, but that's what you want me to say, right?"

Had to give her that. "Want to get out of here for a while? We can't do anything about Bonnie Parker and the funky bunch until I can get in their room tonight."

"Hey, that was a really good one." I earned myself one of those dazzling grins.

"I do what I can, baby."

"I've been trying to work out something with Destiny's Child but I'm struggling." She was so fucking perfect. She knew I needed a distraction from this ridiculous day and she was making a valiant effort to provide one.

"Yeah, that's going to be tough. Which one is Beyoncé?" I considered.

"That's the problem. I love Beyoncé."

"Then I don't think we can use that one but I'll work on it. I swear."

"I have no doubt. There's this amazing breakfast place on The Strip, Blueberry Hill. They have cinnamon pancakes that I swear will give you a mouth-gasm."

Shaking my head at her, I was quite certain I should've just made up some excuse the past few years to spend this day with her. She didn't try to fix what had happened. She knew she couldn't. She wanted to but she was also good with letting it be. Letting the pain live and breathe and stretch its legs because you couldn't keep the damned thing contained. It didn't work. It existed with me, in me, beside me all the fucking time and she was the only person who ever seemed able to put distance between me and the torment. It had to exist because without it Chris, and Matt, and Sunjay and everyone else didn't exist and I would never allow that. But she softened its constant lashes. Took them on for me when I could no longer stand under the weight of it all. I hadn't forgotten about that damned sketchpad but I couldn't go there today. I just couldn't. "A mouth-gasm, huh?"

"Yes. They're delicious." She was already pulling on a pair of short-shorts I wanted to peel right back off of her when she shot me a mischievous smirk. "I mouth-gasm every time I eat there."

"That so? I'd prefer it if I was in charge of all of your gasms of every variety." I marched to my suitcase and located a pair of jeans, even though the heat of July in Vegas was brutal. I wasn't in the mood for pity-glances from every fucking person on The Strip today and you could see my scars when I wore shorts.

"Oh, trust me, you give me mouth-gasms, too." She stood off of the bed. "You taste even better than the pancakes."

Clearly, she was an angel sent to me to make this particular day not suck the balls of every variety of farm animal. "You like that, baby? You like it when I come hot and fast down your throat?" Resolve or gentlemanly behavior might've been something I could summon on any other day, but not today.

"You know I do." Her lips brushed over my jaw before she shimmied out of that tank top. Her tits bounced in my face, mesmerizing me. I had precious little interest in pancakes. She was still within arm's reach so I took full advantage. "I haven't spent near enough time with these." Her nipples obediently throbbed against my palms. A slight shudder worked through her as she stepped closer. My baby loved having her tits worshipped. Like I said, she was perfection all bottled up for me. I caught her nipples between my thumb and index finger and her eyes closed. Oh hell yeah. "Lay down for me. Let me get a fix," I commanded.

"Yes," escaped her lips in a hungry whisper. She crawled back in the bed and I set to work tending her need and making an effort to dam back the pain.

AN HOUR LATER, I watched her devour a stack of cinnamon pancakes. A dollop of whipped cream landed on the tip of her nose. Leaning in to the table, I scooped it off with my finger and laughed. Jesus, I laughed on July 11. How the fuck had that worked out?

She sighed. "Someday, I'll be able to eat something and not get any on me. Today is clearly not that day."

There was already syrup on her shorts.

"I keep telling you I'm happy to eat anything you want off of you so just keep spilling, my adorable little klutz."

She stuck her tongue out at me.

"You looking for something to lick? I can provide."

"I enjoyed licking you an hour ago but I could definitely go for a second course."

I grunted at the angel seated across from me but I wasn't letting her suck me off all damned day as good as that sounded. "What do you want to do today, baby doll?" As massive as it was, our suite just wasn't quite big enough to contain me and the anguish that day. I needed to be outside, closer to the clouds maybe.

"I was thinking maybe we could go get a tat. They have great shops here." Absolutely nothing about her sounded certain and I couldn't stand to think about her hurting herself just because she knew that's occasionally how I dealt. Not one single thing marred my baby's beautiful alabaster skin and nothing ever would as long as I lived and breathed. As much as I appreciated that she would willingly do that with me I wasn't having it.

"You want a tat?" I made no effort to hide my doubt.

"Maybe. I don't know. I could get your initials on my ass or something."

Okay, maybe I'd been hasty in my decision not to allow this. *She doesn't really want that, fucker. She's trying to make you feel better.* Thank God she wasn't naked. My better sense had a fighting chance when she was clothed. "Come on, Hannah baby, you don't really want that and The Sevens will be rounding the bases using snowballs in hell before I'd let some guy stare at your ass long enough to ink anything on it."

"For the record, I like Hannah baby way better than Hannah Banana and how do you know I don't want a tat? What if I do?"

"Because I know my girl. Now come on, anything but a tat."

"I'm assuming based on your comment about another guy seeing my ass you would feel the same way about the Bare Pool back at the hotel." She was teasing me and fuck me sideways if it was working. She managed to give my fury over the people who'd been robbed from the earth directionality.

"That would be a very safe assumption, sweetness. I don't share. You know this."

"And here I thought you were more evolved than that, First Sargent." Her sexy coo wasn't hurting either.

"I'm barely three steps away from the cave and you know it. If I could carry a freaking club around with me to beat back men who stare at you, I would."

That elicited a sweet giggle. "I am aware. I like the warrior side of you, remember?"

My brain knew I needed her to stop saying that. My cock, on the other hand, was lapping it up like it was her pussy asking for it harder. "So I've been told. If you want to go topless in a pool, there is one outside my suite. As long as it's for my eyes only I see no reason for you to wear a swimsuit at all."

"I'll add that to the list of possibilities for today."

"You've been out here a lot lately, right? What are your favorite things to do?" I shoveled another bite of pancakes in my mouth still not really tasting much. Nothing worked right on this day. Even my taste buds gave up the will to function. By the end of the week, they'd stage a resurrection.

"I love to ride the High Roller. It's so fun. You can see all of Vegas when you're at the top."

"That's the big-ass Ferris wheel right?"

She nodded. "Or we could go hiking, or do the fastest go-cart track in Vegas. I've never driven them but they're supposed to be cool. We could walk The Strip."

Fucking amazing. Fast, hard, free-falling, and outside. All the things I needed she just offered up.

For a moment, there was a little space between that day a few years ago and today. I existed between the two. A sudden gasp from her jerked me back to the present time, rescuing me from drowning in memories of moon sand and blood and agony. "I know! Let's go to Range 1020. It's outside. It's huge. That's perfect!"

Had she not been so exuberant I would've batted this off like the tattoo idea but she really wanted to do this. That glimmer in her eyes was legit. My God, how the hell did I get to even spend one single week with her much less all of the fragmented days and weeks I'd gotten to be in her presence? "You'd really go shoot with me?" I had to ask.

"Hell yeah! Please. I haven't been in so long."

"You are aware that you're basically the world's most perfect woman, right?"

She laughed. "I'm glad you think so. You know, I happen to have been trained by the best weapon's sergeant in the army. Bet I can outshoot him now." She waggled her eyebrows.

"Oh, you are on, baby. Get your sexy ass up. Now, I have something to prove."

30

HANNAH

He was almost smiling. I pinched my own thigh. Yep, definitely awake and alive and Griff was almost smiling on July 11. Holy crap, this was working. The fake leather of the ancient Suburban the guy who worked for the range was driving slapped at my thighs as we bounded along the desert terrain. My boobs bounced and Griff's eyes immediately locked on my chest appreciatively. All of that practiced resolve and politeness training wasn't happening today. He didn't have the fight left in him. I was pleased to see it go but hated the reason for its disappearance. Today, he couldn't manage the many versions of himself. Only the one I needed could breathe through all of his pain.

"Either of you ever shot before?" the driver inquired.

Griff smirked. "A time or two."

"How 'bout you, sweetheart? You don't look like you've ever even held a real gun. If you ask me, most of 'em are just too heavy for girls. Ought to leave this to the men. It's men's work."

There were a few ways I could handle this. I could either tell him off now or wait and show him just how well I shot. I'd been trained by a Weapons Sergeant for the Green Berets not to mention a general. Griff smirked clearly thinking the same thing. "First of all, I am not your sweetheart. Secondly, no I've never even *held* a gun before. Are they scary?" I batted my eyelashes for effect.

Griff choked back laughter. I glanced skyward with a silent thank you. I was certain Chris had a hand in this day providing me with so much material to ease Griff's pain.

"Ah, now, don't be scared. I'll hold it for you so you don't have to," the driver spoke to me like I was a toddler but I was in this for the long game. I'd tell him off after I showed off my skills.

"He wraps his arms around you to help you pull, I'm shooting him just be aware of that," Griff huffed under his breath.

"He puts his mitts anywhere near me and it won't be you who shoots him, honey," I matched his whispered tone.

Just as I was beginning to think we were actually being driven all the way out to the canyon, we pulled up at the outdoor range. I hopped out ready to take on both of my opponents.

"Now, you know, man, if you want to give her a little money and let her go shopping back at The Strip you could do our Black Ops Experience. It's the real deal." Our driver continued to make a fool of himself. "Got military grade weapons and everything."

"Dear God," I breathed the words out trying to remain calm. The guy didn't actually know who we were but that little comment about giving me money pissed me the fuck off. Not to mention the fact that it was one thing for us to be sport shooting. It was a whole other thing to make Griff think about all of the real Black Ops missions he'd done.

"The real deal, huh?" Griff glared at the ground the man was standing on like he'd love to set it on fire.

"Yeah, just like real Black Ops."

"Oh, I'll bet." He rolled his eyes. "Where are the guns?"

"Here," he opened the back doors of the Suburban, unlocked a case, and handed Griff the Glock he'd picked. "You sure you don't want an AK? We got 'em. That's a real man's gun. Got a real easy trigger for her, too."

Abject fury flared in Griff's eyes. Burn the house. Scorch the skyline. Fuck their world. Here we go. I braced for impact but Griff shook his head seeming to decide that this guy just wasn't worth it. "I prefer for there to be some degree of difficulty when I shoot. And if you say the words real or man, and associate them with the word gun again I'll shove my boot so far up your ass you can taste the sand still on them from Iraq. We clear?"

The guy took several steps back. Confusion and fear contorted his face. "Sure, man."

"Good. Now shut up and give her a gun."

He removed another Glock from the locked box welded in the Suburban. "I thought you said you didn't shoot much. You sure you're good with this one? It ain't as easy as some others I have and you're gonna have to let me load it for you. It's tricky."

"Oh for fuck's sake, give me that." I yanked the Glock out of his hand, grabbed a box of American Eagles, and shoved bullets in the clip.

"Now, you're gonna need the speed loader when you get a few in there," the guy sounded panicked. "Let me get it for you."

Without missing a beat or a bullet, I shoved all fifteen bullets in the clip and then locked the clip in the pistol, without a loader thank you very much.

"Looks like she's got it." Griff shook his head. "And now you've gone and pissed her off."

I marched to the farthest line from the targets, dragged my sunglasses off my head and placed them over my eyes, took aim, and shot all fifteen bullets in a perfectly straight line down the target sheet.

"Look at that," Griff continued to taunt. "Must be beginner's luck."

"Can't believe any man would let his woman learn to shoot like that," the idiot grumbled.

With that, Griff stood at the line beside me, narrowed his eyes, and turned his Cubs hat around backward. Yep, it was about to go down. He lifted his arms, stared down the barrel, took a few seconds to lower his heart rate and time his breaths. When he barely blinked, I knew this was going to be as impressive as hell. And then, my man shot all fifteen rounds in the same freaking hole. I was both thrilled with the look of absolute awe on our guide's face and bummed because I was so not going to outshoot him. My ears rang. Probably should've grabbed some of those ear plug things.

"So, what you're like Mr. and Mrs. Smith or something?" the guy fumed. "You could've told me that."

"Doubt Brad and Angelina can shoot as well as we do," I informed him.

"Safe bet," Griff agreed. "I didn't get a chance to tell you between all of the chauvinistic bullshit free-flowing out of your face. Might want to wipe that off your chin before you crawl back under your rock."

"It's a range requirement for you to wear ear protection," the guy fumed. "I'm throwing you off the course."

"Seriously?" I huffed. "Then I'm letting every supervisor I can find know just a few of the things you said to and about me."

He considered that for far too long. Griff marched back to the Suburban, got two pairs of earmuffs, and we shot three more rounds.

Our range officer pouted in the truck while we loaded in our last round. "What was that about you outshooting me, sweetness?" He winked at me.

"The sun's in my eyes." I laughed at my own lame excuse.

"I see." He whipped the baseball cap off of his head and pulled it down to shield my eyes from the sun. He ran his fingers through my hair as he eased my ponytail through the back. "That better?"

"Yep. Now I will totally be able to do that all fifteen in one hole thing." I explained in a breathless pant. His hands in my hair always undid me.

"Then get to it, baby."

I considered. "What do I win if I outshoot you this round?"

He chuckled. That was at least ten times he'd laughed today. I made another thank you glance toward heaven. "Guess that depends on what you're wanting."

"Can I have anything I want?" I waggled my eyebrows.

"Do I look stupid?" he teased. Fine, he probably knew I'd want to know why he was so dead set on not telling Smith about us and what it was my father had said to him just before they'd been sent to Eritrea.

"Okay, how about this..." My heart thundered in my chest. I didn't want this nearly as bad as I wanted to know what my father had done but I did want it very, very much. "If I outshoot you this round, then tonight, after dinner, we go to bed and you really show me everything you would do if you had no doubts that I was willing." If I could make him understand that I loved all of him, that no part of him frightened me, I could convince him that I was tough enough to handle whatever it was he refused to tell me.

My eyes locked on his Adam's apple as it bobbed from his harsh swallow. Consideration darkened his eyes turning them more gunmetal than brown in the glaring sun. Wasn't that fitting? "That's really what you want? You're serious?" Disbelief clawed at the hope evident in his tone.

"I'm serious, Griff."

His eyes shifted to the sky and then to his boots. "And if you hate it and then hate me for it?"

The words were almost whipped out into the canyon by the wind.

"I won't hate it and I would never hate you. Please."

"Maybe." The armor was slipping. I wasn't stupid enough to believe that sex could somehow heal any portion of what he'd been through but I did firmly believe my acceptance would suture a few of the wounds.

"It's not like I'll outshoot you anyway, right?" He thought he needed a way out so I provided one. It would all be up to him.

"Come on." He wrapped his arm around me we headed back to the line. "You shoot first."

I tried to do the measured breaths and lower heart rate thing but nervous tension zinged up and down my spine. I was going to end up psyching myself out. Shaking it off, I made a wish even though there were no stars currently available to wish upon. I took aim and tried to remember every single thing he'd taught me so long ago. We used to drive a couple of hours, all the way to the other side of Denver, so no one from Ft. Carson would see us.

He'd stand behind me and wrap his arms over mine. Since all I'd wanted was to be enveloped in him, paying attention to instructions had been difficult. I'd made do. I'd even impressed him which was its own special brand of bliss. If I concentrated, I could still feel his hot breaths as they whispered in my ear and feel his cock harden from being near my ass.

I lined up my shot and pulled. Somehow, my second and third shots actually went in the same hole. "Yay!" I broke my concentration and he chuckled. Realigning, the fourth and fifth enlarged the hole but were still close. The sixth was off, not even in the same ring. I slumped in defeat.

But then he was there. Right behind me. His hot breath over my ear. His arms over mine. His chest a solid foundation behind me and his cock, oh yeah, right there, too. I closed my eyes and let the scent of explosive gunpowder and of him absorb me. His love absolved me. I was completely surrounded by the man I was put on this earth to love and there was nowhere else I ever wanted to be.

He eased my arms a few centimeters to the left. "Deep breath and let it all the way out, baby. You can do this," rumbled in my ear. "Listen to your heart. Let your pulse guide the shot. Remember what I taught you. Look at the clear front sight. Put it right in the center of the blurry target. Slow. Steady. Let the shot surprise you."

"Pull," he urged. And I did and it centered my original mark. "Again," he commanded. And again it went right where I needed it to go. By the fifteenth bullet, other than my own mistakes, I had a perfect round. "Good girl," he murmured in my ear as he tapped my ass with his hand twice. Those two words robbed me of breath and flooded pure lust and adrenaline through my bloodstream. What I wouldn't give to hear that while we were in bed that night. "Not sure that's fair," I managed.

"You pulled the trigger, sweetheart. I was just trying to distract you."

I shook my head at him and stepped back to watch him shoot. The first ten shots were perfect. I had no idea what he planned to do with the last five. Shot eleven also centered the hole he'd made in the bullseye. But with the last four shots, his shoulders eased ever so slightly. If I hadn't been studying him so intently, I would never have noticed. What was he doing?

He pulled and holy fuck it hit the ring three away from the hole. "Damn." He feigned irritation. But then the thirteenth and fourteenth were equal distance due north and due south from the original bullseye mark. I couldn't breathe. He was really doing this. He lined up the last shot and pulled. It was exactly equal distance from the center hole as the others but on the other side of the target. There was a perfect diamond around the bullseye. He was making a point. He turned back and jerked his sunglasses off of his face. "You won, baby doll. You still sure about that prize you picked?"

"Very, very sure."

"Do me a favor and remember you said that tomorrow morning."

31

GRIFF

I'd spent the entire time we'd been on a bus and then in line to ride that Ferris wheel trying to come up with a way to explain to her that she was the only thing I ever really wanted. She kept saying she wanted me to indulge my warrior side, which basically turned me into a fucking dog in heat. I couldn't give her that house she'd been designing or even a real relationship so I fucking owed her this. And it sure as hell wasn't a sacrifice. If she wanted me to indulge her wilder side, even more than we already had, I was all in. It'd taken everything I had in me not to dry hump her leg on The Strip.

The craziest thing of all was that Chris and the team hadn't crossed my mind too often that day. They were there. They would always be there. I wouldn't have it any other way. But when she was beside me it took more effort to access the well of pain I couldn't seem to escape when I was alone.

After our ride, we made our way back to The Obelisk. She wanted to shower before we committed a few crimes, namely breaking and entering, and then had dinner with the wicked powerpuff grannies.

The oppressive sunlight beat down on us from above and

reflected off of the black cement effectively placing the throngs of people crowding The Strip into an oven. Sweat dewed at the nape of her neck, producing curls in a few stray strands of hair that had escaped that ponytail that had driven me to distraction all damn day. My mouth watered.

If she wanted my dirtiest side, I would provide. Fucking her sweaty, inhaling that musky scent of her unwashed, was just the beginning of the things I wanted to indulge myself in. The thought alone made me have to make a quick adjustment of my cock.

Cars sped by and every resort had their own set of outdoor speakers assaulting the desert air with Sinatra and Martin. It all blended into a relatively soothing form of background noise. The pulse of the city kept me from thinking too deeply and that was just fine by me.

Hannah's fingers were laced in mine and her head was on my bicep as we walked. Yep, could definitely get used to that, too. Only I couldn't and I needed to remember that. "One night while we're here we have to go see the Bellagio fountains. I've been wanting to see it since I started working out here."

"Anything you want, baby, I'm game." I planted a kiss on top of her head. "Thanks for planning all of this, by the way. I needed it."

She lifted her head. "We needed it. And thanks for throwing our last round. That was really sweet."

Okay, so, I might've thrown it a little. Never seemed to matter how much training I'd had or how much weight I could bench. I didn't have the strength to tell her no. I had no ability to deny her anything she ever wanted, and that, right there, scared the piss out of me. She'd been more than forthcoming with her intentions for this trip and the longer I spent with her the harder it was to really remember why I was going to have to say no to us ever being a permanent thing. I just wasn't certain I'd ever possess the strength necessary to stay away from my own personal sun. I'd spent too many frigid nights alone being eaten alive by the darkness. "Who says I threw it?" Lying to her had never been an option either so I went on with the smirk forming on my face.

"Well, there was that perfect diamond around the bullseye." She laughed at me outright.

"Couldn't let Gun-range Rick the ass-beagle think I'd lost my edge."

I was indulged with a round of her adorable giggles. I swear if they'd bottle that sound, I'd shoot up with it every fucking day with no remorse. "Ass-beagle? That's a new one."

"Yeah, I'm working on some new material. Just taking it out for a test drive. Not sure I'll stick with that one."

"I like it. And he was definitely an ass."

"Sorry you had to endure that, sweetness. I should've offered to shoot him for you."

She shook her head as we neared the Walgreens across from the hotel. "You going to jail for shooting the teeny tiny balls off of a chauvinist is not how I saw this week going."

"I'm just saying the offer is always on the table."

She stopped walking long enough to stand on her tiptoes and brush a kiss on my jaw. I turned and cradled her face in my hands. "Lips, baby. I need to taste your sweet kisses." I indulged myself in another hit of those lips as she angled her head and offered herself to me. Yep, I was a junkie and I never wanted reprieve. I'd intended it to be a quick kiss, just long enough for me to taste the future I couldn't have, but she parted for my tongue as urgency streamed through me. Her hands traced up my pecs and wrapped around my neck. I gripped her ass and proceeded to rub her up and down my cock in broad daylight in front of The Obelisk and a few thousand people. I didn't give a damn. One of the best things about Vegas is that no one else cared either. We even received a few encouraging wolf-whistles and a, "Get it, man," from a passerby.

That turned our kiss into me trying to suck on her tongue while she laughed which might've been even better than where we started. Suffice it to say that was the best July 11 I'd had in four long, impossible years. I wrapped my arm over her shoulders and dragged her toward the hotel. We'd put on enough of a show for one day and I still had to figure out which hotel room I was breaking into. After that, we'd eat, and then... My heart damn near beat its way out of my ribcage. After that, I'd drown myself in her in every conceivable way I could come up with. The likelihood that I was going to be able to summon enough patience and concentration to find evidence sufficient enough to convict the grannies gone wild gang grew more and more doubtful with every passing moment.

As we rounded the massive waterfall, one of those ever-present photographers stopped us. "Get a picture for a souvenir."

Hannah grinned at him but I saw the disappointment she was trying to conceal. "We can't. Thanks though."

In that moment, I'd fucking had enough. It was one thing for me to tear myself in two trying to live in her world and exist in mine. I wouldn't do it to her. I owed her too much. "It's fine. Take a pic," I ordered as I adjusted my sunglasses to fully conceal my eyes. To keep most of my face covered, I turned and brushed a kiss on her cheek while he snapped the picture.

"You can pick it up in the lobby by the bar," the photographer explained.

"Perfect. Thank you." Hannah beamed. If the guy had managed to capture her exuberance on film I was buying fifty copies, I didn't give a damn how much they were charging. "Let's go see it." Still gripping my hand, she dragged me through the lobby. We joined a line of people all waiting to purchase the pictures popping up on screens behind the attendants.

Making quick work of coming down the few steps from the lobby bar, a guy whose hair was a little too perfect, and who was sporting a collared shirt that was entirely too neat, and who stood far too close to Hannah studied her. "Hey, is your name Hannah Hagen?" He glanced at his phone again and then looked back up at her.

I narrowed my eyes. "No, that isn't her name but just so I have a name to give the cops when they come for your body who the fuck are you?"

Hannah shook her head at me. There was a distinctive snarl to my voice not that I gave a shit.

"Uh..." The guy sized me up and then took two steps backward. Not far enough but it was a start. "I'm Second Lieutenant Ryan Winch, Air Force Academy class of 2017."

Hannah and I both rolled our eyes.

"It's just you kinda look like this picture my dad gave me." He showed us the phone that did indeed hold a picture of my baby.

"Oh for fuck's sake," Hannah huffed under her breath. "Yeah, I'm Hannah. Your father is friends with my father, right?"

"Yeah. He said to meet you here. Hey, did you know you have something on your shorts?" He pointed his fingers far too close to her crotch and scowled at the syrup stain.

The growl that had been churning in my gut sprang free. "Hey, did you know she has eyes?" I menaced.

"I just thought you might want to change before we go out," Ryan explained. "Plus, I was thinking we'd go to the buffet here since you have a room but you need to dress up a little. You'd be prettier in a dress anyway."

I ground my teeth. So, the Academy grad figured he'd use her room to take her out for free and wanted her to dress up for him. Seriously, why was I never armed when I needed to be?

Hannah laughed in his face. "Sorry, Ryan, we're not going out. My father really needs to learn to keep his nose out of my business. I'm here with my boyfriend."

"So...you're the boyfriend?" He stared up at me.

"You're quick, man. That Academy education really took."

"Are you in the Air Force?" Confusion furrowed his brow.

"Does that matter?" This guy was likely to go home and tell Daddy that Hannah was here with someone else. I needed him to have as little information about me as I could get away with."

"He's a Green Beret. Now leave," Hannah fumed. Well, there went that idea.

"Oh, that's like the SEALs, right, only for the army?"

Fuck it. I was tired of pretending to be anything other than what I was. "Yeah, kind of like that. They just don't make movies about us."

Hannah stepped up to the counter when the couple ahead of us left with their photo. "I want ten copies of that," I called as I positioned myself between Hannah and Ryan.

"What am I supposed to do tonight then?" Ryan pouted. Seriously, was there some kind of prick convention in Vegas that week I was unaware of? Their publicists needed to do better promo.

"I literally have a negative number of fucks to give you on that front, man. All I really care about is that you get away from my baby and that you stay away from her. Why don't you go fly something?"

"I'm not a pilot yet."

"Do I get extra points if I pretend that I care because I still don't?"

"So, you two are like together, together. You're hitting that on the regular?"

I stomped closer and towered over Ryan. "Patience is something I only possess when there are witnesses. Keep that in mind."

"Geez, bro. Hostile much? I just wanted to know if she was putting out." He scurried backward yet again.

Hannah spun back around beaming at the pictures. I watched her head lift and then her eyes narrow. "Why are you still here? Go away." She shooed him like a gnat.

"Well, what am I supposed to tell my father?"

"I couldn't care less," she informed him.

"Yeah, see, between the two of us we still have no fucks to give," I huffed. "We tried. We really did but we couldn't even come up with one between us."

"Is he always this protective of you, honey?" Ryan decided to get belligerent.

"Call her honey one more time and you can see for yourself."

"When I said the words Green Beret what did you think that meant?" Hannah taunted.

"Fine. Whatever. Guess I'll see if I can get into the buffet alone." He slithered away.

"Un-freaking-believable." Hannah shook her head. "If anyone on the jury actually had to live with my father, I don't think they'd convict me for taking a roll of wallpaper to his head."

I grunted because talking about her old man wasn't happening. Everything regarding him and us was just too close to the surface that day. Somehow, it had replaced the horrific memories of the past, because it was standing in the way of the future I wanted more than my next breath.

32

HANNAH

There was this constant spiked edge of need that resided in my chest. Annoyance resided there as well. My stupid father running interference and then having to play detective that night with Griff were not anywhere on the list of things we needed to do and yet they were getting top billing.

"The dumbfuckery is at an all-time high today in the Mojave, clearly," Griff grumbled as he wrapped his arm protectively back over my shoulder.

"Sorry about that." I sighed.

"I see your father still has very distinct ideas about what your life should look like." Offense rifled his tone. The wounds I'd spent most of the day trying to help him grapple with returned to his eyes. Now was not the time to discuss my father no matter how badly we needed to. For once this week, I was actually going to stick to my plan.

"Can we just...not talk about the general? I'll deal with him when I get back to Denver."

That earned me a nod but I didn't like the certainty I could now see in Griff's features. I didn't like it at all.

"I have a bunch of questions about dinner tonight." I focused on the current mission like any good soldier.

"You can ask me anything you want, baby, but maybe wait until we're in the suite, okay?" He unlocked the entrance to the suites. Effectively proving his point, two of the other bachelors were heading down the corridor at that very moment. Dammit why did I have to suck so bad at this?

Fred smiled as we turned the corner and approached Griff's suite. "I do hope Las Vegas treated you both well today."

"Very well, thanks." I smiled. Griff only gave him a quick nod as he guided me into the suite.

When he'd sealed the door shut, I scooted to the other end of the suite near the pool. "You don't trust him do you?" I whispered.

"Never assume people are good. They'll almost always prove you wrong. Now, I've got to figure out what..."

"The sassy senile sisters are up to," I offered.

Griff gave me my favorite smirk. "There is nothing sexier than a woman with strong alliteration skills."

I cocked an eyebrow at him. "Nothing?" As soon as he was within arm's reach, I gripped his T-shirt and pulled him closer. "Nothing at all?"

"Well, maybe a few things," he allowed. He wrapped me up in the sanctuary of him. The danger and passion produced by his gunpowder scent was more apparent after he'd been on the range. And once again I was certain there was nowhere else I would ever belong. I was home. Burying my face against his T-shirt, I inhaled. I wanted his scent to permeate my skin while he permeated my body. It was the only way life made any sense at all.

"Like your fucking beautiful ass." He grabbed two handfuls and squeezed. A rush of wet heat gathered in my panties. "I know it's hard to believe but your ass is actually far sexier than your alliteration skills. And your lips. Damn, but you have pretty lips. Both sets. And hair, and eyes, and my God, have you seen your tits? And legs. Fuck me, but I love those long legs wrapped around me, baby."

My chuckle was breathless, the effect of his hands on me. I wiggled my hips back and forth for him. That earned me a rumbled growl. "You keep doing that and I'm going to forget to remind you that you had questions about this ridiculous dinner tonight."

"I wish we could forget about the dinner itself. I'd prefer to take all of my clothes off and join you in the pool."

"You're killing me. You know that, right?"

Lifting my head from his chest, I stared into his gorgeous hazel eyes. "And here I was trying to save you."

Tension locked in his jaw for one heartbeat but then a little of that armor I was trying so hard to pry from his heart loosened. "You've been saving me since the first day I met you. I know what you want me to agree to, Hannah. I'm trying to figure out how to make that happen, okay? Just... I need some time...to figure it out. If I can. I may not be able to."

Holy fuck. I gnawed the inside of my lip. The pain assured me I was indeed awake and not dreaming he'd just said that. "Okay. You know we're a pretty good team. You don't have to figure it all out on your own."

"Yeah." He choked on the word. "I know. But tonight I need to focus on this dinner. My gut says something's coming. I need to know what it is."

I managed a stuttered breath. He'd agreed to the possibility of an us and even to let me help him. If he wanted to distract himself with Victoria Rutherford and the Sequinettes for the night, that was fine by me. We were getting somewhere. That was all that mattered. "About the dinner." *Just focus Hannah. Right now focus.*

He buried his face against my neck and spun his tongue in the hollow above my collarbone. Okay, that was not making focusing any easier. His lips blazed a trail of kisses up to my ear. "I want you so fucking bad." The tiny hairs at the nape of my neck gave him a standing ovation. I sank my teeth into my bottom lip. My eyes fluttered closed.

"Take me," I urged.

Much to my chagrin, he lifted his head. "I swear to you I'm going to give you everything you asked me for tonight."

Words escaped me. However, an embarrassingly needy sound spilled from my lips.

"I want to hear sounds like that over and over again tonight. God, it's all I can fucking think about. Making you moan. Making you show me what I want to see. Making you wrap those gorgeous lips around my cock and swallowing everything I give you. Taking you so hard you can't fucking walk tomorrow. Just promise me if I get too rough, you'll tell me to stop." His callused hands cradled my face again. The abrasion on my cheeks sent a jolt of electricity straight to my pussy.

"I happen to love your particular brand of rough, Griff. Thought you knew that."

His chest contracted with a huff. "Still trying to convince myself."

"I'll figure out some way to convince you but right now we need to talk about dinner, right?"

"And I thought Chris used to be a slave driver." He winked at me. I ordered my face to show no reaction. Did he realize what he'd just done? He'd joked about Chris on July 11. He'd spoken about him in the past tense without it ravaging his determination never to cry. One long blink gave me composure.

"Are you sure I should come with you tonight?" I marched on. That moment needed to live and breathe entirely on its own without me trying to smother it away. The pain had to exist because it was real and pretending it wasn't just wasn't fair to any of them. "They didn't bid on me and then you could teach me how to break into their room and I can do that part."

He shook his head but I could tell he was impressed. "First of all, we never send a soldier in alone. Second, I don't want to do anything without you so no. Third, I'm going to have to use my magnetic override for the deadbolt on the door. I'm not saying you couldn't do it. I'm just saying the one I built a while back is a little shaky and it only works on some hotel locks. If these are different, I'll have to improvise. And last, I want you to go to dinner tonight because I'm betting they'll say things to you they wouldn't say to us and there's a decent chance you being there will frustrate them. Frustration usually leads to letting things slip. That's what we're going for."

"How are we going to get by the room attendant? Every suite has one."

His cocky grin was almost as sexy as his smirk. "That might be a problem if we were using the interior doors."

I studied our own set of exterior doors. "So, we're coming in from outside."

"That's the plan. We need to dress like we've been outside on our own patio. The idea will be to make anyone who sees us assume it's our own room we're entering. Only problem is I still don't know which suite we need to break in to. I can't use the same trick I used to find your suite number. I convinced the attendants I work for you. I can't turn around and work for her.

I grinned. "I may not know how to build whatever it is you just said you had to use to get in the suites but getting a room number I can do." I grabbed my bag and headed toward the door.

"Where are you going?" I hated the panic in his tone. I knew he didn't want to be alone today.

"I'll be right back. I made several friends while I was up here redesigning the suites. I can call in a few favors."

"I'll go with you. I can stay out of sight."

I brushed a kiss on his cheek. "I'll be fine. I promise."

"Be careful, baby. If you see anything you don't like, you call me."

"I really hate that one show they have here with the ventriloquist guy. No normal man shoves his hands up puppet-butts and makes them sing. That's just sick. But his posters are up all over the lobby and I've learned to deal with that all on my own. Also, they keep inviting YouTubers here. What is up with that? You go work on your magnet thing. I'll be right back."

33

HANNAH

Smiling at Fred as I slipped out of Griff's suite, I headed toward the lobby doors. Despite Griff's caution, I didn't think Fred was up to anything. He seemed sweet. Before I made the turn, I heard two women in a heated argument. My heart leapt to my throat. Holy crap that was Ms. Mallory. Slipping into an offset corridor with the Promethean marble console table I'd picked out for the space. I crammed myself between the table and the wall to listen.

I fought not to jump for joy when I heard the grating rasp of Victoria Rutherford's voice. "It's not exactly like you came through on your end either, Megan."

"I did everything I promised you I would do. He does make a lot of money. He works for that government security firm. I still don't understand why you were so insistent that Ashley and Karen come. They couldn't make it. None of that even matters because your check bounced. I have to have that money, Ms. Rutherford. I need it."

"Perhaps you would prefer to take this discussion inside your suite, Ms. Rutherford," a male voice urged. Dammit. That had to be their suite attendant. I didn't need him fucking this up. There was a lengthy pause and I prayed they wouldn't heed his warnings.

"I'll have to move some money out of savings. I'll have you another check by week's end." Outright fury edged in Ms. Rutherford's tone.

"I don't want it by week's end. I want it now. I have to make the down payment on his flight."

"There are a lot of things I want, Megan. The things I enumerated in our agreement to start with. But life's a bitch and we don't always get our way."

I heard a door open. Not even chancing a breath, I slid along the wall and peeked down the adjacent hallway. Victoria Rutherford stalked into suite eleven and slammed the door in Megan Mallory's face. She turned and locked eyes with me. Every curse word I knew, all of the far more creative ones Griff could make up on the fly, and the ones my brother and father favored when they were with other soldiers all staged a revolt on my tongue. I dammed them back with the might of my teeth.

She narrowed her eyes and I tried to think of what Griff would do. He'd play it cool. So I smiled, nodded, and then continued my trek toward the lobby doors. She couldn't possibly have known how long I'd been standing there. Deep breaths, Hannah. You got this.

The click of her heels on the marble flooring echoed against my skull. They disappeared as she crossed one of the inlaid carpet rugs. I picked up the pace. An attendant opened the lobby door for me but she was a half second too late. "Just one moment, Hannah."

It was then that I learned that if you really try you can turn the word fuck into a seventeen-syllable expression in your head. Turning back, I tried to act like I was happy to wait and walk with her. I failed miserably. Trying to ignore the fact that she'd caught me spying on her wasn't going to work. Maybe I could get some more info out of her. "Is Ms. Rutherford okay? She sounded angry."

"You failed to mention that he was a Green Beret when you entered Sergeant Haywood. Was there a reason for that?" Hate oozed from every word she spoke.

Someone needed to send out a mayday because I was going down. I hadn't mentioned anything at all about Griff because I wasn't supposed to be entering him at all. What was she after? I tallied everything she clearly already knew and decided not to lie again. "The form for entering bachelors didn't ask what they'd done in the service. It just asked for their rank. Does it matter that he was a Beret?" If you're ever being interrogated always answer a question with another question. Smith had taught me that. People are inclined to answer whenever they're asked a question. It can keep them off balance.

"Yes, it matters. You've ruined everything."

"What are you referring to Ms. Mallory? What did I ruin?" I'd seen every single episode of the new *MacGyver* and I used to watch *Murder She Wrote* reruns with my mom when I was little. But I couldn't come up with some way to get her to confess whatever it was she was up to.

"Just watch your step, Hannah. You've caused me enough trouble." With that, she stalked out into the lobby and disappeared into a crowd. Holy crap. I turned back and almost walked into Fred. He reached and steadied me.

"I'm sorry, Ms. Hagen. Was that woman threatening you?"

"Sounded that way, didn't it?"

"Perhaps we could move you and Sergeant Haywood to one of the suites on an upper floor. I won't have another guest being rude to you."

Yeah, I liked Fred. "I'm fine. Trust me, when Griff hears about this he'll be on the warpath. You might want to move her to another state."

"I do rather like him. Rough around the edges but he clearly adores you." Fred offered me a reassuring grin.

"Yeah, well, I've loved him since I was nineteen years old. The universe just won't cut us a break."

He chuckled. "In my experience, timing is everything. You never know what the universe has in store. Maybe this whole trip will end up being the break you're wanting. Magic does happen in Las Vegas."

"Thanks. Hey, did you hear what they were arguing about before I came out of our suite?"

"I did but it was largely more of what you overheard. The bank had denied a check. Mistakes made last night." He shrugged. "Does it make any sense to you?"

"Not really but I'll figure it out. Thanks, Fred."

"If I can be of any help, Ms. Hagen, please let me know."

34

GRIFF

Wearing a groove in the tile, I continued to pace and called myself a weak bastard. I needed her to come back. Blinking rapidly, I lost the ability to distinguish the sand colored flooring from the sands that had robbed me of the only family I'd ever really had. I forced myself to breathe. Why the fuck did our suite suddenly smell like chopper fuel?

I stared at the door and willed Hannah to walk back through it. I was using her again and my own self-hatred was readily accessible. I was using her to keep the memories at bay and I was too weak to make myself stop. Flinging open the sliding glass doors that led to the pool I stepped outside and tried to let the chlorinated air anesthetize the sounds of Aaron's groan as he leapt in front of me after I'd taken the first shot, and the echo of the machine gun I'd taught those fuckers to shoot.

We'd been training up a militia to fight alongside us. I'd done my job and they'd turned on us. It was all my fault. Every single gravestone had been hand carved by me.

"Griff?" her breathless call shattered the hellish abyss I'd hurled myself into. "You okay?"

I shook my head because what else could I do? I was here and they weren't and that wasn't okay. It never would be. In two rushed steps of her long legs, her arms wrapped around me and I clung to my own personal saving grace. "God, it just sucks so fucking much. I know it does. And it's okay for you not to be okay. Nothing about any of it is okay. It never will be. It shouldn't have been the way it was but none of it was your fault." She always knew precisely what to say. Always. "Do you hear me? Because I know you all blame yourselves and sometimes life just...sucks. It's never fair and it won't ever be fair. But there was nothing you could've done to stop what happened. Nothing." She was wrong. I could've told my brothers about her, how much I loved her. I should've told them because keeping things from them weakened the bond we needed to stay alive.

"I love you." I strangled on the single truth.

"I love you too, baby. I found out a bunch of stuff. You want to hear about it or I can get Fred to get us a couple six-packs and we can sit out here all night?"

Scrubbing my hands over my face, I shook off the dust of the memories as best as I was able. That damn moon dust. You couldn't ever really remove its choking constriction from your veins. I needed a distraction. She knew that, too. "Tell me."

"Let's stay out here a few more minutes." She took my hand and guided me to one of the cushioned chairs on the lanai. As soon as I was seated, she curled up in my lap. Her touch was the only thing keeping me in the present. My baby knew that as well.

I breathed in the scent of her. The chlorine hadn't done shit but she eased the chokehold. I could no longer smell the scent of fuel laced with sand and blood.

"Want to call Smith?" she whispered.

Yes. I told that answer to fuck off. "No. I'm better now." I couldn't have them both and I didn't deserve either of them.

"You know, the dinner should be over before Lindsen takes the mound tonight."

Jesus, I'd forgotten there was a game. This day fucked me over every year. "We're not watching the Cubs tonight, baby. I intend to keep my promises to you."

"We could still do that later."

"No. Tonight I plan to catch Victoria Rutherford and her arachnid gang. Then I'm taking you to bed and keeping you there for the rest of our trip."

"I thought we weren't sure she killed off all of her husbands." Hannah lifted her head off of my shoulder and attempted to peek around our private cove. "I don't think she did. She seems to be having money problems."

The terror that had been riding hard in my veins ebbed away in light of my need to fix something. I managed to place most of the weight on my good leg as I stood and carried her inside.

I settled us on the bed. "Let's hear what you found out, Nancy Drew."

She beamed at that. "I never read those but I totally read all of the Babysitter's Club Mysteries from the library when we were stationed in Arlington. I wanted to be Claudia because she was an amazing artist only it kind of annoyed me because she was usually painting fruit or her grandmother. Were those the only things she could paint? I mean come on."

And just like that, the consuming fire of the desert sands melted away. She'd smothered out the smoke. I could finally breathe. "Yeah, but I don't know any of those chicks so I can't tease you about them. Plus, you can't be Claudia or your whole company's name doesn't work."

Her laughter rushed fresh breath to my lungs. "That is true. Guess I'll stick with Hannah. But wait until I tell you what I just heard." If I didn't let her tell me soon, she was going to vibrate off the bed.

"Talk, baby."

"I went out into the hallway and Ms. Mallory and Ms. Rutherford were having an argument. I couldn't have timed it better if I'd tried. But Fred said they'd been arguing before I went out there so maybe I could've. I don't know." Her words flew out in rapid-fire sentences.

I fought not to laugh at her outright. "Deep breaths, baby doll. What did you hear them say?"

"Apparently, Ms. Rutherford's check bounced. That's why I'm

wondering about the dead husbands. If she really killed off eight guys for life insurance policies, wouldn't she have plenty of money?"

"Maybe. Keep going." My mind considered every possible angle.

"Obviously, Megan was pissed. Ms. Rutherford said she'd get her another check by the end of the week. Megan said she needed it now because she had to make a down payment on a flight, which makes no sense at all. When you book a flight, you have to pay for the whole thing, right?"

"Depends on the kind of flight." The whole fucked-up thing lay before me in pieces. I needed more to even put the edges of the puzzle together. For half a second, I wished the guys were all there. We worked better together.

"Wait, there's tons more. Ms. Rutherford was really angry and kept saying things about Ms. Mallory not following through on her promises or something. Apparently people named Ashley and Karen were supposed to be there last night and they weren't. Oh, and they were talking about you, too."

"What did they say about me?"

"They didn't say your name. She said something about someone who makes a lot of money who works for a government security firm. Obviously, that's you."

Frustrated with my own inability to figure anything out, I huffed, "Why the hell are they interested in me? Guess it's good I'm a sexy motherfucker. That makes up for me being a dumbass."

Hannah giggled and shook her head at me. "You're not a dumbass. You are a sexy motherfucker though. I can't figure anything out either but isn't that how mysteries are supposed to work? You have to find clues and stuff."

"You're adorable, you know that?" I razzed her hair and then popped a kiss on her cheek.

She combed her fingers through her hair, righting it, and then hemmed. "It gets worse."

"Define worse."

"Well, I know where Ms. Rutherford is staying because I saw her go in her suite. It's eleven. But then Megan caught me spying on them." She cringed. Dammit, how could I have let her do this on her own? I should never have sent her out there untrained. I really was a damned fool.

"Did she call you on it?"

"Yeah. Kind of. She said I'd ruined everything and then told me to watch my step."

With that, I was off the bed. My hip protested the sudden movement but I didn't give a shit. "She threatened you?" I hadn't quite intended it to come out in a roar of fury but it did.

"Griff, I'm fine. I swear. I'm not afraid of her. Honestly, she seems afraid of you. She asked me why I hadn't mentioned that you were a Beret on the form I filled out to get you into the auction."

I tried to think through the haze of rage swamping my vision. My general beliefs ran along the lines of, if you scare or threaten my baby, I'll arrange for you to meet your maker instantaneously. Do not pass go. Do not collect two hundred dollars. "Wait. I thought T entered me in this thing?"

She shook her head. "No, his job was to get you here. I pretended to be you and entered you in the auction. Guess I didn't do that very well since she figured out it was me but what did I ruin? This whole thing is insane. We should just leave and go vacation somewhere else. I'll pay for it. We could go to Hawaii."

"We're not running away. We're staying and we're fighting." Walking away from a mission just wasn't in me. I couldn't do it.

35

HANNAH

The soft fabric of my favorite sundress fluttered down to my thighs while I watched Griff lock and unlock the exterior doors that led from the bedroom to our pool. Nervous energy churned in my stomach. I heard the distinctive click once again and he stepped into the bedroom. "Damn, you're pretty." He grinned at me.

"Are you sure this is okay? I might wear it over a bikini if we were hanging out at the pool so it's sort of legit." I'd purchased an entirely see-through lace cover up to wear over my favorite bikini specifically for the purposes of making him drool but that wasn't on the agenda for this portion of our evening.

"It's perfect, sweetheart." He hooked his thumbs in the hem of his T-shirt and brought it up over his abs. Now my mouth was the one that was watering.

"Damn, you're pretty," I quoted back.

"I know." He laughed and tossed the shirt in the general vicinity of his suitcase. When he shed his jeans I hated Ms. Mallory and Ms. Rutherford even more. "You know, we could be on a flight to Honolulu right now."

Seating himself on the bed, he eased his injured leg into a pair of khaki shorts I knew he hated. The scalpel marks around his knee were more than apparent. "It's like a ten hour flight to Hawaii. I can't wait that long to fuck you. We'd end up trying to join the mile-high club and then we'd get arrested because, baby, you get so damn loud when I bring you. They could hear you over the engines. I look like shit in prison orange. We have to stay here."

"You are so full of yourself," I teased.

"That's right, sweetness, and as soon as we catch the three senior stooges you're gonna be so full of me."

How the hell he figured out how to turn me on with a sentence that also included the words three stooges I had no idea but that's what love can do to a girl. "We can't use trios anymore, remember? Now, Ms. Mallory is in on this, too. There's four of them."

"Fuck and I spent all day coming up with trios. I'm going to have to rethink my whole internal monologue for this dinner. That's bullshit right there. I had good stuff. Wait, how many Spice Girls were there?"

"Five. That's a no-go, plus I like Victoria Beckham."

He cocked an eyebrow at me as he eased off the bed and dug in his suitcase. "You like her or you like looking at her husband?"

"Yes." I laughed. "But he has nothing on shock and awe."

"That's right, baby, and don't you forget it." He flexed one and then the other, making his pecs dance for me.

"Are you planning on attending dinner shirtless? Because I'll bet you could get some answers out of people that way."

"Guess I could." He shrugged.

I rolled my eyes. "Put a shirt on, Sergeant. You're all for me. I don't share. Just ask Smith." That last part leapt out of my mouth without my permission. Dammit, why did I have to bring him up?

"I don't have to ask him. I've tried to get you to give me bites of your ice cream before." He let the comment roll off of his back.

"You know me and ice cream have a symbiotic relationship. It makes me happy and I give it a place to live, on my clothing generally."

One of my very favorite sounds in the whole world was him

laughing. "I keep telling you I'm happy to clean you up with my tongue anytime. I'll see if Jeeves can come up with us some ice cream after our mission."

"I take it Jeeves is actually Fred?"

"Dumbass name," he mumbled.

"He checked on me after Ms. Mallory threatened me and kind of helped me spy on the felonious four..."

"Hey, now that was a good one. Gonna have to step up my game to keep up with my girl."

I slipped my feet into a pair of flip-flops and Griff shook his head. "Do you have anything that doesn't make noise when you walk?"

"Right. Almost forgot we're breaking and entering for an appetizer." I pulled a pair of high-heeled wedge sandals out of the closet and got another head shake.

"Can you run in those?"

"I officially hate these women." I flung the sandals back in and went with my kicks because I had nothing else.

"I can throw you over my shoulder and get us anywhere we need to go but I'd prefer it if you can run without breaking an ankle just in case."

"I feel like we should start calling them all the Rat Pack because that fits, right? We are in Vegas."

"Yeah, but there were five of them, too." He was trying to cover it with our typical banter but I didn't miss him popping the knuckles on his right hand. Something about this made him nervous and the pain of that day still darkened his eyes.

"Yeah, but that one guy no one really remembers."

"You ready, baby?" Griff left his polo untucked and unbuttoned. "We need to be in the casino in a few minutes and then back here."

"I guess so." The plan was for us to hang out near the doors of the casino and wait on the witchy bitches to go by to get to the banquet area where dinner was being held. Once we were sure they were gone, we'd come back to our room, go out our own back doors and then reenter theirs. "Do you break into hotel rooms often? Like is this a common security firm thing?" I couldn't believe how little I actually knew about what he did for a living.

"I do it on occasion. The last time was a few weeks ago. The police suspected a few runaway girls were holed with some piece of human waste trafficker at a hotel outside Omaha but they couldn't get a search warrant."

"Did you find them?"

"Two of them. Never found the third but I did get the sick bastard arrested. He's currently serving thirty to life. Fucker."

Despite all of that, I knew the third girl still ate at him. He couldn't stand it that he'd missed one. He was all or nothing. There were no margins that he'd be proud of.

36

GRIFF

Like a fucker, I asked Hannah to fix me a glass of water, because that shit was the best excuse I could come up with to get her out of the room, while I shoved my personal Glock 23 in the back of my shorts. I didn't want to frighten her. She would insist that the elderly mutant ninja grannies wouldn't be packing and that I was overreacting. Dammit, famous foursomes left me with precious little workable material.

"Thanks, baby." I downed a few sips of the water I didn't really want. That fist that always collided with my gut when shit was about to get ugly had already knocked the wind out of me. She'd threatened Hannah. My brain couldn't work through that.

All I could grasp was that I would forcefully remove anything that wanted to do her harm from this earth. But there had to be a reason. Keeping her safe was all that mattered but I also had to figure out how Megan Mallory had been shoved so far into a corner she'd come out with threats. Rule-makers often made and clung to the rules so they could also create and cling to the loopholes but she didn't strike me as that kind of policy maker. She worked for a freaking nonprofit not Congress. My brain offered me precious little in the way of answers but my gut was crystal clear. Hannah was in danger. Keeping her safe was the only mission that mattered.

"Want to tell me why you look so miserable? I thought you liked missions." She traced her fingers over my scowl.

"I..." didn't know what to tell her. The truth generally worked even if it was only a portion of it. "I love that you did all of this just so we could spend a week together and I hate that we're going to spend even one moment of it chasing down the sisterhood of the traveling girdles."

Based on Hannah's laughter, that was clearly a good one. Maybe I could do the foursomes. Just needed to loosen up a little.

"Hey, we can still do the Golden Girls, too. There were four of them." She gave me one of those grins that took up residence in the depths of my chest. "Let's go catch some bad girls and then I'll bring you back here and be a bad girl all for you."

An overly-eager guttural grunt clogged my throat. My cock immediately sprang to life and got on board. I was starved for her. So damn parched I wasn't sure how long I could go without drowning myself in her creamy pussy. I needed to hear those sweet little gasps and moans she made for me. I was desperate to hold her in my arms where I knew she was safe. Under me, letting me worship her, letting me tend her, letting me protect her above all others. That was the only way my life would ever work. And maybe, it was high-time I manned the fuck up and stopped bowing out of the battles it would take to have her. She was a war worth fighting. "Then let's get this over with because if you want to be a bad girl for me, honey, I'm gonna fuck you senseless, over and over again, fuck you until you're my sweet baby again."

"Oh God, yes." She swayed under the power of my promises. Yeah, we needed to get this mission over with as soon as possible.

After a few kisses meant to assure her that I would make every single one her fantasies a reality, we headed out the door.

"Sergeant Haywood, sir, I don't know if it might interest you to know that Ms. Rutherford has had numerous large ticket items delivered to her room today."

Hannah grinned. "I told you he was sweet."

"I did a little digging on your behalf, spoke with James, her attendant. Seemed to me if checks weren't clearing her shopping might be hampered. Apparently, that wasn't the case."

"Thanks, Fred. I appreciate it."

"Anytime. I'm here to serve and help if I can. Maybe I can give the universe a nudge." He winked at Hannah. No idea what that was all about but I'd take help from anywhere I could get it.

"She's right. You are a good guy." I offered him my hand. We made our way out of the suite corridor and headed toward the casino trying to blend in like your run of the mill tourists.

"Oh, hey, sweet. You're here," bellowed from an all too familiar voice.

"Son of a bitch," I ground out as Ryan Winch class of 2017 bounced into view. He now had five other guys with him.

"These are a few of my buddies. We figured we'd hang out tonight." His eyes zeroed in on Hannah's cleavage. "You wanna hit up the nightclub here? Pretty sure they have poles."

Hannah snapped. "No, we do not want to hit up the nightclub, Ryan, but do me a favor, if my father ever asks you about our encounter, do tell him that you wanted to take me to a place with poles." Before she effectively scalped the air force lackey, I eased her away.

"It's cool. You going to the casino first? We can do that." His buddies all nodded their agreement.

I glared at Ryan and his backup dancers. "Dude, I'm gonna spell this out as clearly as I can for you. You really seem to have vastly more dick in your personality than you could ever even hope to have in your shorts and she isn't interested. The next time you see my face it will be approximately one split second before you see my fists up close and personal. Not just one. Both. Repeatedly. Do you understand what I'm saying to you right now?"

"You don't want us to go to the casino with you?"

"Good, and...?"

"You don't want us to hang with you tonight?"

"Bingo."

"Griff," Hannah spoke through her teeth. Panic set hard in her eyes. "Ms. Rutherford." She gestured her head to the side. I let my eyes take the same path and dammit all to hell but she was heading our way with Moe and Curly in tow.

The Berets are fond of quoting Mike Tyson. He has a saying they goes something like - *Everyone has a plan until you get punched in the face*. We just add to it. Everyone has a plan until you get punched in the face; expect to be punched in the face.

Some kind of promoter for the nightclub approached a gaggle of women nearby and offered them passes and free drinks if they went to party at the club. That was more than enough incentive for Ryan and the Ryanettes to go on with their plans for a night of staring up at women on poles and paying exorbitant prices for drinks. They offered us waves and dissolved into the crowds.

Act intelligently in the worst possible case scenario. That's what I'd been trained to do.

"Why, Ms. Hagen." Ms. Rutherford promptly coughed hard enough to bring up what was left of her lungs. Edith whacked her forcefully on the back with her handbag until she recovered and then sucked down another draw on her cigarette. "We were hoping you'd be joining Mr. Haywood this evening. It'll be a lovely dinner."

Hannah's face said she thought that was a load of bullshit. "You were?"

"Of course, honey," Gladys assured her. "We got four men. We need another gal, right?"

"Hell yeah, the more the merrier. Besides we all want a taste of the Sergeant here." Edith waggled her overly-plucked eyebrows. Okay, maybe she was always this nuts.

"You do?" I watched Hannah grapple with their bizarre change of heart. "Well...uh...we were going to the casino for a few minutes before dinner but we'll see you there." Bless my sweet baby trying her damnedest to stick to the plan. Her big brother had nothing on her.

"Now, you don't want to miss anything. We're gonna sing our rendition of *America, the Beautiful* before we eat," Edith encouraged.

"We wore our sequined bloomers for the routine." Gladys lifted the long skirt of her knitted dress. A flash of red sequins over pink tights burned into my retinas.

"Ma'am, I really think you should keep your dress down in the lobby," Hannah scolded.

"Ah, honey, men love a show. If you can't put one on get out of our way."

"Oh my dear God." Hannah's mouth hung open.

"Yeah, He's really the only one that can save us now." I shuddered. "We'll be in there in just a few. You go on." I spoke with authority, pointed the direction of the room where the catered dinner for the event was being held, and prayed just once that they'd follow orders.

"We'll just wait on you, good-lookin'." Edith wrapped her arm through mine. I shook it off quickly and turned to Hannah.

"Follow my lead." I gently placed my hand on the small of her back as I whispered my instruction barely moving my lips. When I pressed on her right side, she turned into me and caught on to the plan. "Damn, I need another fix baby," I drawled loudly. Caging her between my body and the lobby wall, I leaned in.

"I like this plan," she murmured the words when my lips were millimeters from hers.

"Good. Get into it for me."

I kissed the smile right off of her lips. It was followed by a moan. Since I needed the sequined sisters to believe we would be returning to our suite for a little T and A, I let my hand traverse a course from her hip to the hem of that dress. Then I slid the fabric up her thigh until my hand disappeared underneath it.

My craving groan was audible not only to Hannah but also to our audience who still hadn't left, damn them. I lifted my head, stared her down, and dove back in. Her hands ran the length of my back in an effort to help me put on the show. When she neared the pistol she reversed course, keeping its location from being revealed. She rocked her hips and I had to remind my cock that it wasn't actually going to get to go where it so desperately wanted to be for a few more hours. Damn thing was staging a revolt against my better judgment.

Once again, I backed away and gripped the back pocket of my shorts. "Shit. I...uh think I left my wallet in the suite." I made certain everyone in the general vicinity knew that was a less than covert attempt to get Hannah to go back to the suite. "It's a cash bar at the dinner."

Doing an excellent job at pretending to be dazed, she gave me two slow nods. "We should go get that."

Still playing my part, always a good Beret, I half dragged her back toward our suite. "K, glance back and see if any of them are following us," I breathed.

She did even better. Brushing another tender kiss on my cheek when we paused to let some other tourists pass by, she made her check. "They're not following us but Ms. Rutherford looks pissed."

"Yeah, well she'll get over it."

"Why do you have your pistol?" she whispered.

"Not sure what we might find."

"What are we looking for exactly? Credit cards?"

"Not sure yet. But while I'm breaking into the safe, go through the bags and take pics of everything you see. We'll need that for evidence. Also snap a pic of anything you're going to move before you move it so we can restore it exactly the way it was."

37

HANNAH

"Got it." I could do this. Just because I'd never broken in anywhere in my entire life did not mean I couldn't help.

The rubber soles on my shoes dragged over the rug portions of the flooring, slowing me down. I didn't have time for that. Griff whisked me quickly to his suite door and an idea sprung to mind.

"Fred, would you do us a favor?" I offered him a hopeful smile.

"I would be most pleased to do anything to help you, Ms. Hagen." Such a good guy.

"Do you think you could text me if you see anyone returning to Ms. Rutherford's suite?"

He considered. "I'm not supposed to be on my phone while I'm on duty but I could make an exception for you, dear."

"Thank you. If you see anyone, text me immediately." I entered my phone number in his phone and we headed into Griff's suite.

"Not sure I like that guy having your number." Griff headed straight for the back doors.

"Not sure I like the idea of us getting arrested."

"That's fair," he allowed.

I followed his lead. Heading out of our pool and patio area, we moved stealthily along the concrete walls and rushed by the windows as quickly as possible. Three patios down we had to stop. Thankfully, the drapes were drawn in that suite because a landscaper came around a clump of trees. "Sit down and act natural." Griff settled on one of the chaise lounges I'd picked out and dragged me into his lap. I laughed and nuzzled my head into his neck, like I was loving every minute of this. I also willed the yard guy to go work somewhere else.

The rip of his edger sent a shockwave down my spine. I wasn't afraid but Ms. Mallory's threat was getting to me. I didn't like the implication that I had ruined something especially when my company was tied up in all of this. I'd worked too hard to get where I was to jeopardize it because of some stupid bachelor auction.

"Hey, look at me," Griff murmured in my ear. I lifted my head. "I will never let anyone or anything hurt you. Tell me you know that."

"I do know that. I'm not worried about myself. It's Ms. Mallory and my company. She could spread a lot of bad press if she decides to tell people I used a charity auction for my own gains. I'm sure it would blow over quickly but I don't want the negative attention."

"You didn't let me finish. I would never let anyone hurt you or Palindrome. I'm so fucking proud of everything you've accomplished, baby. I won't let anyone take even a tiny portion of that away from you, okay?"

"Thanks. Kind of hate you have to step in and protect me." Shame clawed its way from my clenched stomach to my cheeks.

"Want to hear some deep shit while the slowest fucking lawn guy on the planet finishes edging that damned tree?" Guilt perforated his offer. I nodded. "Protecting you and taking care of you makes everything that happened four years ago today a little easier to swallow. Like maybe there is a good reason I'm still here."

"Griff, that isn't how..." But I didn't get to finish because the roar of the edger halted abruptly. The landscaper reversed course and headed toward the front of the hotel.

"Quick now," Griff stood me up and we were on our way once more.

We made it to suite eleven's back door. My stomach twisted itself into a knot. He stuck the magnetic tool thing that looked kind of like a screwdriver in the bottom of the lock and I heard the distinctive click. "Why does that work?" I had to think about something but what we were about to do. "I thought the outdoor locks were deadbolts."

"For most hotel locks the magnetic strip for the keycard is wired to the deadbolt. They're not real deadbolts. They're just there to make you feel safe. Hurry." We slipped inside. I glanced around the suite where I'd used a deep plum and gray palette that I adored. I loved the upholstered walls in the living area that framed the custom mural on the master bedroom wall. This was a three-bedroom suite so I'd gotten to really play with my themes. "You know, if I had it to do over I think I'd switch the peonies with cherry blossom stems. That would play off of the pink in the mural in the adjacent room."

I snapped back to reality when Griff waved a pair of surgical gloves in front of my face. "I have no doubt cherry blossoms would rock whatever you just said they'd do, sweetheart, but we need to move." Clearly, I'd zoned out.

"Sorry." I pulled the gloves on and tried to think of where criminals would hide illegal things.

"Pull those curtains for me and check the luggage first. Then check the bedrooms and bathrooms, the places people think of as being private."

I shut the curtains quickly and went to dig through someone else's luggage. To have only been in town for a week, Ms. Rutherford had eleven pieces of Louis Vuitton luggage. If she could afford that, she could surely pay off her bachelor auction bid. Neither of the large rolling cases had anything but clothes, albeit some of those sequins really should be illegal. I went on to the smaller bags. Four quick beeps made me gasp before I realized Griff was opening the safe with the master code.

I dug through a round case. My hand landed on several leather somethings. Flipping the clothes out of the bag, my mouth fell open. Six wallets. Two men's and four women's. "Griff!" I called as quietly as I could.

"Take pictures of whatever it is. I just hit the jackpot," he answered from the closet.

Popping open the wallets, I laid them out on the dresser and took pictures of the inside portions of each. I closed them back and restored them. The next small bag revealed a massive toiletry kit. My stomach turned as I unzipped it. Holy fuck. There had to have been thirty prescription bottles but none of them with Victoria Rutherford's name on them. Working quickly, I snapped pictures of the labels as well.

In the middle of my picture taking, a text popped on my screen. 'Victoria Rutherford is headed toward her suite!'

"Griff! We have to go. She's coming back." I shoved the medicine back in the bag and raced into the closet.

He had a piece of computer paper in his hands and pure, unadulterated rage in his eyes. "What is it?" Probably the only person in the world that would step toward him when he looked like that, I reached for the paper. He jerked it away, folded it quickly, and shoved it in his pocket.

"We have to get out of here." He slammed the safe with enough force that the clothes hung on the closet racks swayed. Time was of the essence, but I paused and made certain the luggage was just the way I'd found it. "The roller bags weren't beside each other." I frantically rearranged them.

Griff jerked the custom draperies open as the sound of Ms. Rutherford's rasping voice reached through the door. She was greeting her attendant.

"Shit." Griff scanned the room. There were too many glass doors outside for us to make an escape.

"Come with me." I grabbed his hand and jerked him toward one of the guest bedrooms. "In the armoire." I pulled open the doors on the antique piece I'd ordered for this room. Thankfully it was empty.

Griff shook his head. The keycard reader on the front door made its click. "If she opens this, there's nowhere to go."

"It has a false back." Sliding open the back doors, I attempted to push him inside without much success. Thankfully, he climbed in on his own just as the front door opened. I joined him and quietly closed the front doors of the massive armoire.

There wasn't room for both of us in the hidden portion. Griff was well over six feet of solid muscle. We couldn't chance any movement and we had no idea where Victoria was or why she'd come back to the room.

The distinctive clunks of her low heels grew louder. I gasped and then Griff's hand was over my mouth again. I ground my teeth but it was probably a good idea. We heard a drawer nearby open and then close.

There was a click and then a slight hiss. Suddenly, cigarette smoke filtered through the cloth panels in the armoire. I'd had to design around at least a half-dozen smoke detectors in every suite. How was she getting away with that? And was that it? Had she come back for a lighter?

Echoes of her footfalls disappeared as she left the room. I slumped in relief and jerked my face away from Griff's hand.

"Sorry," he murmured in my ear. Fishing my phone out of my pocket, I texted Fred back.

Can you tell us when she leaves?

Certainly.

A full minute later, I got the all clear from Fred.

"Let's get," Griff urged. Praying she wouldn't make a return trip, I eased the doors open and crawled out. "Shit," huffed from Griff as he climbed out of the armoire and shook out his bad leg.

"You okay?" I cringed as he took a few awkward steps.

"I'm fine. Let's go."

"I found tons of medicine bottles and some wallets," I explained as he checked and rechecked the rooms according to the pictures we'd both taken.

"Did you get shots of the medicine bottles?" He adjusted the curtains slightly. If they were off, I hoped Ms. Rutherford didn't notice during her return trip.

"Of most of them. They must've stolen them. None of them had any of their names on them."

"K, let's go back to our suite. I can text Voodoo the pictures of the meds. He can tell us what they're used for and might get a hit on some of the names. I want T to check a few things for me as well."

I flung open the sliding glass doors. We stepped outside and immediately heard a splash of water from a nearby private pool. Crap.

Griff relocked the door using that tool thing and beckoned me to follow. "Just act like you don't know we're not supposed to be out here. We wanted to explore the grounds."

Slowly and stealthily we made it back to our own sliding glass doors. He performed the same trick with our door that he'd done on Victoria's.

"Is the actual key too difficult?" I managed a full breath now that we were inside and safe.

"I had it out so I went with it. Sorry about covering your mouth again back there in Narnia."

"You really seem to want to keep me from talking."

"I love it when you talk to me. I just really didn't want you to be caught back there and occasionally you talk your thoughts out when you're nervous. I could see your wheels turning."

"I do not."

His smirk formed on his features. Its appearance actually helped me relax. If he was smirking, we would be okay. "Sure, you don't. It's a complete coincidence that you're the only person I've ever broken into a room with who started telling me about cherry blossoms and murals."

Fine. He had me there. "Talking helps me think."

"Also, you're a damned genius and thank you for saving our asses back there. Seriously, babe, I'm making you an honorary Seven."

I knew I shouldn't have commented. We had way too much going on. We were trying to catch criminals and there was still that piece of paper in his pocket but I was so touched by what he'd just said I went on with it anyway. "As much as I love the idea of being some kind of an interior design superhero, I'd much rather be the wife of a Seven."

His feet halted in our sitting room. He turned to stare me down.

Fervency and doubt flared in his eyes set off by the desert sunset gleaming through the doors. "That club's kinda empty." He tried to clear the uncertainty from his throat.

"Aaron got married last year. I'm good with being one of the founding members."

"I guess Maddie was the original, huh?" he strangled over her name.

I couldn't believe he was even entertaining this conversation. In one declaration, it seemed he was able to recognize that Chris would always be with us in our present, and there in our futures, but that he was also firmly set in our past.

I watched him work his jaw until, "I'm working on it, okay? I swear. I just... I need a little time to figure everything out," sounded from his lips.

38

GRIFF

It finally occurred to me that I didn't owe the general my protection. Maybe he deserved for his kids to find out exactly what he'd done. If Smith and Hannah wouldn't inevitably be hurt in the process, I'd call his ass up right now and let him know precisely what I thought of him. In fact, I'd call up the fucking Chief of Staff and have his ass court-martialed.

Hannah propelled herself into my arms, right where she should always be. I drew her to me, wrapping myself around her. Before I could figure out what to do with her declaration that she wanted to be my wife, I had to protect her from the women out to fuck her life over. Taking down a military nonprofit was not something I'd ever even considered would be a part of my job but I held the evidence in my pocket and my baby in my arms.

Megan Mallory had picked the wrong woman to pick on. Because Hannah was the strongest damned force on this planet and because I would sooner dig my own grave and pitch myself inside than allow anyone to do her harm.

I squeezed her tighter, inhaling the unique flavor of my baby. "I promise. I'll figure something out." And I meant that. I just didn't know how.

She lifted her head. Tears pricked those beautiful eyes of hers. They tore me up. They always did. I'd woken up from one of my surgeries to find her standing beside my bed sobbing. Apparently, there was some doubt as to whether or not I'd recover. Her tears hurt more than the damned wound they'd been trying to repair. "Thank you," she whispered.

"Don't thank me yet. I'm not sure I can make this work. Let's see those pictures you took then we need to get to that dinner."

She handed over her phone. I grouped all of the pictures together and airdropped them to my own phone. I sent them to Voodoo and then checked the time. "Bet he doesn't answer for a while."

"Why?" Hannah stared down at my phone almost willing him to respond.

"Because he's in Austin visiting his parents. I bet he's balls deep in that chick he bangs every time he's home."

"I didn't know Vince had an at-home girl." She grinned at that.

"Does her being an at-home girl make her more special than all of the women he bangs in Lincoln? Guy is a man-whore through and through."

"Be nice to Voodoo. And yes it makes her more special. He has one girl at home and lots in Lincoln and yet he keeps going back to the one in Austin. See where I'm going?"

"You think he's got a thing for her and he's just blowing his load in the others?"

"I think that in far less crude terminology."

"Sorry. Breaking and entering gets my blood pumping." And I was using most of my brain capacity to keep from marching in that ballroom and forcing a confession out of Megan Mallory at gunpoint. I had to know how deep she was in this before I blew the whistle and I had to come up with evidence to convict all of them that didn't depend on what I'd found breaking into their rooms. "Did you know that massive dresser thing had a false back when you picked it out?" I needed her to keep talking. I needed to know she was safe. My mind couldn't seem to believe that.

"Yeah. Most armoires from the twenties have them. Women used to store their wedding gowns or other special gowns back there to keep them for their daughters. I love the stories behind pieces like that. Sorry, I didn't think about it not being quite big enough for both of us."

"You saved our asses. Don't apologize." I texted T the rest of the shit I'd found out and asked him to run checks on every name I saw in the images from the wallets Hannah had located and the stacks of credit cards I'd found in the safe. That damned piece of paper in my pocket set me on fire. I'd figure that out on my own. No one was going to do this to Hannah and get away with it. "We need to get in there with Inky, Blinky, Pinky, and Clyde."

"Pac-Man. Very nice. You really are doing well with the four-somes. I'm impressed." She beamed up at me and I doubled down on my resolve to figure out some way to explain what the general had done.

"Hey, I'm a Beret and I'm pretty much the best at everything I do." I winked at her.

"I happen to agree." She waggled those eyebrows and I momentarily forgot that I needed to go fuck a few people's lives up before I fucked her senseless. "Guess we should go." Her longing glance around our suite made me reconsider all things. I could get Fred to bring us dinner and a few six-packs. Turn on the Cubs. Cuddle up with her and see how many times I could round the bases myself. But that paper in my pocket was all the reason in the world. My phone buzzed before we made it out of our suite.

You're supposed to be fixing your life and fucking your girl not fucking up your life even more and catching a few grandmotherfuckers, T informed me.

Just run the checks. I can multitask, I responded and then escorted her out toward the door.

"Was that T? What did he say?"

"Pretty sure he's just trying to get some kind of high word score by using fuck the most times in a sentence. He'll run the checks as soon as he finishes bitching at me."

Relief washed over Fred's features when we made our appearance. "All's well?" he asked.

"All's well. Thanks for your help. I owe you."

"Perhaps I should've properly introduced myself when you asked my name, sir."

"What's that supposed to mean?" I demanded.

"In my younger days, I was Captain Fred Jones of the Royal Marines."

I offered him my hand. "Served with more than a few Royal Marines. Damned impressive guard."

"Thank you, and for me, listen to Ms. Hagen. I wish I'd listened more when I was your age."

"Will do."

"Thanks for your help, Fred." Hannah waved.

"My pleasure, ma'am."

She fell in step with me as we marched toward the assigned banquet room. I halted her progress outside of the casino, using the crowds and blaring ring of the slots as a cover for the moment. "I need you to remember to give nothing away about yourself. Nothing at all. Don't talk about your family. Don't talk about the army. And absolutely nothing personal. Make up a new birthday. And for fuck's sake do not say anything about Palindrome, okay?"

"What's on that paper in your pocket? Don't you think she'll eventually notice that it's gone?"

"We'll talk about that later. Let's go."

"Shouldn't we come up with a story together? That way we won't make a misstep." Panic was setting in.

"Hey." I pressed my forehead to hers blocking out the world around us. "We've got this. You come up with any story you want and I'll make it work. I've got a few years' worth of training in that area. It'll be fine, sweetheart."

I escorted her into the ballroom. Candlelit tables for two had been set up in secluded corners for most of the couples. There was one large table with ten places directly in the center under one of the chandeliers. We were too late. Victoria was already seated between Watson and Mathis who both shot me an SOS with their eyes. Seeger was being worked over by the other two. Fuck.

Pulling Hannah's chair out for her, I surveyed where we were in this dinner. No one had plates but there was a platter of shrimp in several varieties along with sauces that had been half-eaten.

"Now, Sergeant Watson, you were telling us where you're from," Victoria encouraged. Someone bang the gong. The shitshow had begun.

"Oh, I don't think I'm supposed to tell you that," he informed before turning to me. "You get everything you needed to get done finished?" I deeply regretted his parents' decision to teach him to speak.

I glanced Hannah's way and prayed she'd forgive me for what I was about to say. I resurrected my typical cocky smirk and let my eyes linger on my baby's form until the entire table took notice. "Oh, yeah, I got her all taken care of."

Heat blazed a path up from her cleavage. Blotches of bright pink trailed up her neck and finally settled in her cheeks as she got appreciative looks from every male at the table. Yeah, I'd hear about that one later.

"It is interesting, isn't it, Gladys, that Mr. Haywood planned to be late for our date last evening but then when we saw them outside the casino he conveniently came up with something they needed to go do." Victoria narrowed her eyes.

"Well, you have to give it to him, Vicky. She's pretty. If I had an ass like that I'd never wear pants." Gladys spoke with shrimp in her mouth and I fought not to gag. Hannah was now the color of the Red Cross logo.

"She's not wrong, baby," I informed her through my chuckle. "Maybe you should take her advice."

"I will get you back for that later," she informed me through her clenched teeth.

"I have no doubt."

Victoria wasn't getting any response from me on her inquiry so I simply returned her glare. Had she returned to her room because she thought we were there? That seemed doubtful. Most con men, or con women as the case may be, would get the fuck out of town without leaving any kind of forwarding address if they got so much as a hint that someone was onto their little game. If she'd figured something out, why was she still here?

When I won our deranged glaring contest, she moved on. "Ms. Hagen, why don't you tell us how you met Mr. Haywood."

I had no doubts that my baby would knock this out of the park but damn if I didn't want to bitch slap the women across the table.

"Griff?" Hannah smiled. "I honestly don't know him that well. We met out in L.A. a few years ago when we were both out there for work. We see each other occasionally."

Yep, that would do. I discreetly rubbed her thigh trying to reassure her and also seeing just how pissed she was about my last comment. Thankfully, she threaded her fingers through mine and squeezed my hand. I was at least mostly forgiven.

"I thought you said he worked with your brother?" Ms. Mallory huffed as she loaded a few more shrimp onto her appetizer plate. She looked like someone had puckered both sets of her lips.

Hannah never missed a beat. "He did. That's actually how we got to talking that night at the bar. You know how the army is about their Special Forces teams. I had no idea he worked with...*Steve* until he mentioned he was a Beret. My brother and I aren't that close." Her voice caught on that particular lie. That one cost too damn much. I knew. Smith would always be her hero. I had to remember that. "Do you remember how good that rum was?" She turned to me. There was just a hint of panic on her features. You had to know her as intimately and thoroughly as I did to see it.

"Best I think I've ever had. What was the name of that place? The Caña right?" Want someone to believe your story give them a few superfluous details. A rum bar in Cali? That I could provide.

"That's it," Hannah nodded. "Great music, too."

"My fourth husband, Edgar, enjoyed The Caña." Ms. Rutherford slithered in her seat. Shit. Hannah shifted slightly. She'd never been to The Caña. I could tell. "He always wished they'd had an outdoor area since the weather in L.A. is nice so often." Challenge scorched from her glare. "I was under the impression regulars at the Caña were also investors. Do you hold stake in the club, Ms. Hagen?"

"The Caña does have an outdoor area. Well, I mean they have that glassed roof area where the bands play. They've got that speakeasy feel which wouldn't work with a terrace or anything. And you don't have to be a stockholder to party there. There aren't that many owners." God bless the Screaming Eagles from the 101st. Ryder Mathis had just saved both of our asses. "I'd know since my brother-in-law *is* one of the owners." I owed him the best fucking bottle of rum The Obelisk could provide. "It's cool you two met there. I'll tell him that." Scratch that, I owed him good rum and the truth at some later date.

A waiter approached and I ordered beers for Hannah and me. Edith cut in. "Bring Jager shots for the table, honey. I feel like getting crazy."

Oh the fuck no, we would not be doing Jager shots. And I was more than finished with Victoria driving conversation. I had several questions I wanted answers to. "We're not doing shots," I informed the waiter. "I am curious though, Ms. Mallory, how exactly were the bidders chosen for this auction? Everyone seems to be having fun..." I gestured to the surrounding tables where people were getting to know each other on their forced date, "...you must've chosen well." Steamroll a conversation and you'll squash out a Jager order as well.

The waiter looked momentarily confused. "It's a cash bar, sir. All of the proceeds go to Ms. Mallory. I can get your beer but you'll have to pay for it now."

I slapped a twenty in his hand and he headed toward the bar. Did he realize what he'd just said? Was the check being written to her so she could eventually get the money to Homefront Heroes or was its end stop in Megan's checking account?

She looked at me like I'd just asked her to set her own clothing on fire. “We… uh… well, we reached out to our biggest donors and asked anyone in the area who might have interest.”

“We had a hand in helping her plan the event. Always happy to support our armed services,” Edith announced.

“I’ll bet.” I knew they’d had a hand in it. I just didn’t know why or how.

39

HANNAH

When Griff brought up how the bidders had been selected, I weighed Megan's response. Palindrome was a major donor to Homefront Heroes. I'd even partnered with the organization a few years ago to design houses for homeless vets. My firm had fronted all of the money for my work and the elements I'd used in the home. It was my favorite charity but I hadn't been approached about the auction until I'd run into Megan at The Obelisk when she was here checking out the space for the event. Another round of guilt bubbled in the beer in my stomach. It was my favorite charity and I'd used it for my own purposes.

Covered dishes were brought to our places. When the lids were lifted away plain hamburgers with no sides were revealed. This was supposed to be a charity dinner. That shrimp on the appetizer platter was too limp to have been fresh. What the hell was up with this dinner?

Several crackled percussive drumbeats sounded from a nearby speaker.

"We're on, girls!" Edith leapt from her seat.

On the next low bass beat, my mouth dropped open. Griff wrapped his arm over my shoulders and scooted me closer. "I have no idea what they're about to do but I feel the distinct need to protect you."

Trumpets joined the drums for the first notes of, *Oh beautiful for spacious skies.*

"Thank God it's not the anthem because I cannot salute that," he huffed.

Victoria joined her cohorts at center floor as they began to sing and perform some kind of odd tap-dance. They lifted their skirts thigh high at every available opportunity.

I was close enough to feel Griff's phone vibrate in his pocket. He fished it out and then turned it so I could see the screen. Voodoo had responded. *What the fuck, man? Most of those are narcotics the others are generic versions of Viagra and Cialis. That is a dangerous combo. We're about to take off. I'll run the names on the bottles when I get to the office tomorrow morning.*

"Well, that explains...that." I gestured to the sequined spectacle before my eyes. It was like watching a bedazzled train wreck.

"They're definitely using. Wonder if they're also selling?" He typed back a response to Voodoo asking what effect male enhancement drugs would have on women.

Similar effect as guys. Rushes blood to your crotch which makes it more sensitive. Puts everyone and all of their parts in the mood.

I turned to whisper in his ear. "Last night her fourth husband's name was Robert. Tonight she said his name was Edgar. Did you notice that?"

"I did not notice that and you are a deadly combination. Did you know that my sexy Hannah Banana?"

"You are not allowed to call me that." I laughed anyway.

"Fine. But you are. Fucking perfect sense of humor, both a brilliant and dirty mind, and enough heart to make up for my lack of one. I'm a goner, baby."

"Good." There were recorded fireworks on whatever source of music our insane entertainment was using for their song but they were nothing compared to the ones of victory going off in my chest. By the end of the week, I'd be informing my parents of my plans to move to Lincoln to pursue a permanent relationship with Griff. In time, they'd learn to deal.

Ms. Mallory's gasp jerked me back down from the cloud I was currently floating around and redesigning. Edith and Gladys were pulling red, white, and blue handkerchiefs out of their bras and waving them in the air. I could not believe Ms. Mallory was allowing this at a Homefront Heroes event.

Watson turned in his chair. "I kind of forgot I wasn't supposed to tell them anything so I might've said something about being from Paducah."

Griff gave him a simpering nod. "Just try to keep it under wraps, okay?"

"He also actually signed his name on one of their autograph books," Ryder spat. "I tore the page out while they were practicing their dance."

"Jesus." Griff downed half of his beer in one sip. "Dude, you're in the army and before that you were a chicken farmer has anyone ever asked you for your autograph?"

"No." Again Watson looked confused. "But they said they're fans of military guys. They even have a calendar."

"Wait, why was he not supposed to tell them where he's from?" Ms. Mallory demanded. "They're perfectly nice ladies. They helped me with the event. Just what are you suggesting?"

I watched Griff's impressive form lean in, crowding Ms. Mallory, giving her no room to lie or even to think. "I have a feeling you know precisely why he shouldn't do that and I think you're letting this shit go on"—he gestured to the bizarre dinner entertainment—"because you owe somebody something. Why don't you tell me what that is?"

"I...have no idea what you're referring to. This is all for Homefront Heroes."

Griff's eyes narrowed a half-notch. "Hey, Mathis, you're a Ranger, right? Made it through training and then all the way to the 101st. Tell me, after the army got done flinging your ass out of planes and starving you to death what was the one thing they taught you that's kept your ass alive after you hit the ground in a hostile zone?"

Ryder gave him a knowing smile. "You mean besides killing every living thing and then looking badass in the uniform?"

"Yeah, after that." Griff chuckled.

"How to know when someone's lying their ass off right to your face."

"Figured it was something like that."

"Yeah, but Ranger school is only three months. Don't Berets train for years?" It was like Ryder had been given a script. When he got out of the army, T should hire him for Tier Seven.

"Years," Griff echoed.

Ms. Mallory's chair slid audibly backward and the next second she was rushing from the room.

"Should we follow her?" I prepared to make an escape.

"Nah." He brushed a kiss on my cheek. "Let her simmer in it for a while. I want her good and panicked when I go in for the kill. This whole fucking thing is a sham. I just have to figure out why she did this."

Watson's voice interrupted his explanation. "So, do they like do this on the road or something? I don't get it." He gestured to Edith and Gladys as they did a low-kick routine while Victoria hit the final notes of the song.

"We'll add it to the lengthy list of things you don't get, man." Ryder slapped him on the back. Griff lifted his beer to him. My own laughter caused my beer to spill on the tops of my breasts, the only parts revealed by the sundress.

Griff grinned at me. "Aim's getting better, baby. I'll take care of that later."

40

GRIFF

I*'m not getting anything on a Victoria Rutherford. You sure that's her name?* T's text came in near the end of our bizarre dinner.

It's probably a fake. Hang on I'll get you some pics. Hannah and I spent ten minutes discreetly snapping pictures of our table companions and sending them to T. *Torture the data, my friend. It'll confess to something,* I instructed.

Working on it. Looks like I might've stumbled up on an outstanding warrant. Let me check into this.

An outstanding warrant would make my job a whole lot easier but that still wouldn't explain Megan Mallory's part in all of this. *There are still a few things I have to figure before we call in the cops. I need some evidence that isn't also going to implicate me and Hannah.* I reminded him.

From what I'm seeing. The one in blue's name is Vera Sanders not Victoria Rutherford. I'll keep digging. Leave it. Go enjoy your night.

I intend to do just that. And I planned to get started on enjoying my night immediately. I'd had enough of the sequined freaks and geeks.

Since Hannah was watching our exchange she shot me a sexy, sinful smirk that stirred my cock and whipped my mind into a fucking frenzy of need for her. Her hand slid to my injured thigh and edged ever closer to the semi I was sporting. The cheap table cloth provided a decent cover. Draping my arm over the back of her chair I nuzzled her cheek. "Keep going, baby. I'm so damned needy for you."

She let go of a shaky breath and skimmed her hand higher. Her blinks extended. Those long eyelashes fluttered closed. Pure lust built a fire at the base of my cock as she brushed her fingers over me. The heat of her hand was exquisite. She gave me a dedicated grope and I damn near lost what was left of my mind. "Can we just go?" The heat of her whisper raced over my jaw. "I need you."

Denying her anything at all was laughable. Denying her me wasn't even a remote possibility. "Hell yeah, sweetheart. Just give me a minute to run some baseball stats through my head so I can fucking walk out of here."

That coy grin only served to make me harder, rigid with hunger now. I'd never get enough. I'd made her several promises about that night and I might keep shit from people but I never, not one single time, ever broke my word.

I made a show of awkwardly standing from the table. "Leg's cramped," I explained to Hannah loud enough for everyone at the table to hear me. I had to live with the damned thing for the rest of my life might as well make it work for me on occasion.

She cringed. "You've been sitting too long. Let's go back to the room and you can stretch out."

Mathis shook his head at us. "Old injury or new cobra strike?" Army had done right by him on the training, clearly. He knew I was lying.

Hannah rolled her eyes. She'd heard all of the military slang for a boner.

Normally, if someone wanted to involve themselves in my personal shit I'd tell them to shove their face up their own ass and give it a good lick but I owed the guy. "Both."

"Figured that." He gave me an envious smirk.

I escorted Hannah the hell away from the deranged Andrews Sisters-wannabes. Just having her out of their clutches, my breaths came easier. The desire to throw her over my shoulder and sprint her back to the suite took siege of my better judgment. The erection center of my brain had overrun all rational thought. Damn thing needed some kind of emergency kill switch.

The crowds had gathered around the waterfall outside the doors leaving the hallways relatively vacant. I was thankful for every second I could gain. Rushing her through the suite doors, I damn near ran over Fred.

"How was your dinner?" He smiled politely.

"One of the oddest things I've ever seen in my life and I once watched three camels hump," I informed him. Hannah shook her head at me but couldn't quite hide her laughter. "That's God's honest truth."

"Would you shut up?" she ordered.

"Not 'til I get you in the room."

"Have a lovely night. Can I get you anything before you retire?" Fred's smirk said at least he thought my story was humorous.

"Actually, yeah, I'd like some ice cream. Can the kitchen here do that?"

"Certainly, sir. What flavor?"

All sense of humor vanished from Hannah's beautiful face. Intrigue danced in her eyes. Her favorite flavor was strawberry.

"Vanilla," I informed Fred. Her lungs gave a quick shuddered breath.

"Cone or cup and any toppings?" Fred asked.

"Cup, no toppings, and only one spoon."

"I'll have it delivered soon."

"Good man."

I had her in our room a half-second later.

"Why do I have a feeling it won't be me spilling that ice cream on myself this time?" Her husky tone dripped with need.

"Because you're an incredibly intelligent woman and you know how starved I am for you."

"Before we get to you eating ice cream off of me, I want to know what's on that paper in your pocket." Determination rolled off her. I wasn't getting out of this for sex or anything else.

I pulled the paper from my shorts. "I don't want to scare you, baby. I would never let anything happen to you."

"I know that. I'm not scared but I want to know what you know."

The words I was about to say clogged in my throat. Utter hatred flooded my bloodstream. I unfolded the computer printout. "You're their mark."

"What?" She rushed to my side and studied the spreadsheet of the people who'd donated the most money to Homefront Heroes in the last five years. Four names had been highlighted. Three had been struck through. Hers was the only one that remained. "How did Victoria get that? It had to have been stolen from Homefront Heroes."

"Megan Mallory would have access to this wouldn't she?"

Hannah slunk downward. Her cute ass landed on the sofa. "So, they planned this whole thing to steal my credit cards or something?"

"I haven't put all of the pieces together yet but I'm thinking they wanted more than your credit cards. They're after a much bigger payoff from you. Clearly, they're very comfortable putting on fake identities. Yours would've gotten them a long way and identity thieves are next to impossible to catch. They were targeting donors who make the most money. See, Ashley Kilgore and Karen Winston's names were highlighted and then scratched through. You were the only donor who showed last night. That's probably what that argument you overheard was about. Megan Mallory promised them an A-list event filled with wealthy people. She didn't provide that."

"Wow." Her head fell into her hands. My heart sank right along with it. "I can't believe I was so stupid."

"Hey, you are not stupid. How would you have known that's what she was up to when she asked you to participate in this? And let me tell you something, baby, this"—I held up the list, the first piece of evidence—"is a declaration of war. I'll burn them to the ground and piss on their ashes before I'd ever let anyone hurt you."

"I should never have agreed to participate because I started scheming as soon as she explained the event to me. I can't think when we're apart. I can barely breathe much less make rational decisions. All I could think was that it was a chance for us to really spend some time together, for me to convince you that us staying apart is hurting both of us. I need to call the other board members. She needs to be arrested."

"You could probably get her thrown off of the board but she hasn't technically done anything illegal yet. I need to figure out if the money from the auction is really going to the foundation. If it isn't, then we've got her on fraud and misappropriation. The police are going to need a motive to make either of those charges stick and I have to come up with some way for us to know this without us having to confess to breaking and entering. Plus, my own sick curiosity is getting to me. Why would she do this? She had good standing with the board before this and what's with all of those rules she was so nuts about? It's driving me crazy that I can't figure this out."

"I should never have done any of this. I jeopardized my company, everything I've worked so hard for. I got T to help me trick you. I basically just completely fucked over every single relationship in my life that means the most to me."

"Stop." The rough scrape of my voice had her sealing those gorgeous lips. "Every single day I get to spend with you, Hannah, I swear it becomes the best fucking day of my life. I already know tomorrow will be even better than today was because I get to fall asleep and wake up with you right there in my arms. So, we have a little distraction. We'll get it figured out. But nothing will keep me from taking care of every single thing my baby needs from me. Did you hear what you just said? You jeopardized everything that means anything at all to you and, my God honey, you did it all for me. I'm the one that was stupid not you. Never you. Trying to keep you in one world and the rest of the shit I just exist with in another. I won't do it anymore. I can't breathe without you either. I try. Jesus Christ, I try and it feels like inhaling fire. I told you I'd figure out some way to explain all of this to Smith and I meant that."

Hesitant hope flickered in her eyes. "We'll tell him together. Him and Daddy."

"Let's climb one mountain at a time, okay?" I couldn't go there tonight. I couldn't stomach the general.

"I really am sorry about all of this," she whispered.

"I'm not. All of this bullshit with Homefront and the wicked stepsisters it's just a thing. And you, baby, you are *every* thing."

"There were only two wicked stepsisters." Her teeth scraped over her bottom lip trying to conceal her grin and I was done for.

Sexy little minx. "Guess we better catch them soon. I'm all out of famous trios."

"Tomorrow," she breathed the single word.

"Yeah, maybe. Tonight, I've got a few things I intend to take excellent care of." A knock on the door interrupted the arc of electricity passing between us. "Sounds like my ice cream is here."

"Better get that."

41

GRIFF

I accepted the silver bowl full of vanilla ice cream complete with a mint leaf and a strawberry from Fred. Setting it on the table near the couch I tried to gauge my baby. Her nostrils flared and her quick breaths swayed her breasts in a mesmerizing dance. Her hungry gaze never abandoned mine. If I hadn't memorized every detail of her, hadn't allowed those memories to fuel my very existence for the last seven years, I might not have noticed the hint of nerves evident in the nibble of her bottom lip and harsh swallow of her throat.

"This sure as fuck isn't the first time we've made love, baby. What's wrong?"

"Nothing's wrong." Her head shook as if that would dispel the lie she'd just told.

Moving to her in a few quick steps, I cradled her face in my hands. "Come on. Don't lie to me."

Her gaze attempted an evasive maneuver as she stared out the backdoors instead of at me.

"Hannah, come on."

"Three crazy ladies are trying to steal my identity. That kind of sucks," she placated.

"Yeah, but you know I'm not going to let that happen. You're shaking. Talk to me."

I got a genuine smile. We were getting somewhere. "I still can't believe you let me win today."

A slight chuckle I hadn't expected escaped my mouth. "Trust me, honey, this isn't a sacrifice. Seems to me you like to hear what I want from you. And it seemed like maybe you needed someone to tell you that it's okay if you want that. That it's perfectly natural to want to give up control to a man who knows how to take it. To give it to someone you trust."

She locked her eyes on mine with that statement. "Not just trust, Griff. Someone I love. Someone I want to spend the rest of my life exploring this with."

"The rest of our life starts right now. You sure you're ready for this?" My challenge hung in the air for one beat too long. "Hannah?"

A deep breath lifted her chest like she was trying to inhale courage. It fucking crushed me. If she didn't want this, that was perfectly fine. "There are silk tie-ups in the bedroom. It's just... standing here... I want to touch you so much." She wrung her hands. "I don't want to not be able to touch you." Shame set up camp in her eyes. She tried to shrug it away. So that was it.

"Baby, I have no intention of tying you up. Every centimeter of my skin that your fingers brush over, I swear, it feels like you erase whatever scar happens to be there. I'm not strong enough to deny myself that, honestly. Only people I've ever tied up have been insurgents and I'm not looking for those memories tonight, okay? We're gonna work out every single flavor of your kinks in my bed but I don't think that's one of them."

Relief washed through her. She melted against me, soft gentleness against my broken fragments and metal fixtures. I wrapped her up in my arms. The contentment, I only ever found in her, sated my soul. She lifted her head. The blue pools of her eyes stirred with waves of curiosity and need. I'd answer every single question.

"Let's see some of this lingerie you bought for this trip. Something naughty, baby. Something all for me. Something that's gonna make me want to paddle your delectable little ass for how bad you make me want you."

"Oh God, yes." She spun out of my arms and rushed to the bedroom. A cocky smirk formed on my features. I knew precisely what she wanted to hear. I knew my girl.

Grabbing the ice cream, I tossed the strawberry and mint leaf in the trash before I trailed after her. There was one thing I had to set straight before we got this party started.

She shook her head at me. "I can't dress up for you if you're in here."

"The closet is the size of most people's two bedroom apartments," I pointed out. "I need you to see something first anyway." I dug deep in my duffle and produced the pallet load of condoms Voodoo had provided. "I did not buy these."

Her mouth hung open for the few seconds it took for fury to narrow those cool blue eyes. "You didn't know I was going to be here but it looks like you certainly had plans to get some this week."

Women constantly complain that men don't listen. I get it. We don't but we're not the only ones. "Hannah, what did I just say?"

She did pause for a moment to review. "That you didn't buy them. Then who did?"

"Take a wild guess."

"T?"

"Nope."

Her adorable nose wrinkled. "Please tell me Smith did not buy those for you."

"Oh, hell no. If he had, I would've bought a different box while we were out today. Come on. Who would've bought seventy-two Trojans and thought it was a good idea?"

"Voodoo." She laughed and rolled her eyes.

"Once a medic with a sick sense of humor always a medic with a sick sense of humor."

"You never know. Maybe we'll be sending him a thank you note by the end of the week."

I bit back a comment about also having to get her some chafing cream if we used seventy condoms in a few days' time to avoid completely wrecking the mood. "Believe you were supposed to be dressing up for me, honey. Not going to lie to you. I'm tired of waiting."

Her tongue darted over those lush pink lips. "Yes, sir." Those two words lit through me. Nothing but sinking myself deep inside of her would quell the choke of arousal my cock was barely surviving.

42

HANNAH

The ribbon hook on the gown slipped out of my hand for the second time as I tried to fasten the damn thing. I glared down at my nipples. Was one of them more narrow than the other all of a sudden? *Focus Hannah.* I made another attempt with the strap.

"So fucking gorgeous," rumbled from Griff. I spun in the massive closet and there he stood in all of his naked perfection. Not like those sculptures of Greek gods, no, he'd been chiseled and honed by the American military. All rippled muscle, sinew, tattoos, and scars. The Greek gods had nothing on Griff Haywood. "Need some help, baby?" spilled from his lips in a coaxing rumble.

My gaze tracked down the ropes of muscles constructing his abdomen to the trail of black hair that led directly to his long, solid length. Thick veins protruded along his shaft, crowned with his smooth head fully engorged and all for me. The scars resided there as well, deep purple grooves against heated flesh. Fissures where I could pour in the love I longed to give him. Anticipation tangled me in knots.

His substantial thighs were covered in scalpel markings and

shrapnel penetration points. His bulging arms were proof of his raw power and yet, with me, he was gentle.

He palmed his cock. "Have no clue why you like what you see but I sure as hell love that hungry look in your eyes when you're staring at me." The low gravel of his voice loosed something primal deep within my core.

He tugged and a whimpered moan shook from my lungs. I flung the nightie away and stepped toward him. My fingertips followed after his palm as he gave another pull. An eager grunt filled the air between us. I made another exploratory path with my hand over his slit this time. A drop of pearly need clung there now.

Leaning, I spun my tongue over his crown, steeping my senses in his masculine scent and his flavors. I wanted to be completely immersed in him. The glimmer of heat in his eyes served as my only warning. "You want a taste? Then you get on your knees like a good girl."

A hot blast of pure desire flooded through me from his gruff command. God, yes, this was what I'd craved from him for so long. My pulse fluttered in my throat.

I sank to my knees letting my fingernails trace over the pillows of firm muscle that comprised his chest and abs as I made my descent. The thick carpeting in the closet cushioned my fall, scraping against my knees. Awareness sharpened my focus.

"Now, lick every inch of me." I brushed a tender kiss on his sack instead. His hand threaded through my hair. He gripped a fistful. "I said lick me." Every nerve ending in my scalp rejoiced at his force. Compliant now, I ran my tongue from his root to his tip. He was better than any ice cream cone I'd ever indulged in. God, I wanted to suck but I was no longer in control and that knowledge assured me that we, together, were finally fully alive. Letting my tongue dance at his slit, I reversed course and inhaled his salty flavors all the way back down his shaft. "I taught you to do that so good, didn't I baby?"

"God, yes." And he had. In his apartment on post, I'd been given explicit instructions. I knew precisely how he wanted to be taken in, how he wanted to be consumed.

"Suck me," came from him in a rasping order.

"I was worried you'd never ask." I let my hot breath fan over his cock, watching as it throbbed out his need.

"I don't plan on asking for anything, baby. Tonight, I'm taking what I want. Now suck me."

"Yes," breathed from me as I lapped at his head and drew him in. I hollowed my cheeks and drew him deeper.

Glancing upward, I watched his head fall back in unadulterated pleasure. "Jesus, that's good," scraped from his throat. "Take more. Let me hear how good I taste."

I released him with a pop and then let him guide my head back down. I sucked in earnest now. My hungry moans vibrated down his shaft. His rasping curses and craving groans filled me, surging liquid heat between my legs. Releasing him again, I brushed suckled kisses and teasing strokes of my tongue over the scars that ran along the left side of his cock. The masculine scent of him and his flavors filled my senses. I returned to my work before he made another demand that I do so.

He stared down at me now almost in awe. "So good. So fucking good," and other far less sensical phrases along with ragged sighs drifted through my ears and seized my soul. Tingling sensations raced across my skin and he wasn't even touching me yet. Everything in me yearned for him. I sucked harder, needy for him to let go of the restraints he'd always clung to with me.

"Oh fuck, mmm," groaned from his lips. The sound feathered over my flesh. He seized, tightening his grip on my hair as he pressed himself in farther. I relaxed my throat muscles. I wanted him all.

I cupped his sac as it drew tight. He roared. The warrior freed. "Drink me," was his final command as he came in hard tremors and hot spurts down my throat. I complied, desperate to please him, desperate to love him.

His eyes were heavy-lidded with lust. When he made certain he was steady on his feet, he leaned and lifted me up into his arms, cradling me against him. "Skip the lingerie. I just want you."

That suited me just fine.

43

GRIFF

"My God, baby, the things I want to do to you." The warning shoved its way around the craving greed clogged in my throat. I cradled her in my lap on the bed.

"Do them," she tempted.

I rubbed my hands up from the creamy skin of her hips to those lush tits that drove me insane with need. Her sweet little nipples throbbed, reaching for my touch. Cupping her, I leaned and indulged her right with my mouth. Her head fell back as she offered herself up for my pleasure. I drew her deeper, tending and lathing constantly.

When her breathless whimpers turned to moans, I grabbed the bowl of mostly melted ice cream nearby.

"Griff," panted from her. God, I fucking loved how she made my name sound like sex. She rocked in my lap, unable to remain still. When her back arched, I seized the opportunity to dribble cold ice cream over her fevered tits. It raced over the slight hills and into the underswells. Her nipples were cherry candies in the snow. A harsh shiver coursed through her as the heat of her body juxtaposed with the frozen cream. She writhed for me now.

Dragging my tongue in the valley between her breasts as the dessert raced down toward her navel, I sucked and licked her clean.

"Yes, mmm." She managed a few quick breaths.

Gripping her waist, I devoured the vanilla ice cream as it blended with the flavors of her. I swear every pass of my tongue over her nipples was like a stroke to my cock. She filled my mouth and sutured the broken fragments of my soul. When I'd sucked her clean, I turned her and laid her out on the bed.

Ignoring the slight pull from my hip, I found my place between her legs and pinned her open with the breadth of my shoulders. I wasn't gentle as I spread her for my kiss. "This is just for me, baby. All for me."

"Yes," sang from her like a hymn. And when I let her feel the strength of my fingers separating her swollen folds, she called out my name like a god. My hot breath whispered over her clit. I watched her pussy clench. "Griff, please."

"I love you begging for me." My cock strained against the mattress, so needy for her wet pussy. I rocked against the sheets desperate for relief that would only come from her.

"Please, please." Her hands fisted the blankets. Her head shook back and forth on the pillow. She was just as lost in the need as I was. I would find her, rescue her, and give her the excruciating ecstasy she required.

I bathed that tender bundle of nerves with my tongue, sucking until she was limp and mindless with want.

This time it was her own sweet cream that sated my taste-buds. She dripped faster than I could catch it. Gently, I curled two fingers deep within her channel and began to stroke. I drew her timid clit back into my mouth and sucked to the rhythm I'd memorized years ago. The primal timing of her. My heart knew her pulse. My body knew her rhythms. My cock knew its home. My demons recognized their master. They bowed in earnest to the angel who looked me in the eye, grinned, took my hand, and then willingly freed me from their bonds.

Her thighs tensed against my arms. She was weak against my physical strength and yet she was so much stronger than I could ever hope to be. Her pussy nursed at my fingers so hungry for my cock I damn near lost my mind. I pushed her constantly closer to the edge, needing her to jump, needing her to fly. "Come on my fingers, baby. Just let it come. Then I'll give you what you need." If she would let go, I'd get her to the ground. I knew how to do that. I would never let her fall unless I was there to catch her.

My name rung from her lungs once more and then her climax washed over her in waves of breathless pleasure. She seized and I devoured everything she gave up for me. Her flavors the only sustenance I would ever require for survival.

The thread of fire I'd been walking roared to a blaze.

I climbed up her body and paused for one half second to tear open a condom and roll it on. "I love you," growled from me as I slammed into her, deep and destructive. Tearing away every single thing I would no longer allow to exist between us. "And I fucking need you."

And there was that single truth that could never be undone.

Her eyes flew open. "Yes." Her heels dug into the mattress as she adjusted for my size. "Take me."

I had no choice. We were going down. We could jump or be burned alive. I pounded into her with nothing left to give but pure driven need and all-consuming emotion. I was broken beyond repair. My only redemption lay before me begging me to let her make the jump with me this time and I was too fucking weak to deny her.

The breath tore from her lungs from my force. I couldn't stop. I pressed harder, deeper, ragged with need for her. I rode the delicious friction with no remorse.

That night the only thing I had to prove to her was that this would never be over, not this time. I just wasn't strong enough to deny myself or her any longer. The endless ropes of lies would ultimately either become my noose or be incinerated. Remaining bound was no longer an option.

I thrust over and over, harder with each pass, burying every mistake I'd ever made deep within her where somehow she washed them clean. When I was deep inside her, I could breathe. My mind stilled. My past lay quiet. The future at peace. My present only her.

Every single thing I'd gotten wrong no longer mattered. The heat of her body burned them away. This was where life made sense. This is where I belonged.

"Look at me." She tunneled her fingers through my hair and brought my face to hers. "This is what I wanted all along. Give me you."

Completely unable to keep any part of myself from her, I withdrew and flipped her over so she was lying on her chest. My cock lengthened, desperate to be back deep in her. Gripping her hips, I pulled her up to her knees and slammed back into her with punishing force.

The globes of her ass jiggled against my groin, soft skin pliant to my brutal possession.

And my sweet baby fucking begged for more. The warrior she claimed to need shattered the chains I'd tried so damn hard to hold him in since the first night I'd taken her all for myself. My hand connected with her ass with a snap.

Her body rolled. She shook that ass back and forth against me, begging for it. "You want it dirty, baby? I'll give it to you dirty." I gripped her hair once again with my left hand as my right made another pop of her ass. "All fucking mine. Let me hear my name when I paddle your ass, honey."

Another slap and I rubbed away the sting as my name left her lips on a ragged groan. Her nectar dripped down my thighs with every strike. I sank to my hilt with every smack of my palm against her.

Her pussy flexed constantly against me now, milking every twitch of my cock. "Not yet, baby."

"Please," she cried out into the pillow just before her teeth sank into the cotton.

"I feel it. I feel how bad you need it. It's right there, isn't it." Snap. My hand made another strike.

"Griff," whimpered from her and I lost all ability to stem the tide of my own climax as it barreled through me.

My hands latched to her hips, I jerked her back, holding her against me, burying myself in so deeply she'd ache with the emptiness when I finally freed her. "Now, baby. Come on my cock like my good girl."

She collapsed to the mattress and this time I fell with her. I'd jumped out of hundreds of aircraft. But that night was the only free fall I'd ever made where I knew right where I'd land and that as soon as we touched down everything would figure itself out.

A few minutes later, I had her up on my chest doing my damnedest to gently rub away the heat that clung to her ass.

She traced her index finger over the tattoo she'd designed on my chest. "Thank you."

Her whisper was so faint I couldn't be sure she'd spoken. "Hmm?"

"Thank you for giving me all of that. It was amazing. Pretty sure you broke my halo, soldier."

"Glad to be of service, sweetheart. That halo of yours has been in danger since the first time I set eyes on you. Might as well throw the damn thing away."

Vivid memories of the infinite trust I could see in her eyes the first time I eased her open rushed back into my head. The tender tremble of her body as I touched her virgin lips. The timid wet heat that soaked my fingertips that night. I'd tried so hard to be gentle. She'd overwhelmed me with her strength. It killed me to hurt her and I knew I would. She wasn't afraid. Just like tonight, she'd begged and her need had vanquished my own vows to always protect her. I'd taken her innocence all for myself but I would always guard that with my very life.

"I've been trying to get rid of it for years. But my HALO jumper finally decided to come back home."

"I'm right here. I swear I won't leave you again."

44

GRIFF

My fingers slipped gently through the long fall of her silky blonde waves as she slept on my chest. Vegas never slept and that night I couldn't either. I rehearsed the conversation I intended to have with my best friend. I wasn't lucky enough to hope I'd still be able to call him that after I made my phone call.

It wasn't just that I'd had his baby sister in my bed for years, that I'd popped her sweet little cherry, that I'd had her on her knees begging under my tutelage, that I knew every hungry hollow of her body, that I'd feasted and filled them all. He'd beat the shit out of me for that. I'd let him and I'd survive. It was the lies I wasn't sure we'd ever overcome.

By six, as hesitant sunlight warmed the desert skies, the stirring restlessness was more than I could stand. Easing from the bed, I tucked the sheets and blankets around my sweet baby. "I'm gonna make this right." I made the whispered vow though she slept on.

My hip was still warm from the workout with her the night before. I tried my weight on it and it proved. I threw on a pair of jeans and quietly slipped out of the bedroom. I stared at my cell phone like it was set to detonate at any moment. I couldn't have The Sevens and her. I wasn't certain I could survive without either but she wanted all of me and I owed her that.

"Stop being a fucking coward," I ordered myself. Gripping the phone, I touched his name and counted the rings.

"Griff?"

I could hear the constant whir of the treadmill and the steady slam of his footfalls. "Yeah, it's me."

Several rapid beeps said he was slowing his run. "What's up?"

"Nothing. Something. I don't know."

"What the hell are you doing calling me at six in the morning from Vegas? You just getting in or something?"

"No."

The treadmill clicked off. I could almost see him grabbing a towel to mop up the sweat from his brow. I'd seen him do it a thousand times. "Talk," he ordered.

Smith Hagen was not a man for mincing words, that was for damn sure. "Um..." I couldn't force one single phrase I'd rehearsed all night long past the boulder in my throat. "Have you...have you ever lied to someone? Not like a cherry tree lie. Like one that would really hurt people and then the longer you let it go on the worse it gets."

"Are you okay, man? Want me to come down there?" Deep concern etched his tone. Great, so I clearly sounded like this was a mayday call and I was the one going down for the last time. I hated that almost as much as the fact that I probably was.

"No. Don't come down here. I just need to know if you've ever told anyone you really cared about a lie? A huge fucking lie." My frantic pulse timed the silent seconds.

"I've lied about being sober a few times but I get the impression that's not what you're going for. What the hell's going on? Did you meet someone down there or something? You can tell people we were Berets, man. Most of that shit has been declassified."

"That's not it. It's..." I shook off the vice grip around my neck. "Back in the day. When we first got to Fort Carson..."

"Those were the days right? What made you think about that?"

Hannah. Her name was right there cemented to the tip of my

tongue and dammit I couldn't speak it. The bedroom door opened. She stepped out wearing one of those short silk robes that concealed just enough to frustrate. I tried to blink through the distraction.

"Who is that?" she mouthed.

"Smith." I answered audibly. Her eyes rounded.

"What, man?"

Fuck. "Just know I love her so much. I tried okay. I tried so fucking hard and I just... I can't do this anymore without her. I don't even want to."

"You've been down there a couple of days. Are you seriously telling me you fell in love with someone? Are you drunk?"

"Stone cold sober."

Hannah's eyes closed. I'm sure it was in prayer as she clung to me.

The beep of an incoming call jarred what was left of my nerves. "Hang on." Okay, so I was a complete coward but if the universe wanted to buy me some time, I wasn't going to turn it down. "Haywood," I answered hesitantly. The number wasn't programmed in my phone but the area code was far too familiar.

"Is this Sergeant Griffin Haywood?" a woman asked. Her tone was kind but insistent.

"Yeah. I'm Griff."

"I'm Nancy, a cardiac care nurse from St. Luke's Boise. I wanted to let you know we've just admitted your father. He came to the emergency room in cardiac arrest. You're listed as his emergency contact."

"What?" My brain scrambled. A hum of panic tried to reach through me but it was subverted by the years of distance I'd placed between me and my old man.

"He's stable, sir, but he's asked for you several times. I understand that you don't live in town. Would it be possible for you to make a trip to Boise?"

Suddenly, the bellow of Duke Haywood's voice blared through the phone. "Tell him to go by the house and feed Kilgore."

"He's still alive?" Shock slowly made its way through my synapses.

"Oh, yes sir. The chances of surviving a heart attack are much higher nowadays."

"Not him." I rolled my eyes. "He's too fucking mean to die. I meant the dog."

"Oh. Well, if he needs to be fed, I'm assuming he is also alive. When can I tell your father to expect you?"

I tried to process her question. Hannah was beside me. Smith was in Lincoln. The women out to harm my baby were here in Vegas but that was temporary and I hadn't been back to Boise in years. "Uh, tell him I'll be there later this afternoon. I have to take care of somethings first. And tell him I said to fucking listen to you and the doctors and that if he's a prick to anyone I'll personally whip his ass when I get there." I ended that call. Smith was still on the other line. "Can we put a pin in this? My dad had a heart attack and I have to go feed the dog apparently."

"Holy fuck. You're going back to Boise?"

"Maybe. I don't know. What the hell am I supposed to do?"

"Want me to meet you down there?"

"No. Thanks though."

"What about this chick you think you're in love with?"

"I'll...call you later." I ended that call as well.

Hannah scooped her phone off of the coffee table and began hitting buttons.

I still couldn't quite understand how I'd gone from confessing to Smith to going back to Weed Patch, Idaho to take care of my sperm donor. "What are you doing, baby?"

"I'm booking us a flight to Boise." She squeezed my hand. "Go get packed."

"But...here?" Okay, I had lost most of my capacity to think. What the hell was wrong with me? I couldn't have a week in heaven. I should've known that. Life didn't like me that much.

"Hey." She leaned up on her tiptoes and brushed a kiss on my jaw. "We can come back to all of this after we know your father is all right."

Because I needed one more thing to deal with right that moment, a frantic knock sounded on the door. Hannah was on the phone with an airline from the sound of it. I opened the door before whoever was knocking could beat the damn thing down. "What?"

"Sir..." Fred leaned back to check the vacant hallway, "...I thought it might interest you to know that Ms. Rutherford has carried several bags out to her car early this morning. Odd behavior for someone with reservations through next Sunday."

"Shit. She knowns something's up. Can you stall her? There's one thing I have to figure out before I can take them all down."

"I'll do my best."

"Thanks, Fred."

I did my best thinking on my feet so I paced while I called T-Byrd.

"The Vegas police are waiting on my call," was T's greeting. "Looks like you found yourself quite the band of con-women. I got you seven outstanding warrants."

"Good but don't call them in yet. Help me think this through. The chick that's running this sham of a bachelor auction is all tied up in this somehow. I need to figure that out before we start busting the granny gang."

"What's her name?" I heard our impressive bank of monitors in the control room all click on. Clearly, T, was already at work.

"Megan Mallory. She's on the board of Homefront Heroes but I don't believe they were actually behind this event."

"Yeah, I found her. Let me dig. Nothing I'm seeing looks like anything more than she's trying to earn Girl Scout badges for charity work."

"Time is definitely of the essence," I reminded him.

"I'll call you right back."

The door reverberated under someone's fists yet again. "Jesus, it's six fucking o'clock in the morning. What the hell is this?" I flung open the door again praying I was not about to have to trip three elderly women to keep them from escaping.

Ryder Mathis was covered in sweat and staring back at me. "Need to talk to you," he informed me. "Definitely think you're gonna want to hear what I found out."

I stepped back which he apparently took as an invitation to waltz inside my suite. He stared at Hannah like she was the last canteen in the Iraqi desert. "Damn," he admired.

She was still on the phone and still clad in a barely there robe. Shoving him backward, I was in his face a half-second later. "Literally just thought of seven ways to kill you without even breaking a sweat," I seethed.

Hannah's eyes goggled when she spied our guest. She whisked back into our bedroom and shut the door.

"Sorry, man. You have seen her right? I mean...shit, she's gorgeous."

"Gorgeous and mine. Never forget that last part."

"Got it." He offered me an apologetic glance. "Did I just fuck up any chance of ever working for Tier Seven?"

"You want to work for us?" Well, that explained his helpfulness.

"Maybe."

"After today, I probably won't be working for them so they might need some help."

"I'm interested."

"I'll keep that in mind. What'd you come to tell me?"

"You cool with talking here?" He glanced around my suite.

"Nah, we should see if we can get a reservation at a table with the queen. Talk."

"Geez, you're in a mood. Somebody piss in your Cheerios or something?"

I narrowed my eyes. "I'm sorry, did you come by to admire my girlfriend, insert your dick in my life, and ask me for a job, or did you have something of value to tell me?"

"Sorry for asking. After you left last night, apparently a thought crossed Watson's mind."

"Bet that was a long, lonely journey," I huffed.

Ryder laughed. "That'd be a safe bet. He was rambling on about his friend who Homefront Heroes is helping with his chemo treatments. Guy's last name is Mallory. Watson never thought to mention that to either of us."

"Holy fuck." Sergeant Mitch Mallory screaming in my face during

Basic slammed through my consciousness again. He had the same awkward smile as his sister. I'd forgotten his name but never his face. "That guy was one of my drill sergeants."

"Oh yeah? Mine, too. Out at Fort Jackson, right? Did he make you shovel sun off the sidewalks?"

"Nah, he made us sweep it. What kind of cancer does he have?"

"Tumors are in his brain, which obviously sucks. But it got me to thinking about all of the insanity of this whole auction. Not gonna lie to you. I'm pissed. I came down here thinking I'd get some tail not to have my ass grabbed by the felons of the female *Cocoon* reboot. I found Ms. Mallory at that sports bar here last night. I might've bought her several drinks too many and got her talking." He held up his hands in surrender. "And then I saw her safely back to her suite and I left. I swear. After that, I did some digging. Sergeant Mallory isn't doing well. I used a few clearance liberties, I may or may not have, and read his latest prognosis. Army docs are giving him less than six months. There's some kind of last ditch experimental treatment she thinks can help him but you and I both know Uncle Sam isn't gonna pay for experiments. I'm thinking maybe she did all of this to pay for this treatment thing. I ran six fucking miles this morning but I can't figure out how to prove that. How is she playing Dorothy in those warped old ladies trip to Oz? It's making me nuts."

I almost forgave him for staring at my baby. Almost. I offered him my hand. "First of all, that famous trio and foursome work was impressive as hell. Second, when are you due up for re-enlistment?"

His gaze fell to the floor. Not a good sign. I waited. "I'm up now."

"And?"

His eyes returned to mine. Regret and irritation fought for dominance in their depths. "And I've been recommended with reservation by all of my superiors."

"I see. What would their reservations be?" The likelihood that he'd be offered another four years with that many reservations wasn't good.

He gripped the collar on his T-shirt and used it to wipe the sweat off his face. "Uh, it said something about me failing to place commander's intent over my individual actions."

"That all it said?" I knew it wasn't.

An audible breath hissed from his lungs. "Might've said something about a blatant disregard for authority."

"What'd you do?"

He shook his head. "Man, we..." His explanation was sealed off by the might of his jaw.

"You know, I might've had a few blatant disregards for authority in my career, too."

"Really?"

I shrugged.

"We landed deep in Boko territory in Mubi. Hiked thirty miles in pouring rain, naturally. Embrace the suck or whatever. We fucking had sights on a few of those kids they took. I could see them. Couple of the guys running the show came into view. I saw them hit one of those little girls. Watched it happen through my scope. But then higher called us off. They were right there."

"And you took the shot."

He gave me a single nod.

"Lucky you didn't get your ass discharged."

"Yeah, I know. Also, I don't have a brother-in-law that owns a bar in L.A. I'd just been there and I could tell your girl hadn't."

"What suite is Megan Mallory staying in?"

He didn't even pause to think. "Fourteen."

He was already registering all of the small details. Yeah, he'd make a great asset for Tier Seven. "I have to make a few phone calls but you sure you're willing to relocate to Lincoln? We don't do a lot of jumping out of planes anymore."

Relief rushed into his eyes. "Hell yeah. I've jumped three hundred times in the last five years. I'm good on the ground for a while. Are you serious? I could really come work with Tier Seven? I wasn't a tier one asset or anything."

"If you can keep your sarcasm up, stay on top of your entertainment media humor, and you keep figuring shit out like you did last night, I'd say you're a shoo-in." I smirked. "Of course, you do have to outshoot me."

Poor kid slumped in defeat. "Are you serious?"

I laughed. "No. No one can outshoot me."

Hannah returned fully clothed. This time Mathis offered her a polite grin and never let his eyes drop below her chin, so he was trainable. I could work with that.

"Listen, I've got a thing I have to do this afternoon. Feel like catching Dorothy and the wicked witches of three-quarters of the globe?" I offered him.

"Hell yeah. But we're not cops. How does this work?"

"Watch and learn, my friend. Watch and learn. Also, grab a quick shower. You stink."

45

HANNAH

"Pretty sure you just made his whole life." I studied Griff looking for any sign he was nervous about seeing his father again. I saw none.

"Yeah, well, I would've taken the shot, too."

"Our flight is at four."

"Thanks for booking that. You don't have to come with me." His voice hollowed with his offer.

I shook my head at him. "Of course I'm coming."

"We have to take care of a few things first. I can't leave Watson here to deal with the female felons of the *Cocoon* reboot."

"Wow. That's a good one. You had to dig deep for that."

"Right? Mathis just came up with it. I'm impressed. Not gonna lie."

"He'll fit in very nicely at Tier Seven and I already knew we'd take care of this before we left. Leave no man behind, right?"

"I don't know any other way to be, baby."

"And I don't want you to be any other way." Maybe Smith wouldn't completely lose his mind when we told him about us if there was a new recruit there. I knew better but there had to be some way to get him to remain relatively chill.

"Maybe he can take my place," Griff choked.

"What?" Clearly, he was still unable to think straight. The news about his father had thrown him more than he was showing. "No one could ever take your place in The Sevens, Griff. Why would you say that?"

He shrugged. "Smith."

"Will be just fine. You are not leaving Tier Seven. Not for me."

"I'd do anything for you."

"I know that but you don't have to. Once we tell my father and my brother and they chill the fuck out about it, I'm moving to Lincoln. You have given up enough for ten lifetimes. I will not split up The Sevens."

"You're not moving to Lincoln. You have a whole design firm in Denver." I ground my teeth but another knock on the door interrupted the diatribe I was preparing.

"Grand-fucking-Central here today." Griff swung open the door again.

Fred leaned his head in. "She's made another two trips to a car."

"I'm on it," Griff vowed. "You ready?" he asked me.

"What are we doing exactly?"

"Catching some crooks and forcing a confession. What we normally do before breakfast, baby." He winked at me like all of this was no big deal. He was tugging on a clean T-shirt when his phone rang. "It's T," he explained before answering. "Her brother's a... I'm gonna go with either a Master Sergeant or a First by now and he's sick, right?"

That cocky smirk appeared on his features as T responded. "I'm just that good. You know that." Another pause had him shaking his head. "Fuck off, man. Call in the LVPD but tell them to be discreet. Our con-grannies are nervous. Tell them to meet me in suite fourteen." Griff sank his feet into his boots, bracing the phone between his shoulder and ear. "Yeah, I think I have this all figured. Betting my baby can fill in all of the details I don't have. I'll call you later."

"What details do you not have?" I leapt as soon as he ended the call. "Are we seriously doing this now? What about your dad?"

Griff rolled his eyes. "Duke will still be there when I'm done with this. Trust me. The diagnosis had to be wrong. You have to have a heart for it to attack."

His indifference crushed me. The life he'd lived, the way he'd grown up always tangled my vocal cords and shattered my heart. Griff's mother had abandoned them when he was eleven and Duke hadn't handled it well. But I'd sat with the man in the waiting room of Walter Reed while Griff underwent surgery after surgery. He did love his son. He just had a terrible way of showing it. "I know he wasn't always a great dad but I swear he does love you." I had to try.

His jaw clenched. I watched his eyes. He debated something. "Baby, just because they're your parents doesn't mean they're...decent people. Okay? Making a kid doesn't automatically make you a good human being. Trust me." So, this was no longer about Duke. This was about my father. Before I could press him for more information, he was handing me my kicks and strapping his kit to his thigh. The pistol went back in his jeans.

I slipped my shoes on and followed him out into the corridor.

"Had you ever worked with Megan before on any other fundraisers for Homefront? Was she around before this event?"

We made our way past Fred and down the hallway the opposite direction of Ms. Rutherford's suite.

"She's been interested in moving to a higher position on the board for a while. That's why I can't believe she turned over that document of donors. I've seen her before at events. We made small talk but nothing in-depth. Ms. Donohue told me she was interested in becoming the chairman at a golf tournament I went to last April. She seemed annoyed with Ms. Mallory but I didn't really think much of it."

He pounded on the door to suite fourteen. "And you said the board always attends events right?"

"Yeah, I noticed right off that none of them were there. Every golf tournament, dinner, gala everything. The whole board is always there, except for this one."

"When she first saw you here and asked you about the auction, was she alone?"

I considered that as he knocked again. "I don't know if she was traveling alone but she was by herself when she approached me."

Another knock but still no answer. My empty stomach turned. Where was she at six-thirty in the morning? Griff lifted the flap on his kit and pulled out the same tool he'd used to break into Ms. Rutherford's suite.

Ryder came out of his room, freshly showered. He glanced up and down the hallway. "Are you seriously breaking into her suite?" He was going to need a little more training. I almost felt bad for him having to endure Griff and my brother for the rest of his life. Their bromance was legendary. I said another prayer that Smith wouldn't be too difficult when we made our confession.

"Why don't you call the fucking Pentagon?" Griff growled. "Jesus. Keep your trap shut." With that, the lock on Ms. Mallory's suite clicked and he pushed the door open.

"What if she's just in the bathroom or something?" I fussed as I followed the boys inside.

"Then she needs to zip it up and get out here. I don't have all morning," Griff huffed. "Megan, this is Griff Haywood," bellowed from him. "LVPD is on their way." He stood outside the master bedroom door. "Come out or I'm coming in."

"If I get this job promise to never tell him I said this, but he's supremely badass. Like maximum badassery," Ryder whispered as Griff took a step back and kicked the bedroom door open with his bad leg.

I laughed. "Trust me, he already knows."

The bedroom and bathroom were both empty. "Shit." Griff took off at a sprint. Ryder and I raced after him. Two men in police uniforms were escorted down the locked corridor by hotel staff. "Follow me," Griff ordered.

"They told us suite fourteen," one of the men argued.

"They lied."

The officers followed. With the magnetic lock pick still in his hand, Griff opened Victoria Rutherford's door. The cops exchanged a concerned glance.

"They may be holding a woman hostage in there. Did you really want him to wait on you guys to get approval on that?" Ryder asked. Okay, he'd survive Smith and Griff. I had no doubts.

The cops shrugged and followed Griff into the suite. Megan Mallory stared at us like we'd waltzed in doing the tango naked. Victoria and Edith were headed out the back door.

"Stop right there," one of the cops ordered.

"How did you get in here?" Megan gasped.

"Sit down," Griff ordered. Two other cops approached from the pool area trapping Victoria and Edith. They escorted them back in the suite. Gladys appeared from one of the bedrooms loaded down with packages from stores on The Strip.

"What is going on?" Megan asked again.

"I've got warrants on these three. Not sure about you, ma'am," one of the officers explained.

"Can I have like five minutes to put all of this together? It's gonna bug the piss out of me if I don't get to," Griff asked.

"Sure." The officers all shrugged.

46

GRIFF

I popped the crick out of my neck and grinned. I had a thing for catching bad guys. Always made me smile, even if they happened to be eighty-year-old women. "Let's see how right I am. First off, you three," I gestured to the Rutherford gang. "You lead everyone to believe that you're black widows, right? There's no way to prove that and it's a great explanation for why you're so wealthy. You make jokes about killing off your nonexistent husbands so no one will question how you afford all of the gaudy-ass shit you possess. In reality, you make your fortunes stealing people's identities. Credit cards, checking accounts, whatever you can get your hands on. You book suites in hotels on The Strip using someone else's card then have everything you want to purchase charged back to your rooms, right?"

The women offered me hateful glares. That was probably all of the confession I was going to get. "Doesn't matter. You don't have to answer me. They have outstanding warrants on all of you. But you," I turned to Ms. Mallory, "You were just a fly they webbed, weren't you? No one who comes up with ten pages of rules for an event does it for no real reason. The only thing I haven't figure out yet is if you approached them about the auction or if they approached you."

"I didn't know they did that," Megan pled. "I had no idea. They were here at the hotel when I came down to check it out for the auction. They said if I would let them attend the event they'd..."

"Pay for the medical transport for your brother, right? Either that or they'd pay for the flight and the treatment," I continued to fill in the blanks.

"They said they'd pay for the flight and that they'd help me with the treatments depending on the auction." A terrified shiver coursed through her as she rang her hands. "My brother needs the treatments. I didn't know what else to do."

Hannah shook her head. "What did you promise them you would do in exchange for their help, Ms. Mallory?"

"Nothing, I swear. I just said that I'd get our biggest donors there. I thought they wanted to attend an A-list event and to be sure they won whoever they wanted. I didn't know..."

"They had plans to steal from some of the wealthiest people associated with the military?" I asked.

She nodded.

"Why are you in here with them?" I demanded.

"The check bounced. I saw them loading their car. They were going to leave without paying."

"Oh my gosh!" Hannah gasped. Every eye in the room turned to stare at her. "You weren't supposed to let them win Griff! That's what you messed up!"

Unadulterated fury lit in Victoria's eyes.

"She's a total screw-up," Gladys huffed.

Oh, my baby had struck a chord. "Keep going," I urged.

"You couldn't get the biggest donors to attend because Homefront Heroes didn't actually sanction this event, right?"

Megan erupted. "I'm so sick of having golf-tournaments and galas. I knew this could make real money if I could get the board's support. I thought I could secure a higher position if I proved myself with this event but Edward wouldn't sign off on a bachelor auction. I needed to be chairman to get them to vote to pay for my brother's experimental treatments. When they backed out, I had to do something. I thought if I made a big contribution to the foundation maybe they'd still help me with Mitch's transportation and treatments. Victoria told me she could help me. But then she was furious with me. I didn't understand why until now. I swear."

Hannah shook her head. "When you came up short on A-list donors, they set their sights on me. They wanted to win the guys who they thought made the most money but, mostly, they wanted access to my checking account number which would have been on the check if I'd won."

"It just never occurred to me. I thought they wanted me to pick out the guys who made the most money so maybe they'd be shown a good time this week. I thought they wanted the men to buy things for them or at least pay for a nice dinner or two. I had no idea they were planning to steal from them."

"Doubt that stands up in court." One of the officers shook his head.

"Especially since someone provided them this." I pulled that damned printout from my pocket and handed it over. "If you didn't know what they were after, how did they get that?"

"I swear. I thought they had a lot of money because their husbands left them everything. I had to pay for this whole thing myself. The first few checks they gave me cleared and that's how I secured the deposit here. They said they needed the list of bigger donors so they could contact them about the event. I thought they were helping me. Now, I can't pay the rest I'm going to owe the hotel and I'll have nothing for Mitch. The hotel let me use the ballrooms as long as the guests for the event stayed in the suites."

"That explains the cut-rate food and decor." I sighed. Jesus, this was a deep shithole. "Their first few installments were just a down payment because they thought you were going to be turning over a ballroom full of marks." I turned to the cops. "If you'll search their car, you'll find numerous prescription bottles none of which belong to them. Several people staying here are missing their meds. Talk to the front desk. The narcs and the Viagra help you put on the crazy-old-lady routines, right? Also might ease the occasional wear and tear on the body from running state to state conning people. Stealing meds from hotel rooms, that was Gladys's job right?"

"How did you know that?" Edith gasped.

"The gloves. Always with the gloves. Fingerprints and DNA evidence are a real bitch when you're breaking and entering. You hung around for the dinner last night as a last ditch effort to get some info off of Hannah before you skipped town today."

The officer holding Victoria Rutherford cleared his throat. "We have warrants for the suite and the car. Your friend T knew what was up. Tier Seven always does right by us."

"We try. But there was a bogus waiter here the night of the auction. I can't quite figure out how he fits into all of this, but if you can find him he's got a credit card skimmer," I supplied the police.

"Chad?" Edith scoffed. "He's Vicky's nephew. Had a falling out with his dad. Came to stay with us. Leave him out of it. He's a good kid."

"Shut up, Edith," Victoria seethed.

"Let's go, ladies. Ms. Mallory, I'm taking you in as well. We're gonna need you to explain all of this again to the detectives." The police officers produced four sets of cuffs.

Hannah stopped one of the cops. "If you arrest her officially, call me. I'll cover her bail. And Megan, after you get this all sorted out, call my office. I know what it's like to watch your big brother hurt. I know how helpless you must feel. I'll pay for your brother's transport and I'll talk to Ms. Donahue about Homefront helping to cover the treatments as long as all of the donation money actually goes to the foundation."

"Thank you." Before they cuffed her, Megan threw her arms around Hannah. "Thank you so much."

"Wait," she called before they led them all out, "how did you figure out I'd entered Griff and why were you so upset when you found out he's a Beret?"

If Megan had rolled her eyes any harder she could've checked out her own ass. "I knew as soon as I saw you in the lobby with him. You looked at him like you wanted to climb him like a tree."

The smirk was going to be a permanent fixture on my face at least until we landed in Boise. "That's why she came by my suite with those rules. You went to Hannah's suite first, didn't you? She wasn't there and that's when you decided to see if she was already with me."

Ms. Mallory gave another nod.

"Because Hannah was the only person who'd had any experience with Homefront fundraisers prior to this event. She was the wild card you needed to contain. When you found us in the lobby, you saw your chance. If you made her believe you'd spread bad press about Palindrome because she'd broken some made up rule, maybe she would decide not to notice how fucked up your auction was," I concluded. Damn that felt good.

Hannah shook her head. "I wish you'd just asked me for my help."

"I wish anyone on the board would listen to me," Ms. Mallory came right back.

"Oh, I bet they'll listen now. Take them." I gestured to the door.

"I haven't finished answering her questions." Megan tried unsuccessfully to jerk away from the cop holding her. "Mitch always hated the Special Forces guys. Said they thought they were more god than man. But the thing he hated most was that they seem to really be. I knew if anything went wrong, he would be the one that figured it all out."

"But I wasn't," I pointed out. "Hannah was."

47

HANNAH

"Can I ask you something?" I couldn't stand the quiet anymore. He'd been staring out the window for the last half hour. We were making our final approach into Boise. I think he would've actually preferred it if we'd been landing in some war torn nation.

"Anything, baby." The hollow thrum of his voice made me shiver. His eyes had lost all of the life I'd seen in them the past few days.

"Did you ever tell your father that you found your mom?" As soon as they'd completed the private investigation course they all took as the final piece of the training they'd decided they wanted Tier Seven to offer, Griff had put his new skills to work. In less than forty-eight hours, he'd found his mother working in some dive bar in Missoula, Montana. That was when he'd figured out that his father had been lying to him for most of his life.

"No." Griff took another measured sip of the Coke the flight attendant had poured for him.

"Are you going to?"

"No idea. I plan to make my appearance at the hospital, make sure he's not being a dick to the staff, go feed the damn dog, and then take you back to Vegas."

"We could stay here tonight. It's been a long day. We can always go back tomorrow."

"Whatever you want to do."

I had no idea what I wanted to do except to make him smile again. "I'd kind of like to see where you grew up if you wouldn't hate it." Maybe there were a few good memories we could unearth from the cloud of resentment he'd cast over the entire state of Idaho.

He snorted. That was not a good sign. "There's not much to see. It's a bunch of godforsaken fields and the potatoes that are forced to endure life in Weed Patch."

Definitely time to change the subject. "I think Ryder has a crush on you."

That got me a mere glimmer of my favorite smirk. "He's a good kid."

"He kinda reminds me of you minus your rugged good looks." I laced my fingers through his.

"Poor guy. My good looks are all I have going for me." He squeezed my hand. "That and my baby."

"Always."

With a slight bounce, the wheels touched down in Boise, Idaho. As we unloaded, I opened my Uber app. "I'll get us a ride."

"Doubt you can Uber out here in bumblefuck, baby."

"Stop it. You can Uber anywhere."

"Don't say I didn't warn you if a tractor drives up with a hay wagon to take us to the hospital."

I shook my head at him. "I'd pay good money to see that."

When a Kia Hatchback parked in front of us, I laughed. "Quite the tractor."

"Dad better fucking still have my Jeep in the barn because I am not Ubering around for however long we have to be here."

As he folded himself into the hatchback, I brushed a kiss on his cheek. "I love you even when you're grumpy."

His chest expanded with a deep breath. "I'll try to man-up."

"I'll see if I can't come up with reasons to make you smile. So, your dad has your old Jeep?" A deluge of memories flooded through my mind. That Jeep had been everything when I was nineteen. It was the ticket to him.

"He better. I gave it to him when his truck finally gave up the ghost. Not like I had a lot of use for it in Iraq."

"That was sweet of you."

He went back to grunting then. The rolling hills surrounding us slowly swallowed up the remaining sunlight. We passed a low billboard advertising things to see in Idaho as we drove toward the hospital. My lips folded under the force of my teeth to keep from scandalizing our driver who had, what appeared to be, a solar-powered dancing Jesus and his twelve disciples on the dash of his car.

"What?" Griff elbowed me.

"There's actually a place here called Beaver Canyon?" A slight giggle escaped.

And there was my smirk. "Yeah, Beaver Creek runs through it. Tends to swell when I roll back into town." He winked at me.

Maybe it was all of the insanity of our day or just my need to make him grin, but I doubled over laughing. To my delight, he joined me. "You're adorable you know that?" His arm draped over my shoulder and pulled me closer. "Hey, why the hell did you just drive past South Vista?" he demanded of the driver.

I watched the driver's eyes goggle in the rearview. "There's a potato and lentil festival on the capitol grounds this evening, sir. There will be traffic on Main."

"A carb carnival. Of course."

Despite Griff's protesting the way the driver had gone, we arrived at St. Luke's Medical Center a few minutes later. Griff slung his duffle bag over his shoulder and carried the small bag I'd thrown my toothbrush, a nightie, and a few outfits into.

As we made our way inside the hospital, I kept my thumb rubbing over the pencil case in my bag.

"Hey, Hannah...I meant to say thank you for coming with me," he offered.

"That's how relationships work, babe."

A cringe formed instantly on his features as soon as we stepped through the sliding doors. "I hate hospitals," he spat.

Since he'd spent almost six-months inside Walter Reed, I couldn't blame him. We rode the elevator to the fourth-floor cardiac unit. He guided us toward the check-in desk. "Uh, Duke Haywood's room, please."

Before the woman behind the desk could respond, an infuriated bellow echoed from down the hallway. "I have boils on my ass older than you. You fucking playing dress-up in that getup or something? Find me a real damned doctor and food that wasn't manufactured by Goodyear."

Griff's eyes squeezed shut. "Never mind."

Like he was on a forced death march, he towed me toward his father's room. "You don't have to come in," he offered.

"I'll be just fine."

"You're gonna wear a hole in your pencil case if you keep that up. I'm not sure I could find that little outdoor mall thing where we got it again." He gestured to my hand shoved down in my bag.

I'd suspected all along that it was Griff, not Smith, who had actually picked out my case. I'd ask him about that later. "Sorry." I eased my hand away.

"It's fine, baby. I just hate this whole thing is making you that nervous."

To prove my own bravery, I marched into the room ahead of Griff.

The doctor, who'd just gotten yelled at, sized me up before her gaze ascended to Griff. "And the wayward son returns. Hey there, Griff." When she stated his name like a curse, I had a decent idea the role she'd probably played in his past.

"Do I know you?" Griff spat. Clearly he did not.

"Wow," she sneered.

I didn't know a great deal about his life before me but I knew he'd had a rebellious streak several counties wide before he'd joined the army on his eighteenth birthday. Forcing a smile, I offered her my hand. "I'm Hannah Hagen, Griff's girlfriend."

She whipped off a rubber glove and thrust her freezing cold hand into mine. "Dr. Emma Taylor. Believe I was given that same status for the week it took him to get me in the back of his truck in high school." I forced a smile but kept an eye on Griff. His brow furrowed, realization widened his eyes, and then he cringed. I shook my head at him.

"Well, isn't that...something. How are you feeling Duke?" If I ignored her maybe she'd go away.

"He'll be just fine as long as he changes his diet, stops smoking, and gets some exercise. He was very lucky. The damage to the heart muscle was minimal," Emma informed me.

"'Bout damn time you came to see me," Duke spat in Griff's general direction.

"'Bout damn time you stop treating your doctors like an ass and do what they say." Clearly, Griff was not planning to take any shit off of his father.

Duke mumbled something about lady doctors. It was going to be a long night. Emma still had Griff locked in the death-ray glare coming from her eyes. Girl could certainly hold a grudge. It took a full-minute for me to realize there was another woman in the room.

Her dedication to the windblown look, as evidenced by the sheer amount of hairspray shellacked in her bleach blonde hair, had clearly survived the last three decades. Seated in a chair near Duke's bed, she offered me a meek smile. "I'm Georgia. Duke's lady friend." Unlike Griff's mother, who'd been twenty years younger than his dad, Georgia looked to be about Duke's age. How she managed to put up with him I didn't know.

Judging by the bewildered expression on Griff's face, I assumed he was unaware his father had a lady friend.

"Yeah, Georgie, this is Hannah, the woman my son shoulda married years ago but he's too much of a dumbass to get it done before he went and got his self blown up." Duke made quite the introduction.

"My Glock is in my bag," Griff spoke through his teeth. "Just... shoot me now."

"I'd really rather not." I offered Georgia my hand as well. "It's lovely to meet you. How long have you and Duke been dating?"

"We go play Canasta at the senior center on Tuesdays and Thursdays and Duke takes me to services every Sunday. Been that way for a while now."

"My father goes to church?" Griff gasped.

"Every Sunday. We're working on not taking the Lord's name in vain but he's improving."

"You let me know how that goes."

"Well, I'll leave you all to visit. Duke, please eat the salad we've provided you. You're going to be eating a lot of them while you're here," Emma chastised.

"Needs salt," Duke argued.

"No salt." She gave Griff one final scowl before she left the room.

"It's so nice of you to come home, Griff. I've heard a lot about you," Georgia eased.

"I swear I'm not quite as bad as I'm sure he made me sound."

Her laughter was kind. So far, I liked Georgia. "He's really very proud of you. Duke's just very passionate about things."

Griff studied her like some kind of alien being might be using her as a host pod. "Whatever you say."

"Did you feed the dog?" Duke asked as he picked at the salad on the rolling tray.

"Not yet, Dad. We came here first." Griff settled on a padded bench near the window and pulled me down beside him.

"That was sweet of you. Wasn't it Duke?" Georgia insisted.

"Boy always has done everything he could to get out of chores."

Griff glanced up toward heaven but I couldn't be sure if he was pleading for someone to take his father on now or if wanted to make the trip himself.

"Is there anything you'd like us to get you before we go feed the dog, sir?" I asked.

"Do not call him sir," Griff spat. "Sir is reserved for people actually deserving of your respect. He is a windbag with a bad attitude."

"Fine way to talk to your father." Duke leaned up in the bed.

"Oh, I'm sorry, if you'd ever really been a father maybe I'd have nicer shit to say to you. I'm here. Did I seriously catch a fucking flight from Vegas so I could feed your dog or did you actually want to see me?"

"I see the sinful use of coarse language runs in the family." Georgia patted Griff's hand.

"Don't speak that way in front of Georgia," Duke shouted.

"Jesus Christ, are you serious right now?"

"Why the hell were you in Vegas? Thought you lived out in the cornfields."

Griff rolled his eyes. "Why do you care where I was? I'm here now."

It was going about as well as I'd assumed it would. Where was the father who was so worried about his son he paced for three solid hours while Griff was in surgery? Why couldn't Duke show his son that side of himself?

"And stop giving the doctors and nurses your crap. They're trying to help you," Griff continued.

"Take this thing out of my arm. I'm going home." When Duke reached for his IV, Griff caught his hand.

"Stop, Dad. For once in your life, listen to some voice other than your own."

48

GRIFF

"I hope you don't mind but I drove your Jeep up here." Georgia handed over my old keys. "I thought you might want it."

This woman seemed relatively normal, polite, and kind. What the hell was she doing with my father? "Thanks for doing that. I'm happy to drive you home."

"Oh no, it's fine. I plan on staying the night but I'll take you up on that tomorrow."

Great, so now I was coming back to the hospital the next day. I'd managed to keep my father from removing his own IV and the heart monitor out of pure spite. He'd even chewed and swallowed half the salad. He'd cursed between every bite but it was something. Now, to get Hannah out of that room before it completely closed in on us. Then I was going to have to apologize about Emma, a woman I had exactly no memories of being with.

"All right, Dad, we're going to feed Kilgore. Please give everyone in this hospital a break and try not to be a complete ass."

It was the first time in my life I'd seen fear in my father's eyes. "You're coming back tomorrow, right?"

Sure, because volunteering to put up with an inordinate amount of shit is the very definition of being a Beret. I had a great deal of training. "Yeah, I guess. Do you want me to bring anything from the trailer?"

"Bring me some clean drawers and a pack of cigarettes."

"I'm not bringing you cigarettes, old man. Go ahead and quit now."

He scowled but for once didn't argue. "Fine." After a nervous glance Georgia's way, he motioned for me to come closer. Letting go of my anxiousness to get out of that room and away from the incessant beeps of the monitors, I leaned down. It was the closest I'd been to my father in two decades. "There's a few nudie magazines on the kitchen table. Maybe bring those back tomorrow but, you know, hide 'em in a newspaper or something," he whispered.

My father, ladies and gentlemen. There was no one else like him. Thank God. When he gripped my hand, I stood back to stare at him. Patting our clasped hands, I shook my head. "Let's let your heart recover before you...exert yourself again."

"Fine," he conceded again. Clearly, he wasn't feeling as well as he was pretending to be. I'd never seen him so agreeable.

"We'll be back in the morning." I offered a wave to Georgia and tugged Hannah from the room.

"What did he want you to bring him?" she asked.

My legs were a solid five inches longer than hers and I was having to rush to keep up with her. Clearly I wasn't the only one ready to go.

"You don't want to know."

"But I do want to know." She shot me that beaming grin and life's breath rushed back into my lungs.

We stepped out into the quiet Boise night and it finally hit me. I had no recollection of Emma or of Boise or of the things that used to take my breath away and bring it back. I had no real memories of life before I'd met her.

We located my old Jeep in the parking lot. Hannah bounced on her tiptoes as I reached across to unlock her door. "Excited baby?"

She climbed up into her old seat. "Been a long time since I got in your Jeep. I still love it just as much as I did back then."

"Oh yeah?" I paused to revel in the low metallic hum of the motor. "Me too. You know, I could take it to Denver when I move."

"You are not moving to Denver," she insisted yet again. She was crazy if she thought I was going to let her shut down Palindrome so she could move to Lincoln. One of us needed to have a job and it would take me a little while to get back on my feet after I left Tier Seven.

"I am moving to Denver. You're not shutting down your firm."

"I don't have to shut it down. I already work all over the Midwest. No reason I can't do that from Lincoln."

"Hannah, no. I'll move down there. Just have to apologize repeatedly to your brother. Then I'll pack."

As I merged onto the interstate, she whipped the cute little T-shirt she was wearing up and flashed me a quick glance at her tits caught up in a teal lace bra. My eyes zeroed in on her light pink nipples as they tightened under the blast of the air conditioner. I almost drove the Jeep into the Buick in front of us. "Ha, you've been booby trapped! I win!" she taunted.

"Warn a guy, baby. Jesus. And you do not win."

"That wasn't the deal. I get to win the next ten fights as long as I show you my boobs."

I did recall agreeing to something like that. "You had this planned all along didn't you?"

"I've had a few months to plan for this week."

I shook my head. "We'll discuss this later." After she saw her brother's reaction, she'd come around.

"So, Emma." Her teeth raked over her bottom lip and her eyebrows lifted.

"Sorry about that. I swear to you I have no recollection of being with her. I was drunk the majority of my senior year and clearly, almost as much of an ass as my old man back then."

The miles passed as I flew toward Mayfield. I drove instinctively. I had no conscious knowledge of where I was even heading. It had just been too long ago. The Jeep seemed to remember and that worked for me. It was real. She'd been in it so it existed. Everything else was just faint ghosts of memories I was being forced to look through to find my baby seated beside me.

"You don't remember her at all?" Hannah finally asked.

"I honestly don't remember any of this. It feels like I'm living someone else's life." Taking my eyes off of the road, I offered her my right hand. "I don't recall anything about who I was before you."

That was God's honest truth. It was a bonus that it also elicited a swoon from her. I made the turn toward Weed Patch and willed the bile in my throat to return to my stomach.

Ten minutes later, I was pulling onto the land that had raised me. One slight memory wormed its way through my mind. When I'd left home, Kilgore was some kind of blonde Lab Husky mix who'd shown up when I was a teenager. Now, the dog that trotted out from under the trailer was jet black with a white mouth and neck. "That's not Kilgore."

"Are you sure?" Hannah asked as she hopped out of the Jeep. "He has a collar on."

The dog was smart. He raced up to her and let her pet him before he indulged himself in a few licks of her chin. She caught the silver tag on the collar. "It says Kilgore Haywood."

I grabbed our bags out of the back. "Probably went with the same name to save having to get a new tag when the old dog died. Wonder how many reincarnations of Kilgores there have been since I left here?" I wondered how many reincarnations of myself had occurred as well.

I gave the dog a few pats and then reached for the old key we used to keep on the front porch light on the double-wide I'd once shared with my father. I came up empty. More than the dog had changed. Fishing my kit from my bag, I had us inside in under a minute. "Come on in. I'll open some windows." Breathy memories of the trailer managed to take me back. Cigarette smoke, off-brand 409, and stale newspaper ink. Duke's housekeeping hadn't improved any in the last few years. Mail, copies of the Weed Patch Weekly, and magazines covered the kitchen table. The fan in the living room still clicked with every slow turn. I unlocked the kitchen windows and shoved them open with brute force.

Hannah stepped into the kitchen taking it all in.

"I know it's nothing like growing up in the General's houses. Sure as hell not like the houses you design. I'll take you to a hotel if you want."

Her brow furrowed. "It's perfectly fine. I'm excited to be here." She lifted a fading copy of my senior picture from the mantle and wiped the dust from the corners. As far as I knew, Dad had never owned a picture frame.

"You have to be the first person in the history of this country to ever say that about Weed Patch." I opened the cabinets under the sink. No dog food. The next three cabinets contained a few warped skillets, old Cool Whip containers, and a dozen cans of corn. Shaking my head at that, I searched the pantry and finally located a bag of dry dog food. I fed the new Kilgore and then located two bottles of Budweiser from the fridge. Idaho was known for its breweries. They grew almost as many hops as they did potatoes but Duke would sooner give up cursing than drink a craft beer.

I popped the tops and handed one to Hannah. "You hungry, baby? I can make sandwiches or we can drive back into town. Should've asked that on the way. I got distracted with your tits."

Laughing at that, she clinked our bottles together. "Welcome home, Sergeant Haywood."

"This isn't my home. For the longest time I thought wherever we were stationed was my home but that was bullshit, too. You're my home and that's the only way I ever want it to be."

Setting the beer down on the dust covered coffee table, she wrapped her arms around me. "I think that, too." She squeezed tighter like she believed she could love me enough to put me back together. If anyone could, it was her. She lifted her head and took another inventory of the trailer. "I think that's why I wanted to become an interior designer. We moved all the time. Home was wherever the army sent us." She shrugged. "Then I met you and I finally figured out that it would never matter where I was as long as I was with you. I love giving people a place to call home but I always want to remind them that home has to have a heartbeat."

"I love you, baby doll."

"I love you, too. Show me your old room."

I flipped on lights as we headed down the hallway. Duke's room was much the same. Ancient bedspread wadded up at the end of the bed. My room was at the end of the hall. I did have a distinct memory of making the bed the morning I'd left for boot camp. I never wanted to come back. And the bed had sat just the way I'd left it. A poster of a scantily clad woman stretched out over a Corvette still took up most of the back wall.

Hannah laughed. "She could kill someone with those." She pointed to the chick's chest.

"I was sixteen. Back then, I couldn't even see the car."

"So, he hasn't redone anything since you left?"

"Doesn't look that way." I lifted an old iPod off of the dresser. I'd worked my ass off for that thing. It was still plugged in. To my shock, when I pressed the button the screen came on.

"And what were you listening to back then?" Hannah scooted beside me. "Ha! Maroon 5. Oh, I am never letting you live this down."

"Clearly, someone else messed with this in the last decade." I laughed at my own expense.

"Liar, liar," she taunted. "Better take your pants off before they burst into flames."

"Oh, baby, if I take these off yours are coming with them."

She waggled her eyebrows. "Make me a sandwich then we'll get to the things we could do with no pants on."

"Yes, ma'am." I couldn't believe I was standing in the old trailer in the middle of a town I hated and having a good time. The woman could make hell appealing and take me straight to heaven all in one shot.

49

HANNAH

I proceeded to dance around Griff's childhood bedroom belting out the lyrics to "Sugar." When I wiggled my finger in his face, and asked for a taste of his sugar, he grabbed my hand, wrapped his other arm around my waist, and dipped me low while he ground his pelvis against mine.

I danced my way back up, shimmying all the way. That left eyebrow cocked upward. "Watch it, woman," he teased. "You're gonna get yourself into all kinds of trouble."

"What kind of trouble?"

"The kind that ends up with you naked underneath me in that bed, that hasn't been slept in for years, begging me for mercy."

"Mmm, my favorite kind of trouble."

"There's not another house anywhere near here, baby. Nobody would hear how loud you get for me."

"Good. But we're making sandwiches first. I need sustenance." Shaking my ass for him, I raced back down the hallway to the kitchen.

His laughter echoed after me. There. That's how my big bad Beret should sound. When I leaned to look in the old refrigerator, he scooted in front of me, lifted, and had me over his shoulder in one quick move. I kicked my legs beside his face, laughing hysterically. "I'm trying to make you a sandwich," I reminded him.

"I know." He sat me down on the countertop. "But I dragged you all the way out here and then made you endure Duke. The least I can do is make you dinner." He dug a loaf of white bread out of the pantry and located cheese slices in the fridge. "Looks like I can do grilled cheese. However," he balanced a lopsided skillet on the stove, "I cannot put mayo on it as I am still not over the mayonnaise truck comment."

Still unable to believe everything that had happened in the last few days, I sighed. "I completely understand. I'm good with just cheese. I can't believe Ms. Mallory got herself involved with actual criminals. The police never called me. I wonder if they let her go."

"No idea. Whole thing was insane."

"It was sweet what she was trying to do but damn, when she decides to fall down a rabbit hole she really does it right."

I watched him spread margarine on the bread and set it in the hot skillet. When he flipped the first sandwich, I admired the slight flex of his biceps as the worked. "Until you said that about them not winning me so they could get a copy of your check, I hadn't figured out what exactly the mistake you heard them refer to was. I was flying by the seat of my pants. You saved my ass again."

"I didn't figure it out until you said something about them living off of other people's checking accounts. And your ass is unfairly perfect. Seriously, other men are probably jealous so I'm happy to save it whenever you need me to."

"Oh yeah, the exit wound is quite the sight."

Someday I'd convince him. "Your scars make up the man you are. The man who gave everything for this country and for his team. I love that man, scars and all. It just didn't make sense to me that they'd only want my credit cards. Those can be turned off too easily. With my bank account information plus my address from a check, they could've done a lot of damage. Plus, Victoria said something nasty about a check and a mistake to Megan the night of the auction. I didn't know what she meant then."

He piled the sandwiches on a paper plate. "They were too vague with Megan. She really didn't get what they were using her for. I could tell. She heard the part about letting them win the wealthiest bachelors in the room but she missed that she was supposed to let you win whoever you bid on."

"I guess." I didn't really want to talk about it anymore. I still felt like a fool,even if it had gotten me where I wanted to be. We were standing in the shadow of a whole other mountain now. We still had to tell Smith and my father. I hopped off the counter and tried to clear the table. "Would it be okay if I moved the centerfolds before we eat?" I held up a few copies of Playboy from fifteen years ago.

"That's what he wanted me to bring to the hospital." Griff shook his head. "Sorry. Just put them...wherever."

We devoured the sandwiches there in his father's kitchen as the warm mountain breeze whispered through the open windows. "Hey, Griff?"

"Yeah, baby? You want another beer?" The jangle of beer bottles rattled through the air when he opened the refrigerator.

"I'm good but there is something I think you should do."

Grabbing a towel, he twisted the cap. "What's that?"

"I think you should tell your dad about finding your mom. I think it would be good for you to clear the air, so to speak."

"I don't want to clear the air. I want him to get better and then I want to go back to enduring a phone call to him a few times a year."

I wiped the grease off of my fingers with the same towel he'd used to open the bottle. "I don't think that's really what either of you wants. He's scared and in his own weird way he misses you. I could tell. I think that might be why he always says awful things. He wants your attention."

"Yeah, well..." he downed another sip of his beer, "...I spent eighteen long years wanting his. He'll live." He scooped up our bags and marched back down the hallway to his bedroom.

"Yeah," I breathed. "And until one of you gives a little, both of you will be miserable."

Trailing after him down the worn carpeted hall, I found him

stripping his old bed. He made quick work of locating fresh sheets from the hall closet and stretching them over the mattress.

"Need some help?" I smoothed the blanket he fanned out.

"I got it, baby. I'll scrub the bathroom for you in a second."

While I believe every woman in the world would agree on the supreme sexiness of a man scrubbing anything, I didn't need him to try to clean up his past for me.

"Stop." I grabbed his hands. "You don't have to clean anything. I'm not some spoiled four-star general's daughter. I thought you knew that."

The pain in his eyes was raw, edged with an anger I wasn't sure he fully understood. "You know I never thought of you like that. Why would you even say that?"

I gestured to the freshly made bed. "You've either been apologizing, or cleaning, or cooking since we got here."

"That is not all I have done. You harassed me about Maroon 5 then danced around the room. We talked about Megan Mallory and the..." Irritation swept the pain from his gaze. "Dammit, I've got nothing. I'm out of workable trios or foursomes."

I wrapped my arms around his neck and pressed my cheek to the sculpted wall of chest muscle. "Clearly, it's been a really long day. I don't think you slept at all last night. Why don't we go on to bed?"

"Hey," he tipped my chin upward with his fingers. "Just because I don't want to talk with my dad doesn't mean I don't want to talk to you. You know that, right?"

"I know. I just thought it might help."

50

GRIFF

Her hair hung in limp waves that draped over her shoulders. Her eyes were red-rimmed from that endless day. Exhaustion weighted us both and yet she was trying so damn hard to mend all of the tattered edges of my life.

"I meant to thank you for trying to tell Smith this morning. That means so much to me but I think we should tell him together. We're in this together," she reminded me.

At one time in my life, there had been eleven men I trusted above all others and without any doubt. Half of them were gone and I still had no clue what to do with that. The only thing that stitched the gaping wound was her.

"Together is how I want to do everything, Hannah. You're the only thing on this whole damned planet that..." I forced myself to go on with the entirety of this confession. "That makes me believe somehow everything is going to be all right. You make me glad to be alive. I love you so much. I know your dad is someone who means a lot to you and that you think if I'd just talk to mine it would undo years of lies and anger and abuse, but that just isn't the way it always works, okay? This, right here"—I gestured between us—"this feels really good. The way it was always supposed to be. I'll even buy into your optimism that Smith won't hate me for the rest of my life because I want to believe that so fucking badly. But me and my father....." I shook my head. "That's just a bottomless well of pain I have no intention of throwing myself in anymore." Someday soon, she'd have to see just how badly parents could fuck over your life. I still hated that ultimately I'd have to tell her what the general had done. I wasn't sure I was worth that.

"Okay." She nodded. I studied the tiny dip at the top of her lips and watched her long eyelashes close in extended blinks. My eyes tracked from the hollow at the base of her throat to the plump swells of her breasts tempting me under the V-neck of her T-shirt. I brushed my thumb over the seam of her lips, needing to touch what I was about to devour.

Every single thing about the day had been surreal. We'd existed in other people's warped realities long enough. I needed to ground us in that moment, in that room, in my arms, in my bed.

Her eyes closed as I slanted my lips over hers. Since she'd stepped out in front of me in the lobby of The Obelisk hotel, I'd rushed every encounter. That's how it always had to be. I would try to absorb as much of her as I possibly could because there was always a stopwatch on our time together. No more. Tonight, I was taking my time with her, savoring her, relishing the fact that as badly as I was about to fuck up my life, she was more than worth it.

She parted her lips under the persuasion of my tongue. The flavors of the beers we'd consumed melded with that sweetened spice that was all her. She'd been there for me in every possible way she was able since the first time we'd met. Today was no exception.

Tonight, I was going to prove to her that I'd be there for her no matter what life threw our way. I eased her T-shirt up her waist, desperate to touch her skin. My hand splayed across her abdomen as I pushed the shirt higher. Soft warmth filled my palms. The two sides of my soul went to battle over her once again. Her fierce protector and her ultimate corrupter. This time I would be a warrior over her. I tossed the T-shirt away.

She swayed against me. The cool night air carried her warm

vanilla scent to my lungs as I popped the clasp of her bra. She lifted her head and I sank my lips back to hers, starved for the soft confection of her mouth. When I'd rid her of the bra, I slowed, letting myself really explore the tender swells of her breasts. Her sweet little gasp and delectable shiver took up residence in the very marrow of my bones.

More. I needed more. Trailing my hungry, open-mouthed kisses down her neck, I centered my mouth over her right nipple and felt it bead against my tongue. I took it captive.

A needy moan urged me onward. Wrapping my hands around her ass, I coaxed her closer as I drowned myself in the sheen of sweat that had gathered between her breasts.

Her fingers wove through my hair. Her back arched offering me more of the very thing I needed to go on. I popped the snap on her shorts to reveal a sweet little pair of lace panties that matched the bra.

Unable to help myself, I traced my fingertips lower. A greedy growl kicked up from low in my gut as I encountered wet lace and raw heat. "Why didn't you tell me, baby?" Sliding my hand to the back of her open shorts, I cupped her delectable little ass and pressed the evidence of her arousal against my hard on. She trembled from the friction as I rocked her up and down against my obvious hunger for her. "Why didn't you tell me you were so wet for me?"

Her quick pants of breath only served to stoke the fire already blazing between us. "I need you," she whimpered.

"I know what you need, sweetheart. I'm gonna take good care of my baby." Lifting her up into my arms with ease, I laid her out in the bed of my youth. Somehow she seemed to fit there as well. The only woman capable of mending the two broken halves of my life. I slipped the shorts and panties down those long legs and then painted kisses up her inner thighs. I skimmed my knuckles over her creamy pussy watching her writhe all for me. I indulged my tongue in the flavors of her but she needed more. I knew.

Shedding my clothes, I grabbed one of the condoms I'd shoved in my wallet that morning. I turned off the lamp, and watched the streaming moonlight from the window bathe her slight curves. The very window I'd broken twice with a baseball, the same one I'd stared out of to wonder what life might be like outside of that trailer.

As gently as I was able, I extended my body over hers, needing every square inch of her skin to be in contact with mine. Those cool blue eyes heated with desire. My cock pressed against her warm, swollen folds, blanketing me in heaven. "Let me take you like this, baby." Bracing on one elbow, I drew her hands together and pinned them over her head, pressing them into the mattress with one of my own. I needed to feel her soft body pressed to my hardened strength, needed to be absorbed by her. She would only ever be vulnerable to me and I would protect her until my last breath.

"Yes," she gasped. "Please."

Pausing only long enough to roll a condom on, I rocked forward, guiding my cock against her clit. Back and forth, slow and steady, watching her eyes close and her lips part on a keening moan. Tenderly, I sank deep inside her, drowning out every complication and every bit of insanity the day had provided. Her open thighs cradled my hips. Her nipples pressed insistently against the tats on my chest. All of my scars were hidden against her skin. Her silky channel drew me in like she'd been created for me alone. "Just relax and let me get you there, baby. Let me take care of you."

51

HANNAH

The next morning, I closed my eyes to savor the last few sips of the best coffee I'd had in a long, long time. I'd been to all of the coffee bars in Denver and they had nothing on the hippie eclectic coffee shop in downtown Boise. "Say what you will about Idaho but their coffee rocks," I informed Griff who'd just ordered another basket of muffins for us to share.

"I told you this place was good and my disdain for this state probably has more to do with Duke than the potato capital of the free world."

"Wonder how Duke's feeling this morning." I pulled apart a pumpkin chai muffin that tasted like the very best parts of Sunday brunches mixed with Thanksgiving topped with cream cheese frosting.

"I'm sure he's still giving everyone hell. They're likely to discharge him for being an ass which means I'll be back down here trying to get him to take care of himself." Griff sounded like he'd rather shove a fork in his own eye than return to care for his father.

"I'll come with you but I got the distinct impression Georgia would like to be charged with caring for dear old Duke."

"The woman must be a saint."

"I wonder how they met." I tried to imagine Duke sweet-talking a woman at a bar or maybe at the senior center. "Did he have girlfriends after your mom left?"

"He had women but not any actual relationships that I knew of. He used to tell me to go sleep in the barn the nights he had his dates come home with him. Damn cold in Idaho at night, let me tell you."

Every recollection Griff shared about his father widened the hole in the balloon of hope I'd stupidly inflated in my chest. His father had skirted the border line between terrible and abusive and had crossed that boundary on several occasions. I remembered once when Griff told me he hadn't found boot camp to be all that bad, at least he'd had a bed that was his that he could sleep in every night. Now, I fully grasped what his life had been like before he went from boy to soldier.

"You're sure we can go back to Vegas today?" I studied the available flights on my phone and then accidentally wiped my sticky fingers on my jeans. Griff dipped his napkin in a glass of water and handed it to me to scrub my legs. "Someday I will be able to eat an entire meal without getting it on my clothes," I repeated my mantra though it was yet to come true.

That deep chuckle of his stirred inside of me. "I kind of liked covering you with ice cream myself."

Heat pricked my cheeks. "Did you?"

"Hell yeah, baby."

"I liked that, too. We could do more of that back in Vegas."

"And on that note, yes, I want to go back today. I'll come back out here and check on him after he's out of the hospital. Maybe I can hire a nurse to look in on him if Georgia comes to her senses and decides to get out while she still can."

"More coffee, sir?" the waitress asked as she approached.

Griff considered.

"We should probably stop stalling and get to the hospital," I reminded him.

"Yeah, fine." He fished his wallet out of his back pocket and paid the bill.

Ten minutes later, we drew on deep resolve and outstanding coffee as we headed inside Duke's room.

Georgia was standing beside him trying to get him to eat the small box of high-fiber cereal that was on the tray for breakfast. Duke was not having it. "Tastes like that tofu crap on a slab of concrete. If that's how I have to eat now, I'd rather just die."

Griff rubbed his temples. "First of all, Dad, when have you ever had tofu? I lived ten months out of the year eating MRE's. You'll survive fiber flakes. And if you keep giving her crap, I'll arrange for you to meet your maker sooner than later. Man the fuck up."

"They already gave me two shots this morning so why don't you man the fuck up, son?"

"Believe it was you who told me at the ripe old age of six that the tetanus shot I had to get because you left rusted metal sheeting out in the barn served me right for being a dumbass. Looks like karma rode in on a gurney this time."

Dear Lord. This was going nowhere good and it was traveling rather quickly. "Duke, come on. Aren't you hungry? They're not going to bring you anything else. Just try it. It's not so bad," I coaxed.

Georgia smiled at me. "He just likes to complain."

"Pretty sure it's hard-wired into his DNA," Griff huffed.

Duke did take two minuscule bites of the cereal before he shoved the Styrofoam bowl away, sloshing the milk as it slid and then ordered someone to clean up his mess. Georgia mopped up the milk on the tray with a napkin. God bless that dear, sweet woman. I had half a mind to gag him with the spoon itself.

"Georgie was thinking you and me should talk. Maybe the girls could go to the cafeteria and find me some real food," Duke informed his son. Those delicious muffins I'd indulged in turned to bricks in my stomach. If I left Duke and Griff in a room alone for any length of time there was a decent chance the entire hospital would implode from the detonated rage.

"Talk about what?" Griff demanded.

"Why you never come to see me."

"I don't come to see you because you're an ass. There. Conversation over."

"Well now, I think Duke knows he hasn't always done right by you, Griffin. Maybe he'd like to apologize." Georgia's desperation leaked into her insistence. I met Griff's incredulous gaze.

"If you want to talk, then talk, old man." Griff's arms crossed over the expanse of his chest as he glared down at his father. In that moment, he certainly did look more god than man.

"I don't want to do it in front of her." He pointed his finger three inches from my face.

"Get your fucking finger out of her face," Griff snarled.

Okay, maybe it was time to let them go at it. If Duke was really going to apologize, it might be worth it. Griff deserved his apologies a thousand times over. "It's fine. Why don't we go take a walk Georgia? You can tell me how you two met." I gestured to the door.

"I'd love that." Hope and delight twinkled in her pale brown eyes, weary from spending the night taking care of Duke.

"Text me if you need me," I whispered to Griff as we headed out into the corridor.

52

HANNAH

Georgia and I made one lap around the cardiac unit and then she stopped outside of Duke's room. Apparently, she wasn't as interested in telling me how she'd met Duke as she was hearing him apologize to his son. Spying on a Green Beret was never a good idea. The likelihood of getting caught was extremely high and I didn't want to be intrusive. I wanted Duke and Griff to have their moment whatever might come out of it.

"We could go get Duke some flowers or something from the gift shop," I urged quietly.

"No. I want to hear this." She edged closer to the partially opened door.

The squeak of nurses' shoes as their owners paced up and down the corridor and constant buzz of visitors and machines muffled her explanation.

Okay, then. We were officially eavesdropping. I doubted Griff would care. I knew more than his father did about his past.

"Georgie thinks I ought to be nicer to you. I told her you were a damned Green Beret. You didn't need me to be nice," was Duke's opening line.

"Did it ever occur to you that you're my father not my CO?" Griff sneered. Okay, that was heated but they were sharing real feelings. Maybe this would be good.

"I lied to you," Duke said suddenly. "When you were a kid. About your mom."

Oh holy fuck. Here we go. I dug my fingernails into my palm and glanced toward the skies with a quick silent prayer that somehow Griff might get some closure.

"Yeah, I know that, Dad."

"How the hell do you know that? You don't know anything."

I ground my teeth. *Stop being an asshole!* I wanted to scream.

"I found Mom. She's working in some bar up in Montana with her new husband and the half-brothers I never knew I had. I talked with the husband. Never let on who I was but he mentioned that she'd been married to a real shitwagon and had a kid before they met. Seems she got sick and tired of putting up with the two of us so she met him on the state line and never looked back."

Georgia's eyes rounded with shock.

"Why the hell would he tell you that?"

"People tell me shit, Dad. It's how my job works. People lay their shit on me and I take it. I've watched enough men die to know every fucking regret anyone could possibly have in this life. I had to hear them all."

"Who the hell gave you permission to go looking for her?" Duke sneered.

"I don't need permission to do anything at all, Duke. I'm a grown man. I get to live my life any way I please. Why the hell did you tell me you kicked her out? Of all the shit you could've said why did you lie about that?"

"You needed someone to be mad at." A cold block of realization sank slowly through me, cementing my shoes to the floor of St. Luke's Medical Center. Of all the things I thought Duke might say, that wasn't one of them.

"What?" Griff demanded.

"You were just like me. You needed someone to be mad at and I figured..."

"You figured what?"

"That it should be me. I didn't want you to blame yourself for her leaving."

I placed my palm along the cool painted concrete blocks that comprised the wall trying to hold myself upright. I wanted to go to Griff, to hold him in my arms, but he had to hear his father out.

Silence ate up far too many seconds. "I didn't need someone to be mad at, Dad," he choked. "I needed a parent."

"I didn't know how to do that," Duke admitted. His voice almost somber now. I closed my eyes and prayed Griff would understand that.

"I figured that out all on my own." Griff's tone had been drained of all of its fury.

"What's with you and Hannah? She's been worrying sick over you for years now. You can't keep your damn hands off of her. Why don't you make an honest woman out of her?"

My pulse thundered in my ears. What would he say to that? "I'd marry her right now if I could. It's complicated."

"Complicated," Duke scoffed. "That's a bunch of bullshit coward speak."

"You don't know what the fuck you're talking about, old man. Stay out of it."

"What if I don't want to stay out of it? What if I'm worried about you? I may not have been much of a dad but I do want you to have a better life than I did. You've...been through a buncha shit you... shouldn't a had to go through."

"You want a better life? Why don't you marry Georgia then? And treat her a whole hell of a lot better than you did mom. And for Christ sakes get rid of the Playboys. What are you, fourteen?"

"I can't marry Georgia." Duke sounded like the very idea was preposterous. I glanced Georgia's way. Determination cast those kind brown eyes. I grinned. Duke Haywood was going down.

"Why not?" Griff demanded.

"'Cause, it's like you said, I'm an ass. Now, why can't you marry your Hannah?"

The lengthy pause was agonizing. I leaned closer still and willed him to answer. He could shatter any lock anywhere. Nothing could keep him out if he wanted in. I just needed him to release the things he had in the lockbox of his own soul. "Her brother is my best friend and her father hates me enough to try to get me and his own son killed."

Shock parted at my scalp and sank slowly down my body. What was he talking about? I leaned closer.

"Her brother will get over it. I know I never gave you a reason to but trust me on that. What the hell are you talking about with her daddy? Ain't he a big-time army general?"

"Yeah, that's him." An audible breath pressed from Griff's lungs. My feet scooted even closer to the cracked door. "I never told you but I met Hannah a long time ago. Back when I first got out of Q training. We started dating right off. I swear I fell in love with her the first time I saw her. We kept it a secret. She's a good bit younger than me and we figured if her dad found out he would birth an entire platoon. I got sloppy and we got caught. The next morning I got called into his office. He said if I didn't stay away from Hannah, he'd make certain that I got sent so far away I'd never make it back.

"The next day we were on a flight to Eritrea. I know that's how they make it look in the movies but that's not how it is in real life. We get a minimum of a week, usually more before we're deployed for training and prep, but not that time. We were told to pack and we were gone. The pilot dropped us forty miles from our target zone in the middle of jihadist territory and he did it on purpose. He was court-martialed for it. The general let the pilot take the fall for trying to get us killed all because he couldn't stand that she was in love with me. How fucked up is that? Almost got his son murdered because of me."

Vomit swirled to a maelstrom in my gut. My throat burned as bile shot upwards from my chest. No. No way. My father had done some unorthodox things when it came to me dating but he would never have done that.

"Sonuvabitch," Duke spat.

"Yeah, and that's not all. If I hadn't gotten caught with her, we would never have been sent to Eritrea. The way it works with Beret teams is that we run on a cycle. Your first deployment determines your next and the next one after that all the way up until you retire. If I hadn't been so stupid and reckless and he hadn't sent us to Africa unprepared, we wouldn't have been in Najaf when we were attacked."

Panic drowned out the rest of Griff's explanations. The constant hum in my ears turned to a deafening blare. He couldn't have. Surely. I had to know. I spun on my heels but then turned back. "I have to talk to my father. Please don't tell Griff I'm gone yet," I whispered to Georgia and raced out of the hospital.

Four minutes later, my hollow stomach found ground near my ankles, while I was in an Uber flying to the Boise airport. I already had my ticket to Denver. I wanted the truth and my father was going to give it to me.

53

T-BYRD

I meant every word I'd said to Griff about him figuring his shit out with Hannah. Chris was gone now and it was my job to make sure the rest of Team Seven got the best they could possibly get out of life. But work was hella busy and I needed my weapons expert and the guy who could literally break into Fort Knox to come back.

My cell rang in my pocket as I pulled back into the parking deck from a job that entailed a load of AR's that were not supposed to be where they ended up. "Talk," I ordered Rylee.

"Good morning to you, too. If you're going to give Griff a week off, you're going to have to hire someone to fill in. General Mendoza has called twice about that deal he wants you to look over and that chick who won't ever give me her name wants to know if any progress is being made on her case."

Of course she did. "Uh, I'll take care of Mendoza. Smith's gonna have to take on Miss we-need-secured-servers-and-a-VPN-yesterday."

"Yeah, well, I don't know what crawled up Hagen's ass and lit a fire but he stormed out of here two hours ago."

Shit. "Did he say where he was going?"

"No, but I have never seen him so pissed."

Fuck, fuck, fuckety, fuck, fuck. "K, I'm heading in."

I took the stairs three at a time and flew through the door to Tier Seven. Rylee looked at me like I'd painted my face blue and yanked off my shirt when I raced past her desk and flew into Smith's office. She followed after me. "What are you doing?"

"Figuring out exactly how fucked my day is going to be."

With one quick move of his mouse and my personal override password, I stared at the last thing Smith had seen before he took off. A picture provided him via a Google alert set on his little sister of Griff kissing her cheek outside The Obelisk Hotel. This was not good. Apparently the hotel saw an advertising opportunity with their star interior designer looking like she fell in love at the hotel. They'd run a blog article about her.

And since Smith was a Comm Sergeant turned good-guy hacker, he'd gone on and hacked into the hotel's security cameras and there, for all the world to see, was Griff with his hand up Hannah's skirt kissing her with enough heat to set fire to the rainforest in the background. Jesus, he looked like he was half-mauling her.

Rylee's eyes bugged. "Holy mother of all the world's blue balls is that Griff with...Hannah Hagen?"

I managed a nod.

Two clicks of the mouse revealed the direct flight ticket to Vegas Smith was already on. Okay, we could deal with this. He had to find out sometime. Why not now? I checked the flights to Vegas. There wasn't another one for two hours. Fuck me.

"Voodoo," I shouted.

"You bellowed?" He leaned his head into Smith's office and proceeded to peel a banana.

"We're going to Vegas. Get me a jet and get ready."

"Sweet."

"We are not going to party. We're going to keep Smith from murdering Griff."

"Okay, but after we do that can we party?" He continued eating a banana like he wasn't terribly concerned.

Gripping the monitor I turned it so he could see the images on the screen.

"Holy fuck, is that Hannah?" He spoke around the wad of fruit in his mouth.

"They've been like that for years. For obvious reasons, he didn't feel like he could say anything. But now, we're going to have to play marriage counselor for Smitty and Griff."

"Somebody had their hand up my sister's skirt like that I'd definitely kill them," Voodoo announced.

"Not helpful."

"All I can tell you is he'd reached supreme rage before he even made it out the door. How do you plan to get him to be chill with his best friend shucking his little sister's oyster?" Rylee asked.

"Have I ever gone in without a plan? I have a plan. I just...have to think of it." I considered every possible scenario. There had to be some way to get Smith to see how happy Hannah was with Griff. And then I had it. I picked up the phone on Smith's desk.

"Who are you calling?" Voodoo was on his phone getting us a pilot.

"Backup." The phone rang twice before she answered. "Hey, Maddie, it's T."

54

GRIFF

Every hair on the back of my neck stood. I popped the knuckles on my right hand twice. Something was off. Something more than the oddity of me sharing shit with my father. My heart tripped over its next few beats and then stalled. Staring at my father in a hospital bed, I wondered if I was having a heart attack as well.

But the hollow in my ribcage wasn't an attack. It was a pained emptiness. Georgia returned from her walk carrying a Styrofoam cup of coffee. Guilt was etched in the deep lines surrounding her mouth.

"Where's Hannah?" I was on my feet heading toward the door before she spoke. Realization surged up my spine and my heart flew.

"Well, um, she asked me not to tell you she'd gone but, you know, lying is a sin. I went to get coffee first and there was a line so that's something. Maybe she won't be too mad at me. She left out of here a while ago."

Panic and loss scorched my blood. "Gone where?" I recognized the harsh fury in my own tone. The last time I'd heard it was to shout instructions to Voodoo when the fuckers who'd taken us down turned on us. The abandonment I'd felt for most of my life resurrected itself in my chest.

"I'm not sure exactly. We uh..."

"What? You what?" I seethed.

"We overheard you talking...about her father." Translation: we eavesdropped on a conversation I forced you to have.

"Son, what the hell are you still standing here for? Go after her." That was the first order my father had ever given me that made any sense at all. "You two are meant to be. May not be easy but it sounds like her daddy's an even bigger jackass than I am. She needs you."

"Did she believe what she heard me say?" I had to know what I was dealing with when I got to her. I had to have a plan. Did she run from me and to her father or to him in defense of me?

"I don't really know." Georgia busied herself pulling Duke's blankets higher up his chest.

I burst from the room like a detonated bomb and collided with an orderly pushing a cart of bedpans. Leaping over the shitpan spillage that clattered from the cart, I dodged and ducked around all matter of hospital personnel and visitors, I threw open the doors to St. Luke's and was standing by my old Jeep in record time.

Throwing it into reverse, I backed out and touched Hannah's name on my phone. By the fourth ring, I was out of the parking lot.

"Hi, you've reached Hannah Hagen, Owner and Lead Designer of Palindrome Design..."

"Dammit!" I tossed the cell in the passenger side seat. It landed right where her ass should've been. I'd known better. I should never have let that story breach my mouth. I'd kept it a secret for seven fucking years and it had destroyed everything just like I knew it would as soon as it was given breath. Evil is corrosive and indiscriminate. It takes out everything in its path.

The thing that pissed me off the most was the fact that if she was running from me because she didn't believe her father capable of such a thing, he was about to get his way despite everything he'd done. And that was what kept me flying to the damned airport. Surely, she hadn't gotten on a flight yet. I had to talk to her. I had to make her believe me. She had to know what kind of rat bastard he was. I'd spent years protecting him. Hannah and I were worth fighting for. Dammit, why had it taken me so long to figure that out?

Rolling through two red lights and flat out running one, I made it to the airport in eight minutes. Abandoning my car in the nearest lot, I flew inside. "Hannah!" I shouted in the vicinity of the ticketing lines receiving several odd stares but no answer.

My mind instantly cordoned off the area and searched every face in every line in the airport. She wasn't there. Pulling my phone from my pocket, I did precisely what she must've done. I searched flights. When nothing appeared, I stepped up to a ticketing agent. The people behind me in line would have to get over it. "I need a ticket to Denver now. Preferably one that would allow me to actually arrive in the next ten minutes."

The agent eyed me cautiously. "Okay. Uh..." she hit a few keys on her computer and then forced a smile. "United has a nonstop to Denver at 2:30."

"That's three fucking hours from now. I cannot wait that long. Wait, is that the only flight to Denver today?" If that's the flight Hannah had booked, she was probably at the gate waiting, which would provide me ample opportunity to swear to her that I knew how fucked-up it was to have a shitty dad and that I would always take care of her.

The attendant continued to eye me cautiously.

"Look, my girl just went running out of St. Luke's where my father is because he had a heart attack and I have to talk to her. Can you cut me a break, please? Here"—I pulled my military id—"Special Forces. I swear I'm not crazy just fucked."

She nodded and searched the flights once again. "United had another nonstop that left about fifteen minutes ago."

"Is there any way you can tell me if she made that flight?"

"I'm sorry, sir. I can't do that."

Defeat tugged at my resolve. Dammit. "That 2:30 is the earliest Denver flight, you're sure? Any other airport with an earlier flight?"

"I'm sorry, sir. That's the quickest anyone other than maybe the air force is going to get you to Denver."

"Yeah, had a feeling you were going to say that. I somehow doubt they're going to scramble me an F-15 no matter how much I've done for this country. Give me that 2:30 and tell me the gate that the earlier flight left out of."

"Is your girlfriend really pretty with long blonde hair and would she have been crying?"

"I'm going to go with yes." The knowledge that she would most definitely have shed tears slammed a hammered fist through my gut.

"I think I saw her." She glanced around and edged a few steps away from the nearest ticketing agent a few stations down. "I saw her pull a pack of crackers from her bag and give them to the homeless guy that was outside this morning even though she was the one sobbing. That's the only reason I'm telling you this so listen very closely to what I'm about to say."

Listening, reading, judging, sorting those were all things I did without anyone having to instruct me to do them. They'd been branded in my skull by the United States Army Special Forces. I gave her a single nod.

"Her flight *left* from B19."

She was gone. A boulder with claws strangled me. "How'd she get through security that fast?" I asked but I already knew.

"She has TSA pre-check so she made it through security really fast. For what it's worth, I hope you get this worked out. She was really upset."

"Thanks."

There was only one other possibility for getting to her faster. I touched T's name on my phone. He answered on the first ring. "Listen, man, you need to keep a low profile until we get there..." he began.

"I need a flight to Denver. Now. Can you get me a private flight?" I didn't give a damn about whatever it was T was freaking out about. Hannah was the only thing that mattered.

"Wait. What? Why the hell do you need a flight to Denver?"

"I'm in Boise. My dad had a heart attack. We came up here to check on him and now... Hannah's on her way to Denver and I have to get to her."

"What the hell happened?"

"Not right now." That story would never rattle my vocal cords ever again.

"So, Hannah is in Denver and you are in Boise?" T clarified.

"For the moment, yeah, but if you can get me a flight I'll be in Denver fixing this. If you can't, I won't be there until this afternoon and I can't let her get to her father before I get to her."

"I can't get you a plane. V can't even get us a plane right now. Can you get a commercial flight to Denver?"

"Not for another three hours."

"Do that. We'll meet you in Denver. This is all going to work out. I just need to talk to Smith," T explained.

"What the hell does he have to do with any of this?"

"His sister. According to you there's something with *his* father and also *his* best friend. I'd say he has a lot to do with all of this. I'll see you as soon as I can. Have to pick someone up but then we'll meet you in Denver."

55

HANNAH

I switched my phone back on as soon as we touched down in Denver. I should never have left him there but I had to know the truth. If my father had really done the things Griff accused him of, he needed to say that to my face and I wasn't certain I'd get the truth if Griff was there with me.

Nineteen voice mails and more than thirty texts. Didn't even have to open them to know he'd been trying to explain himself and console me from eight-hundred miles away. Before I could listen to the voice mails, Smith's name appeared on my screen. Talking to him just then wasn't a great idea. I had to know if Daddy had really been insane enough over me and Griff to sacrifice Smith's safety but the knowledge that I could have lost my brother and the love of my life on their first mission had me answering the phone. Besides, he had to know about me and Griff and it had to be me that told him.

"Hey." I tried to erase the emotion from my throat as I stood to file off of the plane.

"Where the fuck are you?" He growled.

"I'm in Denver. What the hell is wrong with you?"

"Sure you are," Smith snarled.

"Hey, I don't know what the hell is up with you but I don't have time for your shit either. If you have something to say, say it."

I momentarily forgot that I was disembarking a plane until mothers started slapping their hands over their children's ears. Dammit.

"Where's Griff, Hannah?" Menace slithered in his question.

My brain, heart, and entire pulmonary system couldn't quite remember what they were supposed to do to function. "What?" That single syllable was the only word my mind seemed to recognize.

"Yeah. That's what I thought. Now, where the fuck are you really?"

"I am in Denver about to go to Mom and Dad's house." Fury rushed the blood back through my veins and the words spilled forth as well. "Knowing Griff as well as I do, and I do know him very well, I'd bet my life that he's already on a flight here as well. Any other questions?" I could just make out someone speaking on what sounded like an intercom system. I swore I heard the words "Welcome to McCarran International Airport."

"Are you seriously in Vegas right now?" I demanded.

"Stay right where you are. Do not leave Mom and Dad's. You got me?"

"No, Smith, I don't. I am not a child. I do not need my big brother or my father to protect me, or to come check on me, or to order me around. I will *go* where I want, when I want, and *do* what I want, when I want, and you need to get that through your head. I need both you and Dad to chill the fuck out but we'll get to that later. I'm hanging up. Do not call me back until you figure out a way to be okay with Griff and me being in love because we have been for seven long years." I ended the call and sprinted down the airport.

Every lane of Denver's highway system was jam packed full of people trying to get somewhere. There was a wreck on I-25. It took me an hour and a half to get out to Castle Pines, the golf-course community where my father had chosen to retire.

As I drove through the quiet neighborhood, it finally occurred to me that I was about to accuse my father of attempted murder. My dad, the army general who had for the entirety of his adult life fought to make sure others were safe. The safety and security of his family was always his top priority. Griff had to have been wrong. He just had to have been.

And there he was studying a boxwood with the hedge trimmers locked in his grip. My father believed that landscaping should be much like soldiers, neat, orderly, and in line. Flinging myself out of my truck, I tried to taste my words before I spat them from my mouth.

"Daddy?" Why did my voice have to shake?

"Hannah B? What on earth?" He set the trimmers on the front steps and met me in the middle of the driveway. "What happened, little one? I thought you were in Vegas. Why are you crying?"

"I am not a little girl. I am not your little one anymore. I need to know every single detail of what you said to Griff the night you caught us together and then I need you to tell me everything you know about Smith's first mission when they got sent to Eritrea. I want every single detail. Leave nothing out because I have to tell you, right now, you're not looking very heroic and I can't quite figure out how that could be possible."

"What are you talking about? What does Haywood have to do with any of this?"

"Do not stall, Dad. Just... don't. Griff and I never stopped wanting each other or being in love just because you decided to interfere. When I leave here, and as soon as we figure out exactly what happened, I'm going to marry him. You can either be there and be happy for us or you can stay here and pout but I'm not going to continue to keep the most important relationship of my life a secret." There. Take that, General.

"I think we better go inside."

"Fine. But I want the truth without margins."

"Fine, but I have one question. Where is Sergeant Haywood?"

"I'm certain he is on his way here so we need to talk now." I followed him inside the house.

"You want a beer?" The hum of the refrigerator was the only sound in their immaculate home.

"No, Dad, I want the truth."

"Understood. You mind if I have one?"

56

GRIFF

I sweet-talked Hannah's admin assistant out of her parents' address as I climbed in a rental Honda at the Denver airport. The amount of damage the general could already have done in the hours it had taken me to get here might've been more than I could undo, but dammit, I wasn't going down until the bitter end. He could look me in the eye and lie to me but I wouldn't allow him to do that to his daughter.

Forty-five long-ass minutes later, I parked on the street and sprinted up the driveway of General Gerald T. Hagen's home.

"What the fucking hell do you think you're doing with my little sister?" seared through the air. I turned back to stare down my best friend. Smith slammed the door on a similar rental car. His long legs ate up the distance between us.

"I'm in love with her. Come on, Smith, you know me better than you know anyone. I would never hurt her. Deep breaths, man. Chill the fuck out."

His hands collided with my chest in his declaration of war. I stepped back. It took everything in me not to respond. Every ounce of training I had sizzled under my skin. It was right there but I wasn't doing this. He had every right to hate me but I had a right to be heard.

"Did you hear me? Come on. I am so fucking in love with her I can't see straight. I can't sleep. I can't even breathe. I know I should've told you. Hate me. I deserve that but don't make me hurt you."

His huff said he doubted my ability to do just that. "You think you can just go around shoving your filthy hands up her skirt?"

I caught his fist with a hard pop as the strength of his fist met my own. Using his force against him, I shoved him back. My blood raced hot and fast through me. Adrenaline flooded out to my limbs but I could not hurt him worse than I already had. "Yes, I do think that and I think that because I am in love with her. Fucking hear what I am saying to you. I didn't choose it. I also can't undo it and I don't want to."

His next swing was another miss. I jerked out of his way.

"Come on, man. We've been through too fucking much. Do not make me do this."

Utterly enraged, he dove in with a hard throat punch, I side-stepped his throw and caught his neck. Instead of bringing his face to my knee, like I'd been trained to do, I shoved him away. Another fist hurled toward my chin, catching my jaw. I landed one in his chest with equal force, enough to rob him of breath for a split second and hopefully knock some sense into him. "No one wins this, Smith. Don't you get that? Equally trained. Equally matched. No one walks away if we go here. We only end up hurting Hannah."

"Fucking fight me!" he snarled.

"No."

He came at me again. Both fists flew. He landed one in my gut as his face collided with my left elbow while my right hit his sternum. We both groaned. Blood seeped from his lip. He wanted more so I locked him up with my arms to keep him from swinging. He spun away. My resolve slipped with every thundered beat of my heart.

I could just make out the squeal of a car and slamming of doors through the anguish in my head.

He went low, diving toward me. Shaking my head, I brought him to the ground. "Stop!" I shouted. "No one wins this."

His fist landed hard against my shoulder. Again, I caught him in his throw and refused to release him.

"Uncle Griff!" split the hot air surrounding us. "Stop! Please!"

Refusing to quit, Smith awkwardly tried to swing again. He hadn't seen her. I leapt to my feet. T and Voodoo were on us a second later, jerking us farther apart.

"Why are you hurting each other?" Olivia's chin trembled. She approached me cautiously and then slowly placed her little hand against my injured thigh. "Please stop."

"Smith, nothing is worth this." Maddie was in his face. "This stops right here, right now."

I lifted Olivia into my arms. She buried her face against my neck and clung to me. "I'm so sorry." I apologized to her, to my team, and to my best friend. "Honest to God, I'm sorry."

Smith tried to jerk away from T.

"Smith. You will stop this now." The commanding voice of General Gerald Hagen shook through his son. I saw a moment of doubt crease Smith's features. "Inside. All of you."

"Are you all right?" Hannah flew into my arms. I balanced her and Olivia but refused to answer. I wouldn't know if I was all right until we got to the other side of this.

"Now." The general ordered again. Not something he had to do too often.

We filed in like the good soldiers we'd once been.

"Have a seat." He gestured to sofas and chairs in the living room. Smith continued to pace and shoot me infuriated glares. "I said to take a seat, son," the general bellowed.

Smith sank down on an ottoman near Voodoo. Olivia gave me another hug and then took the seat beside Maddie. Hannah laced her fingers through mine. That sense of wholeness I only had when I was with her eased the bruises I'd certainly have come morning. But what did it mean? That she believed me? That made no sense. She wasn't crushed by whatever her father would've had to admit to make her understand what he'd done. Other than her worry over us fighting, she seemed fine.

"It seems I have quite a bit of explaining to do, but first and foremost, I owe you a debt of gratitude and an apology, Sergeant Haywood," was the general's opening statement.

I wondered momentarily if Smith had gotten in one of his signature skull punches and now I had a concussion. An apology certainly hadn't been how I expected this day to go. I used to think I had some control over my life, not much, but some. At that moment, my only choice was to sit back and watch the shit show. I didn't respond so the general continued.

"I am very sorry for threatening you when I found you and Hannah together all those years ago. It seems my words have come back to haunt me. And Smith, if you want to be mad at someone about the fact that Haywood kept something from you, be angry with me. I ordered him not to tell you. I was worried a fracture in your team could have disastrous consequences. Turns out my orders fractured my own home. So, for what it's worth, I apologize to all of you."

I tried to process his apology.

"I was initially offended that you believed I had something to do with Team Seven being sent to Eritrea so quickly but given my threat and the extent of my power, coupled with my daughter's good sense explanations, I do see how you would naturally assume I had something to do with that. I'd like to show you something, Sergeant." He handed over a file folder with a classified stamp.

"It's the pilot's court martial papers," Hannah whispered as I hesitantly opened the file. She pointed to her father's signature on the final page. "Dad's the one that brought him up on charges after he heard what happened. He had nothing to do with you being sent to Eritrea. He was the one that figured out the pilot was a sympathizer for the jihadists. He did all of the research. He's who put him away."

"That's true, Griff. I remember that." Maddie offered me a kind smile. "Team Ten had been planning to go to Eritrea. They'd been training for weeks. During one of their last training exercises their detachment commander and intelligence officer were injured. Chris told them Team Seven was ready to go. That's why you all were sent to Eritrea. I'm not entirely certain what all of this is about other than the obvious"—she gestured to me and Hannah—"but I do know General Hagen never had anything to do with Team Seven's missions."

"I would never do anything that would jeopardize my son's life. I understand you may not have experienced that from your own father, but I would also never do anything to intentionally harm the man my daughter loves. I knew she was in love with you the second I saw you two together and I'll admit it frightened me. She was very young. You, much like all Special Forces soldiers, were a little unorthodox. She had dreams and a tremendous amount of talent. I didn't want anything to distract her. I wanted her to achieve the things she'd set out to do."

"She has," I huffed.

"I am aware of that." General Hagen paused. "I have also had to bear the fact that no other man ever made her happy, no matter how many I introduced her to. The rest of what I need to communicate to you I'd prefer to do in my office. He gestured toward a nearby hallway. "While we talk, my son can locate some of his better sense and calm down."

His words prodded at my mind but the barrier I'd built was reinforced and heavily fortified. If our initial deployment as Team Seven had nothing to do with me…everything I'd ever believed was a lie. Unable to either accept or reject that information, I allowed Hannah to pull me off of the couch. I followed her into her father's plush office. His awards and medals were on the walls along with pictures of Smith and Hannah as kids. His own wedding photo was prominently displayed on his desk.

The sound of the door closing jarred me. Nothing made any sense at all. I focused on her. She was here. She didn't hate me. The rest I'd figure out later. I pulled her close and lowered my lips to hers. Touching her, hearing her, seeing her, none of those senses were enough. I had to taste her.

Her hands locked onto my shoulders pulling me closer. Her

father cleared his throat three times before she pulled away. "Perhaps we could save that for the wedding," he ordered.

"Doubt that, Dad."

He pointed to the seats positioned in front of his desk. The general settled in his large leather chair and stared me down. "Hannah expressed to me that you feel what happened to your team was largely your fault due to the fact that you believe you were in Iraq at the time you were because of your initial deployment many years before. That could not be further from the truth. However, I also know no amount of me proving to you that you had nothing to do with where you were at any given moment is going to alleviate your guilt. That's the Department of Defense's job. It is never Special Forces call but you also know that.

"You'll come up with a dozen other reasons it must be your fault and you'll continue to cling to those no matter what I say. Survivor's guilt is a part of every soldier that manages to leave the battlefield. More times than I care to recall I have watched men die. Men I sent into battle. There is nothing anyone can say that will erase that guilt from your conscience. But if I might offer you a little sage advice from my experience, I'd like to. We do not always get closure. There is no worthy reason that half of your team was killed in the prime of their life. No amount of blame or understanding would ever make that fact bearable. I know that and so do you.

"Sometimes in this life we don't get answers. We just get the pain. And let's be real, Jesus Christ himself could walk into this office and give you the explanation you think you deserve and it still wouldn't be good enough, not for any Green Beret. But He did give you something, son. He gave you my daughter's love. And that love will be what sustains you in the darkest moments of memories you'll be forced to endure for the rest of your life. He may not be in the business of always giving answers, but He did give you the very thing you need to go on. And she refused to ever give up on the two of you."

Hannah smiled. "Never surrender. My father taught me that."

General Hagen chuckled before he continued. "Suppose I should be thankful she listened occasionally. But you have also been given a chance to continue to try to make this world a better place. Did it never occur to you that every single path He set you on led you directly back to her?"

"I don't know, sir." I searched the recesses of my mind and only came up with the truth. "I kind of always thought help from above meant there was a sniper on the roof."

The general chuckled. "Trust me, son, it's even better than that and you know the army has some outstanding snipers. Now, as for the business of you two being a couple, as long as you keep my little girl happy and safe that is all I'll ever want. I got an earful this afternoon about the young man I encouraged to meet her in Vegas. All of these years, I'd hoped to make up for taking you away. I assumed you'd moved on. She seemed so miserable. I hated myself for coming between you. She pointed out that she does not need just a man she needs a damned warrior and you are that. One of the finest I've ever seen. Fair warning, my little girl is a dreamer, and a schemer, and quite a handful. I'll admit to you I never quite knew what to do with her."

A flash fire of heat settled high in Hannah's cheeks as she rolled her eyes. I took her hand. "Oh, I know, sir, why the hell do you think I fell so hard for her?"

"Good answer."

"I can also assure you that I will always do everything in my power to keep her happy and fulfilled. She might've thrown you, sir, but she's never thrown me. Probably the difference in a general and a Beret. Nonstandard *was* our standard."

"I'll accept that. She is also a keen business woman, incredibly intelligent, brilliantly talented, and she has done a great deal with what she's been given. As have you." He punctuated the last three words with fervency. "As for my son, he has always been fiercely protective of his little sister. I expect that comes from being the son and daughter of a dad who only managed to come back into town long enough to move them to another new post. Smith will come around. Just give him a little time and maybe go out of your way to show him how much you love her."

"I will, sir."

"I have no doubt."

The phone on General Hagen's desk rang. He glanced at the screen and smiled. "Normally, I wouldn't interrupt a meeting but I always take her calls."

Hannah grinned. "Must be Mom," she whispered.

I tugged on her hand until I had her full attention. "I'm sorry you heard what you heard. That's not how I wanted you to find out. And for what it's worth, I'm sorry I accused him of doing that. It was the only thing that made sense to me."

"After all the hell he put you through and threatening you like that, of course you thought he'd done it. He even sent some guy to Vegas to try to pick me up. He's overzealous but he does love me. I'm sorry I ran out on you like that. That must've made you feel awful. I did it for us but I realized on the plane that all I'd done was abandon you...just like your mom. I'm also sorry I let Georgia talk me into eavesdropping. I shouldn't have."

"Seems like maybe it worked out for the best, and you are nothing like my mother. You threw yourself into battle for us. She retreated."

"Can you give me your exact location, sweetheart? A nearby trail marker?" The general nodded and wrote down a few notes.

"Oh no." Hannah looked horrified.

"No, no, don't keep calling Search and Rescue. If they're that busy, it's not worth it. Besides, something far better than SAR is currently sitting in our home. I'll have to get them some equipment but we'll be there as soon as we can. I love you, Sarah."

As soon as he ended the call, Hannah leapt. "Is she okay? Did she fall? Is she trapped? Oh my gosh. I should never have encouraged her to do this."

"Your mother is fine. She's an army wife. She knows what she's doing. Apparently some kids decided to do some video stunt out on Devil's Head. Something for that ridiculous Facetube thing. They fell more than a hundred feet. One of them is unresponsive. The other can talk but isn't of much help. Your mother found them about an hour ago but she doesn't know how long they've been down there.

She tried to lower down some water and provisions but apparently they didn't understand how the pulley worked and dropped the supplies. With all of the rain and mudslides, Denver SAR is swamped on the more dangerous trails. Sergeant Haywood, do you feel like rappelling down a mountain? As I recall you and Smith were Team Seven's most skilled mountaineers."

As soon as he said Facetube, that idiot's words rushed back into my mind. *After that, Wigs and me are going to Denver for a mountain stunt that should bring killer views.* Jizz Stain you fuckface what have you done? "Truthfully, it's not really on my list of top ten things to do today but why the hell not?"

57

HANNAH

I watched Griff slide back into soldier mode with a mission at hand. He led me out of my father's office. Smith was pacing in the living room. Putting myself between my boyfriend and my brother, I narrowed my eyes. "I really want you to be okay with this. I love you so much but I love him, too. He makes me happy. He keeps me safe. He's pretty much the best thing in the whole world. Can you please just be happy for us, too?"

He grunted which wasn't exactly a yes but I'd keep working on him.

"After all of the hatred you've seen in this world..." Maddie stepped in, "...try not to hate love, Smith. Besides, she's been in love with him for a long time."

"You knew?" I was shocked at that.

"Well, nobody else's little sister came up with very creative excuses to come hang out with The Sevens at my house regularly." She winked at me.

My father cleared his throat. "For right now, I need you to put your irritation aside. Your mother has located two injured hikers out on Devil's Head. SAR is swamped with a mudslide. Would Tier Seven mind filling in? There are injuries. Time is definitely of the essence."

Everyone understood "yes, sir" was the only right answer. Once a general always a general.

"We can do that, sir, but I don't have any equipment. Can you get us a few AMKs?" T requested.

"That I can do."

"I forget what an AMK is," Maddie whispered to me.

Smiling at that, I squeezed her hand. "Army Mountaineering Kit." It was probably good she was letting a few things go.

She nodded. "That's right. I think I still have Chris's in the garage somewhere."

"If there are injuries, sir, I'm going to need saline IV bags and flush syringes. I've got my kit but they're likely dehydrated," Voodoo reminded my dad.

"I'll see what I can do. Give me twenty minutes to call in a few favors then we're heading out."

"Come on, Smith. Would you rather her be with some douche instead of a guy you know and love?" T asked as soon as my father left the room. "He really didn't do anything to you."

Rage seated itself in my brother's eyes again. "He lied to me for years. He took advantage of my sister when she was only a kid. And I'm quite certain he did a lot of other things I don't want to think about."

Griff shook his head but I wasn't letting this go. "No one took advantage of me. I asked him out that night Mom and Dad invited Team Seven over for the first time. Everything we have done has always been me asking him. Never him pushing anything on me because that's the kind of man he is. In fact, it was my scheming that got him to Vegas where he caught a bunch of old ladies who were trying to steal my identity."

"What?" T, Voodoo, and Smith all asked.

I rolled my eyes. "Never mind. The point is he always takes care of me. He always has. He always will."

"I swear to you I will," Griff tried.

"Oh, you swear to me, well that's something," Smith huffed.

"Stop being an ass," I spat.

Smith's eyes narrowed. He shook his head at Griff. "The only thing I can promise you is that from the very pit of my heart I hate you so fucking much right now."

"Smith, please," I urged.

He shook his head. Disbelief was still predominant in his glares. "In theory, I will get over this...eventually. But so help me, motherfucker, you ever hurt her I will end you."

"If I ever hurt her, you wouldn't have to. I'd do it myself."

"I don't like it when you fight." Olivia stared up at my brother with her little finger in the air. She looked remarkably like her father. Everyone grinned including Smith.

"Sorry about that, sweet girl." Smith scooped her up. "Someday you'll understand."

"No, I won't," she argued.

"She's stubborn like her mama." T laughed. Maddie shook her head at him. A coy grin played on her features as she elbowed T and then quickly looked away. And T's gaze lingered on her for two seconds too long. Wasn't that interesting? I glanced around to see if anyone else had noticed their slight flirtation. It seemed the mighty Green Berets were oblivious. *Men.*

"We better get ready to hike." Voodoo sighed. "I'd just like to say this morning I was promised Vegas. Now, I'm climbing something called Devil's Head which clearly has hellish connotations. I deserve a raise."

"Can I climb the mountain with you?" Olivia asked Smith.

"I...don't know baby girl." He glanced Maddie's way.

"It's pretty steep," I explained. "There are rest stops with benches but it's not an easy hike."

"I think we better stay here. Maybe we can get supper for everyone. You can help me," Maddie offered.

Olivia shrugged. "Do you promise not to hit anyone? Hitting isn't nice." She turned those huge doe eyes on my big brother.

"I promise." He set Olivia down on her feet.

"Just to clarify..." T stepped in, "...to her, not hitting includes not throwing him off the side of a mountain or doing anything at all that might require Voodoo to have to repair more than just the hikers. Got that?"

"Yeah. Whatever." He turned back to Griff and spoke through his teeth even though Maddie had sufficiently distracted Olivia with a game on her phone. "Another thing, you are not fucking my baby sister in my house so figure that shit out before you come back to Lincoln."

"I'm not coming back to Lincoln," Griff countered.

"What?" T looked like Griff had just announced his intentions to become a Dodgers fan.

"Her business is here, man."

"My business is anywhere I want to be. We are moving to Lincoln. Don't listen to him," I corrected. "Rachel and Liam can handle things here. I can fly in once a month or so but I design all over the Midwest. I don't have to be here."

Relief washed over T's features. "If I let you two stay at my house until you figure out your own place, will you come back to work? I kind of forgot how much we had to do while I was helping her get you to Vegas. We're swamped."

"We do still have a very nice suite and a week's vacation in Vegas," I reminded everyone.

Griff wrapped his arm around me. "Let's see here, the rest of the week with her in a suite pretty much made for fu..."

My brother made an odd gagging hiss noise.

"Uh, relaxing. Made for relaxing," Griff corrected, "or a week of work while staying at your house. Think I'll go with Vegas." He laughed. "But I do have you a new recruit. He can probably take some of the strain off."

"Oh yeah? Is he a tier one?"

"No, he was a Ranger but he picks things up quickly."

"Also, still pissed with you about this whole Vegas thing." Smith drove his finger into T's chest as he continued to simper.

"Her picture was in his SAPI pocket, man. You don't just keep anyone there. You know that," T vowed.

58

GRIFF

Two hours and a brutal hike later, I was tying myself a seat rappel. Hannah handed me the second locking carabiner. "Have you done this since...?" She gestured to my bad hip.

"Every few months to stay on top of my game, sweetness. I'll be fine. You just be standing right here when I get finished rescuing Jizz Stain."

"Who?"

"Oh, yeah, I met this guy on the plane to Vegas. Famous YouTuber or something. I don't know. He's a douche but he needs help and according to your old man I don't get to ask questions of the universe."

She grinned up at me. "I'll be right here and he didn't say you couldn't ask them just that you might not get an answer."

"I got you. He was right. You are the answer to every question, even the ones I haven't thought to ask yet. But I do have one more question I have to ask before we jump into this with both feet." I cinched my ropes making the ones outlining my package pull tighter.

She laughed. "What's that, you impressive thing you?"

"That? Between the ropes? Pretty sure you know what that is, baby. You seem to enjoy him," I teased.

Smith made another one of those odd gagging sounds.

"Sorry, man." I called over my shoulder.

"I do know what that is." Hannah giggled. "I meant what was your question."

"What if I can't give you everything you want? Specifically...kids." I spoke so low I wasn't certain even she'd heard me.

She gripped both sides of my face. "You know, life is a whole lot like shooting. Listen to your heart. Let it guide you. Look at what is clear right in front of you." She took another step closer so she filled my vision. "Aim at the blurry target and let the shot surprise you. I want us to let life surprise us, Griff. If I have you by my side that is the only fixed point, the only constant, I will ever need. Everything else is a shot in the dark."

"I love you." I brushed a kiss on her forehead.

"I love you, too. Now go rescue those people so we can go crash at my apartment and then go on with our vacation."

I moved my kisses to her lips. I'd rappelled several of the most dangerous cliffs in Afghanistan so this wasn't particularly worrisome but I'd never gotten to kiss her before I dropped myself straight down a mountain so I was taking the opportunity.

I finished my descender complete with a decent friction knot and watched T and Voodoo secure the fixed ropes.

"Is that my Leatherman?" The general gasped in horror as he stared down at his wife's rather odd trail hiking pack.

"I didn't think you'd need it this week," she explained.

"It has my name and rank engraved on it," General Hagen huffed.

"Yes, I know, dear. I had that done for you." She shook her head. "All right, I've spoken with the ranger's station. They're going to meet you at the lookout. When you get them to the bottom, there's a set of stairs due west about two miles that leads to the lookout. And Griff, honey, I'm so thrilled you and Hannah found your way back together. I meant to say that earlier but you know the idiots at the bottom of that cliff have distracted me. Really, who drops the supply line?"

"It's fine, Mrs. Hagen. Thanks for saying that." I made my way over to be roped into the secure lines and to pull on a pair of gloves.

"All right, boys, don't fuck this up," T instructed. Smith and I got into position.

"I still hate you," Smith stated as if I might've forgotten in the last few hours.

"Totally deserved but I am still in love with her."

"Yeah, I know so don't die because if you make her cry, I'll shoot your dead body twice."

"Noted." I kicked off.

He followed suit. We made it down quickly only braking a few times to slow our descent.

Jizz and his woman were slumped over, pale and weak. "All right, stay with me, we're going to get you down," I instructed.

"Dude, thank God you're here. Seriously, I could kiss you. Actually, no," he allowed Smith to secure him over his back in a fireman's hold to carry him to the bottom of the mountain. "You pick a base and I'm there loving it with both hands. You're like a real hero."

"If you touch any of my bases, I will throw you down this mountain," Smith warned.

"Seems fair," I chuckled as I eased the woman over my shoulders and secured a rope around her and back to my own ropes. She was in and out of consciousness. I hoped Voodoo could work his magic.

"Climbing is like way harder than it was on my Wii Outdoor game," Jizz continued to explain to Smith as he lowered them down much slower this time. "I even dropped my camera with all of my footage of us standing on the rails leaning out over the edge. This day blows."

"You don't have to talk to me. It's a complete misconception that we need to talk just because I'm saving your ass," Smith ordered.

"Hey, are you two brothers? You talk the same." Jizz pointed to me tugging on the ropes Smith had tied around him.

"Stop moving," he commanded, "and yeah...we're brothers."

When we hit solid ground and untied our passengers, we managed to get several sips of water down them from a camel pack I'd carried on my chest. They rallied some.

It took us another hour to get them to the lookout station. The rangers let Voodoo hook up IVs and bandage their wounds before they carried them up on stretchers.

"Hey, man"—I slapped Smith's shoulder as the rest of our crew walked ahead of us up the steep staircase—"I am truly sorry for whatever this is doing to you. I'm most sorry about not telling you. I'll answer anything you want to know. I'm doubting you're up for details though. But I'm not sorry I fell in love with her. I never will be."

"I know." He eyed me like he wasn't quite certain what to say to all of that. "She keeps looking at you like you put the stars in the fucking sky. She talks about you that way, too. Guess that's something. Just give me some time to wrap my head around this. Thinking about you...doing night things...hand things...under skirt things...making her *happy* makes me a little queasy. Don't be waltzing into the office in the mornings grinning and shit like that."

"I will definitely keep my waltzing and grinning to a minimum at all times when you're around."

"Good. Hey, is your hip okay? That was a long fucking hike and a rope seat is a bitch."

"It'll hurt like a mother tomorrow but it's just a thing."

"Isn't it always. Hey, I don't want you to move and I wouldn't mind having her in Lincoln close by. So, don't push for coming down here too hard."

"I don't think she's going to let me. I can't stand for her to give up her business for me." I'd always talked with Smith about the hard things. He'd never let me down. It was just the most difficult, most important thing in my world that I hadn't been able to share with him. As fucked up as it was, it felt good not to keep this from him anymore.

"She wouldn't be giving anything up, Griff. She's right. Her business is her. We all gave up a lot of our life doing what we did. Maybe let her give you this. It'd kill her if she thought she'd broken up The Sevens. You know, Triple A brings his wife to our third Thursday thing. You could probably bring her sometimes."

The Sevens had a standing dinner the third Thursday of every month at the Hi-Way diner. I'd never missed one. I couldn't believe I was going to get to keep them and her. After the life I'd lived, maybe things were really looking up.

59

HANNAH

The moonlight glinted off of the carabiner still hanging from the belt loop of Griff's jeans as he made his way up the steps to my apartment that night. I knew he had to be hurting. Rappelling down a mountain with ropes secured around his hips and then carrying a woman several miles to a lookout had taken its toll but he didn't want to take the elevator.

Mrs. Lipscomb was in one of her favorite places, outside her apartment staring up at the moonlight through the atrium windows. This time her husband was in his wheelchair beside her. When we made it to the landing, she grinned. "I see you were successful in distracting the MPs." She winked at me.

Griff's brow furrowed. "Feel like I missed something." He offered Mr. Lipscomb his hand. "Sir."

"The Sergeant returns," Mr. Lipscomb laughed.

"When did you two meet?" I asked.

"Last time I headed out of here on a Monday morning, we ran into each other," Griff explained.

"And I told you then you'd be back. I could see it in your eyes." Mr. Lipscomb's kind grin eased a little of the strain of our day.

"We were very successful. I made it up the gang plank." I grinned at my neighbors. That fact lit a sparkler under my skin that bloomed into a broad grin across my face. If I leaned closer to Griff, I could even smell the gunpowder scent of fireworks on the Fourth of July.

"Well, we're very happy for you, Hannah. The power's out again but I'll just bet your Beret can find some way to help you see in the dark."

I sighed. "I'm sure he can but for the record this is the first time there's ever been a blackout in our building that it actually worked out for me."

The Lipscombs laughed. "If you need some flashlights or candles, just knock."

"I will. Thanks." I unlocked the door by the light of the moon. When I turned back, Mr. Lipscomb was pulling his wife into his lap. The wheelchair had never slowed them down.

"I take it your power is out a lot?" Griff wasted no time collapsing in the massive chair in the corner of my darkened living room. His hungry gaze beckoned me more than the finger he was using to summon me to his lap.

"A few times every month. There's some problem with the substation." I curled up on his legs careful not to put any more pressure on his bad hip.

"I see."

"I'm sorry it's hot in here. I can open the door to the deck," I offered.

"I can think of better ways to cool off, baby. Of course, once I get you undressed I'm just going to get you hot and bothered again." His fingertips drifted down my arms, igniting every nerve ending he encountered. My nipples throbbed out a plea for his touch.

I shook my head at him. "Aren't you tired?"

"Yeah, but I can live with tired. I can't live without having you again. I spent too much time without you. I'm still making up for all that." His gaze locked on my chest. My bra wasn't doing a good job of hiding my obvious arousal. His rough fingertips skated to my breasts and circled just outside where I so desperately needed his touch. "I don't get the impression you're quite ready to go to sleep anyway."

I let my right hand track down his chest and explore the fierce bulge of his zipper line. "There are several things I'd prefer to do before we sleep," I whispered. Heat from his cock poured through the denim.

His greedy grunt filled my ears as his eyes drifted close. "Feels so fucking good when your hands are on me."

"Good." I climbed out of his lap and headed toward the bedroom.

The frustration in his eyes when they snapped open was barely visible in the moonlight. "Where the hell do you think you're going, baby?" His tone riffed with a thirst he wanted satisfied. My warrior had been tied up most of the day either in actual ropes or in the ones we'd stupidly put on this relationship. He needed to be set free.

"Why don't you come see?" I disappeared down the hallway. I heard him cursing his own hip as he took a second longer than he'd probably wanted to stand. I used that moment to peel off my clothes. As soon as he entered my room, I flung my panties in his face. He caught them and inhaled the scent without any hesitation.

I stalked toward him, rather enjoying the darkness now. His hands found purchase on my hips as I tugged his shirt from his jeans and lifted it over his head. He drew me in, pressing my skin to his. I swore every centimeter of my body could be crushed under his and I'd still want him closer.

My fingers snagged on his belt. He stopped me. "I've got it, sweetheart. Go get in bed. Be ready for me."

Oh, I was more than ready for him but this wasn't going to go exactly how he thought it would. Flinging the covers back, I crawled into my own bed and turned on my side, propped up on my elbow. I watched him toe out of his boots, shed his jeans and boxer briefs. I just caught the black ink that spanned from one shoulder to the other across his back. The "Greater love hath no man than this; to lay down his life for his brother," verse was scrawled across two crossed guns. Yeah, my warrior needed to lay down his arms if only for the night.

He crawled in beside me, reaching, seeking, needing me to soften the blows of our day. "Lay down on your back," I instructed.

His brow furrowed. "Thought you preferred it when I was the one giving the orders."

"For tonight, let me."

That wasn't what he wanted but it was what he needed. When he reclined on his back, I sat up on my knees and pressed my fingers gently to his bad hip. I could feel the hardened muscle strain as I began my massage gently.

"I'm fine," he protested.

"I know you are," I assured him and continued my in-depth massage.

He closed his eyes in surrender to my touch. His cock shifted, hungry for my attention. I smiled and kept my hands working and exploring the delineated muscles of his thighs and the tight curve of his ass. A contented sigh preceded his legs widening as I loosened the muscles. I'd half-expected him to watch me do this but his eyes remained closed. It seemed perhaps he was going to trust me enough to let me suture the wounds he'd endured.

Accomplishment flowed through me as I worked. His breaths came steadily now but his jaw flexed. Keeping one hand working his hip, I trailed the fingers of my other over his erection, so hot and thick it was weeping for my attention. Pearly drops of pure hunger clung to his slit. My mouth watered. I traced throbbing veins running up his impressive length and skimmed over the scars there. Pouring all of my love into those fissures that had caused him so much unnecessary doubt.

"Damn, that feels good. Do more of that," he half-pled.

"This?" I smirked as I wrapped one hand around his shaft, leaned, and licked the dew from his crown while I jacked him with my hand.

A ravenous growl, my neighbors probably heard, shook the bed.

"Or more of this?" I drew him in with a hungry suck.

"Jesus Christ, that. More of that."

"Mmm, yes, sir."

60

HANNAH

The following Saturday night I stepped out of our suite on Griff's arm.

Fred gave me an adoring smile. "You look lovely this evening, Ms. Hagen. I do hope you have a wonderful night." He and Griff shared a conspiratorial glance. He was so up to something.

Before we made our way out of the hotel, a man and his little girl headed our way. Griff smiled. "Honey, this is Joe. He's who loaned me the tool belt."

"Yeah, yeah, we wanted to thank you. I took her to get those ice cream cookies from that place down the street and she loved it." Joe lifted the little girl up into his arms. "Said she wanted to come see where Daddy works."

"I told you she would." Griff grinned at the toddler who was hugging her father with all of her limited strength.

"Yeah, and I talked with my ex. She wants to go on a trip with her new guy so I'll have her with me for a few weeks. We're gonna have fun aren't we Lupita?"

The little girl nodded adamantly.

"Congrats, man. Seems things are working out a lot of places lately. I'm happy for you." Griff slapped him on the shoulder.

"Yeah, I still worry I don't get to be with her enough," he confessed.

I stepped in. "Take it from a girl who only saw her father a few months out of the year. It's more about the quality of time than the quantity. She'll understand when you aren't there as long as when you are there you listen and help her spread her wings when the time comes."

"I think I can do that," Joe vowed. "Hey, you look pretty happy yourself." He gestured to Griff. "Happy looks good on you, man. Keep it up." He waved as he carried his little girl toward the hotel pools.

A few minutes later, I leaned up against the railing in front of the Bellagio fountains. I'd spent most of the week in some form of undress either naked in bed, naked in our pool, naked in our Jacuzzi tub, topless at the Bare pool I finally talking him into going to, or scantily clad for the dinners Griff ordered in most every night. This was our last night here. He'd wanted to take me out to see the sights, starting with the fountains.

Since Ms. Mallory had confessed everything to the board of Homefront Heroes, there would not be a final gathering of the auction attendees to present a check, so he'd planned a whole night for us complete with reservations at Costa Di Mare.

In fact, she'd had to email everyone explaining her actions and offering their money back. I'd written a check for her brother to make the trip to Johns Hopkins. I hoped they could do something for him.

Watson and his anesthesiologist had enjoyed the week in Vegas. Ryder was on a flight to Lincoln to meet T and Smith. Even Seth had met someone in the casino to spend some time with. Happy endings had managed to find their way through the insanity.

Griff wrapped his arms around my waist from behind me as the music swelled from the outdoor speakers. I relaxed against his steady strength as he surrounded me, my clear front sight in the blurry target of life.

"You look so damn gorgeous, baby." His hot breath whispered over my ear. "Not sure I'm going to be able to keep my hands off of you all the way through dinner."

"Good." I leaned back and grinned up at him as the water began its choreographed routine through the fountains. The scent of the spray mixed with his gunpowder and cologne. Contentment filled me, and even more than that, I sensed contentment in him. In all of our years together, I'd felt a lot of things inside Griff Haywood. Until the night he'd let me give him a massage in my apartment, contentment had never been one of them.

His father was home from the hospital. Georgia was learning to cook a low salt, low carb diet. She'd also moved herself into the trailer to take care of Duke and to make sure he wasn't sneaking cigarettes.

Griff had promised we'd go see them soon and that he'd think about Georgia and his father at a later date, a much later date.

The water shot several stories high to the crescendo of the music. It was beautiful. As many times as I'd been to Vegas I couldn't believe I'd never stopped to see this. But my father had been right, the entire trajectory of my life had gotten me here. It hadn't all been perfect but this moment was.

After the show, he escorted me to one of the private outdoor cabana tables in front of the water at Costa di Mare. "Wow." I took in the fading sunset over the desert and the most romantic spot in Vegas. The cool water lapped at the lit globes scattered throughout it.

"When I take my baby out, I do it right." He winked at me as we settled at the table.

"This is so romantic. I'm glad our week improved."

"Me, too. Smith even texted me a crude meme this morning so he's coming around."

"Yeah, I know. He texted the same one to me." I rolled my eyes.

Griff had clearly given our waiter instructions. Two craft beers were already at our table. I watched him take a long satisfying pull of the bottle. "It's good," he encouraged.

I tried the beer. It was delicious but I was too curious to really give it much thought. "What are you up to?"

"What makes you think I'm up to something?"

"You've been smiling all day."

"I've been smiling all week. You have that effect, sweetheart."

"Maybe but today's smile is different. I want to know why." A thrill of excitement bubbled in my chest. I had a guess but didn't want to get my heart set on it if he wasn't planning what I hoped he was planning.

"I never could get anything by you." He sighed. "Don't you want me to wait until we have dessert?"

"Wait to do what?" That bubbly zing of hope whipped from my chest out to all of my limbs.

"All right, fine. You're sure you want to do this now?"

"I'm sure." I was practically bouncing up and down in my chair. Suddenly, he stood. My heart performed a high-flying kick routine. "What are you doing?"

"This." He settled on his good knee. "I'm down here so you still good with this?" That smirk of his formed readily. Holy crap. I couldn't breathe. I'd waited so long for this moment and I was going to pass out because I couldn't breathe. I managed a frantic nod.

"Ever since the day I got off the school bus and realized my mom had taken off I've been constantly reeling. I never found another foothold. Not in the army. Not even in Special Ops. Not until the night I walked into your father's house and saw you. And you, my God, baby, you took my hands and that was it. I was done for. So, I decided I was tired of waiting on forever. I'm taking life with both hands right now and I'm never letting go again. I want every morning and every night with you forever. I don't have to look for the good parts in the bad days or the silver lining in the clouds. You're it. You're my sunshine. I'll never deserve you but I'm way past trying to stay away. I want to hold you in my arms every single night. I want to know you're happy, and safe, and I want you to know that I could never and would never love anything or anyone more than you. You were right. You do deserve a warrior and that is precisely what I am and who I will always be for you. So, my sweet Hannah B, will you please do me the honor of letting me be your husband?"

Tears streamed out of my eyes. Breath continued to elude me. "Yes!" I forced the word through the clog of emotion gathered in my throat. "Yes, yes, yes!"

He pulled a ring box out of his suit coat and slid the massive diamond ring on my finger. I didn't care about the ring. I threw my arms around him almost knocking him backward into the pool. He caught me and held me close, just the way it's supposed to be.

Eventually I did settle down long enough to admire the large princess cut diamond set on a white gold band. "Holy wow," I gasped as it glimmered in the lights over our table.

He laughed at me outright. "My baby likes pretty things and the word fuck. She's pretty much the best thing ever. I like to make her smile."

We ate course after course of Mediterranean and seafood and then a chocolate custard that I swear I wanted to bathe in. I dropped the second bite on my cleavage and the collar of my dress. His left eyebrow shot upward. It was good we had a private booth because he proceeded to lick it off of me. "Would you stop?" A fit of giggles burst from my mouth.

"Not in this lifetime or the next. Hope you're okay with that." His tongue feathered over my cleavage again.

"I think I'll manage."

He fed me the rest to keep it off of my clothing. When the dessert course was complete, he took my hand and escorted me back to the Jeep T had rented for him. As we drove down The Strip one last time, a neon sign for The Wedding Chapel caught my eye.

"You know, we are in Vegas." I gestured ahead to the sign.

A broad grin spread across his handsome features. "We are indeed. Might catch crap from The Sevens and our families."

"We might."

"I'm tired of waiting for life though, like I said." He laced his fingers through mine. "I want to officially make you all mine, baby."

"I want the same thing, Sergeant. I've wanted that every moment of every day since you stepped into my parent's house a long time ago." I squeezed his hand.

"I think it's time for us to do what's best for us instead of what may or may not piss people off," he suggested.

"We spent a lot of years making ourselves miserable worrying about what might piss other people off. We put off a lot of things because of it." The twinkling lights of Vegas and the stars above were just a little brighter that night like the universe really was finally cheering us on.

"We did do that," he agreed.

"I don't want to do that anymore."

"Me either."

EPILOGUE

Hannah

I slid into the back corner booth of the Hi-Way Diner between my husband and my big brother and nothing in the entire world could've felt better than the ability to do that. The rest of The Sevens all gave me goading grins as they readjusted to make room for me.

Griff leaned back against the booth and wrapped his arm over my shoulder. "You gonna tell them?"

"I didn't know if there was some kind of grunting contest, or if you all had to scratch and flex or something before we started talking."

"If you're gonna make fun of our ways, Hannah Banana, you can't come," Smith informed me.

"I thought you liked it when I grunt and flex, baby?" Griff smirked.

Smith leaned forward, braced his elbows on the table, and leveled a glare on his best friend. "Speaking of you flexing, numb-nuts, care to tell me how that dent behind your headboard appeared yesterday while I was installing secure VPN's for one of our clients and you said you 'had a meeting'?" He made liberal use of finger quotes and I ordered my face to remain its normal color so my blush wouldn't give us away.

"No idea." Griff made no effort to hide his smirk. "And it is kind of a shit move to call me numb-nuts don't you think?"

"I think you're full of shit." I knew in some bizarre way Smith's ability to tease Griff about his injuries helped Griff accept them.

"Maybe," Griff chuckled, "but I am no longer full of..."

"Erectoplasm," Voodoo chimed in.

"High fructose porn syrup," Aaron, the only Seven who'd opted out of Tier Seven Security, offered.

Natalie, his wife, shook her head at him. "I have clearly been leaving you alone with my brothers too much."

"I've always been fond of layonnaise." T-Byrd laughed.

"Dear God." I rolled my eyes. "Seriously, couldn't you all have just scratched?"

"Did you not hear me at the meeting after we got back?" Griff huffed. "I strictly forbid any references to mayonnaise in any capacity ever."

"I am still not mentally prepared for this conversation." Smith scowled. "You're fixing that wall before you move out, which needs to be soon. What was wrong with your hotel room anyway? Do not fuck my sister in my house. Those were my instructions."

"Housekeeping was in there. I am total shit at turning her down. I'm weak, man. And she was about to tell you we put an offer in on a house today but you all had to play jizz thesaurus instead. Also, how did none of you offer up penis colada. I'm disappointed. Not gonna lie," Griff harassed.

The waitress supplied all of the guys and Natalie with their usual drinks. She offered me a smile. "Haven't seen you in here with them before. Will you be joining the guys every month now?"

"After their last conversation I'm thinking not, but I'd love a diet soda when you get a chance."

She laughed. "Yeah, she said something like that, too." The waitress pointed to Natalie. "But she's usually here so can I put that down as your regular?"

"Sure. Thanks." The waitress made a note on her pad and went to fetch my soda.

T grinned. "Okay, tell us about the house."

Since I'd been waiting on that very opening, I leapt in. "It was built in 1910. Four bedrooms and two baths. One of the bedrooms is perfect for my office. There's a secondary staircase off of the kitchen that goes to another office that will be perfect for a theater room. I'm going to tear out a few walls to re-do the kitchen and of course change the paint. The original hardwoods and fireplaces are in great shape. The basement is finished. The porches are gorgeous and it's on South Twenty-third so not far from Tier Seven."

"I keep telling her if she wants to blow out walls, I can take care of that for her." Griff brushed a kiss on my cheek.

"You are not using anything that requires a cylinder, a metal jacket, or TNT to do demo on our house, honey. I have a crew and when they're finished we'll still have something left to work with."

"You're so picky about that," he continued to tease me. "Just swear to me you'll do something with that blue room at the top of the stairs. It hurts to look at."

"Yeah, retina-burn blue is rarely a good paint choice. I'll make it better."

The even hum of conversation and the soothing sounds of the cooks in the kitchen settled around us. The waitress returned with several platters of sides the guys must've had as a standing order.

To all of our surprise, Maddie stepped hesitantly towards the table. "I'm assuming baby batter and clam sauce must be old school."

"You came." T stood and offered up his seat. I fought not to actually applaud this thing I was watching happen before my very eyes.

She offered us all grins as she scooted close to Voodoo so T could slide back in beside her. "My parents wanted Olivia to spend the night with them. My house was too quiet so I thought I might pop in. I won't stay long."

"We're thrilled you're here," I vowed.

"Hell yeah, girly, have an onion ring, and stay a while." Voodoo offered her the basket.

"Baby batter will never go out of style," T explained, "it's evergreen, but how long were you standing over there?"

"Just a few minutes. I didn't want to interrupt the game. Brought back more than a few good memories. Plus, I kind of wanted to see if I could still sneak by a pack of Berets. Makes me feel like I still have skills."

I grinned at her. "I'm sure they'd be happy to play their game for you anytime and I'm going to need you to teach me that sneaking by them thing."

She laughed. "Never thought that game would be something I'd miss and I will happily share all of my knowledge with you, Mrs. Haywood. Beret wives have to stick together."

I squealed. "I will never get tired of hearing that."

When Griff's brow furrowed, I knew I wasn't the only one who'd noticed T discreetly prop his arm up on the back of the booth behind Maddie's shoulders. Using the waitress's reappearance to take our orders as a distraction, Griff leaned closer and whispered, "Is there something going on there?"

"I'm really hoping so." I nuzzled my head on his shoulder to conceal my answer.

"You think either of them have figured it out yet?"

"Nope. Not yet."

ABOUT THE AUTHOR

Bestselling author Jillian Neal likes her coffee strong and sweet with a shot of sinful spice, the same way she likes her cowboys. In fact, her caffeine addiction is quite possibly considered illicit in several states as are a few of the things her characters do. When she's not writing or reading, you'll find her in the kitchen trying out new recipes or coming up with ~~excuses~~ reasons to purchase yet another handbag or make an additional trip to Sephora. Though she'll always be a Bama girl at heart, Jillian hangs up her hat and kicks up her boots outside of Atlanta with her hunk-of-a-husband and her teenage sons.

For more information...

jillianneal.com
jillian@jillianneal.com

ALSO BY JILLIAN NEAL

Broken H.A.L.O

H.A.L.O. Undone

Camden Ranch

Rodeo Summer

Forever Wild

Cowgirl Education

Un-hitched

Last Call

Wayward Son

Gypsy Beach to Camden Ranch

Coincidental Cowgirl

Gypsy Beach

Gypsy Beach

Gypsy Love

Gypsy Heat

Gypsy Hope

CPSIA information can be obtained
at www.ICGtesting.com
Printed in the USA
LVHW092158161219
640742LV00001B/108/P